BORN
OF THE
SUN

Also by Joan Wolf
THE ROAD TO AVALON

BORN OF THE SUN

by

Joan Wolf

NAL BOOKS

NEW AMERICAN LIBRARY

A DIVISION OF PENGUIN BOOKS USA INC., NEW YORK
PUBLISHED IN CANADA BY
PENGUIN BOOKS CANADA LIMITED, MARKHAM, ONTARIO

Published simultaneously in Canada by
Penguin Books Canada Limited

NAL TRADEMARK REG. U.S. PAT. OFF. AND FOREIGN COUNTRIES
REGISTERED TRADEMARK—MARCA REGISTRADA
HECHO EN DRESDEN, TN, USA

SIGNET, SIGNET CLASSIC, MENTOR, ONYX, PLUME, MERIDIAN
and NAL BOOKS are published *in the United States* by
New American Library, a division of Penguin Books USA Inc.,
1633 Broadway, New York, New York 10019,
in Canada by Penguin Books Canada Limited,
2801 John Street, Markham, Ontario L3R 1B4

LIBRARY OF CONGRESS CATALOGING-IN-PUBLICATION DATA

Wolf, Joan.
    Born of the sun / by Joan Wolf.
        p.   cm.
    ISBN 0-453-00666-3
    1. Great Britain—History—Anglo-Saxon period, 449-1066—Fiction.
I. Title.
PS3573.0486B6   1989
813'.54—dc19   88-39422
                                                                   CIP

Designed by Julian Hamer

First Printing, August, 1989

1   2   3   4   5   6   7   8   9

PRINTED IN THE UNITED STATES OF AMERICA

*For my mother and father,
with love and gratitude*

Near the snow, near the sun, in the highest fields
See how these names are feted by the waving grass
And by the streamers of white cloud
And whispers of wind in the listening sky.
The names of those who in their lives fought for life
Who wore at their hearts the fire's centre.
Born of the sun they travelled a short while towards the sun,
And left the vivid air signed with their honour.

—STEPHEN SPENDER
"I Think Continually of Those
Who Were Truly Great"

THE PRINCE
(555–559)

Chapter 1

THE harper was singing a song about the death of Arthur. Niniane sat in her wicker chair in the corner of the faded Roman room, winding wool and listening to the familiar tragic tale. The song had more poignancy than usual this particular day; word had been brought to Bryn Atha only that morning that, for the first time since the Battle of Badon, the Saxons were on the war road to Calleva.

The last plangent note died away, the spring breeze rattled the loose shutter at the window, and her father said, "Would to God that Arthur was with us today."

Her brother Coinmail got to his feet and went to the window to secure the loose shutter. Then he turned and said coldly, "There is no use in wishing for Arthur. He has been dead these eighty years. Nor will the singing of harpers bring him back."

The harper raised his dreamy eyes. Kerwyn was an old man whose grandfather had fought with Niniane's great-grandfather at Badon; he had been the prince's harper at Bryn Atha for almost all his life. Now he answered Coinmail: "But he is not dead, my lord. He is only resting, making ready to come again when Britain does need him most."

Niniane looked at the ascetic old face with pity and affection. "That may be true, Kerwyn," she said gently, "but until he does, surely he would expect us to try to defend ourselves."

"The cavalry is gone, buried in Gaul," came the crooned reply. "The horses are gone. Bedwyr the lion is . . ."

"Yes, they are all gone. We know." Coinmail sounded almost savage. "And we will shortly be gone too, if we don't do something about the Saxons!"

Niniane sighed. It was true what Coinmail had just said. She frowned down at the wool in her lap. "Naille was quite certain his information was correct?" she said.

"You have asked that question already, Niniane," her father returned impatiently. "Naille was quite certain. The Saxons left Venta two days ago and are on the road to Calleva. Naille's information was that Cynric, the West Saxon king, is looking to expand his territory beyond

3

Venta. Calleva would be a second major city for his kingdom. And if the West Saxons annex Calleva, they will be too close to us for safety."

"We must fight." Coinmail's voice was final.

The wool slid from Niniane's fingers. There had been no battles between her people and the Saxons since Arthur had buried three-quarters of the Saxon army in the Badon pass almost a century ago. Since then the Atrebates tribe had lived in safety, secure in the peace Badon had won for them. But now . . . "How can we possibly fight?" she asked her brother. "We are farmers, not soldiers."

"We will have to learn to be soldiers, then," came the implacable reply.

The harper looked confusedly from Coinmail to Niniane's father, Ahern. "Fight? But who are we to fight? The Saxons all lay dead at Badon."

"My God!" Coinmail turned to Niniane. "Can't you shut him up?"

"He is an old man, Coinmail. Have a little patience." She spoke to the harper in a voice that was almost tender. "It is all right, Kerwyn. There will be no fighting at Bryn Atha." Then, to her father: "Perhaps this is just a raid, Father. Perhaps the best thing for us to do is to wait and see what it is they want . . ."

Ahern was shaking his head. "No, Niniane. Your brother is right. This is just the beginning. If we let them gain a foothold in Calleva, they will soon have the whole of this country under their rule. We must make a stand." His eyes moved to his son. "I have had all the old weapons taken from the storehouse and put in the winter room. I think we had better go have a look at them and see which ones are still usable."

Coinmail moved eagerly to the door and Ahern turned to follow him. Left behind in the silent room were an old harper and a girl with a pool of scarlet wool spilled at her feet.

The sun was streaming through the bedroom window as Niniane came in carrying a brew of herbs. The harper stirred as the door opened. "Did you sleep?" Niniane asked as she set the drink down on a table and came over to the bed.

"Yes." The old eyes smiled up at her. "I dreamed."

She sat in the chair beside the bed and took his hand into hers. "What did you dream?" she asked gently.

"I dreamed of you. It was a happy dream."

She lifted his hand to her cheek. The hand was strong still, a long narrow hand with long narrow fingers; a harper's hand. He began to cough and she slipped her arm behind his shoulders and raised him up a little. She was a small girl, but he was so frail she could support him with little difficulty. When the coughing fit was over he lay back again and closed his eyes.

"I have brought you something to drink, Kerwyn," she said, and he roused himself with obvious effort to drink her potion. Then he fell once again into a restless doze.

Niniane sat at his side, looking at the pale face on the pillow. He had failed very badly this last year. For a long time she had tried to pretend this was not so, but these last few months had seen an undeniable change in him.

She would miss him so, she thought, her heart aching as she sat watching by his side. He had taught her music and in so doing he had changed her life. The harp and the songs it could make had long been her greatest joy. Coinmail might think him an old fool, and her father might tolerate him for the sake of tradition, but Niniane loved the harper more than anyone in the world. And not just for his music. He had always been her friend; the one person she knew would find her concerns of interest, even importance. As the oldest and the youngest in the villa, the two had formed an alliance for years.

"Niniane!" She heard the voice shouting in the courtyard and ran to the window to look out. A man was dismounting from his horse and, even though his back was to her, she recognized him immediately. There was only one person she knew with hair that color. She ran out of the room and down the gallery to the front door of the villa.

Coinmail was holding his horse as she came out into the courtyard. He scowled at her and gestured to the slave quarters. "Where are the servants?"

"With the livestock, as usual at this hour. You will have to put Roaire in the stable yourself."

"It doesn't matter. I cannot stay. I have only come to bring you news."

Niniane stared at him first with surprise, then with apprehension. "Nothing has happened to Father?" she asked.

"No. Father is fine." His deep auburn brows, the same color as his hair, drew together. "The Saxons are in Calleva," he said.

"Oh, no!"

"We could not stop them. It would have been suicide to attempt to block the road. When we make our stand we will need some geographical advantage. They are more experienced fighters than we."

Niniane's small white teeth sank into her chapped lower lip. "What have they done to Calleva?" she asked in a low voice. "Have they sacked it?"

His laugh was not pleasant. "What was there to sack? Calleva has been a dead city for a century at least. I doubt there are two hundred people living there these days. There was no resistance. They opened the west gate and Cynric and his men marched in."

Niniane reached up to rub the forehead of her brother's horse. "All those beautiful Roman buildings . . ." she mourned.

"The man who brought us the news told me that the Saxons were making campfires on the mosaic floors." Coinmail looked physically ill. "*Barbarians*. They are no better than beasts who live in barns."

Roaire nuzzled Niniane's chest. "Let me get him a bucket of water," she said. "He must be thirsty."

He shook his head. "I haven't time. I came merely to warn you. If the Saxon army should get through us, they are likely to come to Bryn Atha. It is too well-known for them to pass it by."

Niniane knew that Coinmail spoke no more than the truth. Bryn Atha had always been one of the more famous of the villas built by the Romano-Celtic ruling class during the days of the Roman occupation of Britain. It had been commissioned by one of Niniane's ancestors, a prince of the Atrebates tribe who had also served as the Roman magistrate in Calleva. Like all the Roman villas in Britain, Bryn Atha had been built as a country home, but after the legions had left Britain to return to Rome, the cities they had built had begun to fall apart. The native Celts were not naturally a city people and gradually the tribes had returned to the pastoral life that was more natural to them. The princes of the Atrebates had eventually given up any residence in Calleva at all and lived off their own farms, administering whatever laws were left from Bryn Atha itself.

Niniane swallowed hard. "I have buried all the valuables. They will find even less at Bryn Atha than they did at Calleva."

"May God damn them all to hell," Coinmail said through his teeth as he looked around the courtyard of his beautiful Roman home.

"I'm sure He will," Niniane replied. "They are pagans."

Coinmail ran a hand through his thick, burnished hair. "Well, we shall do our best to send them hence, you can be certain of that."

Niniane laid her cheek against Roaire's hard face. Her own hair, lighter than her brother's and more brown-gold than red, glinted in the bright sun. "Are you still camped by Sarc Water?"

"Yes. We have a hundred and fifty-three men. About as many as the war band that accompanies Cynric." Coinmail's dark gray eyes were narrowed. "He knows we're there. He will come out to meet us, all right. The Saxon cannot resist a challenge to fight."

Niniane shivered in the warm sun. "I am so frightened, Coinmail."

"Yes, well, you have cause to be. Listen to me, little sister. You must not be at Bryn Atha if the Saxons do indeed get through us at Sarc Water. You are fifteen years old, no longer a child. You are to marry this fall, a good match for the Atrebates. We cannot afford to lose you."

Niniane's eyes were huge. "Lose me?"

"God knows what the Saxons do to the women they take. They are heathens, with no respect for any Christian virtue. Do you understand what I am saying? You must not fall into their hands."

Niniane took a step toward her brother. "Are you going to take me back to Sarc Water with you, Coinmail?"

He frowned. "Of course not. You would be less safe at Sarc Water."

Her face was very pale, the light golden freckles that dusted the bridge of her short, tilted nose more noticeable than usual. "Well, then," she almost whispered, "what am I to do?"

"Go to Geara's farm. If the Saxons get through us, they are bound to come to Bryn Atha, but I doubt they will bother with a poor farmstead like Geara's. You should be safe there."

"When do you expect the battle to take place?"

"I'm not sure, but you are not to wait for the battle. Go now, today."

She frowned. "I cannot go today, Coinmail. Kerwyn is ill. He became ill almost as soon as you and Father left. I cannot move him."

"Then leave him here. Col and Brenna will look after him."

"Col and Brenna can scarcely look after themselves. Besides, how can I ask them to stay if I run away?"

"Neither Col nor Brenna is likely to be raped," he answered brutally. "You, on the other hand, are. You will be no good to us if that happens, Niniane. Father says you are to get away from Bryn Atha."

She looked down at her blue gown, avoiding his eyes. "All right," she said.

"You will go to Geara's farm?"

"Yes."

He rewarded her with an austere smile and threw his horse's reins over its neck. When he was in the saddle he gave her one more piece of advice. "If a Saxon should try to approach you, use your knife." She understood that he did not mean she was to use it on the Saxon.

After Coinmail had left, Niniane turned and slowly walked back into the villa. The main entrance led into a large reception hall, with a lovely mosaic floor depicting Venus hunting a boar. The room was almost bare of furniture. Niniane turned to her left and went down the corridor to the room the family used most. She sat in her father's chair and stared at one faded blue peacock on the decorative scroll that adorned the plaster walls.

Her hands were cold. She was cold all over. Coinmail must be worried if he had come all the way back to Bryn Atha to warn her.

The Saxons. Ever since she was a baby that word had been a source of terror. "Be a good girl or the Saxons will get you," her nurse had said. They were pagans who worshiped the gods of thunder and war. Some even said they offered human sacrifices in their unspeakable rites. She shuddered with cold. *God knows what they do to the women they take.*

Perhaps, in a few days, Kerwyn would be well enough to move. Surely she would be safe enough at Bryn Atha until then.

A brisk wind was driving high white clouds across the May sky on the day the Battle of Sarc Water was fought. The Britons under their prince, Ahern, fought valiantly but ineffectively. The efficient Saxon war machine crushed them with little trouble. The British survivors fled into the hills, leaving their dead on the field. The Saxons did not even bother to make camp to care for their own wounded; they pressed on toward Bryn Atha, home of the princes of the Atrebates.

The sky stayed light for a long time this season of the year, and the sun was still shining when the Saxons marched through the gate and into the courtyard of Bryn Atha. Niniane watched them from the window of Kerwyn's bedroom, her mouth dry with terror. She had not really believed this could ever happen. Saxons. At Bryn Atha. Her breathing was coming quick and shallow as she watched the men pouring into the courtyard. Most were helmetless and carried spears and swords and great embossed shields. They had a large number of packhorses with them, but the war band was on foot, save for two men who were obviously the leaders.

"Niniane . . ." It was the merest thread of sound and she went to kneel beside the dying harper. "Hold my hand," he whispered.

"Of course." She picked up the hand lying on the blanket and held it between her own small ones. It was burning hot.

"I'm cold," he said.

"Shall I get you another blanket?" Her voice was low and husky; Kerwyn had always loved to hear the sound of it. But her mind was not on what she was saying; her ears were attuned instead to what was happening in the courtyard. She heard the sound of the front door crashing open. They were in the house.

Kerwyn began to cough and she put her arm under his frail shoulders to help him sit up. She could feel how burning hot he was even through the linen of his shirt. He struggled to speak, managed one word—"cold" —then slumped down against her. She felt for his heart; it was still. She laid the old harper back onto the bedplace and slowly rose to her feet.

She could hear the clank of mail in the gallery, the guttural sounds of the language they were speaking. They were looking into all the rooms. She could hear the crashing of the doors as they were kicked open. Her hand went to the dagger at her belt and she remembered her brother's words.

The door of Kerwyn's bedroom burst open. Niniane felt an invigorating flash of anger. There was no need to put a foot through it! A big blond-haired man erupted into the room and stopped dead when he saw her. Niniane stood as straight as she could, raised her chin, and stared into his startled eyes.

There was a moment of silence and then he said something to her. She shook her head. "I don't understand you," she answered in British. The Saxon looked from her to the figure of the harper, frowned, and barked a command. Another warrior appeared at the door and the man who was in the room with her said something to him. Niniane could distinguish the word "Cynric." They were sending for their king.

It was the longest five minutes of Niniane's life as she stood there, under the speculative eyes of the big Saxon, waiting to learn her fate. She took some cold courage from the dagger she held hidden in the folds of her gown. The Saxon appeared to be staring at the brooches on her shoulders.

After what seemed to her an eternity, her captor, who had been leaning his shoulders against the wall, suddenly came to attention. Two men walked into the room, and she recognized them as the ones who had been on horseback in the courtyard. One of them was old, with thick shaggy gray hair and a heavy, still-powerful-looking body. He dismissed her captor with a word.

This must be Cynric, Niniane thought. Cynric, son of Cerdic, King of the West Saxons. The king turned to look at her, and for the first time she saw his eyes. They were neither blue nor green, but an extraordinary mixture of both. She had never seen eyes that color before. He was looking her up and down and her hand tightened on her dagger. Cynric turned to the man beside him and said something.

"Who are you?" the other man asked her in accented but perfectly understandable British.

She tried not to show them how frightened she was. "I am Niniane," she answered, almost haughtily. "This is my house."

The British-speaking Saxon raised his eyebrows. He was younger than Cynric, dark-skinned and narrow of face. His clear blue eyes were set under extraordinary high-arched brows. "*Your* house? Who is your father?"

She wondered, belatedly, if it had been wise to tell the truth. She tried to swallow but her mouth was perfectly dry. "Ahern, Prince of the Atrebates," she replied.

The brown-haired man turned to the other and began to speak in Saxon. Cynric answered and then the other man looked at her and asked, "Who is that?" He was referring to Kerwyn.

"My father's harper," she answered steadily. "He became ill and I could not move him. So I stayed . . ."

The brown-haired one walked to the bed and put his hand on the harper's chest. He looked up at her. "He is dead."

She had backed away when he approached the bed. "Yes. I know. He . . . he died just a few minutes ago."

"Poor timing for you, Princess of the Atrebates," the man remarked ironically.

Her hand on the dagger tightened. Her palm was sweating so, she was afraid it was going to slip out of her grasp.

Cynric spoke impatiently and the other answered him. The king's blue-green eyes narrowed thoughtfully as he listened. Cynric spoke again and the British-speaker turned to Niniane, "This is Cynric, King of the West Saxons. I am Cutha, his kinsman. The king tells you not to fear. You can put down your knife. We will not harm you."

Niniane bit her trembling lip. How had he known about the knife? The Saxon king came over to the bed and looked down at Kerwyn's body. Then he looked at Niniane and spoke. Cutha translated: "I too have a reverence for harpers."

Niniane had buried most of the valuable jewelry they still had at Bryn Atha, so there was little in the villa for the Saxons to loot. She was afraid that perhaps they would take their disappointment out on the villa—or on her. But they seemed to accept their slim booty philo-sophically. The Saxons, it seemed, had given up expecting much in the way of gold from the Britons.

They stayed at the villa for two days only, and during that time Niniane was allowed to keep to her room. They brought her food and otherwise left her alone. No one made the slightest move toward raping her. Cutha had even been kind enough to inform her that her father and her brother had escaped from Sarc Water alive.

It could have been much worse, she thought as she stood at her window and watched the Saxon thanes busy in the courtyard. They had taken a number of household items that apparently struck their fancy: the Samianware pottery, the oil lamps, some of the hangings that still covered the walls. The thing that had pleased Cynric most, however, had been her polished metal hand mirror. Evidently the Saxons did not have mirrors.

Yes, it could have been much worse. They had come, and they had taken things that would be missed, but the villa was still intact, her father and brother were still alive, and it seemed she was safe. So Niniane thought as she watched Cynric's men putting the villa's belong-ings into the saddlebags of their packhorses that gray spring afternoon.

An hour later, she was thinking that things could not have been worse. The Saxons were indeed leaving Bryn Atha, but to her horror she found that they were taking her with them. "Am I to be made a slave?" she asked Cutha incredulously when he told her of her fate.

He had given her a reassuring smile. "Certainly not, Princess. You are far too valuable to be a slave. You will come with us as a member of the king's own household. You may pack a saddlebag of things to bring with you. We leave tomorrow at first light for Winchester."

It seemed that Bryn Atha had not been lacking in loot after all. Coinmail would say she should have used the knife.

Chapter 2

CYNRIC, King of the West Saxons, sat his horse in the courtyard of Bryn Atha and watched as his war band made ready to leave. Cutha came out of the house with the little British princess they had found and took her to one of the horses they had captured from her father.

The Britons, Cynric thought with contempt. The young boys in Winchester would fight with more skill than these farmers. Still, it would be wise to go carefully. He would need the goodwill of the Britons if he wanted to expand his territory. There were not enough Saxon ceorls to do all that must be done if Wessex were to become a power in the land. This girl they had found at Bryn Atha might prove helpful in making peace with the Atrebates. She was wellborn, a princess of her line. A useful acquisition.

Cutha mounted and rode over to his place beside the king. The girl followed a little behind, her horse led by one of his thanes. She sat the horse well, Cynric noted. She was small and delicate-looking, but he judged her to be at least fourteen. He could see that she had breasts.

"Ready, my king," Cutha said, and Cynric squeezed his horse forward. The war band fell in behind him, marching four abreast. The packhorses came last, each led by a man on foot.

They did not retrace their steps toward Calleva. Cynric had seen the city; now he wanted to see the rest of the country in the area. So they went west, to the old Roman road that led to Venta from Corinium. Their pace was leisurely. The king wanted to spy out what kind of land lay in this new part of his kingdom. He had eorls back in Winchester to whom he owed much, and there was little in the way of gold to be had from the British. But there was land.

The farms they saw were all deserted. Word had got round that he was coming, Cynric thought scornfully. It would not be difficult to settle Saxons in this country. He would scarcely need to fight.

They filled the packhorses to capacity with the items that took their fancy in the farmsteads, and then, as they were still ten miles from home and it was time to eat, Cynric decreed that they stop for the night. They found a clearing by the road to make camp, fires were made and food cooked. Cynric sat on the rug that had been spread for him, watching his men and fighting his own weariness. No longer could he ride for eight hours at a time. He was getting old.

The girl sat on a rug as well and watched his men out of grave and level eyes. She had ridden behind him all day, her face still and guarded, giving away nothing of what she felt. There had been no whining about how tired she was, how frightened, no questions as to what he was going to do with her. He looked at her now approvingly and said to Cutha, "I am going to lie down. She had better come too. She cannot be used to so much riding."

His kinsman nodded and spoke to the girl, whose eyes flew in alarm to the king. Cynric grimaced a little at what he saw there. She need not fear *that* from him, and certainly not now, when he was so weary he could scarcely stand. "She had better sleep between the two of us," he said to Cutha. "She looks the sort who might try to run away."

Cutha nodded and, standing, reached a hand down to help Cynric up. The king shook him off impatiently and forced himself to get to his feet unaided. He put a hand on the girl's shoulder, ostensibly to guide her but in reality to steady himself, and began to walk in the direction of his bedplace. The girl's bones felt small and fragile under his hand, but she bore his weight with surprising strength. She was tough, this little British princess, he thought. She might make a good alliance for one of his sons.

Niniane was so weary that she fell asleep as soon as she realized that she was indeed going to be allowed to sleep alone. When she awoke several hours later it was to find the camp quiet. All the men were wrapped in their cloaks and sleeping on the ground around the dying fire.

She lay very still. The night was still also and, except for the fire, pitch dark. Clouds had moved in during the course of the evening to cover the moon and the stars. Cynric and Cutha were sleeping deeply. Would it be possible for her to escape?

Slowly and cautiously she sat up. There had to be a guard posted, she thought. But no one stirred. It was possible she might be able to creep out of camp unobserved.

She sat there, alone, the camp sleeping around her, and contemplated the possibility. Once she got out of camp, where would she go?

She could try one of the farms they had passed. Perhaps the people had come back by now and would hide her. But how to get to the farm? The Saxons would look for her on the road. They had horses; they would be able to overtake her before she could reach a safe haven.

She would have to hide in the forest.

Out of the darkness came the call of a wolf. Niniane shuddered. To leave the safety of the fire and go by herself into the fierce darkness of the forest, where there were wolves . . . She could not do it. It was shameful to admit, but she felt safer here, lying between the big bodies of these Saxons, than she would by herself out alone in the forest.

The wolf called again and Niniane lay back down. She was a wretched coward. Coinmail would say it was her duty to take her chances in the forest. Well, she was not Coinmail and she would rather take her chances with the Saxons. They were surely planning to ransom her back to her father. That must be what Cutha had meant when he said she was valuable. It would be wiser not to do anything foolish just yet, wiser to wait and see what was going to happen. There was the gold jewelry she had hidden at Bryn Atha for a ransom. By summer she would probably be home once again.

The Saxons rose early the following morning and were on the road shortly after dawn. "How far is it to Venta?" Niniane asked the thane who was leading her horse and who she had discovered spoke a rough but serviceable British.

"We don't go to Venta," came the surprising answer. "We are for Winchester."

"Winchester? What is Winchester?"

The thane, whose name was Eclaf, turned to stare at her in astonishment. "Winchester is the home of the West Saxon king," he answered. "It is one of the greatest royal enclaves in all of England. You have not heard of it?"

"England?" said Niniane.

"This island you call Britain."

"Oh. No, I do not know of Winchester. I thought the king lived in Venta."

"Venta is the city that serves Winchester, but the king and all his eorls and thanes live in the royal enclave. You will see it shortly, my lady." He spoke as if he were promising her a treat.

They had been riding for several hours and the road before them was still empty, when suddenly the war band stopped. Niniane watched with curiosity as a thane carefully removed a glittering object from one of the packhorses and bore it ceremoniously to the mounted figure of the king. "What is that?" she asked Eclaf.

"That is the royal helmet," he answered. "The emblem of kingship. The king always dons it when he returns to his people after doing battle for them."

Niniane watched with interest as the king raised his hands and placed the helmet on his head. She could see immediately why it was a symbol of royalty. She did not think she had ever in her life seen anything more magnificent. Made all of gold, with a great silver crest and golden garnet-encrusted face mask, it was not something one would risk in battle. Wearing it, the king looked more than a mere mortal. He looked alien, mysterious, powerful . . . frightening.

Once Cynric had the helmet on, the party moved forward once again. As they topped a gentle hill and began to descend toward the valley, Niniane could see a great stockade fence looming before them to the right of the road. At the approach of the war band, a gate swung slowly open. The king turned off the road and began to advance toward the gate.

There was silence in the ranks of thanes as they approached the great wooden gate. Niniane looked from the massive back of the king to the leaner back of Cutha, both of whom were riding before her. Eclaf's head was held high. They passed through the watchmen at the gate and Niniane saw before her a street lined with people, all of whom set up a loud cheer when they saw their king. Niniane could feel the color flushing into her face. Never in her life had she felt so exposed, so naked . . . so humiliated. She thought that Coinmail would die if he could see her now.

She raised her chin and stared straight ahead of her. She would pretend she was alone, she thought. She would ignore the situation, rise above it. The road, she noticed, was made of stone, and at the end of it, straight in front of her, was an enormous timber-built hall. It had a high, steep, shingled roof and very wide gables. All around the hall was grouped a series of other wood buildings, smaller than the great hall but still of impressive size. There had to be fifteen buildings at least, Niniane thought as, forgetting her resolve, she looked around in dazed wonder.

The king and Cutha had reached the great hall and now they halted their horses. There were several steps leading from the paved road to the door of the hall, and at the top of the steps was gathered a line of men. Niniane watched as Cynric mounted the stairs and was formally greeted by the delegation waiting at the top. Then the whole party disappeared into the hall. Behind her, the men of the war band began to break up and move off in different directions toward other buildings. The packhorses were being led away. Still Eclaf stood, holding Niniane's horse, obviously waiting for something.

"Why do we stand here?" Niniane asked him.

"The king is sending for one of the women to attend you," came the cheerful reply. And, indeed, a girl was coming out of the large building that was closest to the great hall.

"Greetings," she said to Niniane in British. "If you will come with me, I will take you to the women's hall." The girl was brown-haired and brown-eyed and obviously a Briton.

Niniane smiled at her a little tremulously and dismounted from her horse. "The lady Fara will see to you, my lady," Eclaf said to her as he led the horse away.

The girl's brown eyes looked her up and down curiously. "You are a princess of the Atrebates?" she asked.

"Yes." Niniane returned her look. "My father will ransom me home."

The girl looked surprised. Then, "I am Nola. Please come this way." Niniane fell into step beside her, looking around at the size of the courtyard and the number of houses.

"I had never even heard of Winchester," she said as they approached the building Nola had called the women's hall. "I always thought the West Saxon king lived in Venta."

"Cynric lived in Venta when first he conquered this area, but as his power grew, the city became too small. He started to build Winchester fifteen years ago. Isn't it splendid?"

Niniane stared at her in wonder. "You look British," she said.

"I am." The brown eyes gave her a friendly smile. "What is your name, Princess?"

"Niniane."

"Well, Niniane, this is the women's hall." She nodded at the doorway. "Please go in."

The front door of the hall opened onto a porch, which appeared to be used as a small reception room. The door from the porch led into the hall itself. This was a very large room, at least a hundred feet long, with a high roof that made it seem even larger. There was a hearthplace in the middle of the room, with tables and benches set along either side of it. The room had no windows, just two doors set on each long wall. Even though it was morning, candles had been lit in the wall sconces and on the tables, where a group of women was engaged in a variety of work. Against the far, gabled wall there were fixed two large looms and women were working there as well.

A dozen heads turned as Niniane walked through the door. Then one of the women rose. "Come in, my dear," she said in British. "You must be weary after such a journey. Would you like something to eat? To drink?"

Niniane had eaten very little for the last few days, and now, all of a sudden, she realized she was hungry. "Yes, thank you," she said with gratitude. "I would."

"Come and sit down," the woman said, and led Niniane over to one of the benches.

This must be the lady Fara, Niniane thought as she took the seat that had been indicated. She spoke almost accentless British, this lady, but she was most certainly a Saxon: tall and fair and strongly made. She was no longer young, but even so, she was beautiful. It came to Niniane that this must be Cynric's queen.

The queen sent a girl to fetch some food and then turned back to Niniane. "So," she said composedly, "you are to stay with us for a while."

"Until my father can ransom me," Niniane replied.

"I see." The lady seated herself beside Niniane, and in the light from the candles on the table she appeared even older than Niniane had originally thought. There were fine lines beside her hazel eyes, and gray in her wheat-blond hair. "Tell me what happened," she said, and Niniane found herself talking easily and comfortably to those calm, kind eyes.

"And Cynric has said he will ransom you?" the queen asked when Niniane had finished her tale.

"Yes." A plate of cold meat and a bowl of fruit were put before Niniane on the table. "That is, Cutha told me I was not to be made a slave, that I would be a member of the king's household. What else could he possibly mean but that I am to be held for ransom?"

The queen gave her a quick smile and then was grave again. "What else indeed?" she answered. "Eat your food, my dear, and then we will show you where you are to sleep."

Niniane ate with more appetite than she had known in weeks. There was something soothing about the calm presence of Cynric's queen. And it was so comforting to be surrounded by women! Niniane ate and watched the women at the end of the hall deftly passing the bobbin back and forth through the warp of flax strung on the large looms. No hands were idle in this room; everyone was busy with spinning or sewing of some sort. Niniane found the atmosphere in the hall strangely solacing.

When Niniane had finished eating, the queen beckoned to Nola once more. "Take the princess to her chamber," she instructed the girl. "I'm sure she would like to rest."

Niniane rose. "I thank you for your kindness, my lady," she said politely, and was dismissed with another lovely but fleeting smile.

"The queen is very kind, is she not?" Niniane remarked to Nola as they left the porch of the women's hall and started toward one of the smaller buildings.

Nola stopped, turned to her, and stared. "The queen?" she repeated.

"Yes." Niniane frowned. "The lady we just left. Is she not the queen?"

"Unfortunately, no." Nola looked around to see if anyone was within hearing distance. "That was the lady Fara. Guthfrid is the queen."

Niniane found herself looking around as well. There was no one near them. "But who is the lady Fara, then? The king's sister?"

Nola gave a snort of laughter. "No. The lady Fara is the king's friedlehe. What you might call his second wife."

Niniane could feel her eyes widen. "His *second* wife? How many wives does he have?"

"Only one legitimate wife, and that is Guthfrid. She is the daughter of the King of East Anglia. Cynric married her sixteen years ago. But the lady Fara has been his friedlehe for more than twenty-five years."

"Then she is . . . she is a concubine," said Niniane.

"No. A concubine is a slave. A friedlehe, in Saxon law, is a freewoman." Nola began to walk once more toward the women's bower, and Niniane followed her, her brow furrowed with thought.

"Who were all those women with the lady Fara, then?" she asked Nola in a resolute voice as they reached the door of the house Nola had called the women's bower.

"The king's household women," Nola replied. She opened the door of the building and Niniane followed her into a long dark center hall. There was a ladder to a loft in the corner, and on either side of the hall was a series of three doors. "These are the private sleeping chambers down here," Nola said. "The rest of us sleep up there"—a gesture—"in the loft." She walked down the hall and opened a door. "This will be your chamber, Niniane."

It was a square room with wood-planked walls and a wooden floor. It was very dark, as there was no window. Nola went to a table and lit the candle that was placed there. In the glow of light, Niniane could see a bed made up with a bright red wool rug, a plain wood table, and a chest for clothes. She walked to the bed and lifted the rug. Underneath, the bedstead was filled with fresh straw and laid on top with clean linen sheets. The wooden floor was also clean. Niniane turned back to Nola. "Thank you," she said. "I'm sure I shall be very comfortable."

The girl, who looked to be a few years older than she, smiled. "There is to be a feast in the great hall tonight, to welcome home the king and his thanes. We are to attend. The lady Fara will send you the appropriate garments. Have a good rest, Princess." And she was gone.

Chapter 3

*F*ARA sent her a complete change of clothes. There was a fine linen undergarment and a saffron-colored tunic that fell in even folds to the tops of her feet. The overgown was deep blue and to clasp it at her shoulders Fara had chosen two circular brooches with garnet inlays on gold filigree. There was also a soft leather belt with a decorated golden buckle.

Niniane sat on the side of the bed and stared at the clothing laid out so neatly on the red wool cover. The workmanship on the brooches and buckle was exquisite; the linen and wool were expertly woven. The materials, in fact, were finer than anything Niniane had ever seen. She dressed slowly and with care. There was no ornament for her hair, so she combed it to smoothness and let it hang loose down her back. Without combs or pins, it reached to her waist.

She had finished dressing and was sitting on the bed, hands folded in her lap, when Nola came to fetch her. The British girl was dressed in bright red and there was the warm color of anticipation in her cheeks. "This is a great occasion," Nola told her as the girls walked down the corridor of the bower toward the door. "Normally we eat in the women's hall."

The lady Fara, with a half-dozen other women, was waiting for them on the porch. "You look lovely, my dear," she said to Niniane. Fara was looking lovely herself in a green gown with a necklace of barrel-shaped gold beads alternating with gold-mounted garnet pendants displayed on her breast. Garnets shone also in the pins that held her hair. The other women too wore fine garments and rich jewelry. All her life Niniane had been told that Saxons were savage barbarians who lived in sunken huts with their pigs and their goats. The reality of Winchester was quite a shock.

"What are all these other buildings?" she asked Nola a little diffidently as they walked across the courtyard in the wake of Fara.

Nola saw the direction of her eyes. "That is the king's private hall," she answered. "And the one next to it is the queen's hall." A group of men also on their way to the banquet passed them without speaking. Nola continued to identify the buildings for Niniane. "That large hall

19

over there belongs to Cutha," she said, "and that one there houses the royal princes."

Niniane's eyes moved from the buildings Nola had named, to the smaller halls nearer the gate. One of them had a huge wooden pillar rising from an enclosed courtyard next to it. "And what is that?" she asked, looking at the building distinguished by the pillar.

"That is the temple," came the reply, and Niniane's smoky-blue eyes widened as she stared at the unremarkable timber building.

"Do they offer sacrifices in there?" Her voice was hushed. Nola shrugged. "I don't know what they do. It is for the men. The women go out to a grove in the forest for their rituals."

Niniane stared at the girl walking so unconcernedly beside her. "Are you a Christian, Nola?"

"My parents were Christians, but Venta has been under Cynric's rule since before I was born."

"Does he persecute Christians, then?"

"Oh, no. He is not a man to care which god you worship, so long as you recognize where your earthly allegiance lies. But there have been no priests in Venta for years. Most Britons are like me; they don't care very much about religion one way or the other."

There had been few priests at Bryn Atha, but the Atrebates had held to their faith. With a flash of contempt, Niniane thought that the Venta Britons sounded like an indifferent lot. They seemed to have given their Saxon conqueror remarkably little trouble.

The women had reached the steps of the great hall and Fara mounted first. There was a set of double doors leading into the hall, and the men on duty there opened them ceremoniously for Fara and her companions. They passed through the double doors and into a porch, somewhat like the porch on the women's hall. This porch was larger, however, and had been partitioned into two rooms, one on either side of a central anteroom. The doors that led into the main room were open and Fara beckoned to Niniane to come up beside her. Niniane obeyed and together the two women advanced into the great hall of Winchester.

It was the largest room Niniane had ever seen. The hearthplace in the middle of the floor was so long that there were two fires on it, one at each end. The room was so broad that the cross-beams were borne up on carven pillars. There were benches fixed along the two long walls, and above the benches hung a magnificent display of arms: great embossed shields and shining swords. Many of the benches were already occupied, and the men ceased talking for a moment as the women entered. Niniane had the unpleasant sensation of being stared at and then the voices picked up again and she walked beside Fara toward the high seat that was set in the middle of the right wall.

This seat, two seats actually, was distinguished from the other benches by its greater height and by the splendor of the arms that hung behind it. Long trestle tables had been set up in front of all the benches in the hall and Fara gestured Niniane to a seat to the left and at a little distance from the high seat. Niniane sat, bowed her head a little so her hair would fall forward to screen her face, and looked around.

The floor was wood but it was polished so brightly it shone.

The wall sconces were bronze and were blazing with torchlight. Even though it was still bright outside, the hall had no windows. The only natural light was from the doors and the smoke vents in the roof over the hearthplace.

The pillars were beautifully carved in a design that Niniane did not recognize.

The room had been quickly filling as Niniane looked around, the sound of male voices escalating. Then, abrupt as summer lightning, the room fell silent. Niniane looked toward the door, expecting to see the king, and saw there instead a golden-haired boy of about her own age, with a woman holding to his arm. The woman was as tall as the boy, and she glittered and shone with magnificent jewelry. Her hair was the same rich gold as the boy's and elaborately dressed with jeweled golden combs.

"The queen," Fara said as she rose to her feet.

"Who is that with her?" Niniane breathed, following Fara's example and standing.

"Her son, Prince Edwin," came the reply. The hall guests all remained respectfully standing until the queen took her place on the high seat. Then they resumed their seats and the murmur of voices began again.

Cutha came in with his wife and sons, and the rest of the eorls took their places as well. No food had as yet been served. They were all waiting, Niniane guessed, for the king.

The woman on the other side of Niniane leaned across her to ask Fara, "Where is Ceawlin?"

"I don't know," the friedlehe replied. "I have not seen him all day."

The door was starting to open again. "Here is the king now," the woman said, and everyone rose once more.

The old king looked splendid tonight, Niniane thought as she watched him cross the polished floor toward the high seat. His wool tunic was a deep, brilliant purple and he carried himself with all the dignity of a Roman emperor. Beside him walked a tall, slim boy with hair so pale and pure that Niniane thought instantly: So must the angels look. "Ceawlin," said Fara. Pride sounded in her voice, and a distinct undertone of fear.

"*Ceawlin!*" Guthfrid almost hissed the name as she too watched the boy who was Fara's son crossing the floor beside his father. Then the queen looked, compulsively, toward her own son sitting on a bench to her right. Edwin did not notice her; he was staring with unwinking concentration at the figure of his half-brother.

Cynric took his place on the high seat beside Guthfrid, and Ceawlin took the bench on his father's left. Guthfrid scarcely listened to the speech her husband was making to open the banquet formally. Her whole mind was preoccupied with the fact that Cynric had chosen to make his entrance with his bastard, not his true-born son, beside him.

What could it mean? Did he suspect anything about her and Edric? Was this his way of punishing her, through Edwin? She looked at her husband out of the side of her eyes as he resumed his seat. His granitelike profile told her nothing. It never did. Sixteen years they had been wed, and still she could not read him. Nor could she influence him. It was one of the great frustrations of her life, this lack of power over her husband. She was a beautiful woman; she had always wielded power over men. But not Cynric.

It was that bitch of a friedlehe, of course. She had put a spell on him. And now she was trying to push her son into a position of prominence over Edwin.

Guthfrid's long sharp nails cut into the palms of her hands and she looked once more toward her golden-haired son. It will never happen, she promised him silently. Mother will never let him supersede you. Edwin. My son.

The first platter of meat was placed on the table before the king and queen and Cynric reached for the parts that were his favorites. Guthfrid took only a small portion.

"You are not hungry?" her husband asked. They were the first words he had spoken to her since his return. He had not come to the queen's hall all day.

"No." She forced herself to smile at him. "I am too excited, my lord, to have you home."

He grunted.

She bit her lip. "Who is the girl you captured?" she asked after a minute.

He swallowed. "A princess of the Atrebates."

Her arched brows rose high. "A princess?"

"Yes. A princess from Bryn Atha."

"So . . ." Her mouth thinned. He had not seen fit to tell her, yet he had lodged the girl with his bitch of a friedlehe. She forced down the words that were hovering on her lips. It had never done her any good to show jealousy of Fara. "You took Calleva, then?"

He shrugged. "There was not much to take. Calleva is a dead city.

But the land up there is fertile. There will be estates enough for all my eorls, and farms for the rest."

Guthfrid's brown eyes, so striking against her golden hair, were calculating. "Atrebates land?"

"Atrebates land. They are farmers up there, not warriors. There is nothing left of the spirit that gave Arthur his victories."

"It will be easy, then, for you to expand Wessex."

Cynric reached once more for the platter. "Easy enough to conquer them, yes. But while I want to conquer the Atrebates, I also need them. There are too few of us. If Wessex is to become the equal of East Anglia and Sussex and Mercia, then I need the labor of the Britons."

Beyond her husband's bulk she could just see Ceawlin's silvery head, turning to talk to Cutha, who was on his other side. Guthfrid's brown eyes narrowed. How had he managed that entrance with the king?

"A good match for Ceawlin," Cynric was saying.

"*What?*"

He ripped the leg off a chicken. "I said this girl may make a good match for Ceawlin. A marriage between the West Saxon royal family and the Atrebates could be beneficial to me. As I said, I need the Britons to work for me, not against me."

"What about Edwin?" The line of her mouth was now thin, like her narrowed eyes. "Why would not this girl be a good match for him? *He* is your heir, Cynric. Not Ceawlin."

His still-strong teeth tore into the meat of the leg. "I did not think you would deem a British princess good enough for Edwin. You have talked too often of matches to other of the Anglo-Saxon royal houses."

This was true, of course. But she had no intention of allowing Ceawlin to gain even a nominal foothold among the Britons. He would push Edwin aside if he could. She had always known that. He was a threat to her child. Over the years she had made several attempts to do away with the bastard, but she had not yet been successful. She had failed only because she had always to be so careful not to show her hand to the king. Cynric cared for Ceawlin. Guthfrid sometimes thought he loved the bastard even more than his true-born son. This, of course, only added fuel to the fire of her hatred.

"Give her to Edwin," she heard herself saying. "It would bind the Atrebates to you for now, and if it became politic in the future, he could always put her aside and make a more advantageous match."

His light eyes scanned her face. Then he wiped his mouth with the back of his hand and shrugged. "I'll think about it." His eyes turned to the servant who was approaching them carrying a great golden drinking horn.

Guthfrid saw the servant too and rose to her feet. She accepted the horn from the servant and stepped to the floor of the hall. The queen waited a moment until silence had fallen and all eyes were upon her. Then she raised the cup and turned to the king to make the banquet pledge: "Take this cup, my lord and king. Be glad, gold-friend of warriors, in your victory. Enjoy while you may many rewards, and be generous to these your followers who have risked themselves at your side."

Cynric nodded to her gravely and she offered him the horn. He drank and she took the vessel next to Edwin. Looking down into her son's face, the mirror image of her own, she knew again the fierce stab of hot maternal love she always felt for this, her only child. His dark eyes looked into hers for a brief, wordless minute, then he gave her back the horn.

With great dignity Guthfrid completed the rest of the ceremony, bearing the drinking horn from one man to the next all around the great hall. The women she passed by, not sparing them a glance. When she reached Edric her heart skipped a beat, but her outward semblance showed no more emotion than she had displayed for any other of the thanes. His pale blue eyes looked back at her with the same cool distance that hers showed to him. Watching them, no one would ever know that they had been lovers for more than a year.

She passed by Fara and her women with arrogant disdain. Let the friedlehe sit there, in her lesser seat, and watch the queen bestow the cup honors, Guthfrid thought viciously. Her eyes flicked to the side only once, to catch a glimpse of the British princess.

A little thing, she thought. Edwin would soon break her to his will.

Finally she had reached the last of the tables, where sat Cutha and his family. First she gave the horn to the eldest son, Cuthwulf, who drank more deeply than he should before he returned the horn to her. Then Sigurd, the second son, whom she disliked intensely because he was Ceawlin's friend. Then Cutha himself: so close to her husband, so enigmatic to her. And then Ceawlin.

She hesitated for a fraction of a second before handing him the horn. I wish it was poison, she thought.

His eyes, an even more brilliant blue-green than Cynric's, returned her look. He had always hated her fully as much as she hated him. He took the cup, being careful not to touch her fingers, drank, and gave it back to her. With head held high, Guthfrid returned to her place. Once she was seated, Cynric rose.

It was the time for the king to reward his men. The hall thanes stirred eagerly. The silence was intense. "Warriors of Wessex," Cynric began. His voice was perhaps not as strong as it had once been, but it filled the hall nevertheless. "You have upheld the glory of your nation. From this time forward, the borders of Wessex will stretch as far as the

Aildon hills. The British have been defeated." A cheer went up from the hall and Cynric waited for silence to descend once again. "There is little in the way of treasure of gold among the Britons, but there is richness of land. Henceforth the West Saxon eorls will be no less than the great eorls of the Franks. This I, Cynric, your king, promise. Lands for my eorls, and lands too for the thanes who have followed me so bravely into battle. From this day forth, the name of the West Saxons will be great in this land."

A roar of approval burst from the hall men and Cynric sat down. After a minute he gestured to the scop, who was supping at the table next to Edwin's. The scop picked up his wooden harp and advanced to the hearthplace. As soon as he plucked a string, silence fell.

He gave them the song he had written for Cynric when the West Saxon army had taken Venta and they had seen for the first time a city of the Romans:

> Firmly the builder   set the foundations,
> Cleverly bound them   with iron bands;
> Stately the palaces,   splendid the baths,
> Towers and pinnacles   pointing on high;
> Many a mead-hall   rang with their revelry,
> Many a court   with the clang of their arms,
> Till Fate the all-leveling   laid them low.

I too have a reverence for harpers. The words of the Saxon king sounded once again in Niniane's brain. She could not understand what the harper was singing, but she was spellbound by the sound of his voice. It was not singing, precisely, she thought; it was more like chanting. It was also profoundly moving. Every note was plangent with sorrow. She looked around and saw that the hallful of pagan barbarians was listening with riveted attention.

The voice died away and a great sigh ran through the hall, as if everyone listening had been holding his breath and had just discovered he could breathe again. "That was beautiful," Niniane said. "I wish I could understand him."

"He is Alric, the most famous scop in England," Fara returned. "He was telling of the fall of Venta." And she translated some of the words.

Niniane stared at her in astonishment. Never had she expected to hear such elegiac poetry on the lips of a Saxon. "Hush now," Fara said. "He will play again."

After the scop had finished, the drinking cups began to pass more swiftly around the hall. Men's voices and men's laughter grew louder and louder. Finally the queen rose.

Guthfrid made her departure in the same way she had made her entrance, on the arm of her son. Then Cutha's wife and the wives of the other eorls rose, and Fara turned to her own women and said, "Come."

In the anteroom of the hall they met Edwin returning to the feast. He halted directly before Niniane and stared down at her. He was not above average height, but Niniane was not tall and had to look up to see beyond his nose.

"Welcome to Winchester, Princess," he said in decent British. The eyes in his fair-skinned face were an unexpected brown. His eyelashes never once flickered as he stared unwaveringly into her face.

"Thank you, my lord," Niniane murmured in reply.

"Your father is prince of the Atrebates." It was a statement that he managed to make sound like an insult.

Niniane raised her chin. She stared back into those strange brown eyes and answered, "Yes, my lord."

He was smiling. Evidently she amused him. "At least they tried to fight, those Atrebates. But it was careless of them, wasn't it, to leave you behind?"

Niniane had learned from years of living with Coinmail how not to answer back. Her spine stiffened but she made no reply.

"We must be going, Niniane," Fara said. For the first time the boy looked at Cynric's secondary wife, and the expression on his face made Niniane recoil. Then the prince turned away.

As they crossed the now-darkened enclave toward the women's bower, Niniane asked Nola, "Who was the boy who came into the hall with the king?"

"Ceawlin. Fara's son," came the reply. Then, in a worried voice, "It was not wise of him to do that. There is little point in provoking Guthfrid's jealousy."

"How many sons does Cynric have?"

"Just two, Ceawlin and Edwin. Ceawlin is the elder by a year, but Edwin is Guthfrid's son and the heir to the kingship."

"If that is so, then why should the queen be jealous?"

"She is jealous of anyone who breathes the same air as Edwin," Nola said bitterly. "For fifteen years she has been like a bear with one cub. Let the king show Ceawlin the slightest notice, and she is livid with fury."

They had reached the women's bower and Niniane parted from Nola and went down the corridor to her own room. Someone had replaced the candle on the table with an oil lamp in her absence, and she lit the lamp with the flame from the candle she had picked up at the door. Then she looked at it with frowning concentration. It was a lamp from Bryn Atha. She sat on the side of the bed and stared at its warm glow.

Bryn Atha seemed very far away tonight. In just two days she had left one world and entered another. Winchester! And not one of her people had even known it existed.

Pictures from the banquet flashed through her mind. Edwin's mocking face. The silver-blond boy who was Fara's son. The beautiful, cold, arrogant-looking queen. The king, who had a reverence for harpers.

What a story she would have to tell to Coinmail and her father!

She undressed, blew out the lamp, and got into bed. She was tired but she did not fall immediately to sleep. This room was as large as her bedchamber at home, but the lack of a window made her feel closed in, suffocated almost. Without the lamp she was in blackness so absolute that she could not even see the outline of the table next to the bed.

Finally, however, fatigue overtook her. Her last thought before she drifted off to sleep was: I wonder what kind of a ransom Cynric will ask.

Chapter 4

"*H*ERE, Bayla!" Sigurd called to the hound who had started to wander back toward the stable. The hound continued to sniff along the ground, ignoring the command. "Ceawlin . . ." Sigurd said, and turned to his friend.

The prince finished pulling up his girth and looked for the dog. "Bayla," he said softly, and snapped his fingers. The hound raised his head, then came obediently to his master's side. Ceawlin slung a bow over his shoulder and picked up his reins. Sigurd did the same and the two boys led their horses out of the stableyard. Three hounds followed, trotting at the horses' heels.

The dawn was just beginning to come up. Sigurd looked toward the queen's hall and said, "I keep hoping we will surprise Edric creeping out of there one morning."

Ceawlin showed his white teeth in a sardonic smile. "They are not stupid enough for that. Unfortunately."

The sky was still gray, with only a few pink streaks in the east to signal that the day would be fine. Ceawlin and Sigurd had been rising this early to go out hunting ever since they were first allowed to venture forth by themselves. The two had been virtually inseparable for almost all their boyhood.

"Who is that?" Sigurd said suddenly in a startled voice. Both boys stopped and stared at the small figure sitting on the step of the women's bower.

"It is the little British princess," Ceawlin said slowly.

"We'd better see what she is doing," Sigurd said, and they both changed direction and began to walk across the courtyard toward the bower.

She did not move as they approached. Sigurd saw that she was huddled into her cloak as if she were cold. Her unbound hair streamed all around her. Sigurd had noticed her hair before and he thought it beautiful. The coppery color made a nice change from all the blond he was so accustomed to seeing in Winchester.

"Why are you sitting here like this so early in the morning?" Ceawlin asked. His British was perfectly unaccented.

The girl's eyes widened with surprise. "But you speak British!"

Ceawlin raised his silver-blond eyebrows. "Most of my generation speak your tongue. But you have not answered me. What are you doing here?"

The girl's widely spaced eyes moved from Ceawlin's face to Sigurd. She was really very pretty, Sigurd thought. So small and delicate-looking. Like a little deer. He smiled at her engagingly. Ceawlin had been too abrupt. "The prince had a British nurse when he was small— that is why he speaks your tongue so well." His own British was perfectly adequate, but he knew he had an accent. "It is too cold out here for you, Princess," he went on kindly. "You should go back indoors."

Her eyes were a dark blue-gray and very steady and grave. "I wanted some air," she said. "I am not accustomed to sleeping in a room without a window."

"Afraid of the dark?" Sigurd asked with sympathy. "You could leave your candle on."

"Not if she's going to sleep in a wooden building," Ceawlin said. His eyes, such an arresting shade of blue-green, were not sympathetic at all.

A little color flushed into the girl's pale cheeks. Ceawlin had sounded distinctly nasty. Sigurd knew what was wrong with him. Cynric was intending to give this girl to Edwin. "I am not disturbing anyone by sitting here," she said a little defiantly. Ceawlin's horse stamped its near front foot with impatience at being kept standing. "You had better go," the girl added, "before *you* wake everyone up."

Sigurd grinned. "She's right," he said to Ceawlin. Then, in Saxon, "She's not likely to go anywhere."

Ceawlin looked from the girl to Sigurd, then to the girl again. "I suppose that's true." He turned without further comment and began to walk toward the main gate. Sigurd smiled once more at the girl sitting on the step and turned to follow his friend.

"Cynric is really going to wed her to Edwin?" Sigurd asked as the two boys vaulted into their saddles and rode through the main gate of Winchester.

Ceawlin acknowledged the salute of the watchman. "So it seems. Guthfrid is urging it. And I can see that it would be a good match for Wessex. It would be well for us to get on terms with the Britons in this new area. Look how useful the Britons in Venta have been to us."

"My father said Cynric originally thought to wed her to you."

Ceawlin said nothing.

"She's such a pretty little thing," Sigurd went on. "It seems a shame to wed her to Edwin."

"It would be a shame to wed any woman to Edwin," came the bitter reply.

"True."

"I think my father meant to wed her to Edwin all along," said Ceawlin finally. "He only told Guthfrid he was thinking of me in order to force her to take the girl for Edwin."

Sigurd stared at him. "What makes you think that?"

"I know him too well. He does not want a match with any other of the Anglo-Saxon kingdoms. Not yet, not while Wessex is still so small."

The sky had become much lighter while they were talking. The hounds ran back and forth across the fields in front of them, eager to reach the woods. There were a number of Saxon vils—peasant farming communities—in the area of Winchester, and Ceawlin and Sigurd had taken it upon themselves to keep the predator population away from the crops and livestock of the local ceorls.

"Well, if the king wanted to trick Guthfrid, he could not have chosen a cleverer way of going about it," said Sigurd. "She can't bear to see you put food in your mouth."

Ceawlin's clear-cut profile was stern. "I know."

"And she is dangerous as a mother wolf. The look on her face when you came into the banquet with the king the other night! You must be more careful, Ceawlin."

"I told you. It was Cynric's doing. He wanted to force Guthfrid to take this girl for Edwin. She has had great plans of wedding him into Mercia."

"Mercia is looking to expand to the south."

"I know." A bird swooped low overhead and Ceawlin's horse gave a little buck. He patted its glossy bay neck. "My mother tells me the girl thinks she is going to be ransomed back to her father," he added.

Sigurd's gray eyes were startled. "Ransomed!"

"Yes. Apparently she is singularly innocent, this little princess."

"Gods," said Sigurd. Then, "It makes me sick to think of giving her to Edwin."

Ceawlin shrugged, and just then they reached the woods. Two minutes later the hounds caught a scent and the two boys tore off in pursuit, all thought of Niniane banished from their minds.

"I am going into Venta today," Fara said to Niniane as they ate their porridge in the women's hall later that morning. "Should you care to come with me?"

"Oh, yes!" Niniane's small face lighted. She had not left Winchester since her arrival, even though there seemed to be a regular flow of traffic between the Saxon enclave and the old Roman city. Winchester was primarily a royal residence. It was Venta that housed the blacksmiths, the armorers, the carpenters, turners, coopers, cobblers, silver-smiths, jewel-makers, soap-makers, and beer-makers who supplied their wares for Winchester's consumption. The staff at Winchester itself consisted mainly of house and kitchen slaves, grooms for the horses, kennelmen for the dogs, gardeners, and fishermen.

"I am going to the jewel-maker's," Fara said. "The garnets in one of my necklaces have loosened."

Venta, thought Niniane with excited anticipation as she spread butter thickly on her bread. But it was not Saxon Venta that she burned to see. It was the Venta that had been a Roman capital, the Venta from which Ambrosius and Uther had reigned as high kings of Britain, the Venta where Arthur had been crowned and where he had lived until he built Camelot.

How she longed for Kerwyn still to be alive so she could tell him all about it.

They rode to Venta in a covered wagon, which had cushions on the seats and was drawn by a matched pair of gray horses. The road between Winchester and Venta was in very good condition; the Saxons evidently kept this part of the old Roman road in repair.

"I don't ride anymore," Fara said to Niniane as the two women stepped into the wagon. "My joints are too stiff for horseback and so my lord king had this conveyance built for me. It serves very well."

It was also a mark of Cynric's regard for his friedlehe, Niniane thought as she took her place on the cushioned seat. She had learned Fara's story from Nola, who was an insatiable gossip and so a wonderful source of information. Fara was the daughter of one of Cynric's father's thanes and Cynric had known her when the West Saxons' only foothold in southern Britain had been the Isle of Wight, taken by Cerdic at the beginning of the century. Then Cerdic had died, leaving Wight to his eldest son, and Cynric had gone to the mainland to win his own kingdom. As soon as he had taken Venta, he sent for Fara. According to Nola, he had held to her alone for six years before agreeing to a marriage with Guthfrid to heal an old feud of his father's with East Anglia.

"She was barren for all those years," Nola said, "and then, almost as soon as Cynric's marriage was set, she conceived. She was old then, in her middle thirties, but she finally bore Cynric a son. Then when Guthfrid had a child almost immediately, everyone thought there would soon be a houseful of princes and princesses of the blood. But there have been only these two: Ceawlin and Edwin. The fault must lie with Cynric. None of the other household women have conceived by him either."

Niniane had been horrified to learn that the women's bower was no more than a harem for the king. And for the royal princes too. In this way the Saxons had fully lived up to her image of them: barbarian, pagan, horrible. The fact that the women seemed to be perfectly content with this arrangement made it even more revolting.

She looked now at Fara, who was sitting beside her. She liked the friedlehe very much. It was hard to understand how she could accept her position with such equanimity. It was even harder to accept that Cynric cared for her, but apparently he did. He had built her this comfortable cushioned wagon, for one thing. He came to the women's hall regularly to visit her, and they would sit talking quietly together, both of them seated in large wooden chairs that were covered with thick rugs to make them comfortable for aging bones. At such times the rest of the women would disperse to the far corner of the hall, or outside if the weather was clement.

Niniane thanked God on her knees every night that she had been born a Christian woman and not a Saxon.

The sides of Fara's wagon were open, and so Niniane was able to see the walls of Venta come into view. They looked very like the walls of Calleva, she thought, but any other resemblance to Calleva died as soon as they were inside the town. This was a city that was alive. The old Roman grid of streets was lined with obviously inhabited buildings.

"We'll show you the city before we do our errands," Fara said. The wagon horses were proceeding at a brisk walk up the main street of the city. "There are the old baths," and Fara pointed to a graceful stone building that resembled the baths Niniane had seen at Calleva. The Saxon woman smiled. "Our scops sing that all these stone structures were the work of giants. My son says the Romans knew how to build. In fact, he says, the buildings will likely long outlast their empire."

"Yes," said Niniane sadly. "Their whole civilization is slipping away from us, all their knowledge . . ." Her voice trailed away and Fara looked at her shrewdly.

"The Romans could build with stone, true, and that is a skill we do not have. But these buildings are the only trace of occupation they will leave on this island, Niniane. You see, they came as conquerors, not as settlers. They came, they built roads and buildings, and then when their emperor called them, they left, like dust blowing away in the wind." Fara shrugged. "So you see, my dear, they were not so successful after all."

And are you not conquerors as well? Niniane thought. She looked at the friedlehe's beautiful profile and prudently held her tongue. But she did not see how the Saxons differed from the Romans in that way.

"There is the forum," Fara said, and Niniane looked in the direction the friedlehe was indicating. The Venta forum was larger than the one at Calleva and there were shops set up under the colonnade arches and a bustle of people going in and out. The tall blond Saxons mingled with the smaller, darker people who were Venta's older inhabitants.

"We'll have a look around the shops, but first I'll show you the building the Britons call the praetorium. And perhaps you would like to visit the Christian church?"

"Yes," said Niniane quietly. "I would."

The praetorium was empty. The centerpiece of Roman rule in this part of Britain, the building which had housed three British high kings after the departure of the legions, was as deserted and bare as most of the buildings in Calleva. Niniane felt tears sting behind her eyes.

"What were the words the scop sang at the banquet the other night?" she asked Fara.

The answer came in a soft voice: " 'The battlements crumble, the wine-halls decay . . .' That is the true Saxon spirit, my dear. *Lif is laene* . . . life is fleeting."

"My father's harper would have understood that," Niniane said. Kerwyn's face came vividly to her mind. "Arthur is gone . . ." she murmured with infinite sadness, her eyes on the empty shell of the praetorium.

"Life is indeed short," Fara said, and now her voice was brisk. "But that does not stop us from enjoying the time and the wealth that we have. Come. Let us do our shopping, and then you shall see your church."

Niniane thought the shops were sumptuous. To a visitor from Paris or Rome or Constantinople, they would have been meager, but to a British girl who had never seen a truly functioning city, Venta was a marvel. The jeweler, a blue-eyed German of some sort, even had a necklace that had been imported from Soissons to show to Fara.

The language generally spoken, even by those who were obviously Britons, was Saxon. The means of exchange was mainly barter, although Fara had some gold imperial coins from the Continent with which she paid the jewel-maker. Niniane's eyes were bright with pleasure as she followed Fara around the marketplace. She had quite forgot the melancholy she felt when she saw the praetorium.

They went to the Christian church before they left to return to Winchester. It was a small building, with plastered walls that had been painted in imitation of marble. The nave had a mosaic floor of red tiles and the floor under the altar was a panel of checkered tile in black, red, and white. The church was perfectly intact, although clearly unused.

Niniane stood before the altar, bowed her head, and listened. Empty and deserted as it seemed, still this room was not dead. There was a presence here, a presence she could feel, a presence that listened to her, a presence that cared.

There were monks still at Glastonbury to the west; that she knew.

Dumnonia and Wales were still strongholds of faith. If the British could not conquer the Saxons in battle, perhaps they could conquer the pagans in this. The thought came to her out of the silent air, and she smiled. She felt quite at peace when she rejoined Fara on the main street of Venta.

Three days later Niniane was sent for by the king. Sigurd's father dispatched him to fetch her from the women's hall for the marriage arrangements. Sigurd did not want to be involved in these particular plans, but he did not dare say so to Cutha. He went.

He waited on the porch of the women's hall with ill-concealed impatience. Ceawlin was being spared this scene; Sigurd did not see why he had to be part of it. His father knew well his feelings about Edwin.

Cynric had sent Ceawlin into Venta that morning to interview the participants in a dispute over a trading license. Cutha had told Sigurd that the king did not want Ceawlin present at this business of Edwin's marriage, but he did not want it to look as if Ceawlin were being deliberately excluded either. By making the arrangements today, the king had an excuse for his elder son's absence.

The women's-hall door opened and Niniane came out onto the porch. Her smoke-blue eyes looked up at him with a mixture of apprehension and anticipation. "Has my ransom come?" she asked.

He could not meet those eyes. "The king wishes to discuss your future," he temporized uneasily. Then, "If you will come with me, Princess?" He opened the porch door for her.

"Are you still afraid of the dark?" he asked as they crossed the courtyard side by side.

"It is not the dark," she returned in her surprisingly husky voice. "It is being shut in. I am used to rooms with windows, you see."

"Windows are nice," he agreed. "We do not have the Roman skill of making glass."

She gave him a quick upturned look. "Neither do we, anymore."

"It is not so bad here in Winchester," he said a little awkwardly. "We may not have windows, but life is comfortable."

"Life is very comfortable, my lord," she replied quickly. He could see she was afraid she had offended him. "It is just different from what I am used to." And she gave him a tentative shy smile.

He felt anger swell in his heart. It was an outrage to think of this girl in Edwin's bed.

They had reached the king's private hall. Sigurd set his teeth and motioned for her to go in before him.

Cynric's hall differed from most of the other halls in Winchester in that the hearthplace was not in the center of the room but in a corner.

The center was reserved for a great carved wood table with eight high-backed chairs arranged behind it. Seated in the chairs today were Cynric, Guthfrid, Edwin, Cutha, and Cuthwulf, Sigurd's brother.

"My lord king," said Sigurd in Saxon, "I bring you the Princess Niniane." Then, in a lower voice to Niniane, "Go and stand before the king."

He watched her walk across the floor and come to a halt before the table. She looked very small. Sigurd then went himself and took the chair next to his brother.

It was Cutha, his father, who spoke. "The king has made a decision about your future, Princess. You will be pleased to learn that you are to marry his son, Prince Edwin."

Every drop of blood seemed to drain from her face. "Marry!" she said. Her eyes went from Cutha to the king.

"Yes, marry," Cutha replied. "The king has deemed it will be wise for Winchester to make a match with the Atrebates."

"But I thought I was to be ransomed . . ."

"You yourself are more valuable to us than any ransom your father might pay," said Cutha smoothly. "You are a princess of your line. A match between you and Edwin will bring the lands of the Atrebates more easily under our control."

The color had not yet returned to her face, but Sigurd could see how her chin rose. "I cannot marry a Saxon," she said. "I am a Christian."

"That matters little. We will not interfere with your beliefs."

"Enough of these questions!" It was Guthfrid, speaking in broken British for Niniane's sake. "You are to marry my son, and that is an end to it. Marriage is not a matter girls are allowed to settle for themselves."

"No, their fathers settle it for them," Niniane shot back. "And I'm quite sure mine will not approve of this. Such a match, my lord"—and here she looked once again at Cynric, knowing that he was the one to whom she had to make her appeal—"such a match is more likely to enrage my people than to placate them. Unlike the Christians in Venta, we take our religion seriously."

Cynric turned to Cutha, who translated for him. Then Cynric looked back at the girl who was standing before him. "Come here," he said in Saxon, and gestured to the place beside him. Niniane began to walk around the table. She did not look at Sigurd as she passed in front of him. Finally she was standing next to the king. He reached out and took her chin into his hand. She looked back into his eyes, her own not flinching.

After a long minute he dropped his hand. He turned to Guthfrid and said in Saxon, "Let us wait. She may be right."

"My lord!"

He held up a hand and looked across her at his son. "We will inform her people of our intentions," he said to Edwin's unblinking brown eyes. "It might be necessary to marry her in a Christian rite. Let us wait and see."

The butter-yellow head nodded. "Yes, my lord," said Guthfrid's son.

Niniane, who had understood nothing of what was being said, stood white-faced between Cutha and the king. "Tell her," Cynric said.

"The marriage will be postponed until we have communicated with your people," Cutha said to her. "Princess, you are dismissed."

Chapter 5

"SIT still, Ceawlin!" His mother gave an impatient tug on the hair she was trimming for him. "I will cut it too short if you keep wiggling about."

Ceawlin let out his breath in an impatient sigh. "It is a good thing you were not born a Frank, Mother," he said, as he had said every time she cut his hair since he was five years old. "Then you would never have an opportunity to exercise your talents with the scissors. The Franks have a law against cutting the hair of their princes."

"Well, you are not a Frank, you are a Saxon, and your hair should not be hanging below your shoulders." Fara made the same response she had been making for the last twelve years also.

"It's going down my back and it itches."

"You can change your clothes later. Now sit still!"

Ceawlin caught the eye of one of the younger bower girls who was working at the loom and winked. The girl giggled, then, as Fara looked up, turned back to her work. Ceawlin crossed his arms and tried to get comfortable.

He did not really mind having his hair cut, but he had played this game with Fara since he was a baby and he knew it gave her pleasure. She did not have much opportunity to scold him these days, not since he had moved to the princes' hall and out from under her jurisdiction.

"I want it short over my forehead," he murmured.

"I know." She picked up a comb from the table and smoothed the hair over his brow. "Close your eyes."

He closed them and then blew upward as the hair fell down and tickled his nose.

"There," his mother said with satisfaction, and he opened his eyes and saw Niniane coming in the door. She stopped a moment in surprise as she saw the unusual scene before her: Ceawlin seated in a chair with a cloth spread under it and Fara hovering over him with scissors.

Ceawlin grinned. "It's a strange Saxon rite, Princess. Called a haircut."

She came toward him with quiet dignity. "We have that ritual also, Prince. I used to cut my brother's hair. He wears it like the Romans, much shorter than yours." She stopped a few feet from him. "You will see for yourself soon enough."

37

Their eyes met. Hers were dark and smoky and carefully expressionless.

Niniane's position in Winchester had changed considerably during the course of the last year. Instead of approving a marriage between her and Edwin, the Atrebates had rallied and reoccupied one of the old hill forts in the mountains northwest of Calleva. The leader of the newly warlike Britons was Niniane's brother, Coinmail. Her father had died three months after Sarc Water.

Since word had come to Winchester of Coinmail's action, Niniane had been waiting to find out what her future was to be. Cynric had postponed all talk of marriage and was taking a war band north in a few weeks' time to meet Coinmail's challenge. Niniane's fate would depend upon the outcome of that encounter. And for the first time, Ceawlin, who had turned seventeen over the winter, was to join his father's army.

"I am looking forward to it," he said now to the level blue eyes that were holding his so steadily.

She did not answer, nor did her expression change. He thought, all of a sudden, that he had never seen her smile.

"I see Alric finished your harp," Fara said in a pleased voice, and for the first time Ceawlin noticed what Niniane was carrying in her hand.

"Yes." Her small hands stroked the wood lovingly. "It was so kind of him."

"Alric made you a harp?" he asked in amazement. The scop was not one to pay much attention to girls.

"Niniane is a very fine harpist," his mother said to him as she brushed the hair off his neck. "There. You're all finished, Ceawlin."

He stood up and brushed at his tunic, which was dusted with silvery hairs as well. "You play?" His voice was frankly incredulous.

"My father's harper taught me when I was a little girl."

It was late in the day but not yet time to sup. He sat himself down in another chair and said, "Play something for me."

Niniane looked at Fara. "Would you mind, my dear? We should all enjoy it," said the friedlehe in her lovely, kind voice.

Niniane came forward with obvious reluctance and sat down on a stool at a little distance from Ceawlin. He leaned back in his chair, stretched his long legs in front of him, and waited. He did not expect much. Everyone knew women had no talent for music.

"The only songs I know are the songs of Arthur's wars against the Saxons," Niniane said. She gave him a sideways slanting look. "And you are not the heroes, my lord."

"That's all right. My feelings won't be hurt." He rested his head against the carved back of his chair.

Niniane looked at him measuringly. His evenly trimmed hair just cleared his shoulders and framed his head like a silver helmet. His

half-open eyes were regarding her with lazy tolerance. Coinmail pa-
tronized her all the time; she did not know why the same treatment
from this Saxon prince should annoy her so much. She decided she
would give him "The Battle of Badon."

As always, all else fell away from her the moment she began to play.
She woke the harp to life. "Arthur, the king . . ." she began to sing in
her rich, husky voice, and the room fell very still.

When, finally, the last note had died away, she raised her head. He
was looking at her, a very different expression in those blue-green eyes.
He said only, "Now I understand why Alric made you the harp," but
for some reason her very breathing altered and she looked in some
confusion at her fingers, resting still on the strings of the instrument.
She did not look back at him until he rose to leave a few minutes later.

He was so tall, she thought as she watched him walking beside Fara
to the door. He topped his mother by half a head, and Fara was a very
tall woman. He was much taller than Cynric, and much leaner too. He
was very much his mother's son. Except for the eyes.

He turned at the door and looked back at her. "Don't expect another
Badon this spring, Princess. The tides of war have changed in England
and it is we who are on the rise." He kindly allowed his mother to kiss
his cheek, and then he was gone.

Ceawlin came suddenly awake. His sleeping room was pitch dark,
but that told him nothing about the time. The walls were so well built
that there were no cracks for the light to creep between. Still, he knew
it was early. He had always had a sixth sense about time.

It was early, but he knew he would not go back to sleep. He was too
keyed-up with anticipation. Tomorrow his father would be marching
north to fight the Britons. Ceawlin had been making ready for this, his
first war band, for the last month at least. Everything was ready: his
sword and spear and sax dagger sharpened, all his leather oiled, his
mail byrnie polished. He and Sigurd had been practicing their sword-
play for hours each day, thinking up new ways to kill their man. His
horse's bay coat gleamed from all the brushing the stallion had been
given recently.

And he still had one more day to get through.

He swung his feet to the floor, lit a candle, and dressed. Then he
opened his sleeping room's door and went out into the main room of
the princes' hall. The door to Edwin's room was closed and the young
men lying on the benches along the wall did not stir. Ceawlin crossed
the wooden floor on silent feet and passed out into the morning.

The stars were still out. It was very early indeed. Ceawlin looked
slowly around the enclave and his eyes stopped as they encountered
the queen's hall.

The bitch. She had persuaded Cynric to take Edwin as soon as she learned that Ceawlin was to join the war band this spring. Was he never to have anything in his life that wasn't spoiled by the jealous envy of his brother and the queen?

He began to walk toward the main gate of Winchester. He had put on only breeches and shirt, and the morning air was cool, but Ceawlin did not notice. He paused for a moment in front of the temple, then, after glancing about once more, walked around to the door set in the long side of the building, and went in.

The inside of the Saxon temple at Winchester was small but complete. The pit for making the offering was next to the door on the long wall opposite where Ceawlin was presently standing. The table for the ritual banquet was on the short wall to his right, while the altar and the images of the gods were in the set-apart area to his left. Ceawlin did not pause indoors, however, but passed through the room and out the door on the other side.

This door led into a fenced-in area which was dominated by a massive wooden pillar. Ceawlin went to stand before it.

Woden, he thought, gazing up at the huge carved image towering above him. Woden, father of battles, fill me with your spirit that I may prove myself worthy to be your descendant. He stood there for quite a long time, until the growing light blotted out the stars; then he returned to the princes' hall to find something to do to pass the day.

Edwin arose after Ceawlin had gone down to the stables. The two boys were forced by custom to share the same hall, but they had so arranged their schedules that they seldom met. Edwin breakfasted by himself and then went to see his mother.

Guthfrid was in her sleeping room in the queen's hall, having her hair done. She caught a glimpse of her son in the hand mirror she was holding, part of the booty from last year's war band and Cynric's gift to her. She smiled at him in the mirror and held her position as the handmaid fastened the last jeweled clasp in her hair.

"You are beautiful as always, Mother," Edwin said as he crossed the floor toward her.

"Oh, Edwin." Guthfrid put the mirror down and motioned to her handmaid to leave. She held her face up and Edwin bent to kiss her on the mouth.

"How are you, my love?" the queen murmured as her hand caressed his cheek.

"Well." He pulled a stool over and sat at Guthfrid's knee. "Mother, I want to make sure that Ceawlin does not win any fame for himself on this war band."

Her plucked brows drew a little together. "The king will not leave him behind. You know that, Edwin. I tried, but I made no headway with your father. He was ready to leave *you* behind, because you are not yet seventeen, but he insisted that Ceawlin must go."

"I know that the king has too great a regard for this bastard," said Edwin coldly. "I want to remedy that."

"But how, my love?"

"You have knowledge of poisons, Mother. I need you to help me."

Her brown eyes widened. "Edwin, you know I would have taken care of your brother that way years ago if I thought I could do so safely."

"I don't mean to kill him, Mother. Just make him too sick to fight. He will look a fool, whereas I . . ."

"Ah," said Guthfrid. Her brow smoothed out. "I see."

"You gave me something once before. He was sick for two days."

She smiled. "All right, my love. But you must be careful. Should anyone see you put it into his cup . . ."

His brown eyes were cold and flat. "No one will see me."

"Oh, my darling . . ." and she put her hand on his golden head. "Please be careful. If ever I should lose you . . ."

He took her other hand and pressed it to his lips. Then he stood up. "Never fear, Mother. I am far too clever to get myself killed."

She stared up at him, her own hair glimmering in the light from the lamp on her table. "Give the poison directly into my hands," he said. "I will trust no one else with this. Tomorrow, just before we leave."

"All right," she said, and watched with a mixture of pride and fear as he walked out the door of her room.

This year's war band was larger than last year's. This year they knew they were going out to fight. The Atrebates had refortified one of Britain's most ancient hill forts, called Beranbyrg by the Saxons and Barbury by the British, and if Cynric wanted to claim land in their territory, he was going to have to win it by force of arms.

Three hundred thanes were lined up four abreast on the main road of Winchester the morning of April 22. It was a week after the Saxon spring feast of Eostre. Ceawlin and Sigurd, mounting their horses near the stables, exchanged grins of mutual delight and felt sorry for anyone who was not lucky enough to be riding out on this beautiful morning to his first battle.

The two boys settled themselves into their saddles, received their weapons from the slave who was holding them, and began to walk their horses toward the mass of men in the courtyard. As he reached the line of thanes, Ceawlin saw his mother come out the door of the women's hall. For a moment he hesitated. Then, with a word to Sigurd, he guided his bay stallion across the yard toward her. She came down the steps and stood beside him, her hand on his knee, her eyes searching his face as if to memorize it. He smiled down at her, his eyes very bright. "I will bring honor home to you, Mother," he said.

Fara smiled back and then was grave again. "I know you will, my son." She dropped her hand and stepped back. As he turned his horse, he saw out of the side of his eyes the little British princess come out onto the steps of the women's hall. He closed his fingers on the reins and looked at her directly.

Her small face was perfectly expressionless but he could see even from the back of his horse that there were shadows under her eyes. It was her brother who was leading the Atrebates. For a brief moment his joy in the day was marred by a flash of pity; then he trotted forward to join his kinsmen, his hair shining brighter in the sun than the metal rings of his byrnie.

They marched north along the old Roman road to Corinium. Ceawlin rode beside Sigurd and inhaled the fresh damp odor of growing things. He felt perfectly happy. Until his eye fell on the golden head of his brother, riding next to the king.

Sigurd saw the direction of his gaze. "I'll watch your back for you," he murmured.

Ceawlin shot him a look, then shrugged and made no answer. There was no answer he could make. They both knew Sigurd's concern was not unwarranted.

"Eager for glory, children?" Sigurd's elder brother, Cuthwulf, pushed his horse between Sigurd and the prince. Cuthwulf had seen battle before, a fact which he never let them forget. He was a big, broad-shouldered man with truculent blue eyes. He was so unlike the suave Cutha that Ceawlin sometimes wondered about his paternity.

Ceawlin said now, mildly, "We only hope to emulate your example, Cuthwulf."

Sigurd's brother gave a pleased smile and started to answer. "I think Father is looking for you," Sigurd said first.

As the boys watched Cuthwulf press his horse forward again, Ceawlin said on a note of suppressed laughter, "Good thinking. We were about to get another rendition of his exploits at Searo byrg."

Sigurd groaned. "At least you don't have to live with him!"

All the laughter fled from Ceawlin's face. "I'll take your brother to mine."

"So will I," said Sigurd, and his face also was now perfectly sober. "So will I."

Beranbyrg was some forty miles northeast of Winchester, along the same road that Niniane had traveled with Cynric and Cutha a little less than a year before. Ceawlin had never been this far north before, and he looked around with curiosity as they drew ever closer to the Aildon hills.

"This is nice country," Sigurd said appreciatively as he too looked over the gently rolling country with its velvety green cover of grass. Farms dotted the landscape and sheep grazed peacefully beside the road.

"The Britons are a strange, solitary people," Ceawlin replied, a puzzled look between his brows. "Our people like to live together. Even the peasants have all their houses in one vil, and then they go out to work in the fields together. We cooperate with each other, help each other. These Britons, though, live in isolated farmhouses and work all by themselves. It almost seems as if they do not like each other."

"That is true," Sigurd agreed. "Look at the way they deserted all the fine cities the Romans built. My father said that only ghosts walk at the place they call Calleva."

There was a steady breeze blowing off the hills and when Ceawlin turned to look at Sigurd his silver-gilt hair whipped across his lean, hard cheek. The expression on his face was stern. "They have no feeling for kingship," he said. "That is why this Coinmail will never be able to extend his leadership beyond his own small tribe. It is their weakness, and our strength."

"They have certainly had no king worth the name since Arthur," Sigurd said. He frowned in puzzlement. "I wonder why they are like that? Surely they must see how their lack of organization weakens them. Is it that they are cowards who don't like to fight?"

"It is that they are Christians," Ceawlin answered. "This Christianity is a faith that takes all power from the king and gives it to the priest. It is the priest to whom they listen, not the king." He reached up to push the hair off his cheek. "That is why it is the religion of defeat." He looked again at the green rolling downs that now surrounded them. "All of this," and he smiled with satisfaction, "will shortly belong to us."

Beranbyrg had been a fort since prehistoric times. The Celts had not used it for centuries, however, and it had fallen into disrepair until Coinmail refortified during the winter for his stand against the Saxons. It lay along the even more ancient roadway that went through the Aildon hills and all the way into East Anglia.

Cynric sent scouts ahead to report on the state of the fort, and they returned with the information that the outer fortifications of Beranbyrg consisted of a substantial dirt bank and a ditch. The Britons had done a good job of repairing the bank; there were no weak points that the scouts could see.

The Saxons made their camp about two miles from the British fort. It was late in the day and cookfires were lit immediately. The king, Cutha, and their sons sat cross-legged on the ground around one such fire and ate their evening meal together.

"We will attack at dawn," Cynric said as he slowly chewed his deer meat. "The less light there is, the better chance we have of getting across the ditch and the bank." He continued to chew as he told them of his plan for the following day. The Saxons were to launch a three-pronged attack led by himself, Cutha, and Cuthwulf. Ceawlin and Edwin were to fight under the king's command, and Sigurd was to fight with Cutha. Ceawlin gave one quick look to Sigurd as these arrangements were discussed, then looked away.

Cynric finished speaking, threw away the rest of his meat, and looked into his empty cup. Edwin jumped to his feet and took the cup from his father, saying quickly, "Let me serve you, my lord." Cynric looked at his son's eager face, smiled, and nodded. Edwin went over to the barrel that held the beer, filled the king's cup, and brought it to him. Then he said to Cutha, courteously, "May I fill yours also, kinsman?"

Ceawlin watched his brother's stocky figure go from one man to the next around the fire. Behind him he heard someone near the barrel offering to fill the cups for Edwin, and his brother's curt rejection. Then Edwin was standing in front of him.

"May I fill yours, brother?" he asked in the same pleasant voice he had used to the others.

Slowly Ceawlin extended his cup. Edwin took it and went to the barrel for the last time. Ceawlin turned his head a little to watch, but saw only his brother's back as he bent over the beer. Then Edwin was before him once more, the cup extended in his hand.

Ceawlin looked up into his younger brother's face. The dark eyes looking back at him were unreadable. Edwin's eyes had always reminded him of an animal's: opaque, unblinking, feral. He took the cup.

The king looked around the circle of his family. "May Woden take them all," he said in the usual Saxon dedication to the enemy host. Woden, god of battles, selected from the men fighting in a battle those who were to be victorious and those who were to be slain.

Cynric drank and the others raised their cups as well. Just as the rim touched his lips, Ceawlin glanced toward Edwin. The dark, unwinking gaze was fixed on his mouth. With sudden decision Ceawlin moved his mouth and swallowed but did not allow the liquid to touch his lips. The failure to drink to the dedication of the enemy host was less dangerous, he thought, than what was likely awaiting him in that cup.

The fire died down and the voices around the fire began to run out as well. Even Cuthwulf seemed to weary of predicting his own great exploits upon the morrow. Cynric began to get to his feet and Edwin jumped up to assist him. Ceawlin made a move as if he too would help his father, but Edwin shook him off. As everyone else was watching the old king rise painfully from his seat on the ground, Ceawlin stooped and poured the contents of his cup into Edwin's.

Finally the king was on his feet. As Cynric walked toward the sleeping place that had been made for him, Cutha at his side, Ceawlin raised his cup. "To Cynric, the king!" he said. "And to victory!"

His cousins and his brother picked up their cups and drank the pledge. Ceawlin went off to his own bedplace with a satisfied smile on his long, beautifully chiseled mouth.

In the middle of the night, Edwin became violently sick to his stomach. By the time the war band had broken camp it was clear that the prince was too ill to go with them. Cynric left his son with a small bodyguard and the rest of the Saxons began the march toward Beranbyrg in the dark.

"The gods were with you," Sigurd murmured to Ceawlin as the two young men rode out of camp side by side.

"He put something in my drink last night," Ceawlin answered. "When he wasn't looking, I poured it back into his."

There was a startled silence. Then, "Gods! What if it had been meant to kill?"

"I was rather hoping it was," Ceawlin said.

Sigurd's silence was even longer this time. Finally, "Someday, Ceawlin, it will be."

"I don't think so. He must depend on Guthfrid to get the poison, and she will not go that far. My father has a fondness for me, and she is afraid of him."

"I cannot understand her! Why does she hate you so? You have never tried to take aught of hers."

"Do you know, Sigurd," Ceawlin said thoughtfully, "we have always blamed the way Edwin is on Guthfrid. What if it is the other way around?"

"What do you mean?"

"I mean we have always thought that Edwin hates me because he had been taught to by his mother. But suppose she hates me only because Edwin hated me first."

"But why?" Sigurd said again. "He is the heir. You do not stand in his way."

"It's the way he is," Ceawlin replied. "He cannot bear anyone to share the sun with him. That is all."

The dawn was beginning to streak the sky with a pale gray light when the fort of Beranbyrg came into view. Ceawlin and Sigurd dismounted and handed their horses to grooms. As Saxon warriors, they would fight on foot. Then the two young men began to check their weapons: the large sword, the lighter spears, the sax dagger both wore thrust through their belts. Before they donned the mittened mail arm covering that would protect their sword arms, Ceawlin held out his hand to Sigurd. The two boys clasped their hands together strongly. Neither spoke but both knew what the other was thinking. Then they finished putting on their mail. They did not wear helmets, as the West Saxons always fought bareheaded.

All around them men were doing the same things they were. The sky was not growing brighter. The day was damp and Ceawlin thought it was probably going to rain. He listened intently but could hear nothing from inside the dirt walls of the fort. Could the Britons really be so unaware of the coming attack?

Cynric's command began to assemble in front of the king. This attack force would take the brunt of the fighting, as the king wanted to draw most of the defenders' attention to one side of the fort while the other two commands got over the wall quickly.

Ceawlin was not surprised when it began to drizzle. The early-dawn air was cold as well as damp. The visibility was poor, a factor which was to their advantage. Through the grayness Ceawlin saw Cynric walking up and down beside his men. Ceawlin exchanged one more look with Sigurd and went to stand in the front line of his father's command. This way, he would be one of the first over the wall. Cynric saw him and smiled.

It was the king's command that was to initiate the attack. They waited fifteen minutes to give Cutha and Cuthwulf an opportunity to circle the fort and find their positions. Ceawlin thought that his father would never give the signal for them to go. Woden, he prayed in a burst of heartfelt intensity, give me glory. Then the signal came and the wedge of men under Cynric began to move.

The rain was coming down harder now. Ceawlin ran forward, light on his feet even with the weight of armor and weapons. As the Saxons scrambled into the ditch, a second rain, this one of javelins, began to fall from behind the earthen bank in front of them. So the British had not been unprepared. Ceawlin raised his shield to cover his head and ran swiftly onward. Without once looking back, he began to climb the bank.

The javelins thudded off his shield. Behind him he could hear men grunting with the effort of the climb. The rain was making the dirt slippery and he concentrated on keeping his footing. Then he was at the top.

Men were lined up behind the protection of the bank. He saw that there were several rows of them and that they all seemed to be staring up at him with open mouths. For a brief, glorious moment he was alone on the top of the wall. Then he threw back his own head, gave his father's great war cry, and, sword drawn, leapt into the men below. As steel clashed on steel, he could hear the sound of his men coming behind him.

A blade was hurtling toward his neck and he raised his shield to protect himself. Then he thrust with his own sword, quick and deadly, and a man went down. Ceawlin grinned. There were more Saxons behind him now and, badly outnumbered, they were being hemmed in against the bank. "Forward, children of Woden!" Ceawlin shouted, and, slinging his shield over his back so that he could wield his sword more forcefully with two hands, he began to press forward. His men came after him.

The fighting was furious. The Saxons fought to achieve the wedge-shaped formation that would allow them to cover themselves on all sides, but under the intense pressure of larger numbers, they wavered. "Stay by me!" Ceawlin shouted. "Forward!" And they held.

Suddenly there was a shout from the far side of the fort. The British had just spotted the second attack party. The pressure on Ceawlin's men lifted and the wedge began to move inexorably forward. Then the pressure relaxed altogether as the British fragmented, not knowing which way to turn. The fort was suddenly filled with Saxons. In five more minutes, the battle was over.

Cynric had been one of the last of the initial attack party, making it up the bank slowly but with no assistance. The first thing that had met his eyes as he topped the bank was the sight of his son, his shield slung over his back, slicing through the Britons like a knife going through butter. Now, as the defeated Britons were being herded into one of the rough shelters they had built for themselves over the winter, he sent for Ceawlin.

The heavy rain had let up and it was drizzling again. Cynric stood in the shelter of an overhang on one of the buildings, his purple cloak pulled over his mail byrnie, and waited for his son. Cutha came up to join him, and then Cuthwulf. Then he saw Ceawlin coming from the far side of the fort.

The rain had plastered Ceawlin's thick hair to his head, and drops still clung to his cheeks and his lashes. He was muddy and bloody and Cynric's heart swelled with pride as he watched him come. What a warrior the boy was going to be! The gods had vouchsafed him only two sons, but they had not stinted him when it came to quality. This one, in particular, he had always known was marked for greatness. He pushed down in his mind the familiar regret that it was Ceawlin who was the bastard. Edwin would have done just as well if he had not become so untimely ill.

Ceawlin went down on one knee before him and Cynric placed his hand on top of the rain-soaked head. Even wet, his hair was unearthly fair. Just like his mother's, Cynric thought. He had never seen another woman to equal Fara as she had been in her youth.

He pressed down on the bent head before him and said, in a voice that was husky but strong, "To you, Ceawlin, my son, I dedicate this day's battle. To you there will be no lack of the good things of the world that I have in my possession. Today you take a place of honor among my warrior heroes."

He could hear the effort the boy was making to hide his emotions, to keep his voice level in reply. "Cynric, son of Cerdic. Great king," said his elder son. "It is reward enough to know that I have won your heart's love by my deeds." And Cynric had no doubt that the boy meant every word he had said.

There was the sound of footsteps, and the king looked over Ceawlin's head to see the other man he had sent for approaching. Then he gestured Ceawlin to rise and stand beside him.

Sigurd was coming toward them with the leader of the Britons by his side, the brother of the little British princess he had in Winchester. "My lord," said Sigurd formally. He too was covered with mud and blood. "This is the leader of the rebellion, Prince Coinmail of the Atrebates."

Cynric saw a man with soaking-wet hair that would be red when it was dry. The British prince had a cut on his forehead that was still oozing blood. He was limping but his head was high and the dark gray eyes that looked from Cynric to Ceawlin and back were bleak and wintry.

"He bore arms against me and thus his life is forfeit," Cynric said to his son. "But I give him into your hands. What shall I do with him?"

Ceawlin did not let the surprise he felt show on his face. The Briton, who was not much older than he, raised his chin very slightly. He understood enough to know his future was about to be decided. There was no fear on his face. So this, Ceawlin thought, is her brother.

Ceawlin spoke to him in British. "My father has given your fate into my hands."

The gray eyes flickered with surprise at the perfect British, but Coinmail said nothing. "If I give you your life, will you swear never to bear arms against me or my father or any West Saxon king again?"

Color flushed into Coinmail's pale cheeks. He hesitated for a moment, his eyes hard on Ceawlin's face. Then the color drained away, leaving the British prince deathly pale. "Yes," he said. "I will swear it."

Ceawlin nodded. "Then you may go free."

Chapter 6

THE air was warm and heavy with mist the day Cynric's war band returned to Winchester. Ceawlin's heart swelled with pride as he watched his father, so majestic in his golden helmet, lead his men through the great wooden gate and up the main street of Winchester.

Bringing back victory for the West Saxons.

"Sigurd! Sigurd!" It was a little girl with long brown hair, who was jumping up and down beside her nurse and waving to them.

Sigurd waved back to his little sister as unobtrusively as he could. "Coenburg has no dignity," he said to Ceawlin as he faced forward again.

"You mean she has no respect for *your* dignity," Ceawlin replied with amusement. It surprised neither of them that Coenburg's welcome had been for Sigurd and not for her father or Cuthwulf. Sigurd was the one who always took the time to notice her.

Sigurd gave his friend a mock-haughty look, then pretended to ignore him. The horses were still moving slowly up the street, past the slaves' hall, past the halls of Cynric's eorls, past the temple where Ceawlin had prayed for Woden's blessing. It was only a few short weeks since they had left Winchester, but it seemed to Ceawlin like a lifetime ago. He had left home a boy and was returning as a man.

His eyes rested once more on the figure of his helmeted father, and a faint frown furrowed his brow. Cynric too had changed on this journey, Ceawlin thought, but the king was traveling a different road from his son's. The rigors of the war band had made obvious what Cynric had largely been able to disguise in Winchester: he was growing old.

A horse moved up on Ceawlin's other side and a voice said, pitched for his ears only, "Well may you fear the day of his death, for then I shall be king." Edwin's dark eyes were narrow and oddly shining. "Brother," he added, the word spoken as if it were an obscenity. Then he pushed his horse ahead of Ceawlin's, crowding him toward Sigurd so that his knee slammed into that of his friend. Ceawlin's horse laid back his ears and Ceawlin closed his fingers on the reins to prevent the stallion from taking a bite out of the rump of his brother's gray. Sigurd cursed as his own horse sidled, but Ceawlin said nothing.

49

They had reached the top of the street and Ceawlin looked toward the women's hall, at the group of women waiting in front of the porch. He recognized his mother immediately, so much taller than the women around her. He did not see Niniane. The war band was dismounting. Ceawlin gave his bay to one of the slaves to take to the stable and crossed the courtyard to where Fara awaited him. Her hazel eyes were smiling as she greeted him. "I hear you were successful, my son." Cynric had sent word of the battle to Winchester weeks ago.

"Yes." He bent his head so she could kiss his cheek. "They are brave, but they are not warriors. We lost fifteen men ourselves, but they died with glory."

"And you. You fought with glory, my son. Your father's messenger told us all about it. Alric has been busy composing a song in your honor."

His eyes blazed. It was what he had dreamed of all his life, to do such deeds that the harpers would sing of them. His mother knew what he was thinking and squeezed his arm. "I am happy that you are safe."

Well, women were like that. He patted her shoulder and said, looking around, "Where is the princess?"

"Inside. Understandably she preferred not to be a witness to the victory parade."

"Oh." He looked at the hall's closed door. "Does she know the fate of her brother?"

"Yes." Fara's eyes were shining. "That was well done of you, Ceawlin."

He shrugged. "There was no point in making him a hero."

Fara took his arm. "Come inside and tell me all about it. Or . . . are you perhaps tired?"

He grinned. "I am not in the least tired." He let her lead him through the door of the women's hall.

He did not see Niniane until just before the feast that Cynric was holding in the great hall to celebrate their victory. She had not been in the women's hall when he had gone in with his mother. He met her accidentally when he was coming back from the stable after checking on his horse. She was on the dueling grounds playing a game with some of the children of his father's eorls. She looked up when he called, "Princess!" and came slowly across the flat dirt field to join him.

"I met your brother," he said. "He does wear his hair shorter than I do."

"I heard about your meeting." She looked up into his face, her own expression very still. She was so small, he thought. The top of her head did not reach to his shoulder. Her nose tilted upward and was sprinkled with faint golden freckles. It was a joyous-looking little nose and did not go at all with the gravity that was always in her eyes. "You were generous," she said. "I thank you."

"Not so generous. I made him swear never to bear arms against us again."

"Did . . . did he say anything about me?"

What Coinmail had said when Cynric informed him that he was going to marry Niniane to Cynric's son was, "Under the circumstances, she is no good to me. Take her if you will."

Ceawlin looked into those apprehensive slate-colored eyes and could not repeat her brother's careless dismissal. "He asked after you, of course. And he agreed to your marriage with Edwin."

Every ounce of color drained from her face. He reached out to grasp her shoulders, afraid she was going to faint. Her bones were as light as a child's. "I'm all right," she said, and swayed. He scooped her up in his arms and looked around for someplace where he could set her down.

"Is Niniane all right?" The children she had been playing with came running up to them. He recognized the speaker as Coenburg.

"She's fine," Ceawlin responded reassuringly. "Just a little tired. Coenburg, you and your friends had better run along home. It's almost time to eat."

The children, accustomed to obeying the voice of authority, ran off. Ceawlin spied a log along the edge of the field and began to walk toward it, still carrying Niniane. "I'm all right," she said again, her voice still not strong.

"I'm just going to take you to where you can sit down for a few minutes." He felt her relax against him as he spoke, and her head fell against his shoulder.

She weighed scarcely more than a child either, but she was not a child. He could feel that very clearly, with her held so closely in his arms. She was small and light-boned, but she was a woman.

He lowered her to the log and she leaned forward, her head resting on her knees. Her long brown hair parted and he could see the tender nape of her neck. Her hair wasn't brown, really, he thought. It was brown and gold and red all together. Pretty. Very pretty.

She looked up and there was now some color in her cheeks. "I'm sorry. I don't often do something as stupid as that."

"That's all right. I thought . . . I thought I had better tell you first."

Even deeper color flushed into her cheeks. Her skin was as fine as a baby's. "Yes. I see. Thank you."

"I'll walk with you back to the women's hall. It is almost time for the banquet."

"Thank you, Prince. But I am not going to the banquet. Your mother was kind enough to excuse me."

"I see," he said, and was sorry she would not be there to see him honored.

For all of his life Ceawlin had dreamed of this: his first victory banquet, the scop singing of his deeds of glory, the light in his father's eyes as he honored him . . . and its purity was spoiled, as was so much else in his life, by Edwin.

Cynric was proud of his son. He wanted all of Winchester to know how proud he was. He could not understand his wife's feeling that every honor he bestowed on Ceawlin meant he was taking something away from Edwin. Edwin would be the next King of the West Saxons. Cynric had never once hinted that he wished to take that right away from his true-born son. It was mean and petty of Guthfrid to begrudge Ceawlin his place in the world.

Women! thought Cynric as he rose to make a speech in honor of his elder son. Guthfrid and Fara had feuded from the first day Guthfrid set foot in Winchester. Women and their sons. Even Woden could not help the poor man who was caught in the middle.

The hall had fallen very quiet, and into that quiet Cynric spoke the words he was so proud to say:

"To you, Ceawlin, son of Cynric, for bravery in battle, I give this sword." There was a gasp from the benches as the king reached down beside him and brought forth a great sword with a jewel-encrusted pommel and scabbard. Cynric knew that everyone present would recognize it as the sword he had had from his father, Cerdic, when Cynric had left the Isle of Wight to go to the mainland to win his own kingdom. Guthfrid would be furious, would deem it belonged to Edwin, but it was not the official King's Sword. It was his, given to him by his father, and if he wanted to give it to this son, then he would. "Carry this sword, beloved Ceawlin," he went on ringingly, "and while you wear it, may all men praise you, as wide as the sea surrounds the shores, wherever the winds may blow."

He looked at the boy kneeling before him, and at that moment Ceawlin looked up. The boy looked so alone, kneeling there before the entire hall. It might be well to give a little sop to Guthfrid and Edwin. He said to Ceawlin, his voice a little lower than it had been, "While you live, Prince, be true to your lord." His son's eyes, so like his, watched him with somber comprehension. There was a brief silence and then he concluded, "Be kind of deeds to your new king when I am gone."

Ceawlin accepted the sword from his father's hands and looked over Cynric's shoulder to where his brother sat beyond. Edwin's face was white and shrunken, the dark eyes blazing. Ceawlin set his mouth and looked back at his father. "I will, my lord," he answered, and, bending, touched his forehead to the king's fingers.

Then Alric, the scop, came forward with his wooden harp and the hall was soon filled with music. He sang of Beranbyrg: of Cynric, the king, and of Ceawlin, his son.

Ceawlin could not enjoy it, this, the first song made of him for this his first battle. He was too conscious of the figure of his brother seated on the far side of the high seat.

Edwin was sick with fury over Ceawlin's success, and Cynric knew it. That promise he had just extracted from Ceawlin in the presence of all had been the king's way of trying to placate his legitimate son even as he honored the bastard. "While you live, Prince, be true to your lord." And, "Be kind to your new king when I am gone."

It would not serve. Ceawlin had seen that clearly on his brother's face as Cynric had presented him with the sword. No one, *no one,* was going to come between Edwin and the sun and be allowed to live.

"Ceawlin, son of Cynric, warrior of Wessex," sang the scop. Ceawlin, listening, felt bitter hatred sear his heart. For all of his life it had been like this, he thought, Edwin spoiling his pleasure in his accomplishments.

There was the scar on his arm from Edwin's dagger; a memento of the time Ceawlin had first won his father's praise for his swordsmanship. He had been eight then, he remembered, and Edwin seven.

There was the time Edwin had killed his hound because of Ceawlin's success in the hunt.

There was the time Edwin had slipped something into his food to make him sick. It was the first night his father had sent a girl to his bed, and he had been too sick to do anything but retch.

The scop was singing something now about his new sword:

> It has
> An iron blade   etched and shining
> And hardened in blood.   No one who wears it
> Into battle,   swings it in dangerous places,
> Daring and brave,   will ever be deserted.

He felt his brother's eyes boring into the side of his head and knew that Edwin had spoiled this moment too.

Guthfrid retched one last time into the large pottery bowl, then motioned to her handmaid to take it away. The queen lay back on the bed and closed her eyes.

There could no longer be any doubt. She was with child.

Could she make Cynric believe it was his?

She lay there in the tumbled bed, the lamplight glimmering on her pale, sweat-misted face, and counted. Cynric had last lain with her shortly before he took the war band to Beranbyrg. That was in April. Gods. This was . . . what? . . . June 30. She had conceived after Beranbyrg, she knew that for sure.

Only a month or so difference. He would never be able to be certain the child was not his.

She pushed her matted golden hair off her forehead. He might even be pleased. He had always been so sensitive about the fact that he had fathered only two children. Now, to have a child in his old age . . . he might be pleased.

Thank God he was still able to perform! Thank God he had come to her before Beranbyrg!

That was it. She would remind him that men were more potent on the eve of battle. Everyone knew that. She would say that was why she had finally conceived.

Edric was not going to be happy. He had been becoming increasingly more fretful of late. He was hungry for power. Guthfrid knew he was only waiting for Cynric to die so he could marry her himself. Then he would have the power he craved; then he would be the husband of the queen.

Edric forgot that Edwin would be the king. Edwin, who was not likely to want to share power with his mother's paramour. Guthfrid was not fool enough to tell that to Edric, however. She needed him. He satisfied her body. When the king's visits had become so infrequent, she had needed someone. She did not want to lose Edric.

She thought, suddenly, that Edwin would probably be less pleased than anyone else at the prospect of a new brother.

The news ran like wildfire around the women's hall. Guthfrid, the queen, was with child.

"It cannot be Cynric's," Nola said to Niniane as they sat side by side on a bench in the sun behind the women's hall spinning yarn.

Niniane looked around. One had always to be cautious in Winchester; an astonishing amount of what was said in the women's hall got back to the queen. "You had better be careful what you say, Nola," she warned in a low voice.

"I am not the only one who is saying it." Nola's brown eyes snapped with feeling. "The king has not fathered a child in sixteen years. It is not likely that he has done so now, in his old age."

"Then who is the father?" Niniane asked.

"Edric, of course."

"How can you be so certain, Nola? The king still can . . . that is, he is able . . . Well, he sends for girls from the bower. Presumably he is not impotent."

"No one is saying Cynric is impotent. I can say from personal experience that he is not. But none of his women has ever had a child. I simply do not believe Guthfrid's child is his." There was silence as the two girls spun their wool. Then Nola added, "Besides, everyone knows about the queen and Edric."

"I shouldn't think the king knows. If he did, he would have done something about it. Cynric does not seem the sort of man to tolerate adultery."

"I suppose that is so. But I am certain that the queen and Edric are more than merely friends. Why else do you think she allowed you to remain in the women's hall this past year? She did not want anyone in the queen's hall she could not completely trust. There is no other reason why she would leave Edwin's future wife under Fara's influence."

"Edwin," said Niniane in a curiously flat voice. She stared at the green wool in her lap without seeing it. In two days' time there was to be a formal betrothal ceremony between her and Edwin. Niniane felt cold with terror every time she thought of it. She looked up at Nola and asked, a note of desperation in her quiet voice, "Is there nothing I can do, Nola, to stop this match?"

"I do not understand you, Niniane." Nola stared at her with frank incredulity. "Cynric is offering you *marriage*. Marriage to the future King of the West Saxons. You will be a queen, you little fool. What is the matter with you?"

"I don't like Edwin, Nola. There is something about him . . . something strange . . ." Her eyes were wide and gray with trouble. "He repels me," she said. Then, in a burst of frankness, "I cannot bear the thought of him touching me!"

Nola laughed. "Little virgin." Her voice held no sympathy. "You will change your mind. It is not so bad, believe me. Just close your eyes and it is soon over. I have never been with Edwin myself, but the bower girls who have say he is good. He has his father's appetite. We must just hope he proves himself a better stud."

Niniane's stomach heaved and just then a girl came running around the side of the building. "Where is Fara?" she panted to the two girls spinning in the sun.

"I think she is in the dye house," Nola answered. "What is wrong?"

"Prince Ceawlin is hurt," the girl flung over her shoulder as she ran off in the direction of the dye house.

Nola put down her wool. "What can have happened?"

"I don't know. He went off with Sigurd this morning. I saw them ride out."

Nola stood up. "I am going to see what has happened."

"All right." Niniane looked up at her. "If you need me, I shall be here." Nola nodded. During the last year they had called upon Niniane on several occasions to sew up a variety of flesh wounds. She was fast and precise and her work rarely left a scar.

Nola left and Niniane sat on, her mind on her upcoming marriage. Unless she did something to stop it, within the month she would find herself in Edwin's bed.

What could she do?

She had thought often of running away, but there was nowhere and no one to whom she could run. The Britons in the area around Winchester were all securely under Cynric's thumb. There was no one who would shelter his son's runaway bride.

She had thought of trying to get home, but she had been certain they would catch her before ever she made it. Now there was no longer even the possibility of trying to get to Bryn Atha. Coinmail had been forced to make peace with the Saxons and she evidently was his peace offering. She could not expect him to take her back; he would not be able to keep her presence a secret. Cynric was planning to give land grants to the eorls who had followed him faithfully during his career of conquest. That was why the war band had stayed north for several weeks after their victory at Beranbyrg; Cynric had wanted to look more closely at the territory. Within too short a time there would be Saxons settled near Bryn Atha. There would be no refuge for her there.

All that was left to her was prayer.

She was still sitting in the sunshine ten minutes later when Nola came to find her. "Fara wants you, Niniane. Ceawlin has cut himself and it needs to be sewn."

Niniane put down her spindle and her wool. "All right," she said. "I'm coming."

Ceawlin was seated on a chair, with Fara standing behind him holding a cloth to the side of his face, when Niniane came in. Fara looked up. "Oh, Niniane. We have need of your skill, my dear. This cut is very deep and needs to be sewn closed."

Niniane came over to the chair where Ceawlin was sitting and turned his face up so she could look at it. The cut was deep and jagged and had missed his right eye by a fraction of an inch. "You were lucky, Prince," she said.

"I know." His sea-blue eyes were narrow with irony. "Can you really sew it up?"

"Oh, yes. It might leave a scar, though. It is very deep."

He shrugged. "Do the best you can. My mother says you are the most skilled of all the women."

Niniane turned to Fara. "Have a lamp brought over here if you please, my lady. It is better than these candles."

As the lamp was being brought, Niniane went to the basin of water that had been set on the table to wash the prince's wound and, picking up the soap, began to wash her hands. She soaped carefully and dried them on one of the cloths stacked there. Then she went over to stand behind Ceawlin. Fara moved out of the way and Nola put the threaded needle into her hand. She took the prince's chin into her other hand and gently pressed his head back against her. "It is important that you remain still," she told him

"Yes. I know."

He closed his eyes and rested his head against her breast. She smoothed his hair back so it would not get into the wound. His hair was very thick and clung to her fingers like silk. It was the color of moonlight, she thought. The weight of him against her was oddly pleasant. She thought, suddenly, that she would not be so frightened if it were Ceawlin she was going to marry.

She frowned at her own thoughts and bent to look more closely at the cut. Then, holding the skin carefully together with one hand, she stitched the jagged edges of his torn flesh together.

She could feel his body tense as the needle went in and out through the sensitive skin of his face, but he never moved. He stayed still as stone under her hand until she had finished. Finally she looked up at Fara. "That is the best I can do, my lady. There will be a scar, I fear, but at least he still has the eye."

Ceawlin moved his gilt-fair head from her breast and looked up. His face was pale under its tan, the striking blue-green eyes heavy. "Thank you, Princess," he said. "You are a skillful needlewoman."

The three of them were alone at the table; the rest of the women had retired into the corner or had gone outside. Niniane nodded and began to put things back into Fara's workbox.

"How did this happen?" Fara asked her son in Saxon.

"I told you. Bayvard came down in the woods and I was thrown. I tore my face on a root that was sticking up in the path."

Niniane continued to put the workbox in order and listened to the conversation between mother and son. Over the course of the last year she had come to understand Saxon very well. She had concealed this knowledge, however, pretending to speak and to understand only a few common words. Her instinct had been to keep to herself any small advantage she might be able to find in this place where she was so alone and unprotected. She had not let even Fara know how fluent she had become.

Fara was going on, "Bayvard is very surefooted. What brought him down?"

There was a long moment's silence. Then Ceawlin sighed. "Sigurd found a vine stretched across the road. It was tied from one tree to another."

"I knew it." Fara's voice was shaking. "I knew he was behind it."

"There is no proof of that, Mother."

"I don't need proof to know who tied that vine! Nor do you."

Niniane slowly folded cloths, listening with an expressionless face. "No," said Ceawlin at last. "But what can I do about it, Mother? He has no compunction about trying to murder or maim me, but I am not so lacking in feeling for my father as he."

"It would kill your father, to have one son slain by the other."

"I know that. There would be no way out for him: not blood vengeance, not wergild. Only grief. That is why I must stay my hand."

"You almost lost your eye!"

He shrugged.

"I have been thinking," Fara said. "Perhaps you ought to leave Winchester, Ceawlin. Perhaps your father might be persuaded to give you a grant of land by the Aildon hills."

"Leave Winchester! You must be mad, Mother." Niniane looked up to see him staring at Fara in astonishment. "What would I do outside of Winchester? Everything I have been brought up for is here. What on earth could I find to do in the Aildon hills? Farm?"

"But, Ceawlin, what else is there to do?" Fara sounded almost desperate. "You cannot stay here until he kills you! And that is what it will be. You know that!"

"He won't. He is afraid of my father. So is Guthfrid."

"Your father will not live forever."

"Well, I won't leave while he lives, that is for certain. So stop this foolish talk about the Aildon hills." He smiled at her and then bent to kiss the top of her head. "I won't let him kill me, Mother. I promise." Next he turned to Niniane and said in British, "Thank you once again, Princess."

Both women stood in silence and watched him walk out of the hall.

Chapter 7

"WHAT is wergild?" Niniane was speaking to Hilda, one of the Saxon girls who dwelt in the bower. They were working together on the looms that hung at the end of the women's hall. Behind them was a bustle of activity as the tables were readied for supper.

Hilda did not look surprised by the question. During the past year they had all become accustomed to Niniane's ignorance.

"Wergild is the price of a man," she answered now in a British that had greatly improved since Niniane's introduction into Winchester. Hilda was a tall, broad-shouldered blond of easygoing temperament. Next to Nola, Niniane liked her best of all the girls in the bower.

"The price of a man?" Niniane repeated, not understanding.

Hilda elaborated. "The fine owed for the life of a man. It is quite clearly prescribed in law: so much for an eorl, so much for a thane, for a ceorl, and so on."

"But by whom is this fine owed?"

"By the man who took the life, of course. The murderer."

"The murderer?"

"Naturally. Who else should pay it?"

Niniane threaded her bobbin through the shed, alternatively bringing the heddle rod back and forth, her hands working automatically, quite independent of her brain. "Let me see if I understand. If a man murders another man, then the murderer must pay a fine to the king?"

"Not to the king, Niniane. To the victim's family." Hilda picked up the old blunt sword which they used to press the weft.

Niniane frowned. "And is there no other punishment? All a murderer must do is pay a fine?"

Hilda carefully pressed the weft upward to make it even. "Oh, no. Wergild is paid only if the victim's family is willing to take it. Most of the time they are not." She put down the sword and turned to Niniane. "It is looked down on a little, the acceptance of wergild in place of vengeance."

"Vengeance? What do you mean by vengeance?"

"Blood vengeance, what else." Then, as Niniane still looked unsure, "As soon as a murder is committed, the victim's family incurs the duty

59

to avenge the death against either the murderer or his family. It is a religious matter, you see. It has to do with the sacredness of blood kinship."

"You mean they must murder the murderer?"

"Yes."

"But that is mad!" Niniane's hands had fallen quite still. "Such a feud could go on for generations!"

"Many have," came the placid reply. "It was because of a blood feud that Guthfrid came to Wessex to marry Cynric. The marriage was a way to end it, you see. That is one way. The other way is for one family to accept wergild. Then the killing is over."

"And what if the victim's family does not want either vengeance or wergild?"

"That would be unthinkable," said Hilda. "Such a person would lose all honor."

Niniane had been among the Saxons for long enough to recognize the sacredness of honor to them. Once again she began to thread the weft through the shed. "If loyalty to kin is of such utmost importance," she said slowly, "what happens if one family member should kill another family member?"

"By the code of kinship, a man is forbidden to kill or to exact wergild from a kinsman."

"Yet, by the same code, he is required to do one or the other to avenge the dead."

"Yes." Hilda smiled, pleased that her pupil had comprehended at last. "That is why the murder of a blood relation is the most horrifying and unforgivable of crimes. It is impossible to avenge."

"I see," said Niniane and, finally, she did.

Niniane's betrothal was celebrated the following day with a splendid banquet in the great hall of Winchester. Among the Saxons the betrothal ceremony far outshone the marriage rite, which was set to follow in two weeks' time. The main features of the marriage were the giving of a ring and sexual consummation. The betrothal was less personal, more of a community occasion.

For their betrothal feast Edwin and Niniane were given the places of honor, Edwin at the king's side and Niniane at the queen's. Out-of-doors the rain was pouring down and it was dark and damp, but in the festive atmosphere of the hall the candles blazed, the food and drink were passed around and around, and the raucous humor got more and more obscene as the banquet progressed.

Edwin listened to the bawdy comment being made by the eorl who sat beside him and gave an appreciative laugh. Left to himself, he would have preferred a marriage with one of the great Anglo-Saxon

royal families, but he knew Guthfrid was right to wish to prevent
Ceawlin from marrying this princess of the Atrebates. It was smarter to
marry her himself and thus keep the bastard from gaining a position
that might prove dangerous in the future. She could always be got rid
of once his father died.

In the meantime, it might not be unpleasant to have a wife. True,
Niniane was not the kind of woman who normally attracted him. She
was pretty enough, but too reserved. She had known for over a year
that she would be his wife, yet she had never done anything to attract
or to please him. Much too reserved. Well, once he had her in his bed
he would teach her soon enough what kind of a wife he wanted her to
be.

Beside him Cynric was signaling for silence. Then, as a relative quiet
fell on the hall, the king called, "Bring in the gifts."

The hall door opened and a line of slaves came in bearing the
traditional gifts of the bridegroom to his bride. There was clothing,
jewelry, a strongbox, linens and blankets, and a list of the domestic
animals that were to become her property. The gifts were placed
ceremoniously on the floor before the high seat. Then Cynric called
forth three of his eorls to witness that these gifts had indeed been
conveyed by Prince Edwin to the Princess Niniane.

The three Eorls duly swore their legal witness to the transaction and
returned to their places. Then Cynric signaled for Edwin and Niniane
to come and stand before him. The betrothal ceremony was always
concluded by a kiss on the mouth, symbol of the union of bodies that
would be consummated in the marriage.

Edwin looked down into the princess's expressionless face. She was
looking at his father, not at him. Stupid cow, he thought. She had been
one year in Winchester and still she did not know Saxon. "We are
supposed to kiss each other," he said to her in British.

At that she looked at him. His dark eyes narrowed, he put his hands
on her shoulders, and pulling her against him, he kissed her mouth
with brutal thoroughness. The hall of half-drunk thanes roared its
approval.

Niniane was trembling when finally he let her go. She kept her eyes
down as she returned to her place beside Guthfrid and clasped her cold
fingers in her lap to keep them from shaking too visibly. She tasted
blood. Edwin's teeth had cut her lip.

Dear Blessed Jesus, she prayed. Help me. The noise in the hall was
deafening. Please, please, dear Lord. Her hands were clenched so
tightly that her short nails cut into her palms.

"Try to look happy, you little fool," said the queen beside her.
"Remember you are to be a bride."

*   *   *

Three days before the wedding of Niniane and Edwin was to take place, Cynric took a bodyguard and rode into Venta to give justice. Cutha went with him, to interpret and to advise. They were not gone two hours before Edwin challenged Ceawlin to a duel.

Duels were not uncommon among the Saxons. In Winchester, dueling was a prestigious way of ending rivalries and quarrels. It was considered both a recreation and a sport. The rules were strictly formulated to avoid serious injury although injury did occasionally occur. A duel was fought until the judge ruled that one of the participants had been officially disarmed. Then everyone usually retired to the great hall to get drunk.

There was no one in Winchester, however, who expected that a duel between the two princes would be at all usual. The bad blood between Edwin and Ceawlin went far beyond the kind of quarrel that was normally settled on the dueling ground. Both Guthfrid and Fara made attempts to dissuade their sons from an action that both mothers perceived as far too dangerous.

"Why did you challenge him?" Guthfrid asked her son as soon as she closed the door of her sleeping room behind him to give them privacy. "You know how good Ceawlin is with a sword, Edwin! Are you mad?"

Edwin was pale with fury, his brown eyes so lightless they looked almost black in the pallor of his face. "I can bear him no more." His voice was flat, cold, and absolutely final.

"But what did he *do*?"

"What he always does. Tried to take what was mine."

"What did he try to take?"

"He knows Hilda sleeps in my bed. He tried to take her away from me. I saw him smiling at her."

"Smiling at her!" Guthfrid almost screamed the words. "What do you care about Hilda?"

"I don't care about Hilda. But she is mine." The set, white look on his face had not changed.

Guthfrid put her hand on his arm. "Edwin, my son, listen to me. This duel . . . he could hurt you."

"He won't. He is afraid to hurt me. But I am going to hurt him." The lightless eyes fixed themselves on Guthfrid's frantic face. "Don't worry, Mother." He sounded irritated, impatient. "I will be safe. And I promise you that today will see the end of the bastard and all his ambition." He pulled his arm out of her grasp. "Now I must go and collect my weapons. Come to the dueling grounds with me, if you like, and see what I mean."

For the first time in the history of their relationship, Guthfrid and Fara were in agreement about something. Fara was so concerned about the proposed duel that she sent a man into Venta to bring back Cynric, even though she knew it would not be possible for the king to return to Winchester in time.

"I hoped that just the threat of the king's return would force them to wait. It seems I was wrong," Fara said to Sigurd shortly after her messenger had ridden out of Winchester for Venta.

"I am sorry, my lady." Sigurd's voice was gentle. He had come to the women's hall in answer to Ceawlin's mother's summons and he had come reluctantly. "Ceawlin cannot in honor draw back. Edwin was the one to challenge him."

"But it is so foolish! All because Ceawlin smiled at one of the bower girls!"

"Edwin was just looking for an excuse, my lady. Everyone knows that."

"Sigurd"—Fara's white face was piteous—"cannot you persuade Ceawlin to wait for his father?"

"If he would not listen to you, my lady, be sure that he will not listen to me."

"I could not move him."

"I'm not surprised," Sigurd said frankly. "I saw his face. Nor do I blame him." He smiled at Fara reassuringly. "There is no cause for such concern, my lady. Edwin cannot best Ceawlin in a duel. This past year I doubt there is anyone in Winchester who could best Ceawlin in a duel. Stop worrying."

Fara's voice was bitter. "And do you really think Edwin is planning to fight fair?"

"He has to," Sigurd answered in surprise. "The rules must be followed. And all of Winchester will be watching him. He will have to fight fair."

"That is what Ceawlin said." Fara's voice was even more deeply bitter. "And you are both fools for thinking so."

Sigurd drew himself up. "It is something a woman would not understand," he said with dignity.

"I am sorry I bothered you, Sigurd," Fara said. He thought, suddenly, that she looked as old as Cynric. "I'm sure you wish to go to Ceawlin."

He patted her on the shoulder, a clumsy gesture of comfort, and left the hall with obvious relief.

Niniane had seen duels before in Winchester but, like everyone else, she knew this particular duel would be different. She had seen Ceawlin as he left the women's hall after talking with his mother. His face had been hard as iron. She was not surprised to learn that Fara had been unable to persuade him to wait for Cynric.

Niniane found herself hoping, with an intensity that almost frightened her, that he would kill Edwin or at least injure him badly enough to incapacitate him. She felt sorry for Fara, but in her heart Niniane wanted the duel to go forward. She saw in it her only hope of escape from this terrifying marriage.

Everyone who could walk in Winchester went to see the duel. Niniane accompanied Fara and the rest of the household women to the flat dueling field near the stables. The squares of pegged-out cloaks had already been set in the ground by the time the women arrived, and Ceawlin was there as well, standing by his cloak and talking to Cuthwulf.

The rules of a Saxon duel were clear. Each man had to keep his feet on his own cloak. If you were forced off your cloak, you were considered disarmed. The first man to be forced off his cloak two times lost. These were rules calculated to produce few serious injuries and thus allow dueling to continue as a major recreation for otherwise inactive warriors.

Niniane followed Fara to the place that had been set aside for the women and looked around slowly. Ceawlin, she saw, was wearing a long-sleeved mail tunic with a leather vest over it. He carried the sword Cynric had presented him with after Beranbyrg. He looked grim.

On the other hand, the thanes who ringed the dueling ground looked distinctly cheerful. Today's sport promised to be more exciting than the usual contest they saw in Winchester. Niniane knew from Fara that Cuthwulf had refused her plea to stop the duel until the return of his father and the king. Dueling was a privilege accorded all Saxon warriors, he had said. Cuthwulf was to be the judge today, and his obvious exhilaration was in distinct contrast to Ceawlin's somber mien.

Men's heads were turning and Niniane looked too in the direction of the princes' hall. Edwin was approaching, with Guthfrid beside him. The queen was as pale as Fara.

She is against this too, Niniane thought.

And, indeed, just before Edwin reached the circle of men, the queen put her hand on his arm and began to say something. He shook her off impatiently and strode forward to stand on his own cloak.

A light breeze was blowing, stirring the hair at Niniane's brow. She could smell the horses in the stable beyond them. The sun shone down on the two blond-haired princes. Gold and silver, Niniane thought, watching the two fair heads shining in the brilliant spring sun. Ceawlin was considerably taller than Edwin, but he was also more lightly made. Edwin was like a bull. Niniane stared at his neck and shoulders. She feared his strength would more than balance Ceawlin's superior height.

Cuthwulf began to recite the rules in a loud, important voice. His rather prominent blue eyes were vivid with pleasure. Cuthwulf loved a fight. After what seemed like a very long time he stepped back, and the two princes were left alone, facing each other, their feet firmly planted on their own cloaks.

It was Edwin who made the first move, raising his heavy sword and bringing it down straight at Ceawlin's unhelmeted head. Ceawlin took the blow on his shield and shook it off, his own sword already in motion. Edwin quickly covered his exposed side, but in so doing was forced to step to his right. Ceawlin pressed him, with a hammering of sword blows landing again and again on Edwin's raised shield. Edwin's shield held steady, but he was forced to give ground under the attack, stepping always to his right, coming closer and closer to the end of his cloak.

Niniane's fingernails bit into her palms. "Go on, Ceawlin!" she found herself saying under her breath. "Go on!"

Step by step, Edwin was being forced to the edge of his cloak. The golden-haired prince was breathing audibly, his lips drawn away from his teeth. Ceawlin followed, relentless, his own face hard and intent, all his concentration on his sword and on the man he was driving so mercilessly before him. He was making no attempt to reach his brother's flesh with his sword; plainly all he wanted was to force him off the cloak.

The power of those blows must be tremendous, Niniane thought. Edwin could not even get his own sword up, so intent was he on keeping his shield in place.

Cuthwulf was standing by the edge of the cloak, ready to make a call the minute Edwin's foot should touch the ground.

"Off!" he shouted, and a great sigh of disappointment went around the watching circle. It had happened too quickly, too easily. Ceawlin dropped his shield and turned to walk back to the center of his cloak. He would have to best Edwin one more time in order to be declared the victor.

Almost everyone present was watching Ceawlin, walking with bent head, sword and shield held by his side, but Niniane was watching Edwin. The snarl was still on his lips; his teeth looked white and canine in the bright sun. And as she watched, he lifted his sword and sprang at his unsuspecting brother's back.

"Ceawlin!" It was Niniane's cry that warned him, and he spun around, shield and sword instinctively lifting. Edwin's strike landed on his blade and not in his back. For a long moment the two swords held, locked together, then Ceawlin slowly began to press his brother's hand back. He must have amazingly strong wrists, Niniane thought with awe, as Edwin's grip began to loosen. Then, as the younger brother's fingers opened, he brought his shield down on Ceawlin's sword arm with a tremendous blow.

Both swords dropped to the ground at once.

Quick as lightning, Ceawlin bent and retrieved the one closest to him. Niniane saw that he had picked up Edwin's sword and not his own.

"Give me my sword!" Edwin's voice was harsh from lack of breath. Then, as Ceawlin stared at him out of narrowed eyes, *"Give me my sword!"*

Ceawlin bent, eyes still on Edwin's face, and picked up his own sword. It was the sword Cynric had presented to him, and now Ceawlin handed it to his brother. "You wanted it," he said. "Now you fight with it. *Brother."*

"No." Edwin began to back away, but Ceawlin raised his brother's sword and followed. The healing scar beside his eye stood out like a line of blood on his white face. Even from a distance Niniane could see the brilliant turquoise of his narrowed eyes. "You rotten little weasel," he said through shut teeth. "Come on. Fight me."

"No!"

"Stop it!" It was the queen's shrill voice, full of panic. "Cuthwulf! Part them. They are incensed."

The entire surrounding circle of men was shifting with uneasiness. As Cuthwulf stepped forward, a sword in his hand to forcibly part the two brothers, Ceawlin came in below Edwin's panic-stricken guard. The blade sliced the flesh on Edwin's bare sword hand.

"Aahh!" His sword clattered to the ground as the golden-haired prince grabbed for his hand.

"Come now," said Cuthwulf. "It is not that bad. You will survive it, my lord."

But Edwin was curled on the ground, moaning. A horrible suspicion began to form in Niniane's mind as she watched him grovel there.

"Edwin. My son." Guthfrid was kneeling beside him now. "What is the matter?"

He held his hand up to her. "Suck it out, Mother! He has killed me. Suck the poison *out!"*

Niniane pressed the back of her hand against her teeth. Ceawlin, standing alone in the middle of the two cloaks, was looking down at the queen and Edwin. Guthfrid had begun to raise her son's hand to her mouth when she was thrust aside by a man.

"You cannot take the chance. You are with child. Let me," said Edric and, bending his head, he sucked the blood from Edwin's hand and spat it on the ground.

Ceawlin stood like a statue, watching Edwin. Niniane found herself hoping that no one would ever look at her the way Ceawlin was looking at his brother now.

They got the prince back to the queen's hall where he could be tended to. By the time Cynric returned to Winchester, his younger son was dead.

Chapter 8

Guthfrid was beside herself with grief at the death of her son. After the burial she had a tremendous fire built on the dueling grounds and thereon she burned all of Edwin's clothing and possessions. When she called for his jewelry to be melted down by the flames as well, Edric tried to remonstrate with her.

"Leave me alone!" she screamed at him hysterically. "I want nothing of him left to remind me. Don't you see? I cannot bear to be reminded!"

First she had tried to get the king to have Ceawlin put to death. "I call for vengeance!" she cried, flinging herself at Cynric's feet in full view of all of Winchester as they stood together before Edwin's burial mound. "A life for a life, my lord. It is my right. I demand it."

"No vengeance," Cynric had replied in heavy voice. "Ceawlin is my son as well. No vengeance, Guthfrid."

"Then send him away. Banish him. *Punish him.*"

"It was Edwin who tried to kill Ceawlin by treachery. He was killed with his own poison. Come," and Cynric had raised her to her feet. His voice was kind. "Come, Guthfrid. Let me take you back to your hall. You bear a new child. Remember that and let it comfort you."

But no thought of the coming child could comfort her. Nothing could comfort her. Only vengeance on the slayer of her son.

Cynric's grief was not so flamboyant as Guthfrid's, but the death of Edwin, and the manner of that death, had wounded him grievously. As the months went by, it could be seen by even the lowest slave in Winchester that the king was beginning to fail.

"He blames me," Ceawlin said to Fara one morning in the women's hall. He had come to see his mother, and all the rest of the women had quickly found errands that would take them out of Fara's way.

"There is nothing to blame," Fara replied. She ached to reach out and take him into her arms as she had done when he was a small boy and had come to her with his sorrows. He looked so bitterly weary, so alone. But she knew he would reject any attempt at comfort on her part. It was many years since he had deemed himself too old for his mother to hug. So she said instead, "The fault was Edwin's, not yours."

"I killed him."

67

"You had no choice, Ceawlin."

"Yes. I did. You were there, Mother. You saw. I did not have to wound Edwin with the sword. He was backing away from me. You can be sure that my father has been well-informed of exactly what happened. He blames me."

"If he does, he is wrong."

Ceawlin shrugged. Then he asked the question he had come to ask. "Has he said anything to you about the succession?"

Fara's heart ached for him. "No, my son. He has said nothing." She paused, then added carefully, "Under the circumstances, it is not a question I myself can raise."

"I understand that." He gave her a shadowy smile. "Well, I must be going. I told Cutha I would go into Venta with him this morning."

"Excellent. It will do you good to get away from Winchester for a few hours."

He met Niniane on the porch; she was coming in as he was leaving. There were two little girls with her, each holding to one of her hands. He stopped and looked at her for a long moment in silence. Her face was tanned to a pale golden color from all the time she spent outdoors, and the freckles on her small tilted nose were more noticeable. "You look remarkably happy for someone whose bridegroom lies under the earth," he said at last.

Her widely set eyes regarded him with serenity. "Good morning, Prince," was all she answered.

"Good morning, Prince," the two little girls piped. One of the children he recognized as Coenburg. Both children spoke in British. He looked down into the round, rosy child faces, and his own face, which seemed to look so much older than its seventeen years these days, softened.

"What are you up to, Coenburg?" he asked.

"Niniane is going to show us how to play a game, but we need some cups."

"And we are going to be very careful not to break those cups," Niniane added, looking at the children as well.

"Oh, yes," they chorused fervently. Niniane smiled faintly, looked up, and encountered Ceawlin's eyes. He smiled back, touched and amused as she had been by the little girls' innocence. Then, with a brief tap on the top of Coenburg's head, he was gone.

High summer came and the harvest was brought in. Wagon loads of food and fodder were trekked into Winchester from the surrounding Saxon vils and British farms, tribute owed the king for his protection. The storehouses were stocked for the winter.

Summer passed and fall set in. Excess cattle were slaughtered and

the meat salted and hung. The dying earth seemed to reflect the mood
of all Winchester, or so Niniane thought as she sat one wet autumn
night listening to Alric sing. Normally it gave her great pleasure to hear
the scop, but the song he was singing tonight was a tale that they had
all grown weary of hearing: the song of the accidental slaying of
Herebeald, prince of the Geats, by his brother Haethcyn. The king was
having supper in the women's hall this night, sitting at a trestle table
before the fire. Fara sat on one side of him and Ceawlin on the other.
Alric's voice rose over the sound of the harp:

> Sad and bitter,   the death of that brother,
> Wrongfully slain,   by shot of arrow.
> The target missed,   the prince lay motionless,
> Bitterly struck,   his friend and his lord:
> The bloody arrowhead   had slain a brother.

Niniane watched as Cynric drank the mead in his cup. His hand was
trembling visibly as he raised it to his mouth. His cheeks and nose were
a dull red in the flickering light from the wall sconces.

"A fatal fight," the scop sang, "without hope of recompense. The
unlucky prince must die unavenged."

Niniane looked from Cynric to Ceawlin, but the prince's face, framed
by its helmet of silver hair, was unreadable. The king knocked over his
cup and the mead spilled on the table. He gestured for more. As the girl
came to serve him, and Fara began to mop up the spill with a cloth, the
scop fell silent. Cynric looked up.

"The rest," he said. "Let us have the rest of it."

"My lord." It was Ceawlin, speaking without looking at his father.
"Enough."

The old man stared at his full cup, then raised a hand and brought it
down upon the table, not with force or with anger, only with a kind of
vague impatience. After a glance at Ceawlin, the scop began to sing
again. "Swa bio geomorlic gomelum ceorle," he chanted.

Alric had told Niniane that this story of Herebeald and Haethcyn was
well-known to all Anglo-Saxons. The West Saxon scop's version of it
dwelt most affectingly on the grief suffered by the aged king whose son
has been accidentally killed by his brother. The king's grief is doubly
great because he cannot have revenge on the killer, who is also his son.
The part Alric was singing now was an embellishment he had himself
composed, comparing the father's plight with the suffering endured by
an old man whose son has been hanged.

"So it is sad for an old man to endure that his son, as a young man,
should hang on the gallows," sang Alric. "He laments his child, who is
strung up as food for ravens; yet, being old, can do nothing to help.
Always, each morning, his son's death is remembered. He does not

care to wait for another heir in the dwelling when the first has felt death's sting. It breaks his heart to look upon his son's dwelling-place, the empty wine hall that is now cheerless and a home of winds. The riders sleep, warriors in darkness; the harp sounds no more in the joyless place."

Niniane looked at Fara. The friedlehe was watching the old king. There was pity on her face, and patience. Cynric was slumped now deep in his chair. Niniane thought he was still upright only because the chair's carved arms supported him. Fara waited as he lifted the cup once more to his mouth. His hand was shaking too much, and after a moment he put it down again. He bowed his head over the cup. Then Fara looked at her son.

Ceawlin put a hand on his father's arm and said something in too low a voice for Niniane to hear. Cynric raised his head slightly, then nodded. The prince rose and came around to his father's side, slid an arm under the king's shoulders, and helped him to rise.

Cynric was a heavy man, and he was leaning on his son like a deadweight, but Ceawlin supported him across the floor of the hall to the door. Watching the two of them, one so young and strong, the other so old and ravaged, Niniane felt none of Fara's pity or patience for the king. What she felt instead was anger. It was not fair of the king to subject his living son to this ordeal night after night. Nor did Edwin deserve this kind of mourning. He had been a treacherous, villainous prince. In Niniane's opinion, the West Saxons were well rid of him. He would have made a fatal king.

The question of who would be the next king was the riddle that was exercising most minds in Winchester these days. Cynric had not named a new heir, although all knew it must be either Ceawlin or the child Guthfrid carried, if that child was a son. Niniane thought that Cynric would be a fool to name a baby over his elder son, but so far Cynric had maintained his counsel. No one knew what he would do. The uncertainty was one of the reasons for the grim mood that seemed to reign now at Winchester all the time.

Fara came slowly back from the door. She had aged too these last months. She felt it deeply, the king's grief and the uncertainty about the future of her own much-loved son.

In fact, Niniane thought, she herself was probably the happiest person in all of Winchester. The king seemed to have forgotten all about her, which suited her very well. She played with the children, learned harping skills from Alric, and helped with the sewing and weaving in the women's hall. Her life had rarely been more pleasant. She had been far more lonely at Bryn Atha than she was at present in Winchester.

Her whole future depended upon who was named the next king. If it was Ceawlin, then she did not think she had to worry. Fara was very fond of her. Fara would see she was treated fairly. But if it was Guthfrid's child . . . Then God alone knew that would happen to her. But God had taken care of her very well thus far. Niniane was content to trust herself to his goodness for the future.

The last of the leaves dropped from the trees and the first frost came. At Winchester everyone waited, waited for a birth and for a death. There were few who did not pray, to whatever god they felt would listen, that the birth would come first. The entire future of Wessex hung on two things: would the queen's child be a boy, and if it was, would the king acknowledge it as his?

Guthfrid, great with child, had retired to the queen's hall at the beginning of November. She was due to give birth around the festival of Yule.

"With any luck," said Nola to Niniane as they were hanging evergreens around the women's hall one afternoon a few days before Yule, "the child will be born dead."

"Nola!" Niniane crossed herself. "That is a terrible thing to say."

"It is true," the other girl returned stubbornly. "Ceawlin should be king. Even if this baby were Cynric's, which I doubt, we do not need a child for a king."

"Well, of course I agree with you. But that does not mean I wish Guthfrid's child dead." Niniane bent her head to sniff the spray of pines she was holding in her arms. She looked again at Nola. "It will be enough if it is a girl," she said half-humorously.

"This is not a laughing matter." Nola put down the armload of evergreens she had just picked up. "I think it is the uncertainty that is the worst. Cynric refuses to talk about it at all, even to Fara. No one knows what he is going to do."

"Perhaps he does not know himself."

"Perhaps not. He might even refuse to recognize Guthfrid's child as his after all. There is scarcely a soul in Winchester who thinks it is."

Niniane arranged a spray of holly. "You know, Nola, whether Cynric recognizes the child or not, he cannot prevent the eorls from choosing their own king once Cynric is dead. They may very well decide they would prefer Ceawlin to a baby of questionable origin. There can be no doubt that Ceawlin is Cynric's son."

"Not with those eyes," Nola agreed.

"So it may turn out well no matter whom Cynric chooses."

Nola was looking at Niniane, an affectionate smile in her dark eyes. "You have the wonderful facility of always hoping for the best, Niniane."

"It is much better to hope for the best than it is to hope for the worst," Niniane answered, and Nola laughed in acknowledgment.

                              *   *   *

It was bitterly cold the day the festival of Yule was celebrated.
Niniane was glad to come into the great hall, all freshly decorated with
evergreens and with the Yule log burning and crackling on the immense fireplace. Yule was a feast dedicated to the god Frey, the Saxon
god of fertility, and the centerpiece of the feast was a great boar's head,
prominently displayed and surrounded with fresh evergreens and ber-
ries. Frey was certainly the appropriate god of the day, for as the feast
got underway, word came to the hall that the queen had gone into
labor.

The news from the queen's hall brought added zest to the feast. The
smoke from the Yule log rose up to the rafters and hovered there,
slowly escaping out the smoke vents; the drinking horns went around
and around; platters of well-cooked boar's meat were served and tren-
chers were filled. Outside, the winter night was cold and dark, but
here, in the warm hall, fragrant with pine, there was life and companionship and hope that soon the uncertainties that had been plaguing
Winchester these last months would be resolved.

Fara ate nothing. Niniane tried to coax her to take a little meat, but
the older woman merely smiled and shook her head. She had grown
much thinner this last month. The strain of watching the failing king
and wondering about the future of her son had taken its toll. There
were hollows at her temples that had not been there before. Her
cheekbones were sharper and her wrists too bony.

I hope to God it is a girl, Niniane thought. She looked from Fara
down the table toward Ceawlin. All she could see of him over the
intervening people was the top of his fair head. As she slowly looked
away, her eyes were caught by Sigurd's. He smiled at her faintly and
she smiled back. She liked Sigurd. She had seen quite a bit of him
lately; he was fond of his little sister, Coenburg, and would often come
to join in their play. Niniane, who loved children, instinctively liked
anyone who shared that feeling. And she thought that Sigurd was
missing the companionship of Ceawlin, who had been spending more
and more time in attendance on his father. In consequence of all this,
she and Sigurd had become quite friendly these last months.

Alric was preparing to sing when there came a hammering at the
door of the hall, as if someone were trying to get it open and it was
sticking. A thane seated nearby rose and went to pull it ajar. In the
doorway a woman was standing, with a bundle of fur in her arms.
Niniane recognized her as one of Guthfrid's handmaids. The baby's cry
was loud in the sudden quiet of the hall.

The girl advanced slowly across the polished wooden floor. Niniane
thought she looked as if she was enjoying her position as the center of
the drama. She stopped when she reached Cynric. "My lord king," she

said in a voice clearly audible to every corner of the hall. "I bring you your son."

Niniane saw Fara's knuckles whiten as she closed her hand hard around the handle of her meat knife. The only sound in the hall was the crackling of the Yule log on the fireplace. Even the baby was silent.

Niniane could feel her heart hammering all the way up in her head. She had learned but recently the full meaning of the Saxon ritual of presentation. If the king accepted the child from the handmaid, it would mean that he recognized the baby as his. If he waved it away, however, then the child was rejected and would be taken out and exposed.

"Exposed!" Niniane had cried in horror to Fara when this had been explained to her. "Do you mean left to die?"

"I am afraid so, my dear."

"But that is horrible! He cannot be so cruel as to do that."

"The alternative is even worse," the friedlehe had replied with a bitterness that was unusual. Then, more gently, "We must all pray it is a girl."

And now the moment had come, and the child was a boy. In the tense silence of the hall, the baby cried again.

Take him! Niniane thought fiercely. She did not care what it might mean for the future, for her or for Fara or for Fara's son. She only cared that this tiny newborn baby, wrapped so lovingly in his fur bunting, should not die. *Take him, Cynric. Take him!*

For a long moment the tableau before her seemed to be frozen in time: the handmaid, the baby, the father and king. Then Cynric held out his arms.

Niniane felt herself go limp. Her eyes closed with relief. When they opened again it was to see the handmaid, a brilliant smile on her face, handing the child to the king. Cynric held it a little gingerly and Niniane sniffled. Then Cutha was on his feet, coming around to stand before the king and his new son. Someone brought a drinking horn to him and he raised it high. Cynric held the baby a little away from him and Cutha poured the contents of the horn over the child's head. The baby screamed.

"Son of Cynric," Cutha said, "with this water I claim you for one of us." He looked at the king. "What is to be his name?"

Cynric signaled to the girl to come and relieve him of the baby. Once the child had been taken from his arms, he leaned his hands on the table in front of him and raised his voice. It was steadier than it had been for many months. "I will call him Edgar," he said. He did not look at the son sitting beside him. "And I name him as my heir."

*   *   *

"*Why did he do it?*" It was Sigurd speaking as he and Ceawlin rode together through the winter woods, hunting the wolves that preyed upon the peasants' cattle. The thin sunlight penetrated the snow-covered trees with a crystal light. The dogs ran around the horses' legs, making brief forays here and there, casting for a scent. It was the day after Yule. "I don't understand it, Ceawlin. He cannot really believe that child is his."

"I understand him very well." Ceawlin's face was pale and bleak and marked with the gray hollows of sleeplessness. "It was the only vengeance he could exact for Edwin."

"Edwin. That viper. He deserves no vengeance. He deserves the place in hel he has surely won."

"Perhaps. But he was Cynric's son and I killed him. Make no mistake about that, Sigurd. I did kill him. You were there; you saw. I did not have to cut him with that sword."

"You did not know the sword was poisoned."

"I had a very strong notion." The line of Ceawlin's mouth was hard. The side of his face that was turned toward Sigurd showed the faint line of a scar at the side of the eye. "I did it quite deliberately, Sigurd. I won't mislead you about that. I wanted him dead."

"I don't blame you. No one could blame you for that, Ceawlin. He most certainly planned to kill you."

Ceawlin's expression did not change. Suddenly the dogs began to howl; they had found a scent. The two boys set off after them, galloping their horses through the snowy woods, jumping fallen branches and narrow streams, the creak of saddle leather and the thud of horses' hooves on frozen ground the only sounds other than the baying of the dogs.

After half an hour the dogs had the wolf cornered. Ceawlin called them off and lifted his bow. The wolf yelped once and blood spurted on the snow. Sigurd jumped down from his horse and went to look; the wolf was dead. Scarcely was he back in the saddle when the dogs picked up another trail.

It was not until they were riding back to Winchester that their interrupted conversation was resumed. "We cannot allow it to happen," Sigurd said. "A child king will be a disaster for all of us."

"I agree." Ceawlin gave his friend an ironic look. "Naturally." Bayvard shied at a noise in the woods alongside the path and Ceawlin patted the stallion's shoulder. "The question is, what can be done about it?"

"Nothing while Cynric still lives. When he dies it will be up to the Witan to choose a successor." Saxon law did not give the king the sole say in the matter of who would follow him. The council of eorls, the Witan, retained always the right to choose the king's successor from among the royal house. It was only in rare cases, however, that the eldest legitimate son was passed over.

Ceawlin was looking down at his horse's withers, his hair falling forward over his cheek, screening his face from Sigurd's view. Sigurd, who knew Ceawlin's mannerisms very well, merely waited. At last Ceawlin said, in an oddly muffled voice, "What does your father say?"

Sigurd's reply was prompt. "My father has no mind to be ruled by Edric's bastard."

At that, Ceawlin looked up. His eyes were blazing. "Gods!" He laughed a little unsteadily. Then, "I wanted you to know, Sigurd. I meant to kill him."

"It doesn't matter. What matters is that we must set aside this bastard and get you named king. That is, if you are willing."

"I am willing." Ceawlin's horse stepped in a puddle and the ice cracked underfoot. Except for the eyes, his face was colorless in the pure winter light. He lifted it to the sky. "That is why I killed him, Sigurd. So I could be king. If I have earned vengeance for that, then Fate may exact it from me."

Sigurd halted his horse and Ceawlin's stallion stopped automatically to stay beside him. "Then I pledge myself to you, Ceawlin, son of Cynric," Sigurd said, his face and his voice very solemn. "You are my lord. And may the fates hunt me to the back side of the wind if ever I fail or betray you."

Ceawlin held out his hand, grave and quiet. The two young men gripped each other hard. Then they rode in silence back to Winchester.

Chapter 9

IT was mid-January and Cynric the king was dying. He lay in the sleeping room of the king's hall in Winchester and looked from under lowered lids at the faces of those who were gathered around his deathbed.

Closest to him on his left was Guthfrid. His queen. She would be glad to see him go, he thought, glad to have the ruling of her new son to herself. She was a wolf-mother, Guthfrid. Fierce and devouring. He had often wondered if it was she who had made Edwin so . . .

He moved his head restlessly on the pillow. Edwin, his son. Dead by Ceawlin's hand. Even now, when all earthly things were slipping away from his grasp, even now, that thought still hurt.

His lids were lowered and the others thought him asleep, but he could see. He moved his eyes from the face of his wife to the other side of the bed, to the son who stood there watching him so gravely. At this moment his vision was amazingly clear; he could see how the light from the wall sconces struck sparks of silver from Ceawlin's thick, smooth hair. The boy's face was unreadable. He had learned early to keep his thoughts to himself. He had had to. It was not easy being a bastard, even a king's bastard. Cynric had always understood that.

His thoughts were so clear, as clear as his vision. He knew he must be dying. Why else would all these people be gathered about his bed? But his mind was so clear.

It was Ceawlin who should be king after him, not this child of Guthfrid's. But he was Edwin's father. He owed vengeance to the shade of his son. He owed it to Guthfrid.

Ceawlin had known what he was doing when he sliced Edwin's hand with that sword. Ceawlin always knew what he was doing. Even when he lost his temper, still Ceawlin was in control of himself. He had killed Edwin so he could be king.

Cynric would have done the same.

His eyes, shielded by their lowered lids, moved from the contained face of his son to that of his cousin standing next to Ceawlin. Cutha. He had been but a boy when he threw in his lot with Cynric, leaving behind Wight and all his family to venture forth to win a kingdom.

They had done well together. He had trusted Cutha more than any other man he had ever known.

Cutha would see to it that Wessex got its proper king.

Next his eyes moved to the woman who stood beside his pillow. He moved his fingers very slightly and felt her take them into her warm clasp.

So fair, he thought. Fara. The fairest woman in all the world.

His eyes closed. He was suddenly so very tired. . . .

"He is dead." Cutha looked up from the bed where he had been listening to the king's chest for a heartbeat. "Cynric the king is dead."

For a moment there was blank silence in the room. It had been coming for weeks, but now that it had actually happened, it seemed unbelievable. Cynric was dead. An era was over.

Cutha turned to Ceawlin. "As his only grown son, Prince, it will fall to you to conduct the funeral rite."

"No!" Guthfrid leaned a little forward, across the body of her dead husband. "I will not allow it! He murdered Cynric as surely as he murdered my son!" Her dark eyes, fixed on Ceawlin, were full of hate. "You are not going to say the dead prayers for him!"

Ceawlin did not answer. It was Cutha who said coolly, "It is right that the funeral ritual be conducted by a man's son, my lady. Your child cannot do it, so it is fitting that it be done by Prince Ceawlin."

There was a general murmur of agreement among the eorls in the room. Guthfrid looked around with wild and glittering eyes. Then Edric was coming in the door of the room.

"Cutha is right, my lady." The big bearlike man came to her side. "This once, I think you must give in."

There was the faintest emphasis on the words "this once." The queen met her paramour's eyes. Then her own dropped and she began to weep and wail and tear her hair.

"Come, Prince," said Cutha to Ceawlin. "Let us go and make ready."

When a king died, the Saxons sacrificed an ox. Ceawlin stood in the sacred courtyard outside the temple as the animal was led in by the priests. The eorls and thanes of Winchester lined the courtyard, watching. It was very cold.

They brought the ox to the place before Woden's tree, and Ceawlin, holding his father's ax, stepped forward. The animal made no protest, merely stood looking placidly up at the great carved pillar of the god. Ceawlin said the prayer of dedication, his breath white in the cold air. Then he brought the ax down. It found the right spot and blood spurted, spattering Ceawlin's white wool tunic. The priest handed him the sacred wand and he dipped it in the blood of the ox, then walked around the group of eorls and thanes, sprinkling them. When this was done, the priest gave him a cup of blood and the men of Winchester moved into the temple where the body of Cynric was lying. The priests took away the ox to cook it for the funeral banquet.

Hours later, after the altar had been properly stained with the blood of the sacrifice, after the banquet had been eaten, after the grave goods had been dedicated, the men began to file out of the temple, leaving only Ceawlin and the priests to keep watch over the body till dawn.

The priests sat at the long feasting table and dozed. The temple had been warm with the body heat of many men, but now it was just Ceawlin and the dead, and it was cold. Bone cold. He stood at the foot of his father's bier and looked at the dead king's face.

He had told Sigurd that he understood why Cynric had given the kingship elsewhere, and he had spoke true. But he did not accept his father's decision. Whatever might come because of it, whatever the price he might be forced to pay, he would be King of Wessex. He felt it was the deepest, strongest thing about him. It was his fate.

He looked around the silent temple, then back to the figure of Cynric. Where was his father now? he wondered. What was it like in the land of the dead? His mother had told him it was a realm ruled by the goddess Hel and that even the gods must go hence one day.

In the end, he thought, looking at Cynric's still face, even the gods cannot help us. In the end, even they must die. But in his life Cynric had won fame for himself. Nothing could take that from him. The harpers would sing his deeds for as long as Wessex endured.

Woden, he prayed, looking from his father to the image of the god, when it is my time to travel the road to hel, let me leave behind me a glorious name. Let not the generations that follow forget that Ceawlin once lived and won greatness for himself and for his people. Let not my name be forgot in the world of men.

For long periods of time Niniane was able to forget that she was dwelling among pagans. The day-to-day life in Winchester was so deceptive, so pleasant, so eminently civilized. Then something would happen to shock her into remembering that the Saxons were not at all like her. Such an occasion was Cynric's funeral.

The biggest shock was the sight of Ceawlin, his clothes all splattered with dried blood. He led the funeral procession to the gravesite, walking at the head of the bier upon which the body of Cynric was carried. The eorls and thanes and women of Winchester followed solemnly behind.

"What happened to Ceawlin?" Niniane asked Nola as she walked beside the British girl in the wake of Fara.

"What do you mean, what happened?" Both girls had their heads bowed and were talking in muted voices.

"He is all bloody."

"That is the blood from the sacrifice, little fool. He watched beside the king's body all night, so he did not have time to change his clothes."

Ceawlin must have killed the ox himself, Niniane thought with repugnance. It was the only way he could have gotten so thoroughly covered with blood. She shuddered. It was even in his hair!

A gaping hole had been dug outside the gates of Winchester, close to the barrow that marked the spot of Edwin's grave. The women clustered around the grave and began to keen loudly as the king, dressed in his finest clothes and covered with a linen shroud, was slowly lowered into the ground. Niniane stood silently in the midst of the household women and watched as Ceawlin placed the grave offerings around his father's body. Cynric's great iron-bound shield, his mail byrnie, several bronze bowls and silver-mounted drinking-horns, two silver spoons, a purse containing forty gold Frankish coins, a gold buckle, a jewelled clasp, and a great silver dish bearing the monogram of the Byzantine emperor Anastasius, all were put into the grave with the king to signify his importance in the land of the dead. One thing that was not included in the grave goods was Cynric's sword. Swords were too precious, and Cynric's King Sword, a magnificent pattern-welded weapon forged in Germany, with a hilt bound with silver-wire, would be passed down to the next King of Wessex.

At last the grave offerings were all in place. Ceawlin, still wearing his bloodstained tunic, stood on the edge of the grave and said clearly, "Take these treasures, earth, now that the living can no longer enjoy them." As the first shovelful of dirt was thrown, the beginning of the great barrow that would mark the spot of the king's grave, Niniane saw Ceawlin meet Guthfrid's eyes across the grave. His face did not change expression, and after a moment he turned away. As the diggers continued their work, the rest of the mourners, huddling in their cloaks for warmth, trailed back to Winchester.

Perhaps the most important part of the funeral ritual was the one that occurred after the burial: the ascension rite. Upon the death of a father, the son formally ascended to the high seat in his father's hall. When the father was a king, the ascension rite was also the crowning of the heir. In the case of Wessex, the heir had still be be chosen.

Cutha had summoned the Witan to meet in the great hall, and he and the five other eorls who made up that council gathered immediately after they returned to Winchester from Cynric's burial. A table had been set up near to the fire and the six men sat around it, ready to decide among themselves who was to be Wessex's next king.

Cutha, as the king's cousin and for twenty years the second-most-powerful man in Wessex, conducted the meeting. He began dispassionately, his clear blue eyes under their high-arched brows going from one face to the next as he talked. "Cynric named Guthfrid's child to be our new king. We all know that. The question we must decide today is: do we want a month-old child for king or do we choose Prince Ceawlin?"

Onela, who was an old man and, after Cutha, Cynric's staunchest follower, cleared his throat. "Ceawlin is a brother-slayer. Do we want such a one as that to be our king?"

Cutha felt deep surprise. He had not expected such an objection to come from Onela. His brows rose even higher as he answered, "Ceawlin acted in self-defense. It was not he who poisoned that sword."

"That is true." The speaker was Agilbert, one of the younger eorls. "But he did kill his brother. That cannot be denied. He ought not to profit from such an action. Surely that is why Cynric kept the kingship from him."

Cutha's surprise turned to uneasiness. He had not thought it would be difficult to get Ceawlin named king. He had been sure that the eorls would wish to avoid the obvious problems that would come with a child king and a regency. He looked to the other eorls, who were sitting opposite him, Oswald and Cynigils, and Egbert. Only Oswald was able to meet his eyes. It was Oswald who spoke next. "It is not only Ceawlin who will profit, but Wessex. If we name Edgar, we will be without a lord to lead us to battle. Ceawlin has shown himself to be a brave leader. My sons fought with him at Beranbyrg and they have told me. Ceawlin is worthy to be our next king."

Egbert's chair scraped a little, then he cleared his throat as if he would speak. He still was not looking at Cutha. "Yes, Egbert?" Cutha said, and now his voice was very soft. The eorls knew Cutha and knew that the angrier he got, the softer he spoke. Egbert did not answer, but looked instead at Cynigils, who stared into Cutha's eyes and said defiantly, "We have talked of this among ourselves, Cutha, and we have decided we want Edgar as king. He was Cynric's choice, and Cynric has always done well by us. We will keep with Prince Edgar."

"I do not agree," said Oswald immediately.

"But the rest of you do?" Cutha looked once more around the table, and four heads nodded yes.

Cutha felt black fury sweep through his heart and he stared at Onela with narrowed eyes. This was not just a rejection of Ceawlin, it was a blow at Cutha's power as well. Everyone knew that Ceawlin would look to him for advice. Everyone knew that his son was closer to Ceawlin than anyone else in Winchester. This was Onela's doing. It must be.

"And whom do you propose to name as regent?" he asked. His voice sounded positively silky.

The answer stupefied him. "Guthfrid," said Onela. "The queen."

Cutha's fury irrupted. "*Guthfrid!* Are you mad? What does a woman know about leading men?"

"We will do very well on our own, Cutha." The speaker was Cynigils again. "The eorls of Wessex are perfectly capable of managing their own affairs."

"Yes." Egbert finally found the courage to speak. "Young Ceawlin would expect to rule Wessex with the same iron hand as his father. Would expect to rule *us*. We don't want that, Cutha. We don't want Prince Ceawlin."

Onela gave Egbert an annoyed look. "Of course, we will follow our rightful king. There is no question about that. But our rightful king is Edgar, named by Cynric to succeed him. And that is our decision."

Ceawlin waited by himself in the princes' hall to hear the eorls' decision. The young men who slept on the hall benches, most of them sons of the thanes who slept on the benches in the great hall, had taken one look at the prince's face and left him alone. He sat on a bench in front of the fire, his long legs thrust in front of him, his frozen feet close to the warmth of the burning logs, and waited.

What would the eorls do? Cutha had been confident that they would not want a child for a king, would choose Ceawlin as his father's only grown son.

He remembered suddenly the first time he had seen his father wearing the golden helmet of the king. He had been perhaps two years old. He had thought Cynric a god come to earth. My father is king, he had thought, and been awed to his very marrow.

That was before he had realized he could not inherit, that Edwin would come first.

And now there was this new child. Guthfrid's bastard. Surely he would not come between Ceawlin and what he most desired? Surely fate would not be so cruel?

Someone had let the dogs into the hall, and now one of them came to thrust his muzzle into Ceawlin's hand. He smoothed the fur on a white head and looked into the adoring hound eyes. His dogs had always loved him.

Gods. They were taking so long.

The call came fifteen minutes later. He knew as soon as he walked into the hall and saw Cutha's angry face that he had lost.

"It was Onela," Cutha told him later, when they were in Cutha's hall, Ceawlin and Cutha and Cutha's sons sitting close to the hearth.

"This is Onela's bid for power, his attempt to oust me. I was a fool not to see it coming."

"But the others went along with him," Ceawlin said slowly. His head ached. He had not slept in thirty-six hours.

"They all knew you would prove to be a strong king and they have a mind to rule themselves. That is why they named Guthfrid regent, because they do not want to be ruled."

"But what can we do, Father?" It was Sigurd speaking now, his voice urgent. "We cannot let them get away with this!"

"We can do nothing. Just wait." Cutha's narrow, dark face was grim. "Winchester must have a strong king. Without one we will see the eorls being to fight among themselves. And Guthfrid will not be strong enough to stop it. Then, when the thanes are tired of the fighting, we will make our move."

Ceawlin looked at his kinsman, his sea-blue eyes heavy with tiredness and with some other emotion. "I swore allegiance to Edgar this night," he said.

"You swore allegiance to Edgar, *Son of Cynric*." A smile that did not denote amusement played around Cutha's thin lips. "I was not the only one to understand your meaning, Ceawlin."

"We should strike now!" It was Cuthwulf. "No one believes that brat is Cynric's. If we move tonight, seize the eorls who supported her—"

"No." It was Ceawlin. He looked at Cuthwulf with weary impatience. "Your father is right, cousin. Hard as it may be, the answer lies in waiting." He stretched the muscles in his tired back. In the far corner of the hall he could see Cutha's wife playing a game with Sigurd's small sister, Coenburg. "And then there is Edric," he added.

Sigurd said, "If she tries to put him in a position of power, the eorls will revolt."

"They will indeed." Cutha sounded satisfied. "Nor will they accept any one of themselves set up over the others. I think it will not be too long before they begin to regret their rejection of Ceawlin." The blue eyes narrowed. "And me," he added, his voice very soft.

January went by, and February. The snow melted from the shingled roofs of Winchester, and the houses' timber walls and the fences and the trunks of the trees in the wood were dark with the damp of winter's end. It was late in the afternoon of a particularly dank day when Niniane was summoned to the queen's hall to play her harp for the baby king. Edgar was a fretful child but his nurse had discovered that music would quiet him when nothing else would. As Alric was considered too important to play for a baby, it was Niniane who was most often called.

The baby slept with his nurse in the hall's second sleeping room, but when Niniane came in she found the nurse in the main part of the hall walking the small king up and down the length of the room. She was alone. The sound of Edgar's crying had driven everyone else away. "Thank the gods you have finally come!" the woman greeted Niniane with weary gratitude. "He has been screaming for hours."

"You've fed him?"

"Of course I've fed him! I've done everything. Nothing will quiet him. I'm at my wits' end."

"Well," said Niniane, "we'll see if the harp will help." She sat on one of the hall benches and ran her fingers over the strings. Then she began to sing, a song Kerwyn used to sing to her when she was a child, about a little girl who lived with the birds. After a few minutes the child began to quiet.

"I am so weary," the nurse said when finally Edgar had gone off to sleep. "I got scarcely any rest last night."

"Give him to me," Niniane said. "I'll put him in his basket and stay with him for a little. You need a change of scene."

The woman smiled thankfully and put the sleeping baby into Niniane's arms. "I'm going to the kitchens," she said. "I haven't eaten all day."

"Go ahead. I'll wait here until you get back."

Once the woman had left the hall, Niniane walked with the baby into his sleeping room. "Such a little mite to have caused so much trouble," she murmured, and pressed her lips to the fuzzy baby head. She laid him gently in his basket and sat down to watch beside him. She had left the sleeping-room door open and so she knew when the queen and Edric came into the hall. Their footsteps moved toward the hearth in the middle of the room and then Edric said, "It is for tonight. I spoke to Wulf and Osric but an hour ago."

The two were speaking in low voices but Niniane's hearing was very acute. She rose from her seat to go to the door, so they would know someone was in the hall, but then she heard the name Ceawlin. She stopped.

"I want him dead," Guthfrid was saying, and now her voice had risen higher. "I don't care how it is done, I just want him dead!"

"I know, I know. I want him dead too, Guthfrid. He is a danger. He makes me nervous, the way he looks at me out of those blue-green eyes. . . ."

Niniane could hear the sound of the queen's feet tapping on the wooden floor as she paced up and down. "So it is for tonight?"

"Yes. Two of the young thanes from the princes' hall will swear that Ceawlin tried to get them to kill the baby king."

"But they will kill him? You said they would kill him!"

"That is right." Edric's voice was soothing. "They will kill him. They will say that when they refused to carry out such a heinous act, Ceawlin tried to kill them first in order to ensure their silence."

"They will pretend they slew him in self-defense?"

"Yes."

"The way he pretended he slew my Edwin." Guthfrid's voice was bitter as gall.

"The way he pretended to slay Edwin." There was a pause, and when he spoke again Edric's voice was closer to the door of the baby's room. "I do not anticipate that the eorls will raise too many questions. Ceawlin is not a comfortable man to have in Winchester these days."

"Cutha?"

"Cutha is powerless without Cynric." Edric's voice sounded as if he were right outside the door. Niniane's heart began to pound. What would happen if they found her here? If they realized she had overheard? Dear God, what was she going to do? She put her hand on the baby's basket as if she were rocking him.

"Is Edgar in his room?" Edric asked, and pushed the door all the way open. He saw Niniane and cursed in surprise.

"What is it?" Guthfrid was hurrying to his side. Then they both were in the doorway, looking with horror at the blank face of the British princess.

"I was asked to play my harp for the little king, my lady," Niniane said politely in British. "Gertrude was hungry, as she had not eaten all day, so I said I would stay with him until she returned." She looked inquiringly from Edric to the queen, none of the terror she was feeling visible on her face. "Have I done something wrong?"

Guthfrid stared at her for a long, frightening minute, then turned to Edric. "It is all right," she said. "The little fool does not understand Saxon."

"Are you certain?" His pale blue eyes were hard on Niniane's small, uncomprehending face.

"I'm certain. She's safe enough."

"All right." Edric moved into the room, his eyes going to the child in the basket.

Niniane stayed until Edgar's nurse returned; then she walked across the courtyard to the women's hall and immediately sought out Fara.

Fara sent for Cutha, and Niniane told her story once again. "He must be got out of Winchester," Cutha said immediately. "We have been lucky this time. The next time, she will succeed."

"I know that." The friedlehe's thin face was white and strained. "I have tried to get him to leave, Cutha. More than once. He will not listen. You know how Ceawlin is. He thinks he is invincible."

"Well, he is not. And if anything happens to him, there will be no son of Cynric's to put in the kingship when once I have got rid of this child. I cannot risk that, Fara. Ceawlin will have to be got to safety."

"Will you tell him that?"

"It would be best if I did not meet with him. I do not want anyone to connect me with his leaving. It is important that I retain my position here in Winchester."

"But I tell you he will not listen to me, Cutha!" Fara was almost weeping with anxiety.

"He will this time." Cutha's blue eyes were looking intently at Niniane. "Listen to me, Fara," he went on, still looking at Niniane, "Cynric's plan to marry Edwin to this girl was a good one. We will keep to it, only this time the bridegroom will be Ceawlin."

Niniane's eyes widened in alarm. "I don't understand you, my lord," she said in Saxon. "Why should the prince marry me?"

"Because your brother is Prince of the Atrebates, and he has sworn to be Ceawlin's ally."

"Coinmail has sworn not to bear arms against him. That is a different thing."

Cutha shrugged. "Nonetheless, if Ceawlin is married to his sister, it will be in his interest to support Ceawlin's claim to the throne of Wessex." The calculating blue eyes moved from Niniane to Fara. "Send him to Bryn Atha with the girl. Edric won't pursue him there. The eorls are greedy for land and won't want to provoke another battle with the Atrebates, particularly when there would be endless fights over who is to lead the war band. They will leave him be. And I will be able to put my hand on him when I need him."

"But will Ceawlin go?" asked Fara.

"Tell him I say he is to go. Tell him if he wants my help, he *must* go."

"All right. But, Cutha, Niniane . . ." The friedlehe's hazel eyes were troubled as they regarded the girl who was standing beside her. "If it were not for her . . ."

"We are offering her marriage with the future King of Wessex," Cutha said, his voice impatient.

"I am not deaf," Niniane said to him coldly. His eyes narrowed at her tone. "And perhaps I do not wish to marry the next King of Wessex. Perhaps I would prefer to go home to my brother unwed."

"You cannot," came the brutal reply. "No man of your people will marry you after you have been two years with us. They will have no way of knowing if you are still a virgin."

This thought was not new to Niniane, but she had an answer for it. "I do not need to marry anyone, my lord."

"Every woman must either be a wife or a concubine. What else are you good for?" He was annoyed by her recalcitrance. "Your birth is noble. Fara has watched over you; *we* know you are a virgin. Your blood is still pure. It is best for you to marry Ceawlin."

"I could go into a nunnery!" Niniane flared. "There are still nunneries in the west. You forget, my lord, that I am a Christian."

"And you forget, Princess, that you are merely a girl and will do as you are told."

"But if she is so unwilling . . ." Fara said unhappily.

"Listen to me, both of you." They were clearly trying Cutha's patience. "First, the princess must go with Ceawlin. Guthfrid is certain to figure out who betrayed her plot to us, and Niniane will be no safer in Winchester than Ceawlin is. Do you understand that?" He was speaking now to Niniane.

"Yes," said Niniane, her chin held high.

"Good. Next, if you go with Ceawlin to Bryn Atha, then you must be married. If you are not, if your people think that he has corrupted you, they will kill him."

"Oh," said Niniane. Then, "I will tell my brother the truth."

"I can't take that chance."

Niniane did not reply.

Cutha turned to Ceawlin's mother. "I will have two horses at the postern gate at midnight. Tell that to Ceawlin. I will see to it that the watchman is one of my thanes. They must leave tonight, Fara."

Fara nodded.

"Ceawlin has gone hunting with Sigurd. I will leave word they are to come to you as soon as they return. Let Ceawlin and the girl take their vows in front of Sigurd before they leave. Obviously," and the fantastic brows rose higher, "there is no time for a betrothal ceremony first."

"All right," Fara said in a low voice, and, looking at her, Niniane knew she had lost her ally.

Sigurd stood beside Ceawlin as Niniane recounted her story once again, and fury exploded in his brain. "The bitch! That she would *dare* . . ."

"Well, she has dared," Fara replied in a tired voice. "And we can be certain that she will dare again." She looked at Ceawlin. "You are not safe in Winchester, my son. I have known all along that she would try to harm you. She hates you. And she fears you as well. You will never be safe as long as she is queen."

They all looked at Ceawlin. His face was closed and hard; it was but one month since his eighteenth birthday, but right now Sigurd thought he looked much older. He said nothing.

"You must leave," Fara went on. "If the knife in the dark does not come tonight, then it will come some other night."

"No," he said.

"Yes. I have spoken to Cutha and he says the same."

"You have spoken to my father?" Sigurd asked.

"Yes. I sent for him as soon as Niniane told me what she had heard. He says that Ceawlin is to take Niniane and go to Bryn Atha."

"Take Niniane!" Sigurd looked at the princess's lovely face. "What does this mean?" he asked her.

Her smoky blue eyes were troubled. "Your father says that Guthfrid is certain to suspect that I was the one who gave the warning. He says I am no longer safe in Winchester."

It was probably true, Sigurd realized, after he had thought for a minute. But he did not like the idea of Niniane leaving Winchester. He did not like the idea of Niniane leaving him. He had only been waiting for the right moment to ask his father . . .

"Marry her," he heard Fara saying.

"*What?*" It was Sigurd, not Ceawlin, whose voice was raised in protest.

"I said that Cutha insisted that Ceawlin and Niniane be married first," Fara repeated for Sigurd's benefit. But she was looking at her son.

"Why?" said Ceawlin.

"Because her brother is Prince of the Atrebates and could possibly become your ally."

"It is the match my father wanted for Edwin," Ceawlin said. His voice was expressionless.

"It is the match he wanted for the future King of Wessex," returned Fara.

Ceawlin slowly nodded his silver head, and for the first time he looked at Niniane. "It might be a way." His voice was slow as well. Obviously he was thinking it out as he went along. "It would give me a base from which to operate." Turquoise sparks began to light in his eyes. "It has been impossible, these last months under Guthfrid's rule. I just did not know where it was best for me to go. This will serve very well."

"Do you mean you will marry her?" Sigurd was whiter than usual, his voice constricted.

"Yes." Ceawlin had come to a decision. "Yes," he said again, his voice more confident. "It is a good move. Cutha is right. We will go to Bryn Atha."

"What if my brother should object?" Niniane's face was as pale as Sigurd's, her soft lips pressed into an unusually thin line.

"Your brother has pledged not to bear arms against me. He is a prince. He will not break his word."

Niniane bowed her head. She was going to do it, Sigurd thought. She was going to marry him.

"Cutha said you were to speak your vows in front of Sigurd before you left," Fara was saying. "You can do it again with more ceremony later, but for now vows spoken in front of a witness are binding in law."

"Niniane?" Sigurd turned to her. "Are you willing?"

She did not look up. "It seems I have no choice."

"No more than I do, Princess," returned Ceawlin pleasantly. "Well, then, let us get it over with. There are things I must do before tonight."

Chapter 10

TRUE to his word, Cutha had two horses at the postern gate when Ceawlin arrived there sometime shortly before midnight. The guard, one of Cutha's men, had been expecting him and said softly, "Prince Ceawlin?" as soon as Ceawlin's shadowy figure moved into his field of vision.

"The girl is not here yet?" Ceawlin responded, looking around.

"Not yet, my lord. But it lacks some minutes until midnight."

The two men stood in silence, listening. The day had been overcast and there were no lights in the sky. "My lord?" Ceawlin recognized Niniane's surprisingly deep voice. She had moved so quietly he had not heard her approach.

"Yes," he answered, looking toward the sound of her voice in the dark.

"You would make a good stalker, my lady," the guard said humorously in broken British. "I never heard you coming."

"I was country-raised," Niniane replied in excellent Saxon.

"What an interesting time you must have had of it these past two years in Winchester," Ceawlin remarked, and even though she could not see him, she could hear the sarcasm in his voice.

"When among the enemy, it is necessary to use what weapons come to one's hand," she replied, her husky voice cool and unruffled. "Lucky for you, Prince, that I did conceal my knowledge of Saxon, else you would be lying this night with a knife in your back."

"I am not that easy to kill, Princess—" Ceawlin was beginning to answer, when the guard cut in.

"Prince, you had best be on your way. If you tarry too long you might be seen."

"Of course," said Ceawlin, annoyed at being caught in a stupid squabble with a girl. Without further speech, he lifted Niniane to the saddle of one of the horses. Then he mounted his own horse and took her reins into his hand. The horses' hooves had been covered with cloth to muffle them, and the silence as they rode out through the gate was almost eerie.

The March night was cold and very dark. Ceawlin seemed to have no

89

trouble seeing, however, and turned without hesitation to cut across the fields that lay to their right. Within ten minutes he had brought them to the road. Ceawlin took the cloth off the horses' hooves and got back into his saddle once more, taking up Niniane's reins.

"I am perfectly capable of guiding my own horse now that we are on the road," Niniane said.

He gave her back her reins without an answer. Then, "Can you ride a canter? We will make better time if we canter."

"Certainly I can ride a canter."

He turned his head to look at her. She was sitting straight in the saddle and her posture looked balanced and relaxed. "All right," he said, and gently pressed Bayvard forward into an easy canter. Niniane's gelding followed, and after Ceawlin had ascertained that she was indeed capable of sitting to a canter, he concentrated instead on thinking about what he was going to do once they reached Bryn Atha.

This Coinmail, her brother, clearly objected to Saxon encroachment into his territory. He had gone to war to try to halt it. He had lost, and now was honor-bound not to take up arms against the Saxons again. But Ceawlin did not anticipate Coinmail would be pleased to harbor a Saxon prince within Bryn Atha. He must be convinced that it was to the benefit of the Atrebates to support Ceawlin over Guthfrid and her child. Any way he looked at it, Ceawlin was going to have to make concessions to the Atrebates.

They rode through the night, the silence growing longer and longer as Ceawlin thought and plotted. He had not had time to do much thinking this afternoon; he had been too much occupied with other things. The marriage itself had been a matter of minutes, a few vows sworn in front of Sigurd, but there had been other people it was necessary for him to talk to before he left. He had *some* faithful adherents among the young thanes who slept in the princes' hall, and it had been necessary to give them instructions.

"What is the chief objection your people have to us?" he said abruptly, turning to Niniane. They had been riding for two hours.

"Wh-what?" She could scarcely speak, her teeth were chattering so much. The night had grown progressively more clear and cold as they rode north.

He brought Bayvard down to a walk; then, when her gelding slowed also, he leaned out of his saddle to feel her fingers on her reins. "You're freezing! Why didn't you say something?"

"I th-thought you w-wanted to get to Br-Bryn Atha . . ."

"I do, but I don't want you frozen to death first." He looked around. "I know where we are and there is a vil not too far ahead. Just a settlement of peasants' huts, I'm afraid, but we could rest and get warm in one of the storage barns."

"All . . . all right."

Ceawlin pressed Bayvard into an energetic trot and began to watch the left side of the road carefully. There was a small track along here somewhere. . . . "Here it is." He turned to where she was riding beside him. "We will have to go single file—the track is not wide. Follow me." And he turned his horse off the road and onto a narrow dirt path. After a short space they came out of the woods and began to cross a series of fields. Niniane concentrated on keeping her stiff, frozen body on top of her horse and let the gelding follow on his own.

"I see it." He turned to look at her. "Only a few more minutes."

Ahead of her Niniane saw a small settlement of sunken huts arranged in a circle. Ceawlin halted and looked around, then began to walk Bayvard toward a large timber building standing some distance from the circle of huts. When they reached the building he dismounted, broke the lock on the door, and peered inside.

It was very dark in the windowless barn and it took a few minutes for his eyes to adjust to the change in light. Then he saw that it was indeed what he had thought it to be, a storage barn for winter fodder. The first floor was almost empty. It was March and most of the fodder had been consumed. He turned back to Niniane and said, "It's all right. We can tie the horses and climb up into the loft ourselves to get warm."

He held her horse's bridle so she could dismount, but when she slid to the ground her knees buckled and she would have fallen had she not held to the saddle to support herself.

"Go in," Ceawlin said abruptly. "I'll bring the horses."

She obeyed him, walking on stiff and shaking legs through the door and into the cavernous blackness of the barn. Ceawlin followed, leading the horses. Niniane stood perfectly still in the middle of the dirt floor and listened to Ceawlin tying up the horses somewhere to her right. Then he said, "I'm just going to climb into the loft to see if there is any hay." She did not hear him going up the ladder, but she heard faint footsteps overhead. Then, suddenly, his voice came out of the darkness beside her. "Yes, there is hay. Come, we'll make a nice nest for you to get warm in."

"How can you see?" He was a virtually invisible presence to her; there was not even light enough to catch his hair.

"I have always been able to see well in the dark. Come. Hold on to my belt. You need to climb the ladder to the loft."

He took her hand and guided it to his belt and she followed him blindly to the ladder. She went up the ladder by touch and he was waiting for her at the top. "Over here." He took her hand. "We can rest for a few hours and be on our way at dawn."

He led her to the place where he had spread a bale of hay to make a bed for them. "Here," he said, picked her up in his arms, and laid her down as if she were a child. When he had picked her up, he felt how uncontrollable were the shivers that racked her. "You should have said you were cold," he scolded, as if she were indeed a child.

"I d-didn't want to hold you u-up. There is d-danger."

He was unpinning the brooch that held his cloak as she was speaking. Then he lay down beside her and, spreading his cloak over them both, gathered her into the warmth of his arms. He felt her stiffen and said in a soothing, comforting voice, "It's all right. We will keep each other warm this way."

"You don't feel c-cold at all."

"I have more meat on me than you do."

He settled her head into the hollow of his shoulder and felt her resistance drain away. She nestled against him. It was ten minutes before her shivering stopped completely. "Better?" he asked in a soft, oddly tender voice.

"Yes." She sounded like a sleepy child.

"Go to sleep," he said. "I'll wake you when it's time to go."

She was asleep almost immediately. It did not take Ceawlin long to follow.

When he woke it was dawn. There was light seeping in between the cracks in the barn wall and he could hear the birds beginning to call in the trees. Niniane was fast asleep in his arms.

Sex had not been on his mind last night when he had made this soft bed of hay for the two of them to sleep in. But his young male body had been aware of the softness pressed against it all night even if his mind had not been that way inclined. He woke and he knew immediately what it was he wanted.

Ceawlin had had his first girl when he was fifteen; Cynric had sent an experienced bower woman to initiate his son into one of the most important rites of manhood. Sex had come easily then and had continued to come easily in all the years since. There were always plenty of women anxious to take a prince, even a bastard prince, into their bed.

Ordinarily he would not have thought twice about satisfying his need. It would not take long, and then they could be on their way. But Niniane . . . Niniane was a virgin. He had never lain with a virgin before. All of his women had known what they were about.

Of course, they were married. She could not complain. It was her duty to satisfy him. He looked down at the small round head that was nestled so trustingly against his shoulder. For some strange reason, this girl made him feel as if he needed to protect her. It was probably because she was so small. He did not want to frighten her.

Her head moved and lifted, and sleepy, smoky blue eyes were looking up at him. He could see the pattern of his tunic's fabric imprinted on her cheek. A strand of long hair had caught in her eyelashes. She looked surprised to see him, then she blinked and tried visibly to collect her thoughts. She looked like a kitten just waking up.

"Come," he said. His voice was abrupt and hard. He was very uncomfortable and he blamed her for it. "If we don't get moving soon, the peasants will find us and I don't want that to happen."

She sat up and pushed her hair off her face. "Of course. The sun must be up. I can see." She smiled at him a little shyly. "Thank you, Prince. I am much warmer."

"Good." He stood up and brushed the hay from his clothes. "Then let us go."

They rode out of the vil without their presence being noted and returned to the road. Ceawlin could see that Niniane was stiff from the long canter the day before, but she made no complaint. He appraised her out of the side of his eyes and decided not to push the pace too hard. She would need all her wits to face her brother when they reached Bryn Atha. And she had wits, this little British princess. There could no longer be any doubt about that.

They reached Bryn Atha in the early afternoon. Cynric had not taken his war band to the villa after his victory at Beranbyrg, so Ceawlin had never been there before. He could not restrain an exclamation of surprise and admiration as he followed Niniane in through the gate and saw for the first time that beautiful Roman courtyard.

It was deserted.

"Coinmail must be at one of the farms," Niniane said. "Come, I'll take you to the stables first. We had better take care of the horses."

He looked at her with distinct approval. She was tired and sore but she was ready to take care of the horses first. He gave Bayvard a long rein and followed along beside her chestnut gelding. "Bryn Atha is beautiful," he said, feeling he owed her a reward of some sort. "When Winchester is naught but ashes, these stones will still be here."

He was rewarded by a smile. Her teeth were small and white and, like the rest of her, perfectly formed. For the first time he noticed that she had a dimple in the corner of her mouth.

The stable was empty too. Empty not only of horses but also of fodder. There was no sign of use at all. Niniane frowned. "This is strange. The chickens are gone too, and the pigs. Wherever can Coinmail be?"

They gave the horses water, then picketed them to graze, as there was no hay. "Let's go to the house," Niniane said. "I cannot imagine what has happened."

They returned to the courtyard, where Niniane shouted first, "Brenna! Col! . . . The servants," she added in an aside to Ceawlin. There was no answer.

"Let's look in the house," Ceawlin said.

Most Roman villas were fronted by colonnades, but Bryn Atha, built by an Atrebates prince to withstand the inclement British climate, had an enclosed colonnade that was more like a long gallery off which all the rooms in the villa opened. The main door led into the tablinum, or large reception room. Ceawlin stood for a moment in silence, slowly surveying the yellow plaster walls with their scrolls of jewellike color. Then he looked at the pictured mosaic floor. It was a hunt scene, with a golden-haired, scantily clad huntress engaged in spearing a giant boar. "What is it supposed to represent?" he asked Niniane.

"Venus. The Roman goddess of beauty," she answered. She went to the windows, opened the glass panes, and then unlatched the shutters. Ceawlin watched as she pushed the shutters wide, then closed the window again, allowing the afternoon sun to come streaming into the room. She turned back to face him, and the sun lit her hair to the glow of autumn.

"I remember," he said slowly. "You don't like the dark."

"I don't like rooms without windows," she said. "Or rooms that are stuffy. The house has been closed up. I don't think Coinmail is living here at all."

"Well, let us look," he answered. The puzzle of Coinmail could wait for a moment; he was curious to see a real Roman house. He looked around the room. "There is no hearthplace. How do you stay warm?"

Niniane explained about the hypocaust. "It still works under the sitting room and the dining room and the small reception room," she said, and showed him where the stoke hole was where one made the fire that would heat the pipes under the house. The dining room was a separate room, with a table that was not taken up after every meal. The bedrooms all had windows, which Niniane opened, and the floors were of brick and concrete and were covered by colorful rugs. The baths were in a separate part of the house, but Niniane said they had not worked for years.

They ended up in the kitchen, with its raised hearth stove fed by charcoal. There was no food.

"Where can your brother have gone?" Ceawlin asked.

"I have no idea. Wherever it is, he evidently plans to be gone for some time. He has taken all the animals."

"How can we find out?"

Niniane pushed her hand through her hair and stared abstractedly at the stove. "Naille would know for sure. He is a cousin and would be chief should something happen to Coinmail." She frowned and looked from the stove to Ceawlin's face. "I'm not sure it's wise to go to Naille until we find out what has happened to Coinmail, Prince. *Naille* did not promise never to bear arms against you."

Ceawlin swore. "We heard no word in Winchester that your brother was gone."

"Why should you?"

"We should. It's true we don't keep watch on the Britons and their doings, but we should."

Niniane did not look as if she agreed. She refrained from comment, however, and said instead, "I had better go and see Geara. He has the nearest farm. He will probably know what has happened to Coinmail."

"How far is this farm?"

"Not too far—two miles, perhaps."

"Then let us go."

There was the faintest of pauses; then, "I think you should stay here, Prince."

At first he looked surprised, then he scowled. "Of course I am not going to stay here! Do you think I am afraid of a simple farmer?"

"I know you are not afraid, but until we find out . . ."

"Absolutely not. I am coming with you."

Niniane set her teeth. "You could get killed."

"Well, it will make a nice gift for you if I do. You will be home again without a Saxon husband to worry about. Come, stop talking and let's go."

He walked out of the kitchen and Niniane trailed along behind him, furious. What he had said was perfectly true, of course. If he were killed, her own life would certainly be easier. But for some reason she did not quite understand, she did not want him to be killed.

They saddled up the horses once again and started along the track that led to Geara's. They rode in silence, Niniane thinking furiously of what she would say to Geara to explain Ceawlin, and Ceawlin trying to figure out how the inexplicable absence of Coinmail was likely to affect his own future plans.

As Geara's farm came into sight, Niniane turned to Ceawlin. "Don't tell Geara who you are. It might not be safe. We'll just say that you are my husband and that the two of us decided to run away from Winchester together."

His eyes always seemed to deepen in color whenever his emotions were stirred. "Run away?"

"Will you think for just one moment?" she snapped, and his eyes grew even more turquoise. "This is not a time for heroics. It is a time for sensible thinking. It is necessary for you to win the support of the Atrebates. Am I right?"

"Yes." His answer was grudging.

"Well, until we find out what the situation is, it will be safest to keep your identity quiet. You are my husband. You fell out with the new rulers in Winchester, which is true enough, and so decided to come to the home of your wife."

For a long moment he did not answer, and Niniane was afraid he was going to be stubborn. He was staring between his horse's ears and his profile looked stubborn. "Prince—" she began to say, and he turned his eyes toward her.

"If I am to be merely a simple thane, you had better not call me prince."

Thank God he was going to be sensible. She gave him an enchanting smile. "Ceawlin. It will be all right to use your name. The Atrebates know nothing of Winchester or its inhabitants."

He looked disgusted but had the sense not to answer.

Geara was a childless old man whose wife was long dead, and he had always been fond of Niniane. She had felt he was the safest person she could apply to for information about Coinmail, and her decision was borne out by the greeting the old farmer gave her when they found him in the pig pen mending a fence. He was so clearly delighted to see her. A further factor in her choice of Geara was that he had only one man to help him do all the work of the farm, so there was little chance of word of her return getting out before she was ready.

He was delighted to see her, but he bristled at the sight of Ceawlin, who was, as Niniane had regretfully realized when she was thinking up her story, unmistakably a Saxon. He might sound British when he spoke, but there was no disguising that silver-blond hair. Niniane waxed eloquent about how Ceawlin had rescued her from marriage to the vile Edwin, risking his own life in the process. It was quite a moving tale, if she did say so herself, and it produced the desired effect upon Geara.

She glanced only once at Ceawlin's face, then hastily averted her eyes.

"Geara," she said at last, getting down to the main purpose of their visit, "where on earth has Coinmail gone?"

"Oh, yes. You would be knowing nothing about that." Geara spat in his hands. "He went to your mother's brother, the one that lives away to the west."

"But why? And when did he go?"

"He went but a month ago." The old man shrugged. "Why? I can't say. He was grim as death after that there battle."

"I can imagine," Ceawlin murmured.

"Well, what did he do with all the livestock?" Niniane persisted. "There is nothing left at Bryn Atha, Geara. He must be planning to be away for quite a long time."

"He did take most of the livestock to Naille to look out for. The two old folk you had at Bryn Atha died this winter, so there was no one there to look after them, you see."

"I see." Niniane folded her lips. "I see also that we are going to be very hungry unless I can get some of the livestock back from Naille."

Geara spat on the ground. "No food in the house, eh?"

"None."

"Well, it were not so bad a winter. I can spare you some."

In the end, Geara gave them flour, corn, milk, cheese, two loaves of bread, and a chicken. He also gave them some grain for the horses. They packed everything onto Niniane's gelding and then Ceawlin lifted her to Bayvard's back and took the chestnut's reins into his own hands. They left Geara's farm, Ceawlin going first on foot, leading the chestnut, and Niniane following.

As soon as they were out of sight of the farm, Ceawlin turned to her and said, "I'm starving."

"So am I."

They looked at each other, then Niniane slid off the stallion's back and they both went to look in the saddlebags the gelding was carrying. Within two minutes they were stuffing themselves with bread and cheese. Ceawlin swallowed, wiped his mouth with the back of his hand, looked over at Niniane, and met her eyes. The two of them began to laugh.

"When we get home I'll cook the chicken," she promised as they restored the saddlebags to a semblance of order. When he came to lift her to Bayvard's back, she said, "Won't he carry us both?"

He looked down at her appraisingly. He was so tall, she thought. "He probably would," Ceawlin agreed. "You weigh scarcely anything." Then he put his hands on her waist and lifted her to the stallion's back behind the saddle. In a minute he was before her, swinging into the saddle itself.

"Who is this uncle that your brother went to visit?" he asked over his shoulder.

She laid her hand on his back to balance herself. Her mother's brother was a prince of the Dobunni tribe whose home was near the old Roman city of Glevum, close by Wales. "My uncle lives in the west," she answered. "I have no idea why Coinmail would have gone to visit him."

"It is very peculiar."

Niniane thought it was extremely peculiar, but she did not say so to Ceawlin. Instead, "Perhaps he went to get married."

He turned his head slightly to look at her over his shoulder. "That is so." He nodded thoughtfully. "Yes, that is very likely. He can fight no longer, so he might as well wed."

Niniane did not answer. She could feel the strong muscles of his back under the palm of her hand. She ought not to be so surprised by them, she thought, remembering the duel with Edwin.

"I will cook the chicken today," she said, changing the subject, "but you are going to have to go hunting if we are to eat tomorrow."

He gave her a quick boyish smile and then faced front again in the saddle. "Certainly." Then he added, "We will have to go and see this Naille. He will perhaps know more about your brother. And we need some livestock if we are to live at Bryn Atha. Livestock for ourselves, and hay and grain for the horses."

"Yes," said Niniane, and was glad he could not see the worried look on her face. "We will have to go and see Naille."

They had the chicken for dinner. Niniane fried it Roman fashion, in oil in a bronze pan on top of the raised hearth stove. She also seasoned it with some herbs that were still left in the larder. Ceawlin ate with obvious relish.

"What did you do to the chicken?" he asked curiously after he had eaten for five uninterrupted minutes. "In Winchester all our meat is either roasted or stewed."

Niniane explained. Then she added, "I shall have to restart my garden, but until it yields, we shall have to buy vegetables and corn from the local farmers."

"Buy?" He raised his fair eyebrows. "Surely the tribe owes you a food tax. Since your brother is not here to collect it, why cannot you?"

"A food tax?" repeated Niniane. "The farms do not belong to us, Prince. They belong to those who work them."

"Don't call me prince," he said irritably. Then, "What does it matter whom they belong to? The fields of the vil belong to the coerls who work them, but still they owe the king a food tax. How else is the king to realize income?"

"The Prince of the Atrebates does not take from the people just because he is the prince." Niniane's large, widely spaced eyes were grave and steady on his face. "We farm our own lands, and what else we need, we trade for."

There had been wine in the pantry as well as the oil and herbs, and she had poured him a cup to take with his dinner. He sipped it now as he thought about what she had just told him. Clearly, he could make no sense of it at all. "What *is* the prince, then?" he asked her at last.

"He is the leader."

"From what you have just told me, he is no different from anyone else in the tribe."

"One doesn't need material things to be a leader," she replied a little haughtily. "Leadership is a moral thing, Pr . . . Ceawlin."

He put down his cup, annoyed by her tone. "Moral?" he said. "You were left all of this," and he gestured to include the room and the villa, "and you make no effort to maintain it or defend it. Is that moral?"

"*You* are the ones at fault there, my lord Ceawlin!" she answered hotly. "You Saxons. You come like wolves, destroying everything civilized that Rome has left."

"Oh, no. Look around you, Princess. Have there been Saxons at Bryn Atha? Not until two years ago, yet the place had already fallen into decay. Silchester—the city you call Calleva—was a city of ghosts long before any Saxon set a foot in it. It is your people who have lost the Roman civilization. You have been in retreat from everything Rome stood for ever since the last legion pulled out."

"That's not true!" Her small round chin rose and she glared at him. "Have you forgot Badon, my lord?"

"Arthur was the only one of you who understood what it means to be a king. And he was half Roman."

She reached for her own wine cup. "And what does it mean to you," she asked, "to be a king?"

His eyes moved from her hand to his own, so much larger with calluses across the palm from holding a sword. "To be a king means that you are responsible for the people," he answered. "These things like the food tax, the poll tax, they are due to the king because he has taken upon himself the burden of that responsibility."

"And what exactly does that responsibility entail?" He felt her eyes on his face even as he looked at his own hand.

He answered slowly but readily. This was something he had thought of before. "The king's responsibility is to lead his people in war, to protect them from famine, to give them justice, to sacrifice for them to the gods." He raised his turquoise eyes. "It is not freedom that a king knows, Niniane. It is responsibility. But it is a responsibility that he takes up gladly, because it is in his blood to do so. The kings of Wessex are Woden-born; the blood of the god gives us our mission."

If she noticed the change in pronoun, she did not say so. Instead, "Do you think that Cynric was a good king?"

"You saw him when he was old." He looked over her head, as if he were seeing a picture in his mind. "But I remember him when he was great. Look what he has done for his people. The poorest ceorls, who came landless from Wight, now have rich fields to farm. The thanes sit each night in a splendid hall; the eorls will soon have great lands of their own." His eyes found hers again. "Look what he has done for *your* people. Venta was dying when Cynric took it; now it is a thriving city." He took a sip of wine. "Cynric made the West Saxon people into a nation," he said. "He was a great king."

"I am sure you will understand when I say I cannot agree with you." Her tone was dry, astringent.

"No," he said. "You will never understand. It is because you are a Christian." And he looked at her with pity in his eyes.

Chapter 11

WHEN they had finished eating, Niniane cleared the dishes off the dining-room table and Ceawlin went to the stable to see to the horses. Niniane washed the dishes in the kitchen and remembered that she and Ceawlin were married and that the night was coming on.

The thought of lying with Edwin had petrified and repulsed her. She was not sure how she felt about lying with Ceawlin.

She finished putting the dishes away, went down the gallery to Coinmail's room, and opened his clothes chest. It was empty save for a few old tunics that he had evidently felt it not worth taking with him. She lifted one tunic out of the chest and held it up. It would be short on Ceawlin, of course, but it might do for a little until she could make him a few more. He had not brought much with him from Winchester.

She heard the door open and then his voice. "Niniane! Where are you?"

"In here," she called back, and listened to his footsteps coming down the gallery. In a trick of memory another scene flashed before her mind: the one other time she had waited in this room and listened to the sound of Saxon footsteps coming nearer. All of a sudden the fear she had felt then washed over her again. Her heart began to pound and she stared at the door with dilated eyes.

It opened gently. "What are you doing?" Ceawlin asked, and came into the room.

She did not answer right away, and he cocked an inquiring eyebrow. She felt her hammering heart begin to quiet. It was all right, she thought in some confusion. It was just Ceawlin. "Looking to see if Coinmail left anything you might be able to wear," she managed to answer at last.

"Oh." He took the tunic from her hand and held it up against himself. "I don't think so."

It was too narrow as well as too short. Niniane was surprised. Ceawlin looked so slim; his shoulders were wider than she had supposed. "Oh, dear." Her voice had still not reached its normal register. "Well, I shall have to try to patch two of them together somehow."

He dropped the tunic on the bed. "At the moment, Niniane, I am not interested in new tunics."

"Oh," she said again, and looked at him out of eyes that were absolutely huge.

He had stepped away from her to model the tunic, and now he moved toward her again. She was standing with the clothes chest directly behind her. She could not back away. "You are my wife," he said, his voice very soft. "You know what that means."

"I . . . I suppose I do."

He was close enough now to touch her. He stopped and looked down into her eyes. They were not wearing the guarded expression so familiar from her days in Winchester. Instead they were apprehensive, unsure, and faintly . . . frightened. He cupped her face in his hands like a flower. "I won't hurt you." His voice now was dark and gentle. He bent his head and began to kiss her.

She was still as marble under his touch. He realized, with pleasure, that no one had ever kissed her mouth before. He raised his head for just a moment and whispered, "Kiss me back." When her mouth began to answer to his, he felt a thrill that was different from anything he had known before.

His lips moved from her mouth to her cheeks, her nose, her forehead. "See? It can be very nice." Then he found her mouth once more. After a while her arms came up to circle his waist. He bent and lifted her in his arms.

"No," she said when she realized he was taking her to the bed. "Not here. My room."

He carried her out of the door of Coinmail's room to the next room on the gallery, kicked the door open, and laid her on the blue wool blanket that covered her bed. Then he lay down next to her.

Niniane could feel his kisses all the way down in her stomach, and when his hand moved to caress her breast, the power of the sensation she felt shocked her. "Ceawlin . . ." she murmured, and her voice was breathless.

He raised his head and looked down at her. "I told you it would be nice." His own voice was hoarser than usual. Then he sat up and said, "Niniane, take off your clothes."

Her fingers were shaking as she began to obey him. First the tunic came over her head, then her gown. She was down to her linen undergarment when she raised her eyes to look at him.

He had stripped completely and thrown his clothes onto the floor. He was standing in a pool of light from the window, and she stared at him with suddenly widened eyes. He looked, she thought in astonishment, exactly like the god pictured on the mosaic floor in one of the houses in Calleva. It was Apollo, her father had told her, the god revered by the Romans for his healing and his power of prophecy. The mosaic had shown a beautiful young man, fair-haired and beardless, with smoothly muscled shoulders and upper arms, flat stomach, narrow hips, and long athletic legs. The god had worn but a cloak draped across one shoulder and had carried a bow and a quiver of arrows. Niniane had thought when first she saw the picture that he was the most beautiful thing in the world. And now he was standing here in her bedroom, alive.

He was like the god when he came to her this time too. Mastering. Overpowering. A rush of feeling and desire that she could not even think of denying. She obeyed his wishes, her heart hammering, her body flooding with foreign and overwhelming sensation.

He did hurt her when he entered her, but she did not try to pull away. Did not want to pull away. And was rewarded by a wild and glorious burst of pleasure such as she had not known could possibly exist.

After a while he braced his hands on either side of her shoulders and lifted his weight from her. She looked up into his face, framed by the hood of moonlight that was his hair. It was Ceawlin, she thought. Not the god. But she was not sure.

"Do you know," he said softly, "I don't think I am going to mind staying at Bryn Atha after all."

Niniane awoke first the following morning. It took her a moment to remember that she was in her own bedroom at Bryn Atha. She remembered instantly who it was sleeping next to her in the bed.

He was lying on his stomach, his arms stretched over his head. She raised herself up a little cautiously and contemplated the part of him that she could see protruding from beneath her blue blanket: a well-muscled back and a tangle of extremely blond hair. He did not look like a god this morning. He looked like a very large young man who had usurped most of the space in her bed.

What had happened to her last night? She looked from the tangled silvery mop on the pillow to the window, as if seeking an answer. Was sex really like that? Or had she drunk too much wine? She looked back toward the pillow and was caught by two sea-blue eyes. He was awake. She stared at him, afraid to speak, not knowing what she could possibly find to say. He smiled at her sleepily and reached up an arm to pull her down next to him. "Oh, no," he said. "You're not going anywhere for a while."

She did not argue.

They had breakfast on Geara's second loaf of bread and more cheese. "I shall have to bake," Niniane said. "Fortunately Geara gave us enough flour."

"We had better ride over to see this Naille this afternoon," Ceawlin responded. "According to Geara, he is the one who has charge of all the villa livestock."

"Thursday is Naille's day to visit the tribe," Niniane replied. "I think we would be wise to wait until tomorrow, Ceawlin. There is little point in traveling to Naille's farm only to find him gone."

He looked irritated, and she added quickly, "Besides, I thought you were going to go hunting today."

His brow cleared. "That is true. You will have to show me where the hunting is best."

"That's easy. The upper wood. I can give you the direction. If I go with you, I won't be able to bake."

"That is so." He looked toward the window. "The day is fine. It will be good to get out in the wood with a bow." His eyes came back to her. "You have no dogs?"

"We had dogs. Coinmail must have taken those to Naille too."

He nodded, finished the cheese he had cut, and stood up. "The horses should have finished their grain. I'll go saddle up Bayvard and put Ruist out to graze."

Niniane smiled and nodded and began to carry the dishes into the kitchen for washing.

She stayed busy in the kitchen, making dough and kneading it, until he had been half an hour gone from the villa. Then she went herself down to the stable and saddled up the chestnut gelding. She was going to Naille's today and she was going alone.

As Niniane had told Ceawlin, Naille was the chief man of the Atrebates after Coinmail, and his farm lay some four miles from the villa. Once, two hundred years before, when Bryn Atha had first been built, all the land in the surrounding area had belonged to the prince. Tenant farmers had worked much of it, and for a long time their labor had been largely responsible for the villa's prosperity. However, as the years went by, much of the land had passed out of the hands of the chiefs. The choicest farms had gone to younger sons of the chief's family, who, as the cities failed, needed to be able to live off the land. In the end, some of these farms had turned out to be more prosperous, though certainly less luxurious, than the original villa.

Such a farm was Naille's, situated four miles to the west of Bryn Atha in a rich, fertile valley. As Niniane rode into the farmyard, a flock of geese screeched and flapped, and the chestnut gelding jumped in surprise. Niniane had dismounted and was calming the horse with reassuring pats when a little girl of about four peeked out the front door of the low stone house.

"Hello, Isolde," Niniane said. The little girl's brown eyes widened when she heard her name from the stranger. "Is your mother home?"

The little girl turned back into the house, and in less than a minute a woman with two toddlers clinging to her skirts came to the door. She squinted a little into the sun.

"Hello, Alanna," said Niniane, coming toward her. "It's Niniane."

"Niniane!" The woman came down the step and into the farmyard. "Good heavens, Niniane! My dear child! Whatever are you doing here?"

Niniane came to give the woman the kiss of greeting. "I got back to Bryn Atha yesterday," she said with a smile.

"But we thought you were with the Saxons!"

"I was, until two days ago."

"Dear God in heaven." Alanna flapped her hand. "Tie your horse to the hitching post, my dear, and come into the house." She turned to the little girl. "Isolde, go fetch your father from the fields. Tell him that Niniane is here." Then, as the little girl hesitated: "Go on, now." Isolde turned and ran out of the farmyard.

Alanna picked up one of the toddlers, who had fallen down the steps and was crying. "Come into the kitchen," she said to Niniane. "Naille will be here shortly." Niniane picked up the other, larger toddler and followed Alanna inside.

"I thought I would find Coinmail at Bryn Atha," Niniane said as soon as she was sitting in a chair before the kitchen hearth and drinking a glass of goat's milk.

"But, Niniane—however did you escape from the Saxons? Coinmail said they were going to marry you to their prince!"

"They were, but he got killed." Niniane leaned a little forward in her chair. "Alanna, where is Coinmail?"

"He went to your mother's brother, near Glevum."

That was what Geara had said, so it must be true. Niniane's delicate brows were puzzled. "But why, Alanna? Bryn Atha is deserted. Has he gone for good?"

"Of course not. I think I had better let Naille tell you about it, though." The woman's lined face wore an expression of mixed eagerness and concern. "But you . . . are you all right, Niniane?"

Niniane read with accuracy the question in Alanna's eyes. "Yes, I am all right. I am married."

"Married? But I thought you said . . ."

"I am not married to Prince Edwin. He was killed before we could be wed. I am married to another man, a Saxon who helped me when I was in Winchester. We escaped together."

"You have brought a Saxon to Bryn Atha?"

"He had to leave Winchester, Alanna. You see, he was the one who killed Prince Edwin. He did it for me, because he knew I was so fearful of marrying the prince. So you see . . ."

But Alanna was crossing herself and muttering a prayer under her breath. Niniane folded her lips. "A Saxon at Bryn Atha," Alanna said again. "Wait until Naille hears."

"He is alone, Alanna. He cannot hurt you. And he is my husband."

Alanna's brown eyes looked piercingly into Niniane's. "Do you know about Beranbyrg?"

"Beranbyrg? Yes. I'm afraid I do know."

"It was fearful. Many men died. The barbarians . . . they overwhelmed our men . . . butchered them . . ."

Niniane was becoming annoyed. "I understood that they offered mercy to Coinmail. That was certainly not the act of a butcher."

Alanna shrugged, then went back to the part of Niniane's story that most interested her. "You say you are married. By a priest?"

"No. There was no priest at Winchester. We were married in a Saxon rite."

"Then there is no marriage," the woman said firmly.

"What is all this about a marriage? By God, it *is* Niniane." It was Naille coming in the kitchen door, a tall, thin, brown-faced man with stooping shoulders.

Niniane repeated the story she had told his wife. Naille's face was grim when she had finished.

"How did your . . . husband kill the Saxon prince?"

"In a duel. That is the way the Saxons settle their feuds."

"Very civilized," said Naille with heavy sarcasm.

Niniane started to explain that dueling was really a sport, then stopped. She said instead, "Naille, why did Coinmail go to my uncle?"

The man sighed and sat down at the kitchen table. His wife put a cup of beer before him. He swiveled it in his fingers and said to Niniane, "We were defeated at Beranbyrg. You must know that."

"Yes."

"Well, after Beranbyrg Coinmail realized that we Atrebates could not fight the Saxons by ourselves. To be successful we must combine with other tribes. That is what Arthur did, Niniane. He brought all the tribes of Britain together into one army to fight the Saxons. And that is why he was successful."

"I don't understand," Niniane said. "I thought Coinmail had sworn not to take up arms against the West Saxons again. I heard he had so sworn in exchange for his life."

Naille shrugged. "What value in a promise given to a pagan?" But he did not meet her eyes.

Niniane was surprised by the outrage that swept through her. Her brother was planning to break his oath. It did not help to reflect that such a possibility had not even occurred to any of the "pagans" he was planning to betray. To the Saxons, an oath was sacred.

"I see," she said at last in a hard, tight voice.

"We were so horrified when we learned you had been taken," Naille said, changing the subject. "Coinmail was furious. He had told you to go to Geara's farm."

"I know, but Kerwyn was ill." Niniane looked up from the scarred wood table she had been contemplating. "Do you mean to tell me that Coinmail wants to form a combined army from the two tribes?"

"Yes."

"Then he will only kill more good men. Listen to me, Naille. I was two years in Winchester and I can tell you that we will not beat the Saxons. I saw what manner of people they are. They are warriors there, not farmers like us. It would be wisest for us to make peace with them."

"Peace," said Naille. "What do they know of peace?" Then he frowned. "What is this Winchester you keep mentioning, Niniane?"

"The West Saxon king has built himself a great capital on the outskirts of Venta, Naille. It is a great enclosed enclave with full fifteen halls within. Great wooden buildings, all hung with gold. The West Saxons will not be easily dislodged from this country, Naille. Coinmail will not be able to do it."

"We shall see," said Naille. Then he leaned his forehead on his hand. "Beranbyrg was very bad. You are right when you say we are unused to war." He raised his head and looked at her. "Where is this Saxon 'husband'?"

"I left him at Bryn Atha. I did not think it wise to bring him here."

"You were right. Wait here with Alanna while I gather some men to deal with this woman-corrupter."

"*No!* You don't understand, Naille. I don't want you to do anything to him. He is my husband."

He searched her eyes. "I understand," he said at last, grimly. "But it was not by your consent, Niniane. We all know that. The tribe will stand behind you, never fear."

"No, you *don't* understand. I went to him willingly."

There was a very long silence. As Niniane well knew, the Romano-British law on the subject of the abduction of a virgin was quite clear. The punishment for a man who took a woman against her will was death or castration. The woman, though she was not at fault, was deemed corrupted and thus unmarriageable, although she was still entitled to the protection of her father or other male guardian. If the woman were proved willing, then the man could make reparation by paying a fine to her father.

"Think," Naille said finally.

"I have. He saved me from Winchester, Naille. But for him, I would still be a prisoner of the Saxons. I owe him a great deal for that."

"All right." His shoulders stooped even more than usual and he got slowly to his feet. "We will leave it for now."

"Thank you." She rose as well. "Geara told me that Coinmail left all the livestock with you."

"Yes."

"Perhaps you could let me have a cow, Naille? For milk. And some chickens?"

"You may have what you need to live on. The rest I hold in trust for your brother."

"Thank you."

"You will have to take them yourself. I have no time to spare. It is sowing season."

"I know. I will come tomorrow with Ceawlin and take one cow and some chickens."

Naille's head came up, arrested. "Ceawlin?" he asked.

"It is a common name among the Saxons," she answered, her heart hammering.

Naille nodded, then scowled, clearly torn between having to go out of his way to deliver the livestock and having to tolerate a Saxon on his land. Finally: "All right. Come tomorrow," he said.

Niniane smiled. "Thank you, Naille. You are very good."

Clouds had come in to cover the sun as she rode back toward Bryn Atha, but she scarcely noticed the change in weather, so deep was she in her own thoughts.

Coinmail was going to try to raise another army against the Saxons. What in the name of God was she going to tell Ceawlin? What was it going to mean for Ceawlin?

She had forgotten how deep was the British fear of the Saxons. Living among them in Winchester, she had come to realize that they were people like herself, albeit people who held to a different set of beliefs. But they were human, as she was. As human as Naille or Alanna.

Cutha had thought that Ceawlin might be able to find allies among the Atrebates. Ceawlin had thought the same. That was why he had married her. Even she had thought Ceawlin might be able to forge a bridge of peace between the two peoples.

She had forgotten how deep the fear went.

You have brought a Saxon to Bryn Atha?

She had indeed brought a Saxon to Bryn Atha. What in the name of God was she going to do with him?

Give it time, she thought as she rode along the forest track that led back to Bryn Atha. Perhaps, once they had a chance to know him, the fear would lessen. She had little doubt that the best thing for her people would be for them to make peace with the Saxons. She had seen the military drills at Winchester, the weapon practice. The Atrebates would never be able to stand against the Saxon thanes.

She was not betraying her own people by harboring a Saxon prince in their midst, she thought as she rode in through the villa gate. She was acting in their best interest. If the Atrebates threw in their lot with Ceawlin, and Ceawlin became king, he would owe them a debt. Surely that would be the wisest course of all.

She dismounted in the courtyard and took the gelding around to the stable. As she came through the small fenced-in yard that fronted the stable, she saw him. He had tied Bayvard to the fence and was brushing him. As Niniane closed the gate behind her, the sun found an opening in the clouds and broke through, glinting off the bay horse's dark winter coat and touching Ceawlin's hair. He heard her and his head snapped around.

"Where were you?" he said angrily. He dropped the brush and began to walk toward her.

Her own step hesitated fractionally, then went forward again. "I went to see Naille," she answered.

"You went to see Naille? Without me? You told me he was not to be found at home." His eyes were bright with temper.

"I know. I'm sorry. But you don't understand how the Atrebates feel about Saxons, Ceawlin. You were likely to get a knife in your heart. I had to see how things were. Surely you can understand that?"

"No. I told you I would come with you. You deliberately went against my wishes."

Niniane clucked to Ruist and began to walk the horse toward the stable. "I know. I know. I did it for your own good."

"I am perfectly capable of knowing my own good."

"Ceawlin." She tied the horse to the fence and began to unbuckle the saddle girth. "Don't you want to know what became of Coinmail?"

He gave her a long, hard look. "I don't like it when people go behind my back," he said at last.

She busied herself with the girth. If he should find out the truth about Coinmail . . . "I'm sorry," she said meekly. "I won't do it again."

He came to lift the saddle off the horse's back for her. "Better not." He took the saddle into the stable and hung it on the wooden pole they used as a saddle rack. Then he came back outside. "All right. Tell me. What has happened to Coinmail?"

"It's as I thought. He's gone to Glevum to marry a girl of the Dobunni. I was to have made a marriage to the Dobunni myself, before I was taken captive to Winchester."

"The marriage you did make is much better."

The dimple at the corner of her mouth flickered. "Do you think so?"

He grunted. "What about the livestock?"

"Naille will give us a cow and some chickens. We must go to his farm tomorrow to fetch them."

"So he is not planning to put a knife in my heart?"

"Not just now. I told him my touching story about how you rescued me from Edwin."

He looked disgusted. "Niniane, that story is sickening."

"I like it. I might even make a song about it."

His eyes widened. "Don't you dare!"

She laughed and began to hum. "Let me see. 'In Winchester . . .' " He feinted a move toward her and she yipped and fled to the other side of the chestnut, putting the horse between them. "All right. I won't."

"Better not. I got a deer today."

"Wonderful. Venison stew for dinner. And I had better see about baking some bread."

"A very good idea." His voice was distinctly sarcastic. "I have had nothing to eat since breakfast."

"Will you take care of Ruist for me?"

"Yes."

"Thank you."

"You're welcome."

"Did you butcher the deer?"

"Yes. And my clothes got bloody. I left them in the bedroom for you to wash."

"How nice."

Niniane went back to the villa and began to pile charcoal into the oven. But no matter how busy her hands, she could not keep the discovery she was trying to avoid from coming back again and again to her mind. It was something she had learned in that brief moment's hesitation before she answered Ceawlin in the stableyard, a realization that was not at all comfortable. It was not for the sake of her people alone that she was protecting the Saxon prince.

Chapter 12

N INIANE dreamed during the night. It was a dream she had had occasionally ever since she was a child, a fearful dream for all that it was so silly. She had first dreamed it the night after Kerwyn told her the story of the giant Ysabadin. She had seen the giant in her dream, huge and hairy, with eyes that shone red. The giant was chasing her. She ran and ran but her legs were very heavy. She could not move them. She had to put her hands on her legs to try to push them forward, but it was no use. The giant was going to catch her . . .

She woke up sweating. Such a silly dream for a grown woman to fear. But her heart was hammering. She lay perfectly still so as not to wake Ceawlin. It was comforting to have him there. It helped to quiet her foolish terror.

It was raining. She could hear the rain beating against the window glass. It was so warm under the covers. Ceawlin was so warm. She laid her cheek against his bare back and closed her eyes. She remembered how safe she had felt wrapped in his arms that night in the barn.

How scornful he would be if he knew she was afraid of a dream. She did not think he was afraid of anything. They were so different, they two. She feared so much.

She feared for him who was so unafraid for himself. They hated the Saxons in this country. How many sons had lost fathers at Beranbyrg? How many fathers had lost sons? How many arrows would be waiting for Ceawlin as he went hunting so fearlessly through the wood?

Under her cheek she could feel his back moving as he breathed. She closed her eyes even tighter and began to pray. She did not want Ceawlin killed.

The following day Niniane and Ceawlin rode to Naille's farm to bring back the livestock. The track underfoot was thick with mud from the night's rain. The sky cleared as they rode, however, and by the time they reached the farm the sun was shining. The track took them through fields that had been newly plowed, and in the distance they could see men at work plowing more.

The geese in the farmyard screeched and beat their wings as the strangers came in. Niniane and Ceawlin tied their horses to the hitching post and were knocking at the farmhouse door when a boy of about six years came running up behind them. "We're out back," he said breathlessly. "Isolde's cat has got caught in a tree."

They followed the child to the yard behind the house. There was a tall beech tree in the middle of the yard, and beneath it, staring upward with concentrated intensity, were a woman and three small children. Far up the tree, clearly visible in the still-bare branches, was a gray cat, meowing piercingly.

"She's been up there since we woke up this morning," the boy reported to the two newcomers. "She's afraid to come down and she's too high for us to climb after her."

"Oh, Niniane," said Alanna distractedly, "it's you. Have you come for the cow?"

"Yes." The children had all turned from their distressed contemplation of the tree to stare at the new arrivals on the scene.

"Alanna," Niniane said gravely, "this is my husband, Ceawlin."

"You seem to have a problem," said Ceawlin in his perfect British. He gave Alanna a charming, boyish smile. Alanna's eyes widened as she took him in.

"My . . . my cat," said Isolde. Her small face was swollen with crying, her voice thick with tears. "She wants to come down."

"So I see," said Ceawlin, looking up. The tree was tall and the cat was at least thirty feet up in it.

"I wanted to climb up to fetch her, but Mama said I couldn't," said the boy. Niniane recognized him as Alanna's third son, Brice. He had been but four when last she saw him.

"You are more precious than the cat," said Alanna in a harried voice. Then, to Niniane, "Isolde tamed her, you see. She was more like a dog than a cat. That is why this is so upsetting."

"I'll go and get the cat for you, shall I?" said Ceawlin to the little girl. Her swollen face lighted. "Oh, yes. Would you?"

"Have you some kind of a bag I can put it in?" Ceawlin asked Alanna. "I won't be able to hold it and climb back down again at the same time."

"Get the leather game bag from the shed," Alanna said to her son, and the boy ran off.

"Are you certain you can climb up there?" Niniane asked doubtfully. "Some of those branches look very thin."

"We'll soon find out if I can or not," he returned. He took off his cloak and handed it to her. The women and children all watched him, wide-eyed, as he looked up measuringly at the tree.

"Here it is!" Brice came panting back with a leather bag strung through the top with a leather tie that could be pulled closed.

"This is just what I need," said Ceawlin, and slung it over his back. Then he went to the tree, jumped to grasp the first branch, and swung himself upward.

Niniane's heart was thudding as she watched his agile figure ascending ever higher. The branches toward the top were much thinner than those at the bottom. Surely they would not hold a man's weight? Surely one would snap and he would come plunging to the ground. She pictured it happening, pictured him plummeting through the branches to come crashing . . .

"He's got her." Isolde's voice sounded as if she were praying. Niniane found she *was* praying. She watched Ceawlin grab the cat by the scruff of its neck and stuff it into the bag.

How could he keep his balance? He was so precariously perched, and on such a slender branch . . .

Please, dear God. Let him come down safely.

Ceawlin slung the bag over his shoulder once more and began to climb back down. As he reached his foot to put his weight on the branch beneath him, there came the sound of a loud *crack*. The women and children gasped. Niniane went deadly pale. But he had reached out and grabbed another branch, hanging for a moment in the air, supported only by his hands. Then he was feeling for another foothold. He found one, and the descent continued.

The children set up a cheer as Ceawlin's feet touched the ground. He handed the bag to Isolde. "Here she is, frightened but safe."

Isolde opened the bag and the cat jumped out and streaked away. Isolde ran after it, calling its name. Ceawlin began to laugh.

"Thank you," said Alanna. "It was foolish to risk your life for a cat, but I thank you for the child's sake."

"It gave me a good excuse to climb a tree," he replied. The short hair on his forehead was slightly damp with sweat. There was color in his cheeks and his eyes were brilliant. "It was fun," he added, and Niniane, staring at him, knew that he was speaking the truth.

Alanna had planned to send Niniane and her Saxon husband on their way as quickly as possible, but now she said, "Please come into the house and have something to eat and drink."

"You are very kind," Ceawlin replied, and they all went into the farmhouse kitchen.

Alanna gave him a beer in her best cup. He drank it and praised her berry bread and talked to her in his perfect British as if he had known her for years. Alanna pressed more beer on him, more bread. The British woman's worn face was brighter than Niniane had ever seen it. A Saxon, Niniane thought with amusement, at Bryn Atha.

Nor was it just Alanna whom Ceawlin put himself out to charm. The children, too, came in for their share of his attention, and soon they were chattering away as well. Niniane watched his performance with rueful comprehension. That it was a performance she had no doubt. Ceawlin was not a man who, left to himself, would waste his time on children. Sigurd was the one who loved children. Not Ceawlin. This effort to charm was quite deliberate.

It was also successful. "I perfectly understand why you married him," Alanna said as she stood with Niniane watching Ceawlin tie the crate of chickens to the chestnut gelding's saddle. "He is not at all like a Saxon."

Niniane's lip curled. There was no one more like a Saxon. But she held her tongue and smiled sweetly.

"And he is so good-looking too." Naille's wife's brown eyes were soft as they regarded the tall, lean figure of Ceawlin packing the chickens. "Scarcely more than a boy. How old is he, Niniane?"

"Eighteen."

Alanna sighed. "You must get him baptized. Then everything will be all right."

Oh, yes, Niniane thought to herself with irony. Just get him baptized. Ceawlin, son of Cynric, prince of the blood. She thought of how he had looked at his father's funeral, his clothes all stained with the blood of the ox he had offered. She heard again the contempt that colored his voice every time he uttered the word "Christian."

If Alanna should know . . .

It was best that she didn't know. Best that she thought him only Niniane's husband, a charming young man, not at all like a Saxon. . . . Let them get to know him this way. Then, when the truth came out, they might be more inclined to help him. That was Ceawlin's thought too, she was sure of it. Else why had he put himself out for a mere farmer's wife?

They were almost ready to leave when Naille came riding into the farmyard. Ceawlin, who was about to lift Niniane to Bayvard's back, turned to look toward the sound of hooves. Niniane recognized Naille immediately. With him was his eldest son, Gereint, a boy of fifteen. Alanna called, "You are just in time to meet Niniane's husband, Naille."

Naille got off his horse and began to walk toward Ceawlin. The Briton's face was as white as if he had seen a ghost. His burning eyes were riveted to Ceawlin's face. *"You!"* he said when he had come to a halt. His voice was a mixture of loathing and fear. *"What are you doing here?"*

"But what is it?" Alanna asked worriedly. "I just told you, Naille, this is Niniane's husband."

"This is Cynric's son," returned Naille, his voice hard as iron. "I saw him at Beranbyrg."

Niniane's mouth was perfectly dry. She looked at Naille and tried to think of something to say. It was Ceawlin who waver. "I'm surprised you recognized me. At Beranbyrg I distinctly remember being covered with mud." He sounded as if he were answering a social amenity.

Naille's eyes widened at the British, but did not waver. "You were the first one over the wall. I remember you very well. And you were the one who gave Coinmail . . ." His voice trailed off.

"Who gave Coinmail his life," finished Ceawlin pleasantly. Niniane stared at her husband's face. He looked perfectly unruffled. Didn't he understand what danger he was in?

"Yes."

A silver eyebrow cocked charmingly. "Well, considering that he was to be my brother by marriage . . ."

Naille's eyes went to Niniane. "Is this really the man you have married?"

"Yes."

"You did not tell me yesterday it was Cynric's son!"

"No." Her voice came out like a croak. She cleared her throat. "But everything else I said was true, Naille. He did kill Edwin and that is why he had to flee from Winchester. The queen, Guthfrid, hates him and would—"

"What my wife is trying to say," cut in Ceawlin, and the pleasant note had quite left his voice, "is that I should be my father's heir, and Guthfrid knows it."

"Who is king now?" Naille asked.

"Guthfrid's infant son. But he is not Cynric's son. Of that I am quite certain."

"It's true, Naille," Niniane put in. "There is no one in Winchester who believes Edgar to be Cynric's son."

Naille's face was a study in conflicting emotions. The West Saxon prince clearly was not behaving as expected. Naille looked from Ceawlin to Niniane, then back again to Ceawlin. "All this talk of Winchester," he said. "We know nothing of Winchester here. Besides, why should an infant inherit before you?"

Ceawlin's face was impassive. "Because I am a bastard," he answered. "But I am my father's son. Edgar is not." Instinctively, Niniane had taken a step closer to Ceawlin as he spoke, and now Naille's eyes turned to her.

"In God's name, Niniane, why did you bring him here?"

"Because he will be King of Wessex one day, Naille, and it would be well for the Atrebates to get on terms with him."

"If we kill him, as well we might, he will not be King of Wessex."

Niniane answered promptly. "No, Edgar will. With Guthfrid as regent. And under Guthfrid you will find the eorls out of control. They have their greedy eyes on our land, Naille. Cynric made a survey after

Beranbyrg. You will be fighting them for your farms if you do not support Ceawlin."

Naille's brown eyes darted back to the prince. "Is this so?"

Ceawlin nodded. "Among my people it is the custom for a lord to reward the warriors who fight for him. Land is a coveted prize, even more coveted than gold or women. My father told his eorls after Beranbyrg that he would give them lands in your country."

Naille's face was bleak. "Then we will fight."

"You will not have to fight if I am king. Support me and you may keep your lands. But if a child is allowed to reign in Winchester, there will be no strong hand to control the eorls. The lack of leadership will lead them to think they can seize what they will." Ceawlin allowed a little silence to fall as Naille contemplated this grim prospect. Then: "There is enough land in this country for both our people, surely."

"The Saxons know only war." It was Gereint speaking, his upper lip curled with contempt. "Everyone knows what they are. They care for none of the civilized things in life: the tilling of the soil, the husbanding of animals . . . these things they have no thought for."

It was what all the Britons thought of the Saxons. Niniane remembered Ceawlin's anger when she had charged his people with barbarism, and held her breath. But his voice was mild as he answered the boy. "Perhaps what you say was true two hundred years ago, when first my people came to Britain. But we have not lived for two centuries on war alone. We too have cultivated our farms, raised our children, put down our roots."

"You are pagans." It was Naille speaking this time.

Ceawlin shrugged. "We do not seek to impose our gods on you."

Naille frowned as a thought struck him. "Coinmail," he began, glancing questioningly at Niniane, "our prince . . ." His voice died away.

"Your prince has sworn not to bear arms against me," answered Ceawlin. "My wife tells me he has gone to Wales to marry. Do not think he will lead you, Naille. He is a prince. He will not break his word."

Naille looked away from those confident eyes. "That is so," he said uncomfortably.

"Well, then, what Niniane has said must make sense. Your people are not warriors. Surely you saw that at Beranbyrg. Allow me the freedom of Bryn Atha and I will promise that when I am king I will not touch any land that belongs now to the Atrebates."

"What do you plan to do at Bryn Atha?"

"Assemble a war band to take against Guthfrid."

Niniane stared at him. This was the first she had heard of this plan.

"You expect me to allow you to keep a Saxon army at Bryn Atha?"

"We will not bother you," Ceawlin said impatiently. "I have given you my word, Naille. My word is sacred."

"Naille . . ." Alanna spoke at her husband's elbow. "He *is* married to Niniane."

"A Saxon marriage. That means nothing."

"I will be happy to marry her in your faith if that is what you want," Ceawlin said promptly.

"There. See, Naille? What better testament of his good faith?" Niniane realized with faint humor that Alanna had become Ceawlin's supporter.

"Oh, yes, Father." Isolde appeared at her father's side and tugged on his tunic. "He is a nice man. He got my cat down from the tree."

Naille looked surprised. "The cat that was in the tree behind the house?"

"Yes. He climbed all the way up and got it down for me."

Naille looked at Ceawlin. "Very shrewd, Prince."

Ceawlin grinned and looked like a harmless boy of eighteen. Naille, who had seen him fight at Beranbyrg, was not deceived, but his wife and children clearly were. "All right," he said slowly. "You may stay at Bryn Atha. For now."

Niniane rode Bayvard and led the cow. Ceawlin walked and led the chestnut, which was loaded with chicken crates. "My heart nearly failed when Naille recognized you," she said as they walked along the track between the plowed fields.

"I was not surprised," he answered.

"You weren't surprised? You never even hinted to me that you thought Naille might recognize you!"

"You went to the farm yesterday behind my back."

"That is not the same thing at all."

He looked over his shoulder at her but made no reply. "Well, I suppose it has turned out for the best," she said after a minute. "You seemed to persuade Naille."

"It was the cat." She could hear from his voice that he was smiling.

"My heart almost stopped when that branch broke under you."

"*Your* heart." He pushed up his sleeve and looked down at his arm. "The misbegotten thing scratched me when I was trying to get it into the bag."

"Let me see." The track had widened and he let her come alongside him and showed her the deep red scratch in his forearm. "Nasty," she said, and had to resist an impulse to kiss it. "I'll wash it out and put some salve on it for you when we get home."

He nodded and walked along beside her for a few minutes in silence. "Did you mean what you said about collecting a war band at Bryn Atha?" she finally asked.

"Yes."

"But how? Who?"

"The young thanes from the princes' hall, for a start. I spoke to some of them before I left. They will join me here at Bryn Atha."

"Ceawlin, it was the thanes from the princes' hall who were going to kill you."

"I did not speak to those thanes, naturally."

Long pause; then, "So you really mean to go to war?"

"Of course I mean to go to war. I will have to, if I am to be king." The track was starting to narrow again and he moved closer to her horse. "We are going to have to find the means of feeding a large group of men, Niniane. This cow and a few chickens won't be sufficient."

"When do you expect the thanes to come?"

"Not until I send word. I had no idea of what I would find at Bryn Atha, of course. I said I would send when I was ready."

"Will Cutha come?"

"Cutha will be my ear in Winchester. I do not want Cutha at Bryn Atha yet, even if he would come. Sigurd will come, though, I doubt I could keep him away."

"I am going to have to plant a very large garden," Niniane said. "And there is the corn to get into the fields . . ."

"I cannot understand this," he said impatiently. "We cannot plant our own corn. There is no one to plant it!"

"My father and Coinmail . . ." Her voice trailed away as he stared up at her incredulously.

"Your father worked in the fields? He was a prince."

"He was a British prince. And there was no one else—"

"I will buy corn," he said flatly.

"Where?"

"Surely there is a local market."

"Well, yes. But, Ceawlin, what will you use for barter?"

"Before I left Winchester, my mother gave me her jewels."

"Oh."

"The track is getting too narrow, Niniane. You will have to drop back."

She halted Bayvard and let Ceawlin get ahead of her. "About your brother," he said over his shoulder, and her heart skipped a beat. "For how long does he mean to stay in Wales?"

"I don't think he is in Wales exactly, Ceawlin. He is near to Glevum."

He shrugged. Where Coinmail was was clearly immaterial so long as he was out of Ceawlin's way. "How long?" he repeated. "Did Naille say?"

"He did not know."

"He is shamed," Ceawlin said. "That is why he has gone away. He is shamed to have taken his life from me."

"Perhaps. I don't know."

"He is shamed to face his people, knowing he can no longer lead them in war. I do not think he will return soon."

"Is that how you would feel, Ceawlin?" she asked. "Shamed?"

"I?" He looked over his shoulder at her. He seemed surprised. "I would have died before I swore such a thing," he said. And looking down into his austere face, Niniane knew that he spoke the truth.

Chapter 13

NINIANE put in her garden and talked Naille into giving her back most of the villa's livestock. She also managed to arrange with Naille for three men to come and help sow Bryn Atha's fields with wheat and rye and barley. It was all very well for Ceawlin to talk of buying what they would need; Niniane knew they would have to grow their own food. It simply would not be possible to feed a group of men over the winter unless they had their own food stored. Come the winter, there would be no food at the market for them to buy. So she got the crops into the ground and thought she would bide her time before telling Ceawlin he and his men were going to have to harvest them.

Ceawlin divided his time between hunting and fixing up the slave quarters. Niniane was surprised at how competent a carpenter he was. "I used to watch the carpenters in Winchester," he confessed a little shamefacedly when she commented on his proficiency. "When I was a child, of course."

"Of course," she agreed gravely.

"My father was still building Winchester, you see. Sigurd and I spent a lot of time making nuisances of ourselves. You know how boys are." He was putting a wooden floor over the dirt floor of the slave quarters and was down on his knees nailing in the boards. Niniane was sitting on the part of the floor that he had already finished.

She hid a smile. "I know."

"Anyway"—he aimed the hammer at a nail—"it has come in useful. We must have quarters for my thanes, and I don't think you would want them in the house with you."

"Decidedly not."

He grunted. "The house is too small. And we will need the reception rooms that have been closed up for the women."

She stared at him. He had finished hammering the nail and was choosing another. "What women?" she asked.

"You will need women to help with the cooking and the weaving, obviously."

119

"Oh." She looked at his lean strong hand setting the new nail. "Where are these women to come from?"

"I haven't thought about that yet. Do you think we could get some of the local girls?"

"With a houseful of Saxon thanes? No."

He looked up from the board he was hammering into the wooden studs he had already constructed. "No?" His brows were cocked in the way she loved, the way that made him look like a little boy begging for honey.

"No, Ceawlin. Too many families lost a son or a husband at Beranbyrg."

He nodded slowly and began to hammer once again. "Do you know whom I think we ought to bring to Bryn Atha?" she asked after a minute.

"Who?" he said around the sound of the hammer.

"Your mother."

He sat back on his heels and pushed his hair off his cheek. "My mother? But why?"

"Because I do not think she is safe in Winchester."

His eyes widened. "Not safe? But . . . do you think Guthfrid would try to do her a mischief?"

"I think she very well might."

He frowned. "Nonsense. My mother is no threat to her now. Cynric is dead."

"The queen hates you, Ceawlin. You didn't hear her when she was speaking about you to Edric." Niniane shivered. "She hates you and would do anything she could to hurt you. And Fara is your mother."

"She wouldn't dare," he said abruptly. But she could see that he had gone a little pale. "Cutha is there . . ."

"Poison is easy enough to administer. And what could Cutha do? Guthfrid has the power in Winchester now."

"Gods." His eyes were getting very turquoise. "I never thought of that. You're right, Niniane. I must get her out of Winchester." His voice became accusing. "Why did you not mention this before?"

"I didn't think of it before," she confessed. In truth, she had thought of little else but him these last weeks, but she did not say that. "It was when you started to talk of bringing women here, and I thought of the women's hall at Winchester and Fara. It just came to me. . . ."

They stared at each other, both realizing they were guilty of forgetting Fara. Ceawlin put down the hammer and stood up. "I'll ride to Venta and see Sigurd."

Niniane stared up at him, but there was no one else who could go. "Yes," she said finally, her voice low. "I think you had better."

*   *   *

Ceawlin awoke early the following morning, the day he was to leave for Venta. The light outside the window was just beginning to turn from black to gray. Ceawlin was finding that he too liked sleeping in a room with a window. It was nice to wake in the morning and see the sky.

Niniane was still asleep, curled under the blankets like a kitten. He had kept her awake for quite a long time last night.

He propped his chin upon his hands and lay still, regarding his wife. Or what he could see of his wife, which was one bare shoulder and a shining stream of autumn-brown hair.

He loved making love to her. She stirred his blood more than any of the more knowledgeable, more experienced women he had known before. She knew nothing except what he had taught her, what they had learned together, yet he found the flicker of her eyelash more erotic than the most blatantly sexual enticements of any of his other women. It could be the isolation of Bryn Atha, of course. They were certainly not leading a normal life cooped up here together with scarcely another soul to speak to from morning until night. It could be. But he did not think so.

He should be getting up. He wanted to get an early start, make Venta before the gates were closed. He had certainly said sufficient farewell to Niniane last night. He remembered suddenly the first morning he had awakened beside her, in the storage barn where they had taken brief refuge on their flight from Winchester. He had wanted her then, and had refrained because she was a virgin and he had not wanted to frighten her. Well, she was a virgin no longer. He could certainly attest to that.

It would not take very long at all, really. . . .

"Niniane." He slipped an arm around her waist and pulled her toward him. She was so light-boned, she weighed scarcely anything. But she held such profound delight. . . . "Niniane!" Her eyes opened and regarded him drowsily, dark and colorless in the gray light of the bedroom. He turned her on her back and slid over her, then into her. Her eyes opened wider. "Mmmmm," he murmured deeply. He lowered his mouth to hers. For a moment she gave him no response, still half-asleep. He deepened the kiss and began to move slowly within her. He waited. He was not looking simply for his own quick relief; he had found that half his pleasure came from the delight he was able to give to her. After a minute her mouth answered to his, then her hips began to move in rhythm with his motion. "Nan," he said against her mouth. "Ah. . . ."

"I have to leave," he said a little while later. "Gereint will be here later this morning." He had made arrangements yesterday for Naille's eldest son to stay with Niniane until he returned.

"Yes. You must."

They neither of them moved. Then she said, "Whom will you go to in Venta? Who will be safe?"

"There is a woman I know," he answered thoughtlessly, and felt her grow rigid against him.

"A woman!"

"An old woman," he lied, "a friend of my mother's."

She relaxed again, warm and pliant in his arms. "Oh."

He kissed the top of her head and got out of bed. She got up too and said, "I'll get your food ready, Ceawlin."

As he dressed, he wondered idly why he had bothered to lie to her. It was easier, he decided, that was all. He knew how women were. He had lived with his mother and Guthfrid for too long not to understand about women and jealousy. The less Niniane knew about his doings, Ceawlin thought, the better it would be for both of them.

He made Venta before the gates were closed, riding in on a horse he had borrowed from Naille. Bayvard would most certainly have been recognized, and quite possibly Niniane's chestnut gelding as well. So, since secrecy was essential, he had taken a roan from Naille. He was also wearing a hooded cloak that had once belonged to Niniane's father. He had protested to her at first that a hood in May would look suspicious. She insisted that he wear it.

"You may perhaps look a little unusual," she had said, "but if you hunch over and pretend to be old, the cloak will cause no comment. Old people are always cold. In any case, the hood will be safer than going bareheaded. There isn't another head like yours in all of Wessex, Ceawlin. You simply must wear the hood."

She was right, of course, and so he pulled the hood up as soon as he was within sight of Winchester and kept it up until he was safe within the confines of Helwig's house in the Lindum street of Venta. Helwig was surprised to see him.

"We heard you had tried to kill the baby king and ran away when you failed," she told him as he sat in her kitchen eating the rabbit stew she had served him.

He scowled. "Is that the story they have given out?"

"Yes."

"Well, the truth is that Guthfrid tried to have *me* killed, but I was warned of the plot and got away first."

"That sounds more probable," the Saxon woman agreed. Helwig was a baker who kept the shop that had once belonged to her husband, a Briton who had been dead for several years. Ceawlin had known her for almost the whole of her widowhood. Helwig was a handsome young woman whose husband, a prosperous shopkeeper, had been some thirty years older than she. She had found the freedom of a comfortable widowhood pleasant and had no wish to remarry. The young prince from Winchester had been a thoroughly satisfactory answer to the problem of an empty bed. "If you got away safe," she said now, "why did you come back? I'd like to think it was for my sake, but I'm not that stupid."

He grinned at her and took another bite of rabbit stew. "I came back for my mother. I'm worried that she is not safe at Winchester."

"Ah." A guarded look came over Helwig's fair-skinned handsome face.

He frowned. "What is it?"

"The word from Winchester is that Fara is not well," she answered.

"What do you mean?"

She shrugged her big shoulders. "Just that. She is not well. She has not been into Venta since before the king died."

"My father's death drained her, that is all." He wiped up the sauce on his plate with a piece of bread. "I need to get a message to Sigurd," he said around the bread in his mouth. "Who goes to Winchester tomorrow?"

"I don't know. I'll ask. Shall I have Sigurd told that you are here?"

"Yes. I need to see him."

"All right."

She left by the kitchen door and returned half an hour later. "The soap-maker is taking a wagon to Winchester tomorrow. He is reliable. He will give your message to Sigurd."

"Good." Ceawlin had been sitting over his empty plate drinking beer, and now he stood up and stretched. "I have been riding since sunup, Helwig, and I'm tired. Can you lend me a bed?"

"Not my bed?"

He gave her a charming smile. "I'd love to, but not tonight."

"All right." She did not seem insulted, but took him to the small bedroom that adjoined hers and left him alone. He was asleep in five minutes.

It was not until late the following afternoon that Sigurd came to the house on Lindum Street. Ceawlin had been growing more and more impatient as the hours went by. The bake shop was in the front part of Helwig's house, with the living rooms behind it. The living area consisted of two small bedrooms, a small salon, and the kitchen where Helwig did the baking in the back. There was not much space. Ceawlin found himself confined to the salon and spent most of the day pacing up and down the room like a lion in a cage. He heard Sigurd's voice in the bakery as soon as his friend came in, but as there were others in the shop as well, Sigurd had to wait until they left before he could come through into the salon where Ceawlin waited.

The two young men clasped shoulders and pummeled each other on the back. "Gods," said Sigurd at last. "What are you doing in Venta, Ceawlin? I thought you were safe at Bryn Atha."

Helwig came to the door and peeked in. "Keep your voices down," she warned.

"We will," Ceawlin promised. Then, to Sigurd, "I came because I'm worried about my mother." Helwig went back to the shop and Ceawlin continued, "I want to take her back to Bryn Atha with me, Sigurd. I don't think she is safe in Winchester."

"Oh." Sigurd's eyes slid away from Ceawlin's concerned blue gaze. After a minute Sigurd sat down in one of Helwig's well-worn chairs and rested his elbows on the wicker arms. He looked at his lap.

"What is it?" Ceawlin's voice was sharp. "Nothing has happened to her?"

Sigurd did not look up. "She is sick, Ceawlin. This last month, since you have been gone, she has failed greatly. There is something wrong with her insides. She is in great pain."

The fair skin of Ceawlin's cheeks, still so boyishly innocent of any trace of beard, went suddenly white. "Could it be poison?" he asked, his voice hoarse.

Sigurd shook his head. "My father thought of that. All her food is tasted first. It is not poison, Ceawlin. It is the crab-sickness." Gray eyes finally lifted to blue. "She is dying."

"I don't believe it." The skin over Ceawlin's cheekbones was stretched taut.

Sigurd remained with his head tilted back, his eyes steady on his friend's. It was Ceawlin who finally turned away. He walked to the farthest end of the room and rested his forehead against the wall. After a long moment he asked, "You said she is in pain?"

"Yes. But the priest is giving her medicine. It helps."

"How . . . how long?"

"It cannot be long now. She is very frail."

Ceawlin did not move. Sigurd looked at him as he stood there, head bent, forehead pressed against the green plaster wall. He did not ever remember a time when Ceawlin had looked so vulnerable. Sigurd's gray eyes were dark with pity.

When Ceawlin finally spoke, his voice was steady. "Can I see her?"

"You cannot come to Winchester, Ceawlin. It would be mad to try. And it would only upset her, to think you had placed yourself in such danger. Her greatest joy right now is the knowledge that you are safe."

Ceawlin's fists clenched at his sides. He did not answer.

"I know it is hard," Sigurd said. "But there is nothing you can do." After a minute he added softly, "She is going to your father."

A long silence fell. Sigurd sat quietly, his eyes on Ceawlin's rigid back and clenched fists. After what seemed like forever, Ceawlin's hands relaxed and he turned slowly to face Sigurd once more. His face was very white, but Sigurd was relieved to see that he had got himself under control. "The world is changing," Ceawlin said.

"That it is." Sigurd judged it was all right now to speak of other things. "Guthfrid is showing herself more and more dependent upon Edric. The eorls are not happy. Edric has his followers, of course, the men who look to prosper under him, but most of the eorls and a number of the thanes don't like him. They see the golden opportunities for power they envisioned for themselves slipping away."

"That is good news." Ceawlin's face was still too pale and he did not seem to be giving Sigurd his full attention.

Nevertheless, Sigurd went on. "It is known that you are at Bryn Atha. When you took Niniane with you, it was not hard to guess where you would go. Guthfrid wanted Edric to take a war band after you, but he would not. He said you were a lordless man, and so harmless. The truth is, of course, that he was not sure he could find the men to follow him. The eorls may not have wanted you for king, but they are not ready yet to see you dead."

"That is even better news." Ceawlin was paying attention now. "I have been fixing up the old slave quarters at Bryn Atha for my own war band, Sigurd. It is a large building and in another month it should be comfortable. The men can come in June."

Sigurd frowned. "My father is not in favor of your collecting a war band at Bryn Atha, Ceawlin. He says to leave all to him."

Ceawlin walked back toward the center of the room. "I have much respect for Cutha, you know that. But I cannot let another man do all my work for me. If he will pursue my cause in Winchester, I will be grateful. But I must do what I can myself." He came to a halt before Sigurd.

Sigurd got slowly to his feet. Cutha, in fact, had been quite adamant that Ceawlin should leave matters to him. "I think my father has hopes of restoring you without a fight," he said as he straightened up.

"There will have to be a fight," Ceawlin answered. "There is no avoiding it. There are too many thanes who will fear for themselves if I become king. And rightly so," he added, his voice and face grim. Then, as Sigurd still hesitated, "If you feel you cannot come yourself, Sigurd, of course I shall understand."

"Don't be a fool, Ceawlin. Of course I shall come." Sigurd was standing close before him now. "Didn't I swear my allegiance to you as my lord?"

The color suddenly came back to Ceawlin's cheeks, flushing them a boyish pink. "No matter who else fails me," he said, and his voice was now much huskier than usual, "I know I can always count on you."

"Till the death," said Sigurd, and they looked at each other, both moved and both a little embarrassed by their own emotion. "Well," said Sigurd more briskly, "I had better be going. People will want to know what I can possibly be finding to do for so long in the bakery."

Ceawlin grinned. "I was known to spend whole afternoons in the bakery. Why should not you do the same?"

"Helwig never had eyes for me," Sigurd retorted. "Not with you around."

"I am not around any longer," Ceawlin returned. "And you know we were always willing to share our treats."

It was not until he had put his hand on the door to push it open that Sigurd asked, "How is Niniane?"

"Thriving," Ceawlin responded instantly. "She is a country creature at heart, you know."

"Well, it was what she was brought up to, I suppose."

"Yes." Ceawlin looked down at his hand, the topic of Niniane clearly not what was on his mind. "Sigurd . . . will you . . . will you give my mother my . . . my love?"

"Of course I will."

Ceawlin gave him a shadowy smile, but still did not meet his eyes. "Well, then, until June."

"Until June," said Sigurd, and pushed open the door.

Ceawlin left for Bryn Atha early the following morning, as soon as the gates of Venta were open. His heart was sore as he rode north, full of trouble for his mother. He wished Sigurd had not told him she was in pain.

Niniane and Gereint were eating dinner in the dining room when he arrived back at Bryn Atha. The dogs, which they had reclaimed from Naille along with the livestock, came racing into the courtyard to greet him, barking and running around his horse's legs. Niniane heard the racket, cried, "Ceawlin is back!" and ran to the front door. He had dismounted and was walking toward the villa leading his horse when she came out into the courtyard. He was alone.

She went to meet him. "You were not gone long," she said, her eyes searching his face. His expression told her nothing.

"No. I talked to Sigurd."

"That is good." Gereint was standing in the doorway and she turned to say to him, "Gereint, will you take the horse to the stable, please, and give him water and grain? I will keep your dinner for you."

Naille's son came to take the reins from Ceawlin, his face sullen. He had not been happy when his father made him come and stay in a Saxon house.

"Come in," Niniane said to Ceawlin as the boy led the obviously tired horse away. "You must be hungry and thirsty. Did you leave Venta this morning?"

"Yes." He followed her into the house and let her pour water into a bowl so he could wash. She asked no questions, just took his cloak and put it away. Then, "Come into the dining room. There is chicken."

As he was following her down the gallery he said, "My mother is ill. Sigurd says she is dying. She could not come with me. I could not even see her." His voice was perfectly steady, perfectly expressionless.

Niniane bent her head and refrained from looking back at him. "She was not well when we left Winchester, but I did not realize . . ."

"No. Neither did I."

They came into the dining room and looked at the table, which was set with two plates of half-eaten food. "Sit down," Niniane said. "I'll get you something to eat." She took a few steps toward the kitchen, then stopped, closed her eyes, and pressed her fingers to her mouth. He made no move to come to her, nor did he speak. After a moment she forced herself to control and went into the kitchen to get him a plate of food. They were both seated at the table when Gereint returned.

"Did you learn anything of use from Sigurd?" Niniane asked as Gereint took his place.

"Yes. It's as we thought would happen. Edric is becoming more powerful. Sigurd says that Cutha does not want me to gather a war band, that he thinks he can gain me the kingship without a fight."

Niniane forgot even the pretense of eating. "Is that possible?"

He shook his head. He was eating steadily, and drinking great gulps of the wine she had poured. "Guthfrid and Edric are not going to disappear so conveniently. If I want the kingship, I am going to have to fight for it. I told Sigurd to come with the rest of the thanes in June."

Gereint was staring at Ceawlin, a mixture of fear and distrust in his eyes. Then he turned to Niniane. "You are really going to let him bring his pagan followers to Bryn Atha?"

Ceawlin put down his knife and looked at the boy. "Your father knows all about it," he said quietly. "You heard the promise I made to him."

"Will you keep your promise, though?" Gereint asked truculently. "That is what I want to know."

Anger kindled behind the blue-green eyes. "I have never broken my oath."

Gereint had obviously been thinking about this, or he had been listening to his elders talk, for now he said challengingly: "What about this new king, your brother? Did you not have to swear an oath to be loyal to him? And are you not about to break it?"

"I swore to uphold the right of Edgar, son of Cynric." Ceawlin's eyes were still blazing at the insult. "That brat is no more my father's son than you are. I know it. Niniane knows it. All of Winchester knows it."

Niniane gave Gereint credit for bravery if not for sense. His eyes never wavered from Ceawlin's. "How can you be sure?" he asked.

Ceawlin did not answer. But it was a fair question, Niniane thought suddenly. The boy only wanted to be certain he could trust Ceawlin's word. She answered Gereint herself.

"Cynric was lucky to get the two sons he had, and he got them when he was in his years of potency, not in his old age. There were no more sons after Ceawlin and Edwin, Gereint. Nor daughters. None of the women in the bower who shared Cynric's bed . . ." Here the boy's eyes widened in shock. "They do things differently in Winchester," Niniane said. "Anyway, none of the women who slept with the king ever conceived." She glanced from Gereint's face to Ceawlin's and was surprised to find that he was looking white about the nostrils and the mouth. She looked back to Gereint, who was watching her with fascinated horror. "It was not the fault of the women," she concluded a little hesitantly. "It was Cynric who could not get a child."

"Well, someone got a child on the queen," Gereint said. His eyes flickered a little at his own daring. If his father ever heard him saying such things . . .

"Edric. The thane we were discussing. It was common knowledge that he shared the queen's bed." Niniane's voice was quiet. Perhaps she ought not to have spoken? Ceawlin was so white, so silent . . .

Gereint ate in silence, digesting what she had said along with his dinner. At last he turned to Ceawlin. "How many men are coming here?"

Ceawlin picked up his knife again. Evidently he had got over whatever it was that had been bothering him. "About a dozen to begin with."

"A dozen? That is all? You cannot win a kingdom with a dozen men!"

Ceawlin grinned at the boy, a cocky, beguiling grin. "It is the start, Gereint. Once the others see that I am able to support a war band, more will follow."

"And then you will go to war against the queen?"

"Then I will go to war against the queen."

There was a reflective silence as Gereint watched Ceawlin eat. Then, "My father said you fought like a madman at Beranbyrg."

Ceawlin grunted around the bread in his mouth. "It's a matter of training," he said. "I've been training for war since I was eight years old."

Gereint's eyes grew very large. "All I ever do is work in the fields," he said. Regretfully.

"Well, that is important work too," said Ceawlin.

"Yes," Gereint answered, but he did not sound so sure.

*   *   *

After dinner Ceawlin went down to the stable to check on the horses. Gereint hesitated as the prince went out, hesitated and looked at Niniane. "Go with Ceawlin if you like, Gereint," she said casually. "He is going to make sure the horses have water for the night. Perhaps you could help."

"All right," the boy said, and turned to follow the Saxon. They came back in forty minutes, both talking easily about the different horses they had known. Niniane was just finishing the dishes. It was later than their usual hour; the sky was growing dark.

Ceawlin yawned. "Gods, but I'm tired."

"Go along to bed," Niniane said. "I'll come in a little while."

He went off down the gallery, and after a minute Gereint said he would go to bed too. Niniane went back to the kitchen and began to set things out for the morning. Her hands worked independently of her mind, however. Her mind was on the news Ceawlin had brought of Fara.

Her heart grieved for the friedlehe. Fara had always been so beautifully kind to her. But her heart grieved even more for Fara's son, who had somehow become more important to her than any other person in the world.

His face had given her no clue as to how he felt. His very impassiveness, however, told her that she could not be the one to offer him comfort. He would have to be the one to make the first move, let her know that he wanted her sympathy, her care. She could not intrude unwanted upon his grief.

She finished in the kitchen and went slowly down the gallery to their room. He was in bed, the blankets pulled up over his shoulders, his back toward the door. She came in quietly and began to undress. She folded her clothes neatly on the chest and slipped into the bed beside him. There was silence. And then he reached for her.

He had never made love to her like he did this night, desperately, recklessly, exhaustingly. For the first time she was conscious that she was just a body to him; she doubted he even knew who she was. She did not resent this, however, but was glad to give him what comfort he could find. When finally he lay quiet, she cradled him in her arms and pressed her lips against his hair as if he were a child at her breast. He slept.

Chapter 14

*I*T was a beautiful warm June day and Niniane decided to take a chair out to the courtyard so she could sit in the sun and dry her hair. She had washed it that morning, and Ceawlin's as well, and now that he was gone for the rest of the day she thought she would just sit quietly for an hour or so and play her harp. She had been feeling very tired these last few weeks.

The sun was strong and Niniane spread her hair like a fan over the back of her chair and picked up her harp. It was the harp Alric had made for her, one of the few things she had brought away from Winchester. She was plucking on the strings, trying to catch a certain melody that had been running in her mind, when the sound of horses broke through her concentration. She looked up.

There was a crowd of Saxon thanes riding through the gate.

Guthfrid! Niniane thought instantly. She has come to kill us. Then she recognized Sigurd.

Sigurd had seen her first. "Niniane!" he called. He turned to say something to the men behind him, then dismounted, gave his horse to someone to hold, and began to walk across the courtyard.

So, they have come, Niniane thought, and the thought was not a happy one. She had never quite believed it would happen, she realized as she put her harp onto the seat of her chair and went to greet Ceawlin's friend.

"Sigurd. So you have come."

"We have come." He took her hands into his and gave them a squeeze. "You look wonderful."

She smiled faintly. "I thought for a minute you were Guthfrid's war band," she confessed. "My heart is still pounding."

He frowned in concern. "I am sorry we frightened you. Ceawlin told us to come in June."

"I know. And he will be so glad to see you." She made an effort to look glad herself.

Sigurd was looking around the courtyard. "Your home is beautiful."

"Thank you."

"Where is Ceawlin?"

"He has ridden into the market today." Niniane's dimple flickered. "He is working very hard at wooing the Atrebates, Sigurd. He seems to be succeeding. They are beginning to think of him as 'that nice boy who is married to Niniane.'"

Sigurd threw back his head and roared with laughter. "Come along," said Niniane, "and I will show your men where they are to sleep."

When Ceawlin returned to Bryn Atha late in the afternoon, the first thing he saw as he came in through the gate was Sigurd and two other Saxons carrying a table into the newly renovated slave quarters. Sigurd looked up, saw him, and dropped the table. Ceawlin jumped off his horse and the two young men met in the middle of the courtyard, clasping each other's shoulders and laughing.

Niniane watched them from the villa doorway. Sigurd was a well-looking young man, she thought, but next to Ceawlin's splendid height and stunning fairness he looked dim and insignificant. They stood together for several minutes, talking. When Ceawlin turned around, Niniane saw that his face had become very grave.

What news of Fara? Niniane thought. She had not asked Sigurd herself, feeling that it was Ceawlin's place to do that, not hers.

Ceawlin did not come to the villa. He went instead into the slave quarters, presumably to greet his new men. Niniane went back to the kitchen. Somehow, all of these thanes were going to have to be fed.

Fifteen thanes in all had come with Sigurd to join Ceawlin at Bryn Atha, ten from the princes' hall and five from the great hall. They were all young. Niniane served dinner in the villa dining room, in which she had set up a second table. In fact, as Sigurd said humorously to Ceawlin around a mouthful of stew, Niniane had had them moving furniture ever since they had arrived at Bryn Atha that afternoon.

Niniane smiled and did not reply. She and Ceawlin were seated in the center of the larger table, with Sigurd next to Ceawlin, and Penda, one of the great-hall thanes, next to her. Across from them sat a row of thanes whose faces were all familiar from her years in Winchester, and behind those thanes was yet another table of men.

I will have to get some women in to help me, Niniane thought as she looked around at the busily eating thanes. I cannot feed all these men by myself every day.

Penda said to her courteously, "The venison is very good, my lady."

"Thank you." Niniane was not hungry herself, and now she put down her knife and turned to the thane beside her. "How did you manage to get away from Winchester, Penda? You surely did not all just ride out as a group?"

"No." He grinned at her. Penda was a few years older than Ceawlin, with yellow-brown hair and beard and light hazel eyes. His arrival had been a surprise; he was not one of the thanes Ceawlin had expected to see. "We all left at different times, some to go hunting, some to go to Venta, and then we met on the road. By the time Edric realized we were gone, it was too late in the day for pursuit."

"Guthfrid may pursue you to Bryn Atha, though. Surely she will guess where you all have gone." It was Niniane's deepest fear.

"I do not think we will be pursued, my lady," the thane replied confidently. "Edric is afraid to turn his back on Winchester. He cannot trust the eorls he would be forced to leave behind. Someone might seize the child and set himself up to rule in Edric's place."

"So Edric has truly become so powerful?"

Penda looked disgusted. "Guthfrid is going to marry him."

"Ah."

"That is why I have come to Ceawlin," Penda said. "There is just so much a man can stomach."

"Yes." It was Wuffa, the thane who was seated opposite to Ceawlin. Slowly he got to his feet, and the men, seeing him rise, fell silent. Wuffa spoke into the quiet with the formal style of the Saxon banquet hall. "We have come to you, Prince, to ask you to be our lord. You are the Woden-born, the only son your father has left to us. We ask you to take us into your service, and we will swear to follow you faithfully all the days of our lives."

The silence was profound as all the men in the room, and Niniane, looked at Ceawlin. Wuffa sat down as Ceawlin rose to his feet. He was so beautiful, Niniane thought, with his new-washed hair and his blue eyes and his splendid height. "I take you as my men," Ceawlin responded to Wuffa's request, his voice and his face very grave. "Be sure that for so long as I live, all that I have I will share with you. You are my comitatus. Together, we shall win back Wessex."

"To Ceawlin!" It was Sigurd, rising to his feet and holding up his cup for the pledge. "To Ceawlin, our rightful king!" All the men leapt to their feet, and Niniane followed more slowly. She drank the toast and looked at her husband and wished she were not so afraid.

"My mother is dead." He told her when they were alone in their bedroom, undressing for bed. "Sigurd brought me word. She died four days since."

"Oh, Ceawlin." She looked at his impassive face and did not know what to say. What words were there for one who believed as he did? For her there was the comfort of a loving God and the reward of heaven. But for him? What did he believe? She was not sure. "I am so sorry," she said at last, conscious of the inadequacy of the words but not knowing what else to say.

"I'm not. It is a relief. She was in pain. Sigurd told me that when I saw him in Venta. Now I do not have to think of her suffering. Now it is all over."

He was sitting on the bed, bent over to take off his shoes, and his hair had fallen forward to hide his face. "You did not tell me that," she said, her voice low. She tried not to feel hurt he had not shared his own pain with her, but she was.

He shrugged. He had unlaced his shoes, but still he bent over them. She realized he was hiding his face from her and she turned away to put her things in the clothes chest. "You were fond of her, I know," his voice said from behind her. "There was nothing to be gained by worrying you too."

He had not told her out of care for her. She felt better and was instantly ashamed that her thoughts were more for herself and Ceawlin than they were for Fara.

Fara had had a truly loving heart, Niniane thought. She had not been a Christian, but surely God, who was so good, would welcome her into heaven. The priest who came once or twice a year to Bryn Atha would say that all pagans are damned, but Niniane could not believe that. Not of Fara. Surely Fara was safe with God. The thought comforted her, but she knew it would not comfort Ceawlin. What would comfort him?

"It is over," he repeated behind her. His voice was flat and hard. "Now it is up to me to see that she is not forgotten. The harpers will sing one day that Fara gave a king to Wessex. I vow it."

"They will. I know they will." She turned from the chest to look at him. Perhaps this was the time . . . The way he sounded . . . She made up her mind. "Ceawlin," she said, "I am going to have a baby."

"*What?*"

She stared at him. "I am going to have a baby."

"Are you sure?" He was standing perfectly still, but there was such an air of coiled tension about him that she was frightened.

"Yes, I am sure. The signs are all there, and I talked to Alanna yesterday . . ." Her voice trailed off. His eyes were blazing purely turquoise and his cheeks were flushed. "Is something wrong? Are you not pleased?"

"Pleased? Pleased? You cannot know how pleased. Oh, Niniane," and he came to envelop her in a crushing hug. "My good luck," he mumbled into her hair. "You have always been my good luck."

She put her own arms around his waist and leaned her cheek against his chest. She was bewildered by this violent reaction, had never expected such a thing from him. Well, she had said the right thing, that was certain. "Your mother would be pleased," she murmured softly.

"Yes." His arms tightened. Then they relaxed and he held her away from him so he could look down into her face. "We must get some women here," he said. "You cannot be doing the work for all these men by yourself."

"I think I can get some British girls to come and help me. You have done a good job of wooing the local families."

He grinned. "You should have seen me at the market today. I was even invited to eat with Naille and Col and Conmach."

"You were?" The three men Ceawlin mentioned were the three most important of the Atrebates leaders after Coinmail.

"And Gereint asked me to show him how to use a sword," he added smugly.

Niniane laughed.

"Little Niniane." He flicked her cheek with a finger. "My good luck."

"Why do you say that?" she asked curiously.

He dropped his hands from her shoulders and began to take off his tunic. "You were the one who warned me on the dueling grounds." His voice was muffled by the tunic coming over his head. "Weren't you?"

"Yes. Everyone else was watching you, but I was watching Edwin."

"Why?" He dropped the tunic on the floor and looked at her inquiringly. His hair was ruffled into a halo of silver, and she smiled.

"Because I didn't trust him." She bent to pick up his tunic. He took off his shirt and she took it from his hands and went to put them both on the clothes chest.

"I did not mean why were you watching him, I meant why did you warn me?" He stood on one foot to remove a shoe, then on the other. Niniane picked up the shoes as well and put them in the corner. Then she came back to him and placed her hand upon his lean, muscled back. She loved to touch him.

"Where did you get all these muscles?" she asked.

"Wrestling, I suppose. I never had much weight, so I had to be strong." He sat on the edge of the bed so their eyes were on a level and drew her close to him. "I have always wondered why you warned me. You were to marry him. He would have been king. I should have thought your interest lay with him, not with me. Was it for my mother's sake?"

"Partly." Her small face was grave as she looked back into his eyes. "But I did not want to marry Edwin. He . . . he frightened me."

He frowned and reached a hand up to smooth her hair. "Did he? Why?"

"I don't know." Her eyes were very gray. "He was just . . . strange." She grimaced a little. "He repelled me, if you must know."

Ceawlin looked over her head. Then he said, with extreme quietness, "I don't think he had a soul. Even a man one dislikes, distrusts . . . still one can see he has a soul. It's there, in his eyes. It was not in Edwin's."

Her eyes almost engulfed her small face. "Yes," she whispered. "He was like that. He made my flesh creep."

"Mine too." Their eyes met and held. "Guthfrid and Edric I can deal with . . . but him . . . and he was my brother." There was a faint trace of horror in his voice.

"I was glad when you killed him," she said.

"So was I." The horror had been replaced by a note of distinct grimness. "I will have to pay for it one day, I know. Fate does not allow a brother-slayer to go unpunished. But I will face it when I must. For now, fate is on my side. I can feel it."

"Ceawlin, it was not your fault. Edwin was going to kill you."

He smiled a little crookedly. "No, Niniane. One cannot hide from the gods what is in one's heart. I wanted him dead. I wanted to be king. And whatever may come to me in the future because of what I did"—his eyes narrowed to slits of turquoise—"it will have been worth it."

Niniane had been very tired these last few weeks, falling asleep as soon as she settled herself in the bed, but tonight she lay awake, her mind busy with what had happened between her and Ceawlin.

Never had she expected such a reaction to her news. Never would she be able to understand him. He was so utterly different from anyone else she had ever known.

He fascinated her. She lay curled against his warm, sleeping body and thought about her marriage. Was what she felt for him a sin? She supposed it was, at least until they were married by a priest. But he had agreed to a Christian marriage, so that would be all right. Naille had told her the priest was due to come in August. Then they could be properly married.

What she felt might be a sin even when they were properly married. She did not think it was right to do such things with a man . . . to want to do such things. Yet she could not help herself. She could not even think of saying him nay.

He fascinated her. Nor was it just the things they did together in the night. There was something about him, a power she recognized though she could not put a name to it. He would get what he wanted, Ceawlin. Of that she had no doubt.

Her eyes began to close. Her bed had been so lonely those nights he was away in Venta. Finally she slept.

Ceawlin woke with the dawn. Niniane was still asleep. She was lying on her back this morning, one arm flung above her head with the abandon of a sleeping child. The inside of her elbow was delicately veined and fragile. Her lashes lay quietly against the pale honey of her tanned cheeks. She did not look old enough to be having a baby.

He felt again the surge of triumph he had known last night. He had fathered a child! His wife was going to have a baby!

Ceawlin had never confided this to a living soul, not even to Sigurd, but for years now he had gone in terror that he would never father a child. True, he was only eighteen, but none of the women he had lain with had ever conceived. And his beard had yet to grow. In vain had his mother assured him that fair-haired men grew their beards late. "Your father was late in growing his," she had said, striking fear even deeper into his heart. All of Winchester knew that Cynric was a poor breeder.

And now Niniane was with child. His child. She was no Guthfrid, his Niniane. Of that he was sure. He looked down at his wife's sleeping face.

She was so sweet, so yielding, she gave herself to him with such heart-searing trust. It was that quality in her that moved him most, that trust. For some reason, when he was with her the carnal flame of passion was always tempered by a tenderness he had never felt for any other woman. It was because she had been a virgin, he supposed, and had known nothing of love until he had taught her.

He had never given her a morgengabe. He frowned as this thought struck him, and it was his frowning face that Niniane saw when her eyes first opened. She blinked, then blinked again. "But what is wrong?" she asked, her voice husky with sleep.

"I was just thinking that I have never given you a morgengabe."

She rubbed her eyes and yawned. He laughed at her efforts to wake up. "What is a morgengabe?" she asked.

"The gift a husband gives to his wife the morning after their wedding. It is to signify that she was a virgin, that her blood is pure."

"Oh."

He was very grave. "I will give you a morgengabe one day, Niniane. I promise you that. One day, when I am king."

She smiled sleepily and yawned again. "That will be nice."

"Go back to sleep," he said. "You're tired."

"Not at all. I'm fine," she said. He got out of bed and began to dress. When he turned around to the bed once again, she was asleep.

Niniane waited until the thanes had been at Bryn Atha for a week before she approached Ceawlin with a subject she knew was going to be unwelcome to him. "The hay is ready to be cut," she said.

"So?" He cocked his eyebrows. "Then get it cut."

She had ridden out to their hayfields that morning to inspect them and had sought him out as soon as she returned to Bryn Atha. She took him into the kitchen so they could be alone. "I cannot cut it myself," she returned.

"Of course you cannot cut it yourself. No one is suggesting such a thing. Get Naille to send some men over."

"Ceawlin, you don't understand. Every man within miles is cutting his own hay. There *is* no one to cut ours."

"They can come here after they finish their own."

"The hay will not last that long. It must be cut now, while the weather is fine. One rain and we will have lost it."

His eyes were beginning to deepen in color. "What are you suggesting, Niniane? That I cut it?"

She raised her small round chin. It was going to have to be said sooner or later. "Yes. You and the thanes are going to have to cut it."

"No."

"Then your horses will have no hay. The cattle will have no hay."

"I told you I will buy what we need." The scar at the corner of his eye was becoming whiter, the way it always did when he was angry.

"No one will sell you hay, Ceawlin. They need it for their own beasts."

"We were always able to buy hay for Winchester."

"You had your own farms for Winchester, worked by ceorls who owed tribute to Winchester. There are no ceorls among the Atrebates. No one owes us tribute. What we eat, what we feed our animals, we must grow ourselves."

There was an ominous silence. The smell of her stew filled the kitchen. Niniane had known this was going to be his reaction. The Saxon thanes considered themselves a warrior elite; the very idea of farming would revolt them. It clearly revolted Ceawlin.

"Are you suggesting that I ask my thanes to work in the fields like common ceorls?" His voice was dangerously quiet.

"If you don't, then you will starve," she answered.

"I told you months ago. I will buy what food we need in the market."

"You cannot. Oh, there is food available right now, I grant you. But let the winter come, Ceawlin, and it will be a different tale. Then there are no more vegetables, and the hunting grows sparse. If we do not have grain and corn stored up, and fodder for the animals, we will all starve. Do not expect Naille to feed your war band for you. He will not."

"I can buy from the Saxon vils."

"And when Fara's jewelry is gone? What do you expect to use to equip your war band? To reward your war band? When your money is all spent for food."

"How can I send my men out to plow the fields?" His nostrils flared. He was becoming really angry. "They are Saxon warriors. Not farmers."

Niniane did not back down. "Tell them that if they don't farm, they don't eat."

"I am their lord. I am responsible for seeing to it that they eat!"

Niniane stared up into his blazing eyes. He knew she was right, of course. That was why he was so furious. "Well, you may be a Saxon and a prince, my lord, but if you want to live to be a king, you will learn to farm."

"Don't talk to me as if I were a child."

"Then stop acting like a child."

He clenched his fists and took a step toward her. She did not move. "That's right. Hit me. That will solve everything."

He turned on his heel and left the room.

That night he told his men they were going to have to harvest the hay.

Chapter 15

"**I** don't care what may happen in Winchester! I want him dead, do you hear? Dead! Dead! Dead!"

"Guthfrid, try to calm yourself." Edric cast a harassed glance at the door of the sleeping room.

"No, I will not try to calm myself! I will never be calm again until that bastard murderer is lying under the earth like my Edwin." The queen's brown eyes were glittering as if with a fever, and there were hectic spots of color in her cheeks. She had been hounding Edric on this subject ever since their marriage, but never before had she been so close to hysteria.

"I have told you," he said with controlled patience. "Once I am secure here in Winchester, I will raise a war band and go after him."

"I know what you have told me. And he has been gone for five months now, and you have done nothing!"

"What can I do? If I turn my back on Winchester, the eorls are likely to seize control of Edgar."

"And do you think to keep Edgar safe by allowing his brother's murderer to go free? Who knows what spies Ceawlin has inside Winchester? Fifteen of your thanes deserted to him. Who is to say what followers he has left within our gates? What dagger may be poised even now at Edgar's heart?"

Edric looked at his wife. Since their marriage he had been openly sharing the queen's hall and the queen's sleeping room, and he had been hoping for a very different greeting when he came in this night after having dinner with Cutha. Guthfrid's golden hair was loose for the night and she wore only a thin robe over her nakedness. She was very beautiful. He desired her as much as he ever had. But she was becoming obsessed with this need for revenge against Ceawlin. It was not getting better with time. It was getting worse. Nor was she wholly in the wrong, he thought. The desertion of the thanes had been a nasty shock.

"Guthfrid." His voice was sober now, almost grim. "I cannot turn my back on Cutha. You know that. No matter what he may say to my face, he is Ceawlin's supporter. He voted for him in the Witan over Edgar.

139

His son is one of the thanes who deserted to the bastard. I cannot leave Cutha in Winchester while I am gone."

"Then get rid of him."

"How?" He put his hands on her shoulders and moved his thumbs to caress the silky skin beneath the robe.

She tipped her head back to look up at him. "Send him to East Anglia." The heaviness of her eyelids gave her a sultry look at all times, but when she half-lowered them as she was doing now, she was enough to ignite a fire in any man's blood. His fingers dug into her shoulders. "We will send him on a mission to my father, Redwold. That will get him out of the way."

"What kind of a mission?" His eyes were on her mouth.

She shrugged. "I will think of something." Her eyes were so dark they were almost black. "Once Cutha is gone, you can take a war band and go after Ceawlin."

"I suppose I could do that."

The tense, strung-up look relaxed and she slid her arms around his thick neck. "You *will* do it. For me, Edric." She leaned her body against his.

"Yes," he answered. She was rubbing against him now and he groaned. "Yes, Guthfrid. I will do it." And he tore the robe from her body and pushed her down on the bed.

The priest arrived in Atrebates country in August and, after a discussion with Naille, agreed to marry Niniane and Ceawlin. As Naille pointed out when the priest had first demurred, the Franks had been converted when their king married a Christian princess. Father Mal, a Welshman who had trained at Glastonbury, had seen the truth of this and so it was with visions of glorious conversions for Christ running through his mind that he went with Naille to meet the Saxon prince.

Bryn Atha was bustling with activity when Naille arrived with the Welsh priest early on the afternoon of August 14. Ceawlin had set up training grounds for his thanes all over the villa: wrestling area, javelin-throwing area, area for sword practice, for large spear practice and, for stamina, a running path that encompassed the perimeter of the villa walls. As Naille rode in through the gates, the priest by his side, the first thing he saw was his son and several other British boys throwing javelins at a target. He checked his horse.

Gereint was doing very well, he was pleased to see. But he had not realized how many Atrebates boys were coming here.

"All of these men are Saxons?" Father Mal inquired in shocked surprise. "I had not thought there were so many."

"Not all are Saxons," Naille replied a little grimly. "About half are Britons."

"Britons are joining with Saxons in fighting?"

"In training to fight," Naille corrected. "The boys can use some training. I saw that well enough at Beranbyrg. We outnumbered them, and they beat us into the ground. We have never learned the skills of battle. It will be well if the young ones do."

The priest turned to him in incredulity. "And this Saxon prince . . . this Ceawlin . . . is training the boys who will fight against him?"

Naille slanted the priest a return look. "He does not think we will take up arms against him again. Coinmail swore he would not when Ceawlin gave him his life at Beranbyrg."

"Did Coinmail swear for all the Atrebates?"

"No."

"Ah," said the priest. "But this Ceawlin does not realize that?"

"I do not know what Ceawlin realizes. All I do know is that Gereint wanted to train with the Saxons and I said he could. Ceawlin and I have not discussed the subject further."

"He is very young, this prince," Father Mal said as they progressed across the yard. "And naive."

"Young he may be," Naille returned, and now the grimness was more pronounced, "but I do not think Ceawlin is ever naive. Ah," and he raised a hand as the door of the villa opened and a girl came out. "There is Niniane."

Father Mal was favorably impressed with the Princess Niniane, who was young and lovely and gentle of manner. Such a wife, he felt, would make an excellent missionary for Christ. "I will send for Ceawlin," she said to Naille after she had greeted the priest. She turned to call something in Saxon to one of the thanes within earshot. The young man looked up, grinned at her and went off.

"Where is Ceawlin?" Naille asked.

"He could be anywhere. He says it keeps the men alert and doing their best if they are not sure when he will suddenly appear to watch them." She gave Father Mal a pretty smile. "I am so happy you have come, Father. It means so much to me, that I am to be married in my Christian faith."

"I am happy also, my lady." He looked fleetingly at her figure. Naille had said she was to have a child, but there were no visible signs as yet.

Niniane said, "Let us go insi . . . Oh, good, here comes Ceawlin now."

Father Mal looked in the direction she was looking and his eyes widened with surprise as they alighted on the young man who was coming across the courtyard. Ceawlin had evidently been with the wrestlers, for he was still stripped to the waist, and as he came up to them he said to his wife, "Sorry. My shirt and tunic got lost somewhere." Then he looked at Naille.

"Prince," Naille said instantly, "may I introduce Father Mal. He has said he will be happy to marry you in the Christian faith."

Ceawlin smiled at the priest. "I am pleased to meet you, Father." His look and his voice were perfectly gracious, his British flawless. "Such a marriage means a great deal to my wife."

Father Mal looked with stunned surprise at the half-naked young man before him. Naille had deferred to him unhesitatingly, had presented the priest as if they were in the great hall of Camelot and Ceawlin were the high king. The prince's teeth were very white in his tanned face, his eyes an extraordinary shade of blue. Father Mal found himself smiling back. He was a tall man himself, but he had to look up to meet the Saxon's eyes. He realized he was staring and searched his brain for a reply to the prince's pleasantry. Then behind him he heard Niniane say, "I'll get you another shirt, Ceawlin. Come in, please, Father, and let me offer you something to eat."

The Saxon prince held the door for the priest and they went in out of the sun. Niniane led the way to a room that was comfortably furnished with well-worn wicker furniture and then disappeared to get a shirt for her husband. Ceawlin sat down, not at all embarrassed by his lean brown shirtless torso. He smiled engagingly at Naille and said, "Gereint is doing very well."

"I saw him as I came in," Naille answered. "But I admit I was surprised to see Ferris and Owain and Druce as well."

Ceawlin shrugged his shoulders and the motion set off a ripple of muscles in his upper arms. "You know boys. Once they find out there is weapon training going on, nothing can keep them away."

"How old are you, Prince?" Father Mal asked.

"Eighteen," said Ceawlin.

Father Mal looked at Naille but the Briton did not appear to share his amusement that this eighteen-year-old should be speaking so easily of "boys." Niniane came in with a shirt for her husband and he put it on. Then she sat on the stool that was next to Ceawlin's knees and looked expectantly at the priest.

"When will it be convenient for you to marry us, Father?" she asked.

"I shall be here for at least two weeks," the priest replied. "Whenever you like within that period."

A girl came in the door of the room carrying a tray. She put it down on a table and Niniane smiled and said, "Thank you, Meghan."

"Meghan is happy here, I understand," Naille remarked as the girl left the room. "I was speaking to her uncle at the market last week."

"I am glad to hear that." Niniane handed cups of beer to the men. "She is a very good worker. And it is nice for me to have a few women around. All these men!"

"Niniane likes to put people to work," said Ceawlin. There was an undertone in his voice that the priest did not quite understand.

His wife came back to her stool and sat down again. "Ceawlin and I think it would be nice to have a wedding feast," she said, ignoring her husband's comment. "We would like to invite all the families who have been so good to us these last months. What do you think, Naille?"

Naille stared at her small, innocent face. He was not sure he liked the idea at all. Lately he had been wondering if perhaps he had allowed Ceawlin to insinuate himself into the Atrebates tribe a little too easily. He had never intended the prince to become so integral a part of local life when he had agreed to allow him to stay at Bryn Atha. He had envisioned Bryn Atha as an isolated island of Saxons, safely under his eye. It was not working out as he had expected. Even this business of Gereint . . . It had seemed such a good idea at the time, to get the Saxon to train his own enemies. But . . .

"I know so little of Christians," Ceawlin was saying to the priest with his most charming little-boy look. "My thanes would find it of great interest, to see a real Christian wedding."

"A wonderful idea!" the priest said heartily. "We shall invite all the faithful who can come."

As Naille met Ceawlin's celestial sea-blue eyes, he had the distinct feeling that he had been outmaneuvered.

They were married a week later, on a day of cloudless blue sky and brilliant sun. Ceawlin and his men had hunted all week, bringing in a wide variety of game which Niniane and the three girls who were now living at Bryn Atha cooked for the company along with vegetables from the villa garden and loaves of white bread baked from wheat. Tables had been set up all over the large reception room, and the food was put on big wooden platters so the guests could serve themselves. Ceawlin had made sure there was a quantity of beer.

Naille found himself seated next to Sigurd at the main table, with Alanna and their older children on his other side. Naille thought the Saxon seemed a little subdued today and said, with seeming casualness, "You do not mind that your prince weds in a Christian ceremony?"

"Of course not." Sigurd was clearly surprised by the question. That was not it, then, Naille thought. "It was very nice," the Saxon added courteously. They were all courteous, these Saxons. It was a constant surprise to Naille, who had always had very different visions of the ancient enemy.

What would Coinmail think, Naille wondered, to see his people supping cheek by jowl with Saxon warriors? Of course, Coinmail had given Niniane to them. Naille had been present when Cynric had asked for her for his son. He could not complain, then, about this wedding.

And what Naille had said to the priest might, after all, prove true. Niniane might convert Ceawlin. He knew Alanna thought she would. Why, then, did Naille himself find the thought so unlikely?

The noise in the room was growing louder and louder. Naille leaned a little forward so he could see Ceawlin, who was on the other side of Sigurd. Niniane was speaking to the priest, who was seated to her right, and Ceawlin was staring at the door, an alert look to the tilt of his head. Naille had a clear view of his profile: the faint hollow under the hard cheekbone, the straight nose, the long, firm mouth. He looked very sober, not at all like a bridegroom. Then someone was running into the room, pushing his way through the tables, heading for Ceawlin. Naille realized with a little ripple of surprise that Ceawlin had heard him coming over all the noise.

"My lord! My lord!" It was one of Ceawlin's thanes, Naille saw. He thought it was the one they called Bertred. He was very young. "They are coming, my lord!" he gasped out. "I saw them. Edric and a war band. They are coming!"

"You were watching the road to Corinium?" Ceawlin sounded perfectly calm. The voices were dying away now as everyone realized what was happening.

"Yes, my lord. I saw them from the sentry point, my lord. They are seven miles away. Less now. I had to get back here."

Ceawlin said something in Saxon. Then, "How many?"

"I counted forty, my lord."

"All right." Ceawlin stood up. "We will stop them at the ford, the way we planned it." To Bertred, "They are on foot?"

"Yes."

"Good. We have time, then." He looked around the room and said, "I am sorry, my friends, to have to leave so precipitately, but it seems we have business elsewhere. The queen has sent a war band for me and I do not want to disappoint it." His eyes were a blaze of color in his tanned face. "Stay and enjoy your food. I will be back later."

"There are forty of them, Prince!" It was the voice of the priest. Naille looked his way and saw Ninane's white, stricken face.

The Saxon thanes were all heading for the door. "Well, there are seventeen of us." Ceawlin gave the priest a cocky grin. "The odds are about right."

"Eighteen, my lord!" It was a young British voice and it was a stunned moment before Naille realized it was his son who was on his feet and heading after the thanes.

"Nineteen!" said Ferris from a table in the middle of the room, and he was standing too.

"Twenty!" said another voice.

Then, "Twenty-one!"

Naille stared in numbed horror as the boys of his tribe all began to pour after the Saxons. Then he got his voice. *"Gereint!"*

His son was already in the doorway, but he turned. "This is not your fight," Naille said over the heads of the diners. All activity in the room had stopped, as if frozen in time.

"Yes, Father, it is." The boy's voice was respectful but firm. "If the Saxon eorls ever get a grip on Atrebates land, they will push us out. That is what Ceawlin says, and I believe him. If he wins, he will be our good lord and take care of us. I believe that too. So it is our fight, you see."

Naille's head whipped around to where the Saxon prince was standing. Ceawlin's face was very grave. "You have done this," Naille said to him.

"I have said nothing to Gereint that I did not say to you," the prince replied. His voice was very quiet, very calm. "But I will say this to you now, Naille. You are the leader of your people. If you do not want these boys to follow me, then I will not take them."

"No!"

"Quiet, Gereint." Ceawlin spoke very softly but Gereint fell silent. Naille looked at his son. It did not seem as if anyone in the room was even breathing.

"All right," the Briton heard himself saying. His voice sounded oddly far away. "They may go."

Gereint's face lit like a candle. "Thank you, Father!" and he turned and ran out of the room. Sigurd had already left the table, and when Naille sat back down, it was just himself, Alanna, their two daughters, and the priest. Niniane was following the men out the door.

"Are you mad, Naille?" Alanna cried at him. Her face was ashen. "They will still be outnumbered!"

"He will be safe, Alanna."

"How can you say that?"

"I saw Ceawlin fight at Beranbyrg. He is worth ten men by himself alone. And the boy is right. Our best interest lies with Ceawlin."

"How did this happen?" Alanna wailed. "I don't understand. No one expected such a thing. No one!"

"Ceawlin did," Naille replied tiredly. "Else why did he keep a guard posted on the road?"

There was a long silence. Then, "He never said anything to us."

"I always thought he was a very clever young man," said Naille. "But I realize now that I have underestimated him. Gereint is right. He is not a man to make an enemy of." He looked around the room, now in a state of upheaval. "Well, I suppose I had better go and find a weapon as well."

"You are not going!"

He stood and looked down into his wife's appalled eyes. He gave her a crooked smile. "You know, Alanna, it will be nice to be on the winning side for a change." And he followed his son out the door.

"And to think I almost didn't post the sentries on the two roads today," Ceawlin said to Sigurd as they saddled their horses in the stableyard. "I almost didn't, you know. It seemed a shame to have two of the thanes miss the banquet. There is little enough fun around Bryn Atha these days, with everyone sweating in the fields every time Niniane says something is ready to be harvested."

"Niniane is only being careful for our future. It's well we have someone who knows about growing food."

"I know, I know. Niniane is always right." But Ceawlin did not look at all irritated. His eyes were blazing. "Gods!" he said. "What luck! Edric *did* come after all."

"I don't know that I would call it luck," Sigurd replied a little dryly. "He is obviously hoping to surprise us. He took the longer Corinium road." Sigurd raised his eyebrows and for a moment looked very like his father. "You were right to post guards on both roads, Ceawlin. But I cannot understand why my father did not warn us."

"Edric got Cutha out of the way somehow." All around them men were saddling up, Saxons and Atrebates together. "I want everyone in the courtyard in two minutes!" Ceawlin called. Then, to Sigurd, "Bring Bayvard for me, Sigurd. I must see Niniane before I leave." Sigurd was busy tightening his girth and merely nodded in reply. Ceawlin tied his reins to the fence and left the stableyard.

She was with Alanna and the rest of the women in the courtyard in front of the main door of the villa. They all turned together to watch Ceawlin come, long legs covering the ground with his characteristic swift grace. When he had almost reached them, Niniane moved forward to meet him. They stood together some ten feet from the huddled group of women and he looked down into her eyes. They were more gray than blue, a sign that she was not happy.

"You never told me you were keeping a lookout for a war band," she said.

"There was no point in worrying you," he replied. "It was only a precaution."

"You said Edric would never dare leave Winchester."

He shrugged. "Well, he has."

"And you're pleased." She sounded bitter. "Your eyes are bright as stars. You are absolutely delighted."

"I'm a warrior, Niniane. Of course I'm delighted. It would be strange if I were not."

"But, Ceawlin," and despite herself her voice trembled, "suppose you are killed?"

"Death must come to us all, Nan." His voice was perfectly matter-of-fact. "There are worse ways to go than with glory in battle." He put his hands on her shoulders. "But I do not think it is my time yet. This is a good thing, Nan. I feel it. And your people are joining with me. It is the start. I know it. The start of the road back to Winchester."

She stared up at him. He was so confident, so unafraid for himself. It was unfair of her to burden him with her own fears. She forced herself to smile. "I will pray for your victory, Ceawlin. And for your safety. God go with you."

"There speaks a good wife." He bent his head and she held up her face for his kiss. "I'll be back in time to celebrate our marriage properly, I promise you that," he murmured in her ear. Then Sigurd was bringing Bayvard into the courtyard and he turned away. Five minutes later, the courtyard was empty of horses and men, and the women trailed disconsolately back into the house.

Niniane had spent some fear-filled hours in her young life, but she did not think anything had ever been as bad as the waiting she was enduring now. What would she do if anything should happen to him? How should she live? She had been his but five short months, yet she felt she had belonged to him forever. It was for him, for him and for his child that she carried, that she had been striving and working ever since they came to Bryn Atha. It was for him that she had endangered her immortal soul, ignoring all the strictures of her own faith about the sinfulness of physical passion. She had lived with him in sin, gladly, joyously, intensely, holding nothing back even though she knew their union was unblessed by the church.

And God had not punished her. God had softened Ceawlin's heart so that he had agreed to a Christian marriage. God had given her a child. Out of her sin had come all her happiness.

If he should be killed now . . . Surely God would not be so cruel? Not on her wedding day.

Ceawlin. . . . my love. . . .

"Niniane."

She opened her eyes and turned to look blankly at Alanna. "If we are all to wait here for the men to return," Naille's wife said practically, "we might as well be busy. I'm sure you have work we can help you with."

"Oh. Yes, Alanna. Of course. Thank you." Niniane focused her brain with difficulty. "The animals have to be fed, and the men are not here . . ."

"Just tell me what must be done."

Niniane smiled. "You are very good. Well, then, the chickens . . ."

They fed the animals and then ate themselves and then gathered once again in the large reception room, a party of women and the priest. It was growing late and the sky was beginning to darken. The sixteen women left behind in Bryn Atha all had husbands or sons or brothers with Ceawlin, and the apprehension in the room thickened with the dusk. Finally Niniane fetched her harp. She was singing one of Alric's songs about a storm at sea, singing in Saxon and translating for the benefit of her British audience, when one of the women leapt to her feet. "I hear the horses!" she cried.

The harp stilled. The shutters and windows were open, and now they all could clearly hear the noise of hoofbeats. Then came the rumble of male voices, then laughter. Niniane sat perfectly still as the rest of the women ran to the door. Over all the noise of men and horses a clear young voice floated, full of pride. "We won, Mother!" It was Gereint. "We killed half of them and chased the other half back to Winchester!" Niniane's fingers relaxed their deathlike pressure on the wood of the harp and she went to join the rest of the women in the courtyard.

They had indeed won, surprising Edric at Cob Ford. The ground on the Bryn Atha side of the ford was high, and Ceawlin's men had come out of cover, pouring down on the men still wading through the water. The attack had been completely unexpected, and their charge, with the impetus given them by the hill, had been ferocious. The men in the water had struggled to raise their weapons, but their shields had been slung across their backs. The men in the front line perished before they could even begin to defend themselves.

"The Saxons went first," Naille told Alanna as they lay down to sleep later. There were people sleeping all over the floors of Bryn Atha this night, but Naille and Alanna had been given the bed in Coinmail's room. "Ceawlin was scrupulous about keeping our men safely to the rear. We just followed the Saxon line. It was surprisingly easy."

"But weren't you outnumbered?"

"Not by much. And it didn't matter. The charge was too strong. They could not stand against it. The river was running red with blood by the time we were finished. And we have only a few flesh wounds!"

"You sound as if you enjoyed yourself," Alanna accused him.

"I rather think I did." Naille was surprised at himself.

"What I want to know is what Coinmail is going to do when he hears all this." Alanna raised herself on her elbow to look down into her husband's face. "You know his plans. He would never have agreed to fight alongside Ceawlin. To Coinmail, Saxons are the enemy."

"He may change his mind. When he meets Ceawlin—"

"Coinmail never changes his mind. The world could fall down around him, but he would never change his mind. You have known him since he was a child. You know that."

"He gave his word not to take up arms against the West Saxons again."

"He never had any intention of keeping his word."

"I know. And I am not sure that he is right. If a people cannot trust in their prince's word . . ."

"He did not give his word to his people; he gave it to a pagan."

"I know. And that pagan has implicit trust in it. Because to Ceawlin, his word is sacred."

Alanna sighed and lay back down again. "Perhaps he will become a Christian. Then even Coinmail could not object to him."

Naille yawned. "God in heaven, woman, but I'm tired. Let me go to sleep."

"It is all very well for you, Naille . . ." Alanna was beginning, but her only answer was a very gentle snore.

Ceawlin was one of the few other men in Bryn Atha to share the privacy of a bedroom with his wife that night. But, unlike Naille, he did not waste his time talking. Nor did he get much sleep. But he woke the following morning, ablaze with energy, and immediately put the women to work cooking a victory banquet for his men.

Niniane did not have the heart to tell him that the corn crops of wheat, barley, and rye were due to be harvested.

Chapter 16

*T*HE harvest was a good one and the storehouses and barns and bins at Bryn Atha were consequently well-stocked for the winter. Ceawlin celebrated the Saxon Autumn Festival with a great banquet. There was, of course, no Saxon temple at the villa and he decided against creating one. To do so would clash with his policy of placating British sensibilities. So they had the banquet in the villa dining room, with prayers to Woden and Thor and Tiwaz in lieu of a formal sacrifice.

November went out in a downpour of cold, heavy rain and the sullen gray skies of December set in. Ceawlin worked hard at keeping his men busy. No snow had fallen as yet, so he had them out practicing on the iron-hard ground and riding madly through the woods in crazy competitive games. The thanes were joined as often as not by the British boys who had fought with them at Cob Ford. The cold and the grayness were no rival for the youthful high spirits that reigned at Bryn Atha.

Niniane was heavy with child and found the dreariness far more stressful than did the men. As her time drew nearer she began to have fearful dreams and fantasies. Would the babe be healthy? She had seen children before who had been born without limbs, with horribly deformed mouths. Surely, surely, such a thing could not happen to her child. Surely God would not punish a little innocent child for the sins of its mother?

Ceawlin wanted to celebrate the feast of Yule and she worried about that. She had been too lax in permitting all these pagan practices. Surely she should be striving to convert him, to convert all these poor souls to Christ.

The thanes decorated the reception room and the dining room with evergreens they had picked in the wood. At Winchester it had been the women's work to prepare for Yule, but the only women at Bryn Atha were Christian and so the thanes did it themselves. Niniane and the three British girls stayed in the kitchen and listened to the laughter of the men as they hung the pine and the holly. Ceawlin's voice was clearest of all.

"They sound as if they're having fun," said Meghan a little wistfully.

"Filthy, pagan doings," replied Amena. She was the oldest of the girls, and the homeliest.

"They're not doing anything so terrible," Wynne said. She was a pretty girl with red-gold hair and green eyes. Ceawlin had said to get rid of her, that she was too pretty to be let loose around a pack of hungry-eyed thanes, but Niniane needed her help and there had been no one else willing to come to Bryn Atha. So Wynne had stayed. "It's nice," Wynne added now, "decorating the house with greens. It's cheerful."

Amena snorted.

"I think it *is* nice," Niniane said firmly. "And I don't see any reason why we cannot celebrate Christmas at the same time the thanes are celebrating Yule. The feasts fall on almost the same day."

"Celebrate the birth of Christ with a bunch of filthy pagan rites?" Amena was horrified. "Never!"

"You know what Father Mal said when he was here in August, Amena." Niniane turned from the bread she was kneading to give the girl a stern look. "He said we were all missionaries for Christ. That it was our duty to do our best to bring the word of Christ to the Saxons. And Yule does not have any 'filthy pagan rites.' It is merely a happy feast. We have a special banquet for Christmas too. There can be no harm in combining the two. It will be a way to tell the Saxons the story of Christ's birth."

"I think that is a splendid idea!" said Wynne.

"Yes." Meghan smiled shyly. Then, to Amena in her gentle voice, "Niniane is right, Amena. It is our duty to be missionaries for Christ."

"I don't agree," said Amena.

"Then you do not have to come to the banquet," Niniane said with perfect pleasantness. "Perhaps you would prefer to go home to your family."

Amena glared but did not answer. After a minute Niniane went back to kneading her bread.

The sky was full of snow the morning of Christmas-Yule. Niniane went out into the backyard for a few moments to get away from the smells in the kitchen, and saw that the sky was growing darker. The clouds had taken on an ominous yellowish tinge and the wind was strong enough to blow her hair and whip her skirt around her knees. It looked as if a storm was coming.

The baby kicked and she put her hand on the rounded mound of her stomach. Her back ached. Just a few more weeks, she thought. Surely it could not be any longer than that. She was so weary of always being weary. So weary of the clumsiness, the burden of weight she must carry wherever she went. Would she never be slim and vigorous again?

She looked once more at the sky, sighed, and went back to the kitchen.

The combined feast was a great success. The men had roasted a boar for the traditional Yule meal in honor of Frey, and the women had baked for days in order to load the table with special delicacies. There was plenty of mead to go around. The dining room was bright with candles and evergreens and the sound and the laughter of young voices.

When the food had been finished, someone called upon Bertred to play the harp. Niniane had not been able to hold the harp for some time, having lost her lap, and so Bertred, the youngest of the thanes, had been pressed into service as a substitute.

Niniane sat at the big table, with Ceawlin on one side of her and Sigurd on the other, and listened to the sound of Bertred's pleasant voice. There was a fire going at the stoke hole of the hypocaust, and no one else seemed to feel at all chilled, but Niniane's hands and feet were freezing. Her hands and feet seemed always to be cold these days. It was as if the babe were drawing all the blood from her, she thought as she pulled her cloak more closely around her shoulders.

"Are you cold?" It was Sigurd, concern in his kind gray eyes.

"I'm always cold now," she answered, and gave him a rueful smile. "Feel my hand."

She extended her fingers and for a moment his hand, large and callused and wonderfully warm, closed around hers and engulfed it.

"You're freezing!"

"What is it?" Their soft voices had caught Ceawlin's attention.

"Niniane is freezing," Sigurd said. He sounded almost angry.

"Are you?" Ceawlin unpinned the brooch that was holding his own cloak and settled it around his wife's shoulders. It was warm from his body and she huddled into it gratefully. Ceawlin turned back to the music.

"Shall I get you a rug to wrap up in?" Sigurd asked her.

"No. No, thank you, Sigurd. I shall be all right."

"The tip of your nose is red."

Ceawlin looked at them again, a slight frown between his brows. "You are distracting from the music."

"Sorry," said Niniane, and looked dutifully to Bertred. Sigurd's mouth tightened but he did not reply.

Bertred was giving them a familiar Saxon lament for lost youth. It was the sort of song only the young could enjoy, Niniane thought as she listened to the chanted words:

> and he dreams of the hall-thanes
> The giving of treasure,   the years of his youth,
> When his lord bade welcome   to wassail and feasting . . .

The thanes were all lounging in comfort around the tables, listening cheerfully. The candlelight flickered on blond and brown heads. Not a gray hair in the room, Niniane thought. Nor was Ceawlin the only one still without a beard. Her eyes halted at the table where Penda sat. He was looking at Wynne. As Niniane watched, the girl's eyes turned toward him. The Saxon raised his mead cup slightly and smiled. Niniane was just in time to catch a returning smile on Wynne's full mouth. Then the girl saw she was being watched and gave Niniane a wide-eyed innocent look before turning back to the harper.

Niniane frowned. This could be trouble, she thought. If Wynne should ever . . . Perhaps she ought to tell Ceawlin. But he would make her send Wynne away, and she could not do without that extra pair of hands. Not now, not when she was feeling so wretched.

She would keep an eye on the girl herself. Penda was not one of the young thanes from the princes' hall. He was older, a man, not a boy. And the Winchester thanes were not accustomed to celibacy. Perhaps she ought to tell Ceawlin.

"And now, my lady . . ." It was Bertred, finishing his song and turning to her. "I believe you have a story you wish to tell to us."

All eyes in the room were turning her way. Niniane put Wynne firmly from her mind and concentrated on the words she had prepared to say. "Yes. This day of Yule is also the feast day of our God, the Christ. I would like to tell you the story of his birth. I hope you do not mind."

A murmur of courteous encouragement ran around the dining room. "Well, then," Niniane began. "Once there was a woman named Mary . . ."

The thanes listened in attentive silence. Outside, the wind was picking up; Niniane could hear it rattling the shutters they had closed against the cold. "And the shepherds from the fields saw the star as well," she said. Next to her she saw Ceawlin's fingers moving restlessly up and down the curve of his mead cup. Meghan's brown eyes were huge as she listened with breathless attention to Niniane's words. Bertred was looking at Meghan, not at Niniane.

"And that is how the Christ was born," Niniane finished. She did not want to talk too long. "We believe he came to save the world from sin and death, and that is why we worship him."

"Save the world from death, my lady?" It was Wuffa speaking. "How is that? People still die."

"They die, yes, but not forever. After death we believe we go to live with Christ in a land called heaven."

"It is not where we go when we die that concerns me, but how we live." Ceawlin's voice sounded perfectly pleasant but Niniane could hear the undertone of irritation. He suspected what she was about and he did not like it. "And I rather think we are getting our first winter storm. We had better see to the animals now, before the snow comes too heavy."

There were groans and complaints from the comfortable thanes, but everyone rose to his feet. Outside, it had already begun to snow. The thanes fought their way through the snow and the wind down to the barns. By the time they returned to the house, the gray day had slipped into the dark.

The Yule feast in Winchester was more lavish than the one held at Bryn Atha, but not nearly as joyous. The defeat of the war band by Ceawlin still rankled. But it was more than pride that had gone down with Edric's men at Cob Ford. Two of the eorls had lost sons in that skirmish, and they had sworn vengeance against the man who had shed the blood of their kin. Come the spring, that debt would be paid.

There were others in Winchester who were waiting for the spring also, waiting to see how Ceawlin and his thanes got through the winter. If the prince proved he could keep a war band, there were those who preferred Cynric's son, a Woden-born prince of his line, to the usurper they were faced with in Winchester these days.

Cutha left the Yule feast early to return to his own hall. He had been furious when he returned from East Anglia to find that Edric had outwitted him. Of course, it could have been worse. The boy had beaten the attackers, turning their own surprise back on them. But still Cutha had not been happy.

He sat now before his own hearth, with his elder son beside him, and brooded. The temper in Winchester was just what he had hoped it would be. He knew that come the spring there would be a goodly number of thanes ready to throw in their lot with Ceawlin. The lines were beginning to be drawn. Why, then, was he so discontent?

"What a gloomy feast!" Cuthwulf stretched his legs to the fire. "It is enough to put any man off his food, the sight of that lowborn thief sitting in Cynric's place."

Cutha watched the figure of his wife moving back and forth on the far side of the hall. Coenburg had not been feeling well these last few days and her mother was nursing her. "Yes," he said after a minute, in response to Cuthwulf's comment. "The hall seemed quite empty, I thought."

"No Ceawlin, no Sigurd, no Penda. Fara is gone." Cuthwulf drained his cup of beer. "Just a bunch of old graybeards left around Winchester these days."

"That is not true." Cutha was distinctly annoyed.

"Well, the best of the young ones are with Ceawlin. You can't deny that." Cuthwulf grinned. "Myself excluded, of course. And, come the spring . . ."

"You are not planning to join with him?"

Cuthwulf's prominent blue eyes stared. "What is the matter, Father? I thought you were supporting Ceawlin."

He was, of course. The problem was, Cutha had intended to win the kingship for Ceawlin himself. He had not counted on the young prince taking such an aggressive role in his own destiny. It discomposed him. Cutha's aim was to put the new king heavily into his debt. The eorl fully intended to be as important a figure in the reign of Ceawlin as ever he had been in the reign of Cynric.

Things were not going as he had planned.

"We will see how he gets through the winter," Cutha said now to his elder son. "Ceawlin is a great fighter. We all know that. But he has no experience at keeping men. In Winchester it is easy. The food is readily available. It will not be that way at Bryn Atha. And these Britons who fought with him will need their own food to feed their own people. We shall see."

"My lord?" It was his wife's soft voice. She was his second wife, and much younger than he, the mother of Coenburg but not of Sigurd or Cuthwulf. "May I fetch you some more mead?"

"Yes." He watched her figure as she went to fill his cup. Normally Cutha was a frugal drinker, unlike most of the Saxon thanes and eorls. But tonight he was feeling gloomy. It was blowing hard outside and the snow was coming heavily.

"Gods," said Cuthwulf at his side. "This is going to be a long winter."

The January world was white with snow. There had not been so much snow in ten years, so Naille told Ceawlin when the prince rode home with Gereint one day to share a meal at the farm. Ceawlin had come mainly to see Alanna. He wanted to make sure Naille's wife was ready to come to Bryn Atha to help Niniane during childbirth.

"Of course I will come," Alanna assured him. "I promised Niniane long ago that I would."

"Why not come back with me now?" Ceawlin asked. "That way you will be sure to be there. Suppose we should get another storm and you cannot get through?"

Alanna restrained herself from patting his hand. "I will get through. It may be another week yet, Prince, and I cannot leave my own family for so long a time just to sit around Bryn Atha waiting. First babies are often late. Do not worry so. I will be there."

She stood at the door of the farmhouse and watched Ceawlin ride away. Then she turned to her husband, her face wearing the bemused smile it always wore for Ceawlin. "Such a sweet boy," she said. "He is worried about her."

Naille grunted but said nothing.

It was snowing the following morning, and in the afternoon Niniane's pains began. Ceawlin saddled Bayvard and rode out into the blinding whiteness to fetch Alanna.

He had been afraid of this, he thought grimly as he pushed on through the snow-heavy woods. Why wouldn't the stupid woman come with him yesterday? Now he had to get her back through a snowstorm. And it would be dark too. She would probably not want to come, would probably say it was too dangerous.

She would come if he had to take her by force. Those girls at Bryn Atha knew nothing of childbirth. They were all virgins! Alanna would have to come. Niniane needed help. Something might go wrong. The baby might die . . . *she* might die . . . Alanna would have to come.

It was already dark by the time he rode into the farmyard. As soon as Alanna saw his snow-covered form in the doorway, she knew what was happening. "You must come," he said. His face was grim and he did not look young at all.

Alanna sighed. "Why do babies never come when it is convenient? All right, Prince. Come in and get warm. I must put some things together."

Ceawlin's face relaxed a little when he realized she was not going to object, and he stamped the snow off his feet and came into the room. He would not take off his cloak, however, and in ten minutes Alanna was in the saddle of one of the farm horses. Ceawlin took her reins and led the way out of the yard.

The ride to Bryn Atha was one Alanna never forgot. The snow was blinding, covering the path so that the horses were up to their knees. Alanna buried her face in the blanket she had wrapped around her shoulders for warmth. The going was very slow, but Ceawlin never faltered, never once lost his way. He had to be guiding them by instinct alone, Alanna thought. It simply was not possible to see. She had never been out in such a storm, and she was very cold, but she was not frightened. She had implicit faith that he would get them there.

And get them there he did. They were in the courtyard before she realized they had made their destination; the snow was so thick she had not seen the walls until they were on top of them. He lifted her off her horse and said, "Go in. I must see to the horses."

She nodded and toiled through the snow to the door. It opened immediately. They had evidently been keeping a watch. Ceawlin saw her go in and then he turned to lead the horses to the stable.

Niniane had not known there could be such pain. At first it had been endurable; there had been a respite between one onslaught and the next. If this is all it is, she thought, I can bear it. She clenched her teeth and her fists and fought against crying out. She wanted very much to be brave. But then the pains came closer and closer and soon there was no respite. There was nothing but pain. Her body was delivered over to it, eaten up by it, torn apart.

She was so grateful to see Alanna. She had been afraid the woman would not make it . . . there was a storm . . . she could hear the wind rattling the shutters. "You are here!" she gasped when first she saw Alanna's face.

"I am here, my dear. Your husband brought me safe and sound. How are you doing?"

"I . . . All right." Then the pain came again. Alanna took her hand. "Squeeze," she said. "It's all right, my dear." She looked around at the frightened girls behind her. "Get some hot water in here," she said. "And a hot drink for me. I'm freezing."

The girls scattered to do her bidding, grateful for a chance to escape from the pain.

The pain came in constant waves, washing over Niniane, rending her. . . . Finally her will to be brave gave out and she screamed aloud in pain and terror. She would never live through this . . . she would die in this terrible agony. Alanna, still holding her hand, said, "Scream, my child. It will do you good to scream." And Niniane screamed again, not caring if Ceawlin heard and deemed her a coward.

The night went on. Ceawlin stood at the window in the small family chamber and stared out at the snow. Sigurd sat in a chair and stared at the floor. Both young men were white as the winter world outside. Neither spoke. From down the gallery came the sound of Niniane's screams.

Niniane's child was born into the pitch dark of a January morning. She was exhausted, soaked with the sweat of pain and fear, her throat raw from screaming. "It's almost done, my child," Alanna was saying. "Just a little more." Then there came a last great agonizing spasm that she was sure would tear her apart, and Alanna was holding something up in her hands. "A boy!" the woman said into the sudden silence.

Niniane heard the words, heard the sound of a baby crying, and closed her eyes. She felt nothing but a weariness so immense she thought she would die from it. She forced her eyes to open and asked, "Is . . . is he all right?"

"A beautiful baby, my dear," said Alanna. "He is perfect." Niniane closed her eyes again.

She lay in a half-conscious stupor all the while the women washed her and dressed her in clean linen. Then they brought her her son to feed. She looked with wonder at the tiny head under her chin and instinctively her arms moved to cradle him. She felt his mouth against her breast, and her heart was suddenly pierced with tenderness. She touched her lips to the soft silky head. When she looked up a few minutes later, Ceawlin was coming into the room.

He looked as tired as she felt. His eyes were hollow and his skin tinged with gray. He had been listening all night to her screams, she thought with sudden shame. He came to the bed and stood looking down at her.

She remembered the Saxon custom and said softly, "Will you take up your son, my lord?"

He reached down and she gave the child to him. The baby cried at being taken from the breast, and Ceawlin laid his cheek against the tiny face. The crying stopped. When Ceawlin raised his head again, Niniane could see that the color had returned to his skin.

"You gave your mother a hard time, my son," he said to the small bundle in his arms.

"I was not brave," said Niniane.

He put the baby back into her arms. "Once, when I was a boy, I came across a sheep that had been attacked by a wolf. It was half-eaten, yet it still lived. I remember still how it cried. . . ." He looked at her out of shadowed eyes. "That is how you sounded this night."

"Niniane must sleep, Prince," said Alanna, coming forward. She took the baby from its mother. "The girls have brought the baby's basket, my dear. Let me put the little prince to sleep there so you may rest undisturbed."

Part of Niniane longed to reach for her baby again, but she was so tired, so very tired . . . Her eyes closed and she slept.

When she wakened many hours later, the storm was over. Someone had opened the shutters and the sun was streaming in the window. She saw with surprise that Ceawlin was still in the room. A shaft of sunlight from the window drew sparks of silver from his hair. He was standing before the basket, looking down at his son.

Chapter 17

CEAWLIN named his son Cerdic, after Cynric's father, who had first brought the West Saxon folk to Wight. Cerdic was a beautiful baby, with large blue eyes and a fuzz of downy golden hair. Niniane thanked God on her knees every night for his goodness in giving her such a fair and healthy child.

One thing only gnawed at her joy. Ceawlin refused to allow Cerdic to be baptized.

"No," he said flatly when Niniane spoke of the priest's coming the following summer. "No Christian priest is going to cast his spells on my son. He is Woden-born, a future King of Wessex. I will not allow your priest to come near him."

Niniane had been astonished. He had been so accommodating about their marriage, she had never expected him to take such a stand. But nothing she could say would move him. His son was not to be baptized and there was an end to it. Niniane decided to let the matter drop for a while. Cerdic could not be baptized until Father Mal returned in the summer anyway, so it seemed pointless to argue.

Toward the end of winter, Ceawlin sent Sigurd south to Venta to try to get word from Cutha of what was happening in Winchester. Sigurd was to do as Ceawlin had done the previous year, stay at the bakery with Helwig and have her send a message to Winchester.

"I must know what I can expect," Ceawlin said to his friend as he sent him off one gray-blue morning in late February. "Are any more thanes likely to join with me? If so, they must come soon. I cannot tarry here at Bryn Atha through the spring waiting for Edric. I must be the one to make the first move."

Sigurd left and Ceawlin took the rest of the thanes out to hunt for a wolf that had killed a sheep and a newborn calf in their pastures the previous two nights. Niniane and her women were alone at the villa, sitting in the winter room, which Niniane had set aside as the women's room, when Naille came riding into the courtyard.

Meghan went to the door to let him in. Niniane looked up from her spindle and smiled when she saw who it was. "Naille! How good to see you. But Ceawlin is not here. A wolf got one of our calves last night and he and the thanes went after it."

The clan leader's face was very somber. "I did not come to see Ceawlin, Niniane. I came to see you." He looked at the girls working at the looms. "May we speak alone?"

Niniane kept her surprise from showing on her face. "Of course," she said. Then, as the girls prepared to leave the room, "No. Stay. I will take Naille to the dining room." She rose, put down her spindle and wool, and led the way down the gallery.

"Coinmail is at the farm," he said as soon as he closed the door behind them.

Niniane felt all the color drain from her face. She stared at Naille, who looked as pale as she felt. "Wh-what does he want?"

"He heard that you and Ceawlin had come to Bryn Atha and that we had joined with the Saxons at Cob Ford. That is what has brought him home."

"But how did he find these things out, Naille? I thought he was in Glevum. That is on the other side of the Aildon hills!"

"One of our people rode to Glevum to tell him. Not everyone is pleased to see British boys coming so under the influence of the Saxons. Not everyone is in agreement with my decision to support Ceawlin."

"Who told him?" Niniane demanded fiercely.

The Briton shrugged. "What does it matter? What matters is that he knows and that he is here to put a stop to any cooperation between the Atrebates and your husband."

Niniane sat on one of the dining-room benches and stared at Naille out of worried eyes. "What are you going to do?" she asked.

"I don't know. But he wants to see you, Niniane. And I think it would be well for you to talk to him. Perhaps you can make him understand what it is that we hope to gain by supporting Ceawlin."

"Do you want me to come now?"

"Yes. While Ceawlin is out hunting. I think it will be best if we can keep Coinmail and Ceawlin apart."

"Yes," Niniane agreed fervently. "That is true. Very well, Naille. I will tell the women that Alanna wishes to see me."

"Good."

"I must feed Cerdic first."

Naille sighed. "All right. But hurry, Niniane! I don't want Ceawlin coming to the farm looking for you. He and Coinmail—"

"I know. I know. I will do my best, Naille. Why do you not go down to the barn and get Ruist saddled?"

"All right." And the Briton went to ready her horse.

*   *   *

Niniane waited until they had left the courtyard of Bryn Atha and turned onto the track that would take them to Naille's farm before she asked the question that had been worrying her most. "Has Coinmail made an agreement with the Dobunni?"

"They have not agreed to fight for Atrebates land, if that is what you mean," he answered. "Coinmail was not able to impress them with any sense of their own danger. Close as they are to Wales, the Dobunni have been safe for too many years. The Saxons did not threaten Glevum even in the days of Arthur."

"Then Coinmail has failed . . ."

"Coinmail is to marry a Dobunni princess," Naille said. He added, his voice dry, "In many ways, he and Ceawlin are very like."

Niniane did not answer, but she turned Naille's words over silently in her mind. Perhaps, in a superficial way, what Naille had said was true. Both Ceawlin and Coinmail were ambitious men, both fighters and leaders. Both had a strong sense of their own mission in life. But the personalities of the two were utterly opposed.

Niniane had not seen her brother for three years, but she remembered vividly the years she had spent under his domination. She had admired him, striven to please him, allowed him to rule her naturally spontaneous feelings with his relentless iron judgment. Her only escape from him had been Kerwyn and music; he had known that, and that was why he had so disapproved of the old harper. His was a nature that demanded utter submission.

It was not until she went to Winchester that she realized how subjugated she had been at home.

Ceawlin was not like that. Ceawlin released her natural feelings, her natural vivacity. His was fully as dominant a personality as Coinmail's, yet she never felt with her husband that she must watch her tongue, hide her emotions. . . .

"He is very angry," Naille said, his voice breaking into Niniane's thoughts. "He feels I have betrayed him." There was pain in Naille's face, in his voice. "I have only done what I felt was best for the tribe, Niniane."

"I know that, Naille. Most of the Atrebates know that too, else they would never have gone to fight with Ceawlin at Cob Ford."

"I had to restrain Gereint from physically attacking Coinmail at one point," Naille said, his voice still a little shaky. "Ceawlin has certainly won the young ones to his side."

"He is so young himself, you see."

Naille turned to look into her face. "So is Coinmail," he answered.

Niniane's smile was wry. "But Ceawlin is much more fun."

"Yes." Naille's voice held the same note as her smile. "He is."

They rode the rest of the way in silence. The road was a quagmire from the melting snow, and the horses and riders were splattered with mud by the time they reached Naille's farm. Gereint had evidently been waiting for them, for he appeared in the yard as soon as they did and came to hold their horses.

"I am glad you have come, my lady," he said to Niniane. His cheeks wore bright spots of color.

"I hope you have not been arguing again with your prince," said Naille sharply. Gereint looked mutinous but did not reply. Naille's mouth settled into a thin line. "Go and clean these horses," he said, and Gereint led the animals away toward the barn.

Coinmail was in the kitchen with Alanna and the younger children. The first thing Niniane saw was the dark, burnished red of his hair. He got to his feet and stared at her, his eyes like dark gray ice in his fair-skinned face. "So," he said. "Here is my sister. The wife of the Saxon."

Niniane looked back at him, her own eyes level, her face composed. "Greetings, Coinmail," she said.

"Take off your cloak, Niniane, and let me get you a hot drink." Alanna was coming toward her and Niniane smiled faintly and allowed the woman to take her cloak. Then she came forward to stand before her brother.

She had thought once that he was so tall. He was considerably taller than she, of course, but his size did not intimidate her as once it had. She had grown used to looking so much higher. She raised her brows and said, "Why have you come?"

There was a flicker of surprise in the gray eyes. He was not accustomed to his little sister speaking to him in that particular tone. Then he frowned. "I have come to put an end to this Saxon occupation of Bryn Atha. This . . . husband of yours must go elsewhere. And his followers with him. I will not have a Saxon on my land."

Niniane stared at her brother, at the features she had known since childhood. Coinmail was an extraordinarily good-looking man. Almost as good to look upon as Ceawlin. But Coinmail's features, though beautifully regular and harmonious, were always severe. There was never any softness in the line of his perfectly cut mouth, never any tenderness in his face as there was in Ceawlin's when he looked at his sleeping son, or talked to Bayvard, or made love to her.

Coinmail had intimidated her for years, she thought, because he had held her in awe. She had always felt she must admire a man who was so dedicated, so fanatic in his single-mindedness. He had dominated her father as well. Ahern had deferred to Coinmail from the time Coinmail turned ten.

But she looked now at her brother and saw a man as fallible as she herself was. Coinmail was no more perfect than any other of God's creatures, and that thought gave her courage. "Bryn Atha is my home," she said. "And Ceawlin is my husband. You approved the marriage, Coinmail. After Beranbyrg—where I understand you took your life from Ceawlin's hands."

His eyes were like gray ice. "I had no choice but to approve the marriage. It was your fault you were taken, Niniane. I told you to go to Geara's farm. But you did not listen."

"Kerwyn was too ill to move."

"The Saxons would not have been interested in a sick and dying harper. But they were interested in you, a princess of the Atrebates. I told you that. I made a special trip back to Bryn Atha to warn you. Once you were taken, there was nothing more I could do for you."

Niniane read unerringly what was in his mind. He had washed his hands of her because she had disobeyed him. Bitterness rose in her heart.

"You made a mistake also, Coinmail, when you left Bryn Atha to go to Glevum," she said. "The tribe made its choice while you were gone, and its choice is to make peace with the Saxons. Ceawlin will be king of this country one day and he has sworn to protect the land of the Atrebates as if it were his own. My husband is a man of his word—unlike my brother."

There was silence in the kitchen. Alanna and Naille were but shadows in the corner of Niniane's eyes. Coinmail stood before her, his face looking as if it had been carved in stone. Niniane read well in her brother's iron silence what he was feeling. Not shame, but fury. Cold fury. Buried like an iceberg below the controlled surface of his face and his mind.

"I see you have been tempted by the enemy," he said at last.

"Ceawlin is not the enemy." It was Alanna speaking now, trying to diffuse the hostility that had so palpably arisen between brother and sister. "I have tried to tell you, Coinmail. He has married Niniane in the Christian faith. And he is truly a good boy. Why, he even climbed a tree to rescue Isolde's cat!"

"He has the cleverness of Satan," said Coinmail. "I see that well. He has won you all, has he not?"

"We were beaten into the ground at Beranbyrg." It was Naille speaking now. "And you say you have not been able to make an agreement with the Dobunni. So what do you offer us, Coinmail? A repetition of Beranbyrg, with more of our men and boys slain by Saxon spears? We cannot fight them! I was at Cob Ford. Ceawlin put the Britons in the rear and all we did was follow the Saxon charge. They come down like an avalanche, Coinmail! It's Ceawlin who does it. You saw him at Beranbyrg. I doubt the first Saxon line there would have held were it not for him. He would make a formidable enemy. But I think he will also make an honorable friend."

"You speak of honor from a Saxon?" Coinmail's voice was cold with contempt. "He is using you, that is all. And once you have helped to win his kingship for him, he will show his true colors."

"I do not think so," said Naille. His brown eyes held Coinmail's steadily.

There was a tense silence. Then Coinmail said slowly, "Even if all you say is true, even if this Ceawlin keeps to his word and protects our land, still I say he is my enemy. He is a Saxon and I am a Briton. He is a pagan and I am a Christian. He and his kind are my enemy, and I will never rest until they are purged forever from this land."

He meant every word he said, Niniane thought. That was why he was so impressive. She had been petty to accuse him of betraying his word. He would not look at it that way. Simply, he would take any course, follow any path, that would bring him his goal of destroying the Saxons.

It was Naille who answered him. "You are not another Arthur, Coinmail. And even if you were, the will to join together in common battle is no longer with the Britons. The Saxon kingdoms are spreading all over this land, and nothing you can do will stop them. But there is another difference from the time of Arthur. As Ceawlin once said to Gereint, the Saxon folk are no longer the same barbarian pirates who first landed on our shores. They have become civilized, Coinmail. The thanes at Bryn Atha are as gentle and courteous as the highest-born British prince. Niniane says that under Cynric Venta has once again become a thriving city. And one day they will turn Christian. Look at the Franks. Why should not the Saxons go the same way?"

Coinmail's skin was very white against the red of his hair. "I will never accept what you say, Naille. Never. As long as breath is in me, I shall fight them. I am a Briton. Never will I bow my head to a Saxon king."

"This Saxon king will have a British queen," said Alanna suddenly. "And the king who follows Ceawlin will be your sister's son, with royal Atrebates blood running through his veins. *That* is the way we will conquer the Saxons, Coinmail. Not by the sword."

"The men who summoned me home do not agree with you," Coinmail said.

"The men who summoned you home number but a handful." It was Gereint coming in the door. He was very dirty from cleaning the mud off the horses. "The rest of us are for Ceawlin."

Coinmail's eyes went from Gereint's defiant young face back to Niniane. "You were right about one thing, my sister," he said at last. "I made a mistake when I left Bryn Atha."

Niniane felt an unexpected stab of pity. He was, after all, her brother; and he looked so alone. "Come home with me, Coinmail," she said impulsively, and ignored Naille's look of horror. "Come home with me and meet Ceawlin. See my baby. We are one family, after all. Let us be friends."

His eyes searched hers. "No," he said after a long moment. "What you ask is impossible. The Saxons must be crushed; that belief is stronger in me than anything else in the world, stronger even than the ties of blood. You cannot have it both ways, Niniane. If you choose him, then you are my sister no longer."

She was as pale as he, but her answer came without hesitation. "He is my husband, Coinmail. My husband and the father of my child. God's law on the subject is quite clear: my duty lies with my marriage."

"Then farewell," he said. He might have been carved out of marble. "You had best return home before you are missed."

"Come along, my dear," said Alanna when Niniane neither moved nor spoke. "Gereint will see you safely back to Bryn Atha." And Niniane allowed Naille's wife and son to take her out of the room.

It was dark when Niniane returned to Bryn Atha; as she rode into the courtyard, she saw that the windows of the thanes' quarters were yellow with candlelight. Niniane's already heavy heart sank further. It was the hour for dinner, and the thanes were not at the villa. That meant they had not yet been fed.

There was one thane waiting at the villa, however, for a man came out of the front door to hold her horse while she dismounted. "The prince was growing worried about you, my lady," he said.

Niniane recognized Wuffa's voice before she could clearly see his face, and she asked him the question that was most concerning her at the moment. "Have the thanes eaten, Wuffa?"

The reply, as she had feared, was negative. "Oh, dear," she said, "and it is so late. You must be hungry. I will see to dinner right away."

"I'll help Gereint with the horses," Wuffa offered.

"Yes, Gereint"—she turned her head—"it is too late for you to go home now. Stay the night and return to your father's farm tomorrow." Niniane was certain Naille had sent the boy with her to keep him out of Coinmail's way.

"Thank you, my lady," the boy replied. "I will." The two men began to walk the horses toward the stable, and Niniane went into the villa.

Amena was waiting for her in the atrium. "The prince took the baby to your bedroom, my lady. I was walking Cerdic myself in the sitting room, but there was nothing I could do to quiet him. I did my best, but he is hungry."

Amena's feelings had evidently been wounded by Ceawlin's removal of the baby. "Thank you, Amena," said Niniane. "I understand dinner has not yet been served?"

"No, my lady. The thanes returned from the hunt only a short time ago."

Niniane frowned. "Well, then, go to the kitchen and make sure the food is being readied. I want it served as soon as possible. If the men have been hunting all afternoon, they will be hungry." Then Niniane turned away to walk along the gallery, leaving Amena to follow.

She heard her son as soon as she passed the kitchen. The crying lessened instead of increasing, however, as she drew closer to the bedroom wing of the house. She reached the door to her room and pushed it open. The crying was intermittent now, not angry as it had sounded when she was farther down the gallery.

Ceawlin was walking up and down the room, his son in his arms. He looked at the door as Niniane came in, but did not pause in his pacing. "Where were you?" he demanded. His eyes sparkled with temper but he kept his voice quiet so as not to frighten the baby.

"Naille's farm."

"In the name of all the gods, what were you doing riding out to Naille's farm so late in the day? You must have known it would be dark by the time you returned. There is no dinner ready here and the thanes are hungry. The baby is hungry. *I* am hungry." He was really in a temper. "Those girls are worse than useless. I arrive home to find no dinner, no wife, and my son screaming because the stupid slut who is taking care of him is jiggling him up and down and making him sick!"

Niniane came to take the baby from his arms. "Did you get the wolf?" she asked. She sat in the old wicker chair they had brought into the room and began to unfasten her gown. Cerdic, sensing he was soon to be fed, began to scream with impatience.

"I know just how he feels," Ceawlin muttered.

"You didn't get the wolf."

"No, we didn't get the wolf. I will have to put a guard on the livestock until we do."

Niniane put the baby to her breast, and silence fell on the room. She looked up from her son and found Ceawlin watching her. He sat on the edge of the bed directly across from her chair. "Why did you go to Naille's farm?" he asked.

"Coinmail is there," she answered.

His eyes opened wider. "Your brother?"

"Yes. He heard that we were here at Bryn Atha. He heard about Cob Ford. He came home to find out what was happening." In his greediness, Cerdic lost the nipple and began to scream. Niniane gave it back to him and returned her eyes to her husband. He was looking thoughtful.

"What did he say?"

"He told Naille he did not want the Atrebates cooperating with you."
Ceawlin quirked his eyebrows. "And Naille?"

"Naille said that in his judgment, cooperating with you was in the best interest of the tribe. That the tribe agreed with him. Coinmail is going to go back to Glevum, I think. He is to marry a princess of the Dobunni."

"Hmm," said Ceawlin. His eyes were on his son's head but they wore an abstracted look. He was thinking about Coinmail. Niniane shifted the baby a little, also thought of Coinmail and their interview, and looked assessingly at Ceawlin.

He had turned nineteen last week and Niniane and the girls had cooked for days, preparing a great banquet to celebrate the occasion. The biggest sign of his advancing age, however, was the fact that he was finally beginning to grow a beard. Niniane could see it now, glistening like silver thread under his skin.

"Have you ever thought of shaving, Ceawlin?" she asked, following this train of thought. "My father's razor is still here at Bryn Atha. Coinmail was nicely clean-shaven this afternoon. The old Roman razors still work well."

A pair of blue-green eyes moved from the baby to meet her own. "Shave? Take off my beard?"

"Yes. Your skin is so nice . . ." Her voice trailed away. The astonishment in his eyes was almost funny. "I suppose that is not the Saxon way," she ended.

"It certainly is not. If your people wish to take off their beards on purpose so they look like women, that is their business. But don't expect me to do it!"

Cerdic's sucking had slowed down considerably. She took him from the breast and put him on her shoulder to pat his back. "The next thing, you will be wanting me to cut off my hair," Ceawlin said.

"I will never want you to cut off your hair. I love your hair." She frowned. "Except, it needs to be washed."

He got off the bed. "Niniane, there are more important things to talk about than my hair and my beard! Did Naille come back to Bryn Atha with you?"

"No. Gereint brought me home."

"Ah. And how did Gereint deal with your brother?"

"Not well. Gereint has become your devoted admirer—as you well know, having gone out of your way to attach him."

"I have done nothing in particular," he replied blandly.

"Take him wolf-hunting and he will love you even more."

Ceawlin gave her a long thoughtful look and left the room. Niniane put the baby in his basket to sleep and went to the kitchen to see about the dinner.

*   *   *

Sigurd met with his father in Helwig's bakery the day after his arrival in Venta. Cutha was glad to see his son and anxious to learn how Ceawlin's thanes had survived the winter.

"Very well," Sigurd replied to Cutha's question. "Bryn Atha has much fertile farmland and the harvest was a good one. There has been plenty of food for the winter."

"I wondered how you would fare," Cutha said slowly. "Ceawlin can lead a war band into battle, of that I have no doubt. But I was not sure how he would fare as a provider."

"It was Niniane more than Ceawlin whom we have to thank for our well-being," Sigurd replied evenly. "She is the one who insisted we grow our own food. She is a careful and a thrifty manager. Ceawlin is fortunate in his wife."

"Grow your own food? You are not saying that you worked in the fields yourselves?"

Sigurd grinned. "Yes, Father. We worked in the fields ourselves. It was not so bad."

"None of the thanes revolted at being put to work like common ceorls?"

"How could we object, when our prince was out there working with us?"

Cutha's clear blue eyes searched his son's face, but, "I am surprised," was all he said.

"Well, we are in good heart and good health, Father. Ceawlin has sent me to you to find out if there is any hope of further recruits for his war band. The good weather is coming and he is getting ready to move."

"What is he planning?" Cutha's voice was as expressionless as his face.

"I don't know, precisely. He just said he has no intention of sitting at Bryn Atha to wait for Edric. He will go on the offensive, somehow. I know Ceawlin. It is not in his nature to do otherwise."

"I have been thinking I would move to Banford myself," Cutha said carefully. Banford was the property east of Venta that Cynric had given his cousin soon after the king had begun to build Winchester. It had at one time belonged to a prince of the Belgae tribe and consisted of a large farmhouse with surrounding fields.

Sigurd's gray eyes were puzzled. "But why, Father? If you are going to leave Winchester, wouldn't it be wisest to go to Ceawlin at Bryn Atha?"

"I might be of more use to Ceawlin by leading a war band of my own. That would give Edric two fronts on which to fight. He would have to split his forces."

Sigurd frowned. "I do not think Ceawlin would want you to do that." His voice was positive. "If there are thanes in Winchester who wish to fight for Ceawlin, send them to Bryn Atha."

Cutha was annoyed. "I was fighting with Cynric before Ceawlin was born. Allow me the wisdom of experience. I do not doubt Ceawlin's courage, but he has had limited experience of battle and even less experience of the strategy that makes for success in battle. You may tell him that I will be taking the field myself this spring, on his behalf of course. Let him keep to the north. I will see what I can do about driving Edric, the queen, and her bastard out of Winchester."

Nothing Sigurd could say would change his father's mind. It was a matter of pride; the son finally saw that. His father, Cynric's kinsman and eorl of Winchester, did not want to put himself under the command of a young and untried prince. He would fight for Ceawlin, but he would do it his way.

It was a distinctly troubled Sigurd who rode north to Bryn Atha the following day. Ceawlin was not going to like his news. Of that he was quite certain.

Chapter 18

C EAWLIN was indeed angry when Sigurd brought him the news of Cutha's plan. "He is tying my hands behind my back by doing this," he said to his friend as he paced up and down the floor of the family chamber in Bryn Atha. "Surely you could have made him see that? My forces must be concentrated. It will do no good at all to have two war bands in the field."

"I told him you would not like it, Ceawlin," said Sigurd. His troubled eyes were on the hard, angry line of the prince's mouth. "It is a matter of pride with him, you see. He is so much older than you, so much more experienced. He does not wish to put himself under your command."

Ceawlin stopped in his pacing and looked directly at Sigurd. The rest of his face was as hard as his mouth. "Does he wish to be king also?"

Sigurd's eyes widened with surprise. "Of course not! That is not what is in his mind. He is fighting for you, Ceawlin. He does not seek the kingship for himself."

Ceawlin's mouth did not relax. "So he told you."

"So he told me. And I believe him." Gray eyes held blue with unflinching honesty.

Ceawlin's mouth looked fractionally less grim. "All right. But it is still a mistake not to join our forces. Divided we are less strong, less effective than we would be united. Cutha is playing into Edric's hands by doing this."

"Perhaps. But that is the way it is to be. He will go to Banford and bring with him the thanes that are loyal to him and to you. Edric will have to move against him. With any luck, my father will make away with Edric's forces before ever we have to lift our spears."

Ceawlin did not look as if he placed much hope in that happening. But all he said was, "Who is likely to go with Cutha?"

"Oswald is the only eorl. The others do not care for Edric, but my father says they are likely to wait and see who will emerge the victor before they declare themselves."

"A fine council of eorls my father created," Ceawlin said with scorn.

"They were loyal to Cynric, but now the power is there for the taking and things are different."

Ceawlin rubbed the palm of his hand against the silvery down on his cheek. "So there will be Cutha and his thanes, and Oswald and his thanes, against the rest of Winchester."

"My father says he can count on others from the king's hall to join with him."

Ceawlin cursed, thrust his hand through his hair, and resumed pacing up and down the room. Sigurd sat in silence and watched him with resigned sympathy. There was nothing Ceawlin could do—which was why he was so frustrated, of course. The door of the room opened and Niniane looked in.

"Ceawlin? I have something I must speak with you about." Her eyes fell on Sigurd, sitting in Coinmail's old chair. "Sigurd! I did not know you were back."

He smiled at her. "I just rode in, Niniane."

Her small face lighted with a returning smile. "I am glad to see you safely home. These trips to Venta make me nervous." Then, to Ceawlin, "I shall come back later."

"No, you might as well come in now." He continued to pace the floor, not looking at her. "Well, what is it?" This, when she closed the door but stood in silence, her back against it, watching him. "I warn you, though, Niniane, do not say anything to me about the livestock or the fields. I am in no mood for playing farmer just now." His tone of voice was noticeably disagreeable. Sigurd frowned.

"I wish that was all I had to bother you with," Niniane said.

Ceawlin stopped pacing and stared at her. "What is it?" His voice was hard.

"Wynne is pregnant," she answered. "She has named Penda."

Ceawlin's eyes narrowed to slits of turquoise. "You are saying that Penda has corrupted her?"

"Yes."

He cursed, long and fluently. Then, almost shouting, "I told you to get rid of that girl!"

"I know you did, Ceawlin, but I needed her help. With all these men, there is so much to do—"

"I don't want to hear about how much you have to do! Gods! For the sake of a few miserable meals and lengths of cloth you have put me in an impossible position! Gods," he repeated, his voice becoming less furious as he began to think about what he must do. "I could choke you, Niniane."

"*Ceawlin.*" Sigurd was horrified by the way Ceawlin was speaking to his gentle wife. "It is not Niniane's fault. What did you expect? There are no women here and the thanes have healthy appetites. I'm surprised you haven't had a rape on your hands all this long winter. If it wasn't Wynne, it would have been some other woman."

Ceawlin's eyes flicked his way, but otherwise he ignored Sigurd. "He will have to marry her," he said to Niniane.

"I know."

"He will marry her and I will pay a fine to her family."

Niniane nodded. Her eyes looked huge in her small face. "I am sorry, Ceawlin," she said miserably. "I suspected there was something between Penda and Wynne. I should have told you . . ."

Her voice trailed off. He was looking at her in utter disgust. "You suspected something and yet did not tell me?"

She bit her lip and nodded. She looked so small, so helpless standing there in the blaze of Ceawlin's wrath. Sigurd wanted to reach out and gather her safely into the shelter of his arms.

"Well, pray to your crucified god that Naille and her parents will accept the fine and the marriage as recompense for the loss of their daughter's virginity," Ceawlin said to his wife. "If they do not, then I will be forced to have Penda executed. And he is a man I cannot afford to lose." His voice was deeply bitter.

All the color drained from Niniane's cheeks. She looked stricken. "You wouldn't do that," she whispered.

"I will have no choice. I cannot lose the goodwill of the Atrebates." He picked up a small pottery cup from a table and threw it on the tile floor, smashing it into pieces. "*Gods!*" he said again forcefully, pushed by Niniane as if she were not there, and slammed out the door.

The two left in the room listened to the sound of his footsteps going down the gallery. Then Sigurd said, his voice very gentle, "It is all right, Niniane. It is not your fault. Ceawlin should have foreseen something like this was bound to happen."

"But he did, Sigurd." She was still standing forlornly by the door Ceawlin had slammed closed. "He told me to send Wynne away and I wouldn't. And at Christmas I saw a look pass between them . . . Ceawlin is right. I should have told him." She looked so distressed that he crossed to her side and put a brotherly arm around her shoulders.

"Do not fret. It will all come right. Ceawlin will make Penda marry her."

He could feel her shoulders trembling under his arm. "I knew he would be angry," she said.

"It is not just your news that upset him. I had to tell him that my father is planning to lead his own war band, not join forces with Ceawlin. He was angry before ever you came into the room. He just took his temper out on you." Sigurd did not sound as if he approved of his friend's behavior.

Niniane's shoulders had stiffened as soon as he spoke of Cutha's plans. Now she said, her voice sharp with alarm, "What does this mean, Sigurd? Cutha is going to lead his own war band? Does this mean he is seeking the kingship for himself?"

"No." He let his arm drop away from her. "Ceawlin asked me the same question. I cannot believe that either of you could think such a thing. It is merely that my father, as the older and more experienced warrior, feels he can serve Ceawlin better by leading his own men."

Niniane tipped her head back to look searchingly into his face. Her neck was long and slender as the stalk of a flower. Her bright hair hung straight to her waist, a shining fan of coppery brown. "Ceawlin was counting on additional men," she said.

"I know. But my father may strike the decisive blow for him."

Niniane's small white teeth bit into her lower lip. Ceawlin would not like that either, she thought, and the thought was plain on her face for Sigurd to read. But all she said was, "I can well see it was not the time to tell him about Wynne."

"No." His eyes on her upturned face were oddly still. His voice was perfectly normal, however, as he added, "But he had to know sometime. He will get them married, Niniane. Do not worry. Everything will be all right."

A beautiful rose color flushed into her skin along the lines of her cheekbones. "How could I have been so stupid as not to tell him what I suspected!"

He raised his hand as if he would touch her, then dropped it again. His mouth tightened. "Stop blaming yourself." His voice sounded short. "It was as much Ceawlin's fault as yours."

Niniane caught the change in his voice and thought he was annoyed with her. "I'm sorry, Sigurd," she said apologetically. "I did not mean to bore you with my guilty conscience. You are wanting to go to Ceawlin and I am keeping you." She gave him a small smile to indicate that he could go without hurting her feelings.

"You are not boring me. You could never bore me." Now he sounded angry. "I just do not want you to think you have failed Ceawlin. You have not."

Niniane's smile became more genuine. "Thank you, Sigurd, for trying to cheer me up. You are a good man." She reached up to touch his cheek with gentle fingers. Then she sighed, put her hand on the door, said, "I had better go and get something to clean up this mess," and was gone.

Sigurd stayed on in the chamber for several more minutes, his eyes on the smashed pottery on the floor, his fingers on his cheek.

Ceawlin had an extremely unpleasant interview with Penda, who said the same things to him that Sigurd had said. "*You* have a woman here, Prince. For how long did you expect the rest of us to do without?"

The truth of Penda's words only made Ceawlin more furious. He controlled his temper, however, and got Penda's agreement to marry Wynne. Then he went to Naille's farm, where he stayed the night, and the following day he and Naille together called on Wynne's parents.

"Yes, it will be all right," he said to Niniane irritably when finally he returned to Bryn Atha from his rounds. He had gone into their bedroom to change his tunic, and found her there, feeding Cerdic. "They agreed to the marriage. A Christian marriage, of course, so it cannot be done until the summer. It is costing me a big fine in gold, I might add." He pulled his good tunic, one Niniane had recently finished making for him, over his head and threw it on the bed. Then he went to the clothes chest to get his old one. "This has been a lesson to me, though," he said as he bent over the chest. "I cannot keep the thanes idle any longer. Next week we take to the war road."

Her body jerked with surprise and Cerdic lost the nipple. "All right, love," she said to the baby as she replaced him at her breast. Then she told Ceawlin, "But Sigurd told me that Cutha was going to lead his own war band."

"I don't care what Cutha is going to do. I will have to set my hand to what is available to me right here. I cannot challenge Edric to battle, that I know. But I can take some vils, perhaps even pick up some ceorls who are tired of the farm and wish to see what the life of a thane is like. That is one way to increase my war band."

Niniane stared at him as he put on the second tunic. She longed to cry out that he should not go, that he should wait for Cutha, that it was madness to think some two dozen or so men could successfully defy the army of Winchester. But she said nothing. He would do what he felt he must do, and nothing she could say would make a difference.

"Bertred is interested in Meghan," she said instead.

"Well, that decides it then. I will get them away from Bryn Atha. We will raid some vils and collect some women. Otherwise I will be spending my life facing the irate parents of Atrebates girls!"

Niniane's mouth fell open. "You are going to bring women back to Bryn Atha?"

He was buckling his sword belt over the tunic. "You will have to find some place to house them."

"Are you planning to turn my home into a brothel?" Her voice was shrill with outrage.

He finished with the buckle and looked up. "Do not argue with me on this, Niniane. Sigurd and Penda are right. It was unreasonable of me to expect Saxon thanes to live like your gelded priests. I shall raid a few vils—Saxon vils . . . do not worry, I won't bother your precious Britons— pick up some women, and perhaps some men for the war band. That will enliven the thanes a little and let them know that they have chosen a lord who knows how to look out for their welfare."

"You will scandalize the Atrebates if you bring such women here," she said. "Christians have a very different view of such things."

"Well, then, they will have to be scandalized. I have sworn not to interfere in their lives, so let them not interfere in mine. I must have women for the thanes, and there is an end to it." He picked up his sword, which he had dropped on the bed along with his good tunic. "Tell your people the women are here to work in the kitchen. The gods know you have certainly whined enough that you don't have sufficient help! Now you will have some." And he left the room, slamming the door behind him.

"Cutha has not gone to join Ceawlin after all." Edric was speaking to Guthfrid in the privacy of the queen's hall one wet and blowy afternoon in March. "He is at Banford."

"Banford?" Guthfrid's slim shoulders were very straight as she sat on the edge of the bed and looked at her husband. "What is he planning? Does Cutha desire the kingship for himself?"

"He says not. He has declared for Ceawlin. But it is certainly strange, the fact that he has not joined forces with the bastard. The eorls do not like it. They do not trust Cutha. Nor do I. He has known power for too long to relinquish it lightly."

"How many men went with him?"

"Fifty."

Guthfrid raised a thin, arched eyebrow. "You have three times that number."

Edric smiled with satisfaction. "I know. Cutha thinks he is a war leader, but all his successes came under the direction of Cynric. We shall see how he does on his own, and outnumbered three to one."

"You will go after him?"

"I will go after him. And quickly, before he has a chance to prepare his defenses or change his mind and join with Ceawlin." Edric patted the queen's shoulder with his thick, callused fingers. "It could not have fallen out better," he said. "With Cutha and Cuthwulf out of Winchester, I no longer need to fear the knife at my back. Now I can take a full war band on the road. And once I have dealt with Cutha, we shall turn north and finish Ceawlin once and for all."

"Bring Ceawlin's head home to Winchester," said Guthfrid, "and I will lay it as an offering on Edwin's grave."

There were a number of Anglo-Saxon settlements in the valley of the upper Thames, established by settlers who, since the time of Arthur, had come up the river valley from Kent or along the Icknield Way from

East Anglia. It was an area of Britain that had not yet been successfully claimed by any of the Anglo-Saxon kingdoms, and this was the place Ceawlin chose for his first raid. "I have sworn to increase the borders of Wessex, to make her equal with the other English kingdoms," he said to Sigurd when first he told his friend of his plans. "We will start with the upper Thames. I hear the land there is rich, the farms prosperous. Let them swear allegiance to Ceawlin of Wessex."

Gereint and his friends wanted to accompany the Saxons, but Naille refused to allow them to go. It was one thing to fight when their own land was being threatened, he said, and quite another to fight for the expansion of a Saxon kingdom. Ceawlin had accepted his refusal with perfect good humor and even reprimanded Gereint for protesting his father's decision.

The war band left Bryn Atha on a chill overcast March morning and Niniane saw it off with ill-concealed resentment. The thought of Ceawlin's bringing women into Bryn Atha was eating like acid into her heart. He knew how she felt but he did not care. He needed women, "and there was an end to it." They parted with each one feeling the other was being unreasonable.

Ceawlin thought that she was being a prude. It was not that at all, she thought as she watched the last of the war band ride out the gates of Bryn Atha. She had lived for too long in Winchester to be outraged by the easygoing morals of the Saxons in regard to sex. The thanes could bed a hundred Saxon girls for all she cared. It was Ceawlin who was on her mind. She could not forget Cynric and the women's bower: the harem that had existed solely for the pleasure of the king.

What would she do if Ceawlin should take one of these women into his bed? The very thought drove her into a blind and jealous fury. She had never thought of herself as a possessive person, but with Ceawlin . . . She was not like Fara, she thought despairingly as she turned to go back into the house. She was not made to love and share. She could not stand by and watch another woman . . . she could not even think about it without her hands clenching into tight fists at her sides.

He would not do that to her.

But in this, as in so many other things, the gap between pagan and Christian was wide. He would not do that to her, she told herself as she buried her face in the comforting baby-smell of Cerdic. But she was not sure.

Ceawlin was gone for almost two weeks, and when he rode back into Bryn Atha it was with a herd of cattle and an additional ten men for his war band, but no women.

"What happened?" It was Sigurd whom Niniane asked about the

raid, managing to get him to herself while Ceawlin was seeing to the disposition of his new men and beasts.

"The country up there is very rich," Sigurd replied. "British and Anglo-Saxon farms stretch all over the valley. They had no idea that we were coming, of course, and no time to organize resistance. We marched from farm to farm, and the mere sight of an armed war band struck terror into their hearts. Ceawlin treated them very gently. He declared himself their king and exacted a tribute of cattle. He also wooed a group of the less prosperous farmers' sons with promises of glory in Winchester. They are the ones we have brought back here with us."

Niniane listened with concealed impatience. She was not interested in the men. "I thought he was going to bring women back also, Sigurd. He told me you were right, that it was unreasonable of him to expect his thanes to live like celibates."

"Oh, the women. Yes, there are some women coming. One of the East Anglian settlers had several East Saxon women slaves. Ceawlin bought them. It was a better policy than taking freewomen, he said. Ceawlin has hopes of adding that country to Wessex permanently. The land is really very rich."

"Where are these women now, Sigurd?"

"Not far behind us." Sigurd grinned. "Ceawlin put Penda in charge of them. Penda was furious."

"How many are there?"

"Five, I believe."

"I don't know where I am to put them," she muttered, her brow dark with rebellion.

"Put them in the thanes' quarters," Sigurd answered cheerfully. "They can keep the place clean. They were kitchen sluts for the Anglian, so they will be able to help you with the cooking and the gardening as well."

Niniane stared at his smiling face, her eyes gray and stormy. "I think you are disgusting," she said. Slowly and clearly. And watched his smile dissolve to a look of surprised shock. "Disgusting," she repeated emphatically. She left him standing in the middle of the sitting room with the silly look of surprise still on his face.

The women arrived several hours after the men, escorted by Penda and one of the younger thanes. Ceawlin had disappeared with the rest of the men and the cattle, so it was left to Niniane to greet the new arrivals. Penda turned them over to her care with almost comical relief.

There were five in all, two middle-aged women and three girls. They spoke East Saxon, which was a slightly different dialect from the one spoken in Winchester, but Niniane was able to understand most of what they said. She made out that two of the girls were sisters, daughters of the eldest of the women and the Anglian who had sold them. Slavery had not been practiced among the Atrebates for years, and Niniane was horrified by the way these women had been treated.

The women, however, did not seem unhappy with their fate. They were impressed by Bryn Atha. They were impressed by Penda. They were impressed by the silver-blond king who had bought them. None of them seemed perturbed by the suggestion that they live in the thanes' quarters. Niniane escorted them there, her face stony, and found them a room by the simple expedient of tossing the belongings of the thanes who had formerly occupied the room onto the floor outside the door. "You can live here," she said, looking around at the planked wooden walls Ceawlin had put up over the old crumbling plaster.

The women were impressed by the thanes' quarters. Niniane sniffed and wrinkled her small upturned nose, noticing indoors what had gone unnoticed outside. They smelled. "I will fix a tub of hot water for you in the kitchen," she said ominously to the greasy-haired women who looked at her with such pleasure. "You all need a bath. And clean clothes. Come with me."

The Saxon women had never in their lives been submerged in water, and protested vigorously as Niniane relentlessly forced one after the other into the large wooden tub she had Amena set up in front of the kitchen stove. Amena also assisted with the scrubbing; indeed the British woman seemed to get an almost fiendish satisfaction out of the amount of dirt she scoured out of Saxon skin. By the time she finished, the women's complexions were glowing bright red. Then Niniane gave them clean clothes to put on, and combs to pull through their hair. They were miserable, but they were clean. The two sisters were even pretty. Once their hair was combed, Niniane put them to work cooking the dinner and went to her own bedroom to feed her son.

Cerdic was there, lying unswaddled and kicking with delight on the bed, but it was Ceawlin who was playing with him, not Meghan. Niniane stared at her husband's back, and bitter gall rose in her throat. "Those women were filthy," she said in a cold, hard voice.

He was bent over the delighted baby, tickling him. He did not turn around when she came in, but continued to play with his son. "I know." His voice sounded unconcerned. He knew, of course, how she felt on this subject. "I thought they would clean up decent, though. Did they? I heard the screams and splashes from the kitchen and thought you must be working on them."

"They had bugs."

"I imagine they did." He was still bent over the baby, not looking at her.

She could withhold it no longer. Her voice, now low and trembling, came from somewhere behind her clenched teeth. Her hands were balled into fists at her sides. "Ceawlin, if you so much as lay one finger on any of them, I will murder you."

At that he straightened up from the bed. The blue-green eyes opened wide as he took her in. A slow smile spread over his face. "Nan. You're jealous."

"I am not a Saxon wife," she answered fiercely.

He picked her up and sat down on the bed next to the baby, holding her in his lap. "No, you're not, are you?" He began to nuzzle her throat. "I have no interest in those women," he said. "They are for the thanes. I have enough to keep me busy right here."

She slid her arms around his neck and twined her fingers into his hair. His lips moved lower. The baby felt a pang of hunger and screamed. Ceawlin cursed and looked up. She smiled at him.

"Tonight," he said, and she kissed his mouth before picking up Cerdic to be fed.

Chapter 19

CEAWLIN and his men were home two days when the thanes from Banford arrived at Bryn Atha. Wuffa, the sentry on duty for the Corinium road, was the first to see them. When first he spied the obviously Saxon group he thought it was Edric again, and then he recognized the men as belonging to Cutha. He rode down the hill on which he was hidden and walked his horse onto the road. The little group raised their spears when they saw the mounted figure, then someone shouted, "It's Wuffa!" and all the spears dropped.

"Ine," Wuffa said, his eyes falling on the man who stood at the head of the weary group. "What happened?"

"Edric surprised us," came the grim reply. "Cutha was not expecting him so soon. He came at dawn and we were not ready."

"What of Cutha?"

"He got away. But we left a good twenty men dead in the farmyard before we ran for it. We were but fifty and they numbered at least two hundred. We hadn't a chance."

"You are heading for Bryn Atha?"

"Yes. We lost contact with Cutha and the others and so I thought our best chance was to come north and hope to find Ceawlin. I was at Bryn Atha with Cynric and thought I would remember the road."

"You did. Follow me and I will take you there."

Ine looked up at Wuffa's mounted figure. "Would you mind if Erick rode your horse?" he asked. "He was wounded at Banford and has been finding the going hard."

"Of course not." Wuffa dismounted immediately and Ine boosted his comrade into the saddle.

"How many miles to Bryn Atha?" Ine asked as he walked along beside Ceawlin's thane.

"Eight."

"And someone is always on watch here?"

"Yes. Here and on the road to Calleva. That is how we spied Edric coming last year." Wuffa forbore to point out that Ceawlin had not allowed himself to be taken by surprise. He did not think he needed to. The point was clear enough to anyone with eyes.

"You look well," came Ine's next comment.

"We have been very comfortable," Wuffa said. "In fact, we have just returned from a raid to the north. The prince wanted to claim the valley land there for Wessex. We brought a herd of cattle and some women back to Bryn Atha."

"I see," said Ine.

"We shall have you all comfortable in no time," Wuffa promised cheerfully.

Ine looked back at the fourteen tired men he was leading. "That will be nice," he answered, and sounded as if he meant it.

There was not enough room in the thanes' quarters for fifteen more men, so Ceawlin put the new arrivals in one of the storage barns he had cleaned out over the winter for just such a purpose. Niniane washed and bandaged Erick's wounded shoulder and served up a hot meal for all the thanes in the main reception room of the villa. There was not space enough in the dining room to accommodate them all now.

After dinner Ceawlin took Sigurd and Penda and retired to his bedroom to talk. Niniane and the women cleared the tables and one by one the thanes began to head toward their sleeping places. Dinner had been later than usual and the sky was dark. Cerdic was in the kitchen with the women, kicking and babbling in his basket. When he began to cry, Niniane fed him and then it was time to put him down for the night.

The three men were still in her bedroom, Ceawlin pacing up and down the floor, with Sigurd and Penda sitting on the bed watching him. The three of them glanced her way, then ignored her as she brought the baby to his basket and knelt to change his cloths.

"We cannot meet him in a pitched battle," Ceawlin was saying. "Not yet. The numbers are too much in his favor. And he has veteran warriors, too, not untried boys. The thing to do is harry him, madden him, and pray that Woden will send us more men."

Niniane pinned Cerdic's new cloths and swaddled him in his blanket for the night. The men were silent and she turned to look at them. "Where is he?" she asked Ceawlin.

He flicked a glance her way. "I don't know. I have sent Bertred and Octa out to scout."

She forced her voice to remain calm. "Are they likely to come here, do you think?"

"I do not want them to come here. The walls of Bryn Atha are strong and perhaps we could withstand a siege, but I do not want that. There is too much to lose."

"They would lay waste all the area farms," Niniane said.

"I know that. I told you I do not want them to come here." Her remark had irritated him, and he frowned. "What are you doing here, anyway? This is warrior business, not yours."

"It is time to put Cerdic to bed," she answered. The baby, as if to second his mother's statement, began to cry. Niniane put her hand on the basket to rock it, and said to the men, "If you must talk, please keep your voices down."

The three men stared at her. She smiled at them sweetly and began to sing to the baby. "Come into my room," Sigurd said to Ceawlin. "We won't disturb the baby there."

"Yes. It seems you are the only one with the luxury of privacy in this woman-infested place," Ceawlin replied. The three men tramped to the door and went out, but Niniane noticed Ceawlin took care to close it gently so as not to disturb his son.

Cerdic was asleep and Niniane was in bed herself when Ceawlin finally came back into the room. "Are you awake?" he asked softly.

"Yes." She pushed herself up on her pillow a little so she could see him.

He sat down on her side of the bed. "I knew it was a mistake for Cutha to go to Banford. And then the fool lets himself be surprised. That pride of his Sigurd talks about cost me twenty men. I cannot afford to lose twenty men!"

Niniane wrapped her arms around her knees. "Naille may see things differently now, Ceawlin. When you went on that raid to the north, it had nothing to do with the Atrebates. This does. Edric knows that you had Britons with you at Cob Ford. If he comes into this country he will be out to teach us a lesson. I think Naille will let Gereint and his friends fight with you now."

They had not lit the candle and the only light in the room came from the moonlight streaming in through the unshuttered window. Ceawlin looked down at the hands he had clasped on his knee. His hair was like a spill of moonlight inside the room. "As soon as the scouts return with news of Edric's whereabouts, I will march after him."

Her knuckles whitened as her fingers dug into the blue blanket around her knees. "I thought you did not want a battle."

"I don't. I want a chase. I want to lead him away from Bryn Atha."

"Yes." Her voice surprised her by being perfectly steady. "I see."

"You will have to manage here on your own for a while, Nan."

"I can do that. Do not worry about me. I can take care of myself and Cerdic."

He raised his head at last and looked at her. "I will leave you three men. Keep the guards posted on both the Roman roads at all times. If you see Edric coming, get away from Bryn Atha."

She stared into his face. His words were an eerie echo of another time, another man's warning. "Do not fall into Guthfrid's hands,"

Ceawlin said somberly. "You are the one who said she hates me. And you are my wife, Cerdic my son."

Niniane ran her tongue around suddenly dry lips. "Yes," she said at last. "I understand."

His face looked grim. "I do not mind risking my own life," he said. "I am a warrior and that is my fate. But you . . . my son . . . that is another story."

"I can hide in Geara's cellar if I have to," she said. "No one even knows it is there."

He put his hands on either side of her face. "Do not let any dying harpers keep you here this time."

"No, I won't. I promise." He bent his face down to hers and she flung her arms around his neck.

They did not get word of Edric's whereabouts for three days. Apparently he had gone in pursuit of Cutha before turning north. When Ceawlin's scouts finally located Edric, his war band was some twenty miles south of Bryn Atha, on the Calleva road.

Within four hours of learning his whereabouts, Ceawlin was on the war road himself. With him went his own thanes, Cutha's thanes, and ten Britons. Two of the British volunteers and the wounded Erick were left at Bryn Atha to guard the approaches to the villa. Ceawlin's command numbered forty-nine in all, and according to Ine and Cutha's other men, Edric was leading some two hundred. One difference was that all of Ceawlin's men were mounted.

"For the kind of tactics I have in mind, speed will be essential," Ceawlin had told Naille, and though the Briton had grumbled, he had provided horses for all of Cutha's thanes as well as the British boys.

"Arthur's successes came because of his cavalry," he said to Ceawlin when the horses were delivered to Bryn Atha. "Never did I think I would be mounting Saxons to follow in his footsteps."

Ceawlin privately thought that the British stories about Arthur and his cavalry were greatly exaggerated. It simply was not possible for a horseman to keep his seat under the shock of a heavy lance-thrust. Ceawlin himself was one of the finest horsemen in Winchester and he knew he would be unseated should he try to fight foot soldiers from horseback. But, prudently, he said none of this to Naille, only smiled and thanked the Briton for his valuable contributions.

Bryn Atha seemed deserted once the men had gone. Niniane and the women stood in the courtyard and looked forlornly at the gate through which they had ridden. Then Niniane straightened her shoulders. She had told Ceawlin she would manage on her own, and so she would. She turned to Meghan and said briskly, "With the men gone, we will have to do all the work for the livestock and the farms ourselves. We will have enough to keep us busy until they return, that is certain. Come now"—her voice sharpened to catch the attention of the rest of the women—"into the house. There are things to be done."

Ceawlin took his men to a point eight miles south of Calleva where he knew there was a British farmhouse half a mile to the west of the Roman road. The British farmer was terrified when a thundering wing of fifty horsemen came riding into his yard, but Ceawlin had Gereint talk to him and soon the Saxons were feeding and watering their horses and waiting for the scouts Ceawlin had posted to return with news of Edric's approach.

It was growing late as Ceawlin and Sigurd stood together at the edge of the farmyard and looked toward the road. "There is a perfect place to make camp a mile south of here," Ceawlin said. "I am hoping that is what Edric will do. Then, when they are all sleeping, we will make our move."

The scouts returned within the hour to say that Edric was doing exactly as Ceawlin had hoped. The thanes ate the bread and cheese they had brought in their saddlebags. Then there was nothing to do save wait.

The day waned. Great piled banners of blood-red light stretched across the sky and dyed the clouds. Then came the dark.

The thanes waited, sleepless, for the word to be given. Ceawlin had told them earlier exactly what they were to do: "Ride down on that camp like warriors out of hel. Use your javelins and get as many men as you can. *Do not stop for anything.* I want no hand-to-hand combat. We are in and out as fast as possible, and we kill as many as we can with javelins alone. I cannot afford to lose a single man of you. Is that clear?"

When they assured him it was, he went on: "We will come up on the camp from the south, go through it to the north, and keep on going up the Roman road. We don't stop until we reach Calleva."

"Where do we go after Calleva, Prince?" It was Ine, Cutha's thane, speaking. "Edric will follow us, that is for certain."

"I want him to follow us. After Calleva we head for the Aildon hills, Ine. To the Badon pass."

"The Badon pass?" Ine frowned. "Isn't that where Arthur . . . ?"

"Yes." Ceawlin's silver brows rose. "I have been there since coming to Bryn Atha, and I promise you a few dozen men can easily hold that pass against a full war band. That is where we go and that is where I want Edric to follow."

It was after midnight when Ceawlin and his men moved out. The British farmer knew a way through the forest that would bring them up to the road south of Edric, and Gereint persuaded him to guide them. They went single-file, leading their horses, as the path was narrow and overgrown and they did not want to hit their heads on the overhanging branches of trees.

Ceawlin went first, directly after the guide. It was very dark in the forest and only his excellent night vision allowed him to keep the figure of the farmer in his sight. It was easier for the men behind him, who had the larger bulk of a horse to follow. After what seemed to him a very long time, but what the clock in his head told him was but half an hour, he saw the moonlight shining up ahead. At last the long tree-tunnel was coming to an end.

The road looked almost bright after the blackness of the tree-canopied forest. Ceawlin mounted Bayvard and kept the horse at a halt as he waited for the rest of his men to reach the road. No one spoke. They were all well aware that sound carried clearly on the night air and they were but a quarter of a mile from Edric's camp. They could see the dying campfires clearly from where they were gathering. The sound of the horses' hooves on the gravel of the road seemed unnaturally loud to Ceawlin's sensitive ears, but there was no alarm shouted from the camp up ahead.

Finally the last of his men had reached the road. They lined up as previously instructed, six abreast, eight lines deep. Ceawlin was holding a javelin in his right hand when he raised his arm. There was a moment of intense silence; even the horses seemed to stand frozen in stillness. Then he brought his arm down and the wing of horsemen began to gallop up the road.

They were on Edric's camp in less than a minute. Ceawlin swerved off the gravel road and rode directly for the rows of thanes sleeping on the grass around the campfires. His men came thundering behind him.

He saw a face in the light of the fire, recognized a thane from the king's hall standing and beginning to raise his sword. Ceawlin's javelin got him in the center of his chest. Ceawlin galloped his horse over the bodies on the ground and grabbed the other javelin he had stuck through his belt. He got another thane in the back as the man turned to run from the murderous hooves bearing down on him. Then Ceawlin was through the camp and turning back to the road. He turned his head to see who was beside and behind him. The wing was still intact. The gravel of the road was under Bayvard's feet and Ceawlin settled down to ride.

They rode through to Calleva, where they stopped to count heads. They had not lost a man.

Ceawlin had stopped only once before Calleva, to post a man on the road three miles south of the city with instructions to wait until he saw Edric's war band before he rode to Calleva to sound the warning.

The city gates were open, as the inhabitants had no idea that there were Saxons in the vicinity. Ceawlin rode in and quartered his men and horses in the old forum. He then commandeered hay for the horses and food for the men from the townspeople, who gave slightly less grudgingly when they saw that Britons were among the Saxon invaders. After they had eaten, Ceawlin had each man fill his saddlebag with as much food as he could carry. Then they all settled down for a few hours' sleep.

It was an hour after dawn when Octa came galloping into Calleva with the news that Edric was coming. Ceawlin woke his men and they started northeast, toward the hills.

Ceawlin knew it was a risk to pass so close to Bryn Atha. But he had too few men to do aught else but hide in the hills and try to draw Edric after him. He was counting on Edric being too anxious to catch him for the queen's husband to think it worth his while to make a stop at the villa. And if he did . . . if he did, Niniane was smart enough to get herself and the baby away.

Ceawlin did not travel too swiftly. He wanted Edric to feel he was within reach of the prince so he would not be tempted to give up the pursuit. Once or twice they spied several of Edric's horsemen a mile or so behind them. Edric was scouting his quarry.

One advantage Ceawlin had over Edric was that Ceawlin numbered among his band men who knew the country. The West Saxons had only once been this far north, the time they had beat the British at Beranbyrg. The terrain was largely unfamiliar to them.

They did not realize they were being led toward the Badon pass.

It was very late in the afternoon when Ceawlin's men reached the cleft in the hills that was known to the Britons as the Badon pass. This was a five-mile-long ravine between the two highest mountains in the Aildon hills, Mount Badon and Mount Dall. The Roman road from Venta to Corinium ran farther to the west, where the hills were low. Here the heights on either side of the pass were very steep, the ground rocky and uneven, the width narrow. It was in this pass less than a hundred years before that Arthur had buried an entire generation of Saxon warriors. Now the leader of a new Saxon generation, helped by British allies, was using the pass again.

Horses were useless in the terrain of the Badon pass and Ceawlin had half his men lead two horses apiece straight through the pass to the other end, where they were picketed and left with three men to watch them. The rest of the men trudged the five miles back to where they had left their fellows; then everyone sat down to eat the bread and cheese that was all they were carrying. Ceawlin was certain the thanes from Winchester would not make the pass this day; they were on foot and moving through unfamiliar territory. Nevertheless he did not wait until morning but posted his men on the heights of Mount Badon and

Mount Dall for the night with instructions that they were to remain there until Edric appeared.

Gereint was ecstatic. He had been weaned on stories of the Battle of Badon, and here he was, on the very same mountain, following the very same strategy as the greatest hero of his race.

In fact, the strategy was not the same. Ceawlin had little hope of luring Edric into the pass. He did not have the element of surprise Arthur had had. Ceawlin's hopes were to keep Edric tied down at the mouth of the pass while the prince pursued some further strategy of his own.

The sun rose on a beautiful, clear blue day. The early-morning air was chill, but Gereint huddled behind the rock that was to protect him from enemy arrows and scarcely noticed the cold. Wait until his father heard what he had done! The morning dragged on interminably as he trained his eyes to the east, searching for the enemy. Ceawlin was posted on the heights directly across from him. You couldn't miss Ceawlin, Gereint thought. There was not another head like his in all of Britain.

Finally, in the distance, he saw the first lines of the marching war band. Edric had come.

Edric had known for the last two hours where it was that Ceawlin was leading him; he had sent out scouts to find a local farmer to question. When he heard the words "Badon pass" he had recognized them immediately. He had heard, of course, of the Battle of Badon, knew it had been a decisive victory for Arthur against his own people. But of the particulars he knew little. It was not the Saxon way to dwell on their defeats. So as he rode along in front of his marching men, Edric remained optimistic about finishing with Ceawlin and returning to Winchester by summer.

Then he reached the pass.

He saw the men stationed on the hills, bows at the ready. They disappeared quickly behind the scrub and the rocks that were serving as their cover, but not quickly enough to avoid being sighted. He saw the narrow ravine that cut between those steep, chalky hills.

It would be suicide to try to enter that pass. His men would have no cover from the bowmen on the heights above them. Nor would it be possible to send men out over the mountains to try to find the hidden archers. They would be shot down almost as quickly as if they were on the floor of the pass. Edric had had enough of being a sitting target for Ceawlin. He had lost twenty-five men back on the Calleva road.

"We will wait them out," Edric said grimly to the eorls. "They have only the food they are carrying. They are trapped in those mountains. They will have to come out sometime, and we will be waiting."

"Where does the pass lead?" one of the eorls, Agilbert, asked. "Might they not go through to the other side?"

"The British farmer said it leads nowhere—only deeper into the hills. If they choose that way, they will have rendered themselves useless. If Ceawlin wants to be the king of a pile of barren hills, he is welcome to them. But I do not think that is what he wants. He wants Winchester. He will come out. He will have to come out."

Edric made camp on the gentle slope near the front of the pass, out of the range of Ceawlin's bowmen. Occasionally an arrow came down from the heights as one of the Winchester thanes ventured within range. No one was hit. Ceawlin's men finally resorted to shouted taunts.

"They are desperate to get us to enter the pass," said Edric with satisfaction. "Good."

Night fell and the Winchester war band posted sentries all around the camp. Edric was taking no chances of being surprised again. The night passed quietly. When the sun rose in the morning, the bowmen on the slopes of the mountains were gone.

"They have gone deeper into the hills," Edric said. But he was uneasy. It was not like Ceawlin to give up so easily. "Find me someone from this area," he ordered. "I want to know exactly what is on the far side of that pass."

It was noon before he found out. The pass led to the old Roman road that went from Corinium to Calleva. Ceawlin had never had any intention of luring Edric into the pass. He had merely fooled him into remaining in the hills for the night while he and his horsemen galloped back to Calleva. And from Calleva the road to Winchester lay wide open before him.

Edric grimly turned his men and retraced his steps east, out of the hills. They did not pause to eat or to sleep, but marched on through the night. When they reached Calleva it was to find that Ceawlin had been through the previous day and had taken the road south. The tired Winchester war band set out in pursuit.

Chapter 20

CEAWLIN feinted a move to Winchester, then veered west toward Searobyrg, where Cynric had begun his conquest of Wessex so many years ago. For the rest of that spring and early summer, the two war bands played cat-and-mouse throughout Wessex, living off the British farms and Saxon vils that lay in their paths. Ceawlin was hoping desperately to get some word of Cutha, but the eorl and his remaining followers seemed to have simply dropped off the map.

In early July Edric wearied of the chase and returned to Winchester. Guthfrid greeted her husband with public respect and waited until she had him alone in the queen's hall to tell him her thoughts.

"He is making a fool of you!" Her brown eyes were almost black with anger and contempt. "Gods. You are like a hound who cannot sniff out his quarry. He has run you the length and breadth of Wessex, and still he eludes you!"

"What can I do?" Edric shouted in return. "He has no intention of fighting me. He is merely trying to—"

"To make a fool of you. Well, let me tell you, Edric, he is succeeding."

He threw himself into a carved wooden chair and stared at her truculently. "At least I got rid of Cutha."

"Where *is* Cutha?"

"Gone to earth. No one has heard of him since he fled with his tail between his legs from Banford."

Her thin, arched brows drew together. "I don't like that."

"I like it better than learning that he has joined up with Ceawlin."

"Where is Ceawlin now?"

"Somewhere to the west. Near Selwood."

"Has it ever occurred to you, Edric," said Guthfrid, crossing the room to stand before him, "that all this while Ceawlin has kept you away from the north?"

Edric looked up at her from under his brows.

"Away from Bryn Atha," she said.

There was silence.

"The British there are for him," said Edric at last. "He had some with him at Cob Ford, and there are a number riding with him still."

"And he has a wife there."

"A wife," said Edric, "and a son."

Her eyes widened and a strange glitter came into them, making them look almost feverish. "A son?" Her voice was sharp.

"So I hear."

"I did not know that."

They looked at each other. Then, "He killed my son," she said.

He contemplated her for a long moment before he smiled. "What would you say if I promised to leave for Bryn Atha tomorrow?"

She came to put her hands on his shoulders, and lowered her face until her mouth was almost on his. "I would be very pleased," she murmured. "Only don't kill them. Bring them here."

"It will be my pleasure," he answered, and pulled her down onto his lap.

Ceawlin was not in fact near Selwood, the great forest that separated Wessex from Dumnonia. He had followed Edric back to Winchester and was now quartered but seven miles north on the road to Calleva. As Guthfrid had noticed, he was always concerned with making sure that Edric would not slip off to the north. Consequently, when the Winchester war band took to the road, the small troop of horsemen that followed Ceawlin knew of it very quickly.

It soon became clear that Edric was not out on a hunt for Ceawlin but had other prey in mind. He was marching purposefully north, toward Calleva, even though he must still believe Ceawlin to be in the west. And from Calleva it was but ten miles to Bryn Atha.

Ceawlin and his men turned their backs on Edric and rode north as well.

Bryn Atha looked just the same as they rode through the gates on a warm and overcast July afternoon. The dogs raced to greet them, barking noisily. A woman, hearing the dogs, came out the door of the house as the men and horses crossed the courtyard. Sigurd recognized Wynne by the color of her hair. Her lovely face lighted as she spied Penda.

The men began to dismount and two other women came out into the courtyard. Still Sigurd looked around. Bertred was talking to Meghan, and Penda had his arm around Wynne's shoulders. "Where is Niniane?" Ceawlin asked, echoing Sigurd's thoughts. He was squatting on his heels, rubbing the white hound's ears and looking around.

"Oh, my lord, she is seeing to the chickens," Wynne answered a little breathlessly. "Something got at them last night and she is setting a trap."

"Gods," said Ceawlin, torn between exasperation and amusement. "Niniane and her farm!" He gave the hound one last caress, straightened, threw his reins to one of the thanes, and strode off in the direction of the chicken coop, followed by three dogs. Sigurd directed the thanes to take their horses to the stable and, like Ceawlin, gave his reins into someone else's charge. Then he moved slowly toward the house. A man had opened the front door of the villa and was standing there, framed in the doorway. As Sigurd approached, he recognized the Christian priest Father Mal.

Sigurd greeted the priest courteously. "We are pleased to see you," the man replied. "Is the news you bear good or ill?"

"Not good, I fear. Edric is coming north, Father Mal," said Sigurd. "We think he may be heading for Bryn Atha."

The priest did not answer, but his face set into harsher lines.

"For how long have you been here at Bryn Atha?" Sigurd asked.

"A week. Naille told me I was to marry Wynne with one of the Saxon thanes, so we have been hoping you would return before I have to leave."

"Oh, yes." Sigurd had almost forgotten about Penda's marriage. "Well, you will have to do it quickly if it is to be done at all. Ceawlin wants to get everyone out of Bryn Atha before Edric arrives."

The two had been standing in the doorway all this while, and now the priest looked over Sigurd's head. "Here is the prince now," he said. Sigurd turned and saw Ceawlin and Niniane approaching, escorted by the dogs. He was looking down into her face and talking. The top of her head did not reach to his shoulder. As Sigurd watched, she slipped her hand into her husband's and said something in reply. He nodded, his face grave.

"Greetings, Sigurd," Niniane said when they were almost to the villa and finally she noticed the men in the doorway. She smiled. "Why have you not gone into the house?"

Sigurd forced himself to smile back pleasantly. Her own smile was brilliant, her eyes a deep dark blue. She and Ceawlin had not unclasped their hands.

"We were waiting for you," Sigurd answered.

She laughed a little unsteadily. "Well, come along in and let me get you something to eat!" They all went with her into the house, except the dogs, on whom she firmly closed the front door. Niniane directed them to the sitting room and then went along herself to the kitchen. She was back shortly with the news that food was being prepared. Then she said to her husband, "Do you want to see your son?"

Ceawlin, who had been standing by the window, moved with alacrity toward the doorway. "Where is he? Sleeping?"

"He should just be waking from his nap. He has grown so big. Wait until you see him."

They walked down the gallery side by side, walking closer to each other than was necessitated by the width of the hall. Ceawlin opened the bedroom door, then shut it behind them. The shutters had been closed to keep out the summer daylight, and there was silence from the baby's basket. Cerdic was still sleeping.

Ceawlin stood over him, looking down. For a long minute he said nothing. Then, "You must get away from here, Niniane. Both of you. Edric is coming north."

"I see." Her voice was very soft. "I thought perhaps that might be the reason for your coming." The baby's lips moved as if he were sucking, then he put his finger in his mouth and fell quiet again.

"He's sucking his thumb!" said Ceawlin. Niniane smiled at the wonder in his voice.

"We are the reason you have stayed south all this time, aren't we?" she asked.

"Yes. I told you I did not want Edric at Bryn Atha. I was also hoping to get word of Cutha."

"You have heard nothing?"

"Nothing." He sounded bitter. "He seems just to have disappeared.

"Ceawlin." She drew a long breath. "Ceawlin," she said again, "I will take the baby and go to Glastonbury with Father Mal. We will be safe there and, more important, we will not be in your way. You will be free to act as you will without the necessity of protecting us always on your mind."

He turned from the baby to look down at her, at the small, great-eyed face that always stirred him so. She was right. She was a burden to him just now. She was tying him down, she and the son who carried his love. There was a short silence; then, "Where is Glastonbury?" he asked.

"In Dumnonia. Dumnonia is British still, has always been British. There is a convent at Glastonbury, a group of religious women sworn to serve God. I can stay with them, Father Mal says. We will be safe there until you send for us."

"You have thought this all out."

She nodded. Even in the dimness of the room he could see the coppery strands in her hair. "I knew it would come to this. I will not leave you vulnerable to Guthfrid's vengeance."

"Nan." At the changed note in his voice she stepped toward him, raising her face. His kiss was hard, hard and hungry. Her arms went around his waist. "Gods. It has been so long," he said. Her body was pressed against his, her head bent back against his arm so her hair spilled over his wrist in a stream of coppery silk. He straightened a little so her feet came off the ground, and began to walk toward the bed.

"Ceawlin . . ." Her husky voice was huskier than usual, and unsteady. "Not now. They are waiting for us . . ." But despite her words, her body was calling to him. He felt it, felt the fire in his own blood, and laid her down on the bed. When his mouth came down on hers once more, she wrapped her arms around his neck and made no further protest.

When Ceawlin finally returned to the sitting room, it was to issue a series of orders. Niniane and the priest were to leave at dawn the following day for Glastonbury. The British girls would go back to their families, while the Saxon slaves were to remain at Bryn Atha. "If there is to be a marriage between Wynne and Penda," Ceawlin said to the priest, "you will have to do it tonight."

It was not until the thanes had fed and watered their horses that Ceawlin learned there was another marriage requested for the evening. Bertred came directly to the villa from the stable and asked to speak to Ceawlin privately. Meghan was with him. "Meghan and I wish to marry, my lord," said Bertred, respectfully but firmly, as soon as he and Meghan were alone with the prince.

Ceawlin raised his brows. "This is a surprise."

"I said nothing to you before because Meghan wished to wait for the priest," Bertred explained. "And then, of course, we have been on the war road. I know that we must leave on the morrow, but still . . . we wish to marry." His jaw set with unusual stubbornness.

Ceawlin regarded his young thane thoughtfully. "Do you have the permission of her parents?" he asked after a moment. "It is all right with me, Bertred, but I cannot have the Atrebates at my throat over this."

"My guardian does not mind so long as we are wed in the Christian faith." It was Meghan, who rarely had the courage to talk to Ceawlin, speaking up bravely to second Bertred.

"Your guardian?"

"My uncle," the girl replied. "My parents are dead."

Ceawlin gave them both a long level look. "Do you swear Meghan's uncle has given his permission?"

"Yes, my lord," they chorused together.

"Very well," said Ceawlin. "It seems that Father Mal will have a busy night." He gave Bertred an infectious grin. "As will a few other people around here."

Bertred grinned back and Meghan blushed.

Ceawlin had taken the two lovers into the dining room when they had asked for privacy, and now he dismissed them and walked back to the sitting room, where Niniane was talking with Sigurd and the priest. The three looked up at him when he reentered the room, identical looks of inquiry on their faces. "They want to be married too," Ceawlin said.

Sigurd looked surprised; Niniane did not. "They swear they have permission from Meghan's uncle," Ceawlin continued. Then, to his wife, "Do you know aught of this?"

She shook her head. "Meghan has said nothing to me. But I have had my suspicions. I told you about them, Ceawlin, don't you remember?"

He grunted. She went on, "This is not another case like Wynne and Penda, of that I am certain. They have waited. And Meghan has no parents living, only an uncle, who will be glad enough to relinquish responsibility for her. That is why he let her come to Bryn Atha in the first place."

Ceawlin cocked one eyebrow. "I see." Then, to the priest, "Your services are much in demand, Father Mal."

"That is always the case when a priest comes to an area so rarely," Father Mal replied. "Marriages and baptisms pile up. I have been busy indeed this past week. There was your own son, Prince . . ." He stopped as he saw the look on Ceawlin's face. There was a moment of ominous silence.

"What do you mean, there was my own son?" The priest stared in horror at a suddenly transformed Ceawlin. The affable, civilized prince he had been talking to was gone as completely as if he had never existed. Ceawlin took a step toward the priest, and Father Mal, who was not a coward, found himself backing away. Ceawlin's face was white, his eyes twin blazes of slitted turquoise. *"Did you baptize my son?"*

"I . . . Yes . . . the princess asked me to."

Ceawlin looked at his wife. She was pale, but her chin was up. He took a step toward her and she did not back away. "Is this true?" he asked.

"Yes." Her eyes met the blaze of his and held steady.

His hands were opening and closing into fists at his sides. "I told you I did not want a Christian priest near him. He is my son. How could you dare—?"

"He is my son too, Ceawlin. I could not do otherwise. This is a matter of his immortal soul."

Fury such as he had never before known swept through Ceawlin. She had done it. Cerdic, his son . . . bewitched by this mewling priest . . . lost. . . . He took one more step toward her and raised his fist. He wanted to kill her. He did not hear the priest's cry of protest or see Sigurd jump forward to stop him. He had eyes only for Niniane, who did not flinch or try to protect herself, only looked back at him, her face very still. At the last minute he opened his fingers and hit her across the face with his open hand. She fell to the floor.

"Ceawlin! Stop it!" It was Sigurd, grabbing his arm and dragging him away from his wife. Ceawlin shook him off and, turning, crashed out of the room.

The dogs dashed up to him as he left the villa by the rear door. The day had brightened and the late-afternoon sky was now partly blue. Ceawlin noticed nothing, however, as he strode toward the stable. His only desire was to get away from Niniane, to be alone. There were several thanes talking in the stableyard, but they fell silent as soon as they saw his face. He did not even bother to saddle Bayvard, just bridled him, leapt on him bareback, and rode out of the villa grounds toward the fields.

She did not understand what she had done. He realized that as he walked Bayvard around the edges of the hayfield that was filled with high grass getting ready to be cut. She was not Saxon. She could not understand. He had told her once, had tried to explain how he felt about who he was, what he was. Not just a man, but a man born to be king. Woden-born, with the blood of the god running in his veins. And now she had claimed his son for another god, this god who was born in a stable among animals. This weak, gentle god who was good enough for women perhaps, but was not a god for a king.

His son. Her son too. She had said that, and he was too essentially just a man to deny the truth of it. He remembered still her screams the night Cerdic was born.

But she had betrayed him. She had promised never to . . . He thought back. She had not promised. He had said he did not wish his son to be baptized and had assumed she would obey. She seemed so mild, Niniane, so soft and yielding. . . . He was beginning to realize that about some things she was not yielding at all. There was the farm, and the food she had made them grow last year. And now, this baptism. . . .

He could not allow them to go to Glastonbury with the priest. Niniane was too much under the influence of this religion as it was. But where else could he take them that they would be safe?

He rode around and around the hayfield, his brain going in the same large circle as his horse. It was dusk before he realized that he had better be returning to Bryn Atha.

Niniane had not been knocked out by Ceawlin's blow, just stunned. She opened her eyes to see Sigurd's white face bending over her. "Are you all right?" he asked her, his voice sounding as strained as his face looked.

"Yes. I think so." She put her hand to her cheek. It stung badly. She flexed her jaw. It hurt. She looked around the room and then at the door.

"He's gone." It was Father Mal, also looking very pale. "My daughter, I am so sorry. I did not realize . . . I should not have said anything about the baptism. You should have told me not to say anything."

"It is all right," Niniane replied. Sigurd lifted her to her feet. "He had to be told. I would not keep such a thing from him."

"He should not have hit you." Sigurd's gray eyes were harder than Niniane had ever seen them look. "I understand how he feels, but he should not have hit you."

"Ceawlin's anger is hot, not cold," Niniane replied. "But I have never seen him as angry as this." She was shaking, and stepped away from Sigurd so he should not notice. "Where has he gone?"

"I don't know," Sigurd replied.

Niniane was feeling sick to her stomach. She had known Ceawlin would be angry, but she had not quite expected this . . .

"He should not have hit you," Sigurd repeated.

The trembling was becoming worse. Niniane looked at Ceawlin's friend with troubled eyes. How could she explain that it was not the blow that was distressing her so much as the fear that Ceawlin would never forgive her for what she had done? She clasped her arms across her chest and said determinedly, "We will have the marriages first, then dinner. I am going to put it out in the dining room, as there is not room enough in the reception room to seat all these people. The thanes will have to serve themselves and eat standing up."

"Are you sure you are feeling all right?" the priest asked. "You should put a cold cloth on your face, Princess."

"I will," she answered. Then, "Sigurd, would you mind telling the thanes to come to the reception room in an hour? We will have the marriages then."

"All right," he answered, looked at her cheek with those hard eyes, and left the room.

Niniane and the priest were alone. "He is a pagan through and through, is he not?" Father Mal asked. He was not speaking of Sigurd.

"Yes," said Niniane, her voice low. "He is."

"Your duty is to your children, my daughter. You did right in having your son baptized." Then, carefully, "If you wish to remain at Glastonbury, I think that can be arranged."

"No!" Niniane stared at him with horrified eyes. "Leave Ceawlin, do you mean? I cannot do that, Father. I love him."

"He is a beautiful young man, my daughter, and I can see how a woman would find it easy to fall under his sway. But I must tell you that in remaining married to him you may well be endangering your immortal soul."

Niniane shook her head. "No, I cannot believe that. Ceawlin is a truly good man, Father." At the priest's look of skepticism she added impatiently, "Don't tell me no Christian man ever hit his wife!"

"I cannot tell you that, of course . . ."

"Well, I will tell you this," Niniane said passionately. "I would far rather live with a man like Ceawlin, who loses his temper and knocks me down, than with a 'good Christian' who rules by icy despotism and blights every honest emotion with his disapproval."

"Princess, I do not know of whom you speak, but I can assure you that the church does not wish to blight honest emotions."

"I'm sorry." Niniane pushed a shaking hand through her hair. "Forgive me, Father. I'm upset. I shall go and put some cold water on my face."

"Do that, my daughter," the priest said kindly. "In the meanwhile, I shall prepare to perform the marriages."

The evening seemed to Niniane to go on forever. Ceawlin did not return for either the marriages or the feast, and Sigurd had to make the gift pledges over the beer cups. Niniane's cheek bore a distinct bruise, and while no one asked her about it, there were a great many speculative looks.

"I will let the beer cups be filled one more time," Sigurd said to her when the platters of food were empty. "We must all be fit to ride in the morning."

"Thank you, Sigurd." She smiled at him. "You are a good friend." She looked around the room, filled with the noise of male voices and male laughter. "I am going to go feed the baby now. I will be back later."

He nodded. She could feel him watching her as she made her way out of the room.

Her bedroom door was closed. Niniane frowned. It was always left open when the baby was there by himself, so that if he cried, someone might hear. She pushed the door open softly, so as not to wake him if he were sleeping, and stopped in surprise as she saw that someone had come into the room before her. It was Ceawlin. He was standing beside the baby's basket, looking down at his son, a distinctly apprehensive expression on his face. Niniane suddenly understood. He was looking for some outward sign of the baptism.

"Ceawlin," she said softly, and came into the room, closing the door behind her.

His head came up and he gave her a wary, almost hunted look. Her heart swelled with compassion. "Nothing has happened to Cerdic, I promise you. He is just the same as he always was."

"If that is so, then why did you need to have him baptized?"

"It is for the afterlife, not for this life. If he is baptized, then he may go to heaven when he dies."

"I don't care about the afterlife," he said. "I care about this life. I care about fulfilling my fate in this life. And that is what I care about for my son."

"That has not been changed. His destiny, his fate, whatever that is, has not been changed by the baptism. He still has all his strength, all his power."

"A king must answer for his people, must stand between his people and the gods."

She drew a long breath. "You believe in many gods, I in one. Whatever Cerdic believes, he will be able to answer for his people. He will be a king. He is your son, Ceawlin. Nothing can change that."

He turned away from the basket and went to look out the window. After a minute she followed him. She put her arms around his waist and laid her cheek against his back. He stiffened but did not pull away. "I don't want you to go to Glastonbury," he said. "I do not trust that priest."

"All right. If you don't want me to go, I won't."

There was a long silence. She kept her arms around him and closed her eyes, feeling the strong muscles under her uninjured cheek. "Perhaps I could go to Coinmail," she said doubtfully.

He turned around, freeing himself, and looked down at her. The pale light from the dying day illuminated her face and the bruise on her cheek. "No."

She searched his eyes, trying to read his thoughts. "I will stay with the women in Glastonbury," she offered. "I will swear not to let the priests do aught else to Cerdic."

His face was closed. "You will swear?"

"Yes."

"All right," he said after a minute. "You may go to Glastonbury."

They were standing close to each other but not touching. "It is just that I cannot think of anywhere else," she explained. "I do not want to go, Ceawlin." Her white teeth bit into her slightly chapped lower lip. "I wish I could go with you."

He sighed, as if a hard vise that had been squeezing his lungs had just given way. "Nan," he said. He touched her cheek with his forefinger. Gently. "Did I hurt you?"

"Oh, Ceawlin." Great tears brimmed in her eyes. "I did not want to disobey you. It was just . . . I *had* to." She flung her arms around him and began to cry.

"It's all right," he said. Very briefly his cheek came down to touch the top of her head. "Stop crying, Nan. It's all right." Then, "Look, now, you've waked the baby."

Chapter 21

W HEN Edric marched into Bryn Atha the following day, he found it deserted save for a few female slaves. The slaves were East Saxons and remarkably stupid; all they knew was that the prince had come to Bryn Atha several days ago and taken the princess away. Where he had taken her, they did not know.

Edric set fire to the house and the stable and the storage barns before leaving, in a fury, to wreak the same vengeance on the tribe who had dared to shelter his enemy. The day was hot and the air was still thick with smoke from the burning buildings when the Winchester war band began its march along a forest track that gave promise of leading them somewhere. The Saxons had gone but a mile when, out of the trees on either side of the path, came an unexpected shower of arrows. The thanes shouted and cursed as they raised their shields to protect themselves from the death that was flying toward them from the wood.

"Go after them!" Edric shouted, and several thanes began to run toward the forest, toward the men they knew must be hidden in the summer foliage of the trees. A new barrage of arrows flew through the greenish air and found their targets. Those thanes still standing retreated.

"We must get under cover!" one of the eorls shouted to Edric.

"Make a shield wall!" Edric shouted. "Those in the middle, hold the shields over your heads." The thanes crowded together on the track, which, even when they jammed together, was only wide enough to hold three abreast. They formed a long line, shields turned outward, middle shields overhead. The arrows continued to fly for perhaps another minute; then there was nothing. The thanes searched the wood, shields up, javelins at the ready. They found no one. Finally Edric called his men back to the path. They had four dead from arrows and two wounded.

"We will return to Bryn Atha," Edric said bitterly. "If we go on, we are likely to find the same ambush waiting for us up ahead." Then, as the war band began to retrace its steps, "Name of the gods, when will we find an enemy to fight?"

*   *   *

Summer passed into autumn. Edric quartered his war band in the old Roman houses in Calleva and the eorls quarreled among themselves as to what course they ought to pursue: return to Winchester or continue the hunt for Ceawlin. The Saxons were disgusted by the progress, or the lack of progress, of the war. They had lost over one-fifth of their own men and, so far as they knew, had not wounded Ceawlin in the least.

Edric finally prevailed. "If we allow him to go free, he may very well rouse more of the British to join him. Then we will be facing him outside the gates of Winchester." The truth of this statement was reluctantly acknowledged by the other eorls. Edric's proposal also won reluctant approval: "Our first step," said Edric, "must be to lure him out of the hills, where he is safe. He cannot stand against us in battle. If he could, he would not be running and hiding like a fox with the hounds on its tail."

After a great deal of discussion, the eorls finally agreed on a plan. They would lure Ceawlin out of the hills by pretending to return to Winchester. Then, when the prince had been fooled into thinking himself safe, they would fall on him and cut him to pieces.

It was a day of unusual warmth for October when the scouts Ceawlin had posted to keep watch on the Saxons in Calleva came galloping into Bryn Atha. Ceawlin had been at the villa for the last month, for almost all the while the Saxons had been at Calleva. He had kept his thanes from idleness by having them rebuild the parts of Bryn Atha that Edric had burned, but the time had dragged. Now it seemed something was finally going to happen.

The news was even better than Ceawlin had hoped. "My lord," said Bertred, one of the two scouts who had returned to report, "Edric has put all his men on the road to Winchester. It seems they are going home!"

Ceawlin looked toward Calleva, as if he could see the road from where he stood. "Are you sure?" he asked, and then looked again at Bertred.

"Yes, my lord. We watched them for at least ten miles before we came back here to report to you."

Ceawlin let out his breath. "Well, that is good news, indeed. They must be going into winter quarters at Winchester. They have done nothing in the north for the last month, that is for certain."

"They made themselves comfortable at Calleva, Prince, I can tell you that." It was Ine, Bertred's fellow scout, speaking. "They had wagon loads of food brought in from the vils near Winchester. I doubt they have taken it back with them."

Ceawlin cocked an eyebrow. Edric had burned Bryn Atha's storehouses, and extra food would be needed for the winter. "Perhaps we ought to pay a visit to Calleva," Ceawlin said.

Ine grinned. "There will be women there too. They came from all around this last month, once word got out that the gold-rich Winchester thanes were at Calleva."

"A further enticement," said Ceawlin. "Food and women. Most certainly we shall march for Calleva."

Ceawlin's men rode into Calleva late on the morning of October 22 and found the city as Ine had said, well stocked with food. There was beer as well, and the thanes broke open a barrel almost immediately. Most of Calleva's residents, having experienced one Saxon invasion, stayed inside their houses with the doors locked. As Ceawlin had given orders that none of the British in the city were to be harmed, they were left largely undisturbed. Of far more interest to Ceawlin than the impoverished British were the sackfuls of grain he and Sigurd discovered stacked in the Christian church.

Ine had been right about the women as well as the food. There was a gratifying number of British and Saxon whores in the city who had gravitated to Calleva in the hope of earning gifts from Edric's men. These entrepreneurs seemed perfectly ready to offer their services to Ceawlin's thanes, and by and large the offers were enthusiastically accepted. Between the beer and the women, the thanes were in no mood to load sacks of grain, and Ceawlin prudently decided to give them a day and a night before reminding them of their real reason for coming into Calleva.

He was standing on the steps of the forum, contemplating the grid of city streets lined with Roman houses, when a feminine voice said to him in Saxon, "My lord, would you care to come and see my room?"

Ceawlin looked down to the step below him and saw a girl with corn-colored hair and long-lashed blue eyes gazing up into his face. When she saw she had gotten his attention she smiled. "It is not far," she added enticingly.

He had not had a woman in months, not since Niniane had left for Glastonbury. This girl was extremely lovely and his body let him know, instantly, that her offer was very welcome. Without thinking, he put out a hand and touched her sunny hair. She lowered her lashes and gave him a long, seductive look. "Follow me, my lord," she murmured, certain from his gesture that she had won a customer. He moved down a step to stand beside her, but then, when she turned to lead him further, he stopped.

He was surprised by his actions himself. Don't be a fool, he told himself impatiently as he stood irresolute beside the golden-haired whore. You need a woman. Niniane will never know. Then, when still his feet did not move: It could be years until you see her again. Do you intend to remain celibate the whole time?

The girl was looking at him out of puzzled eyes. "My lord?" she said when still he did not follow.

It was impossible. Of course he could not stay away from other women. It was ridiculous even to contemplate such an idea.

But the irrational, instinctive, superstitious part of him was saying something else, was saying that Niniane was his luck, that if he betrayed her, then his luck might betray him. He remembered suddenly the words she had whispered to him as he saw her off on the road to Glastonbury. She had been sitting on the quietest horse they had in the stable, holding Cerdic in her arms. "When next I see you," she had whispered as she bent down to kiss him good-bye, "perhaps you will have another son."

No other woman had given him a child. Niniane had given him Cerdic and she would give him more children. He was certain of it.

He moved back up to the top step. "No," he said to the girl, and smiled to soften the rejection. "I cannot, sweetheart. Someone must keep watch on the road, I'm afraid, and I appear to be the only one sober enough for the job." Then he turned away from her and went down the steps on the opposite side.

Ceawlin scowled furiously as he walked along the main street of Calleva toward the city walls. He was sure he had been a fool. His body was telling him he had been a fool. He almost turned and went back to find the girl. But he didn't.

He was standing on top of the city walls watching the road when Sigurd joined him an hour later. He could tell from Sigurd's rumpled clothes that his friend had not been too scrupulous to enjoy the town's offerings. For some reason, this put Ceawlin more out of temper than ever. He glowered at Sigurd and said, "Is there a sober thane in the whole of this city?"

"I doubt it." Sigurd ran a hand through his disordered hair. "Why don't you join in the fun?"

"Someone has to keep watch on the road," Ceawlin returned disagreeably.

"I don't see why," Sigurd said. "It is evident that Edric is returning to Winchester. He would not have traveled so far south if he were not."

The ill temper left Ceawlin's face with startling abruptness, to be replaced by an alert look that Sigurd knew well. "He left too much food here," he said to Sigurd, but absently, as if he were not paying attention to his own words.

Sigurd's eyes had followed Ceawlin's, but he could not see whatever it was that had brought that look to the prince's face. "What is it—?" he was beginning when Ceawlin suddenly swore.

"It's Edric," Ceawlin said, his voice cold and hard. "By the hammer of Thor, Sigurd. It's Edric. And he's got us trapped." Ceawlin swore again.

Still Sigurd could see nothing, but he did not doubt Ceawlin's word. The prince's vision was legendary among his men. The blood rushed to Sigurd's head, then drained away. He felt instantly sober. "What shall we do?" he asked.

"Get the men out of here," Ceawlin answered. "Now, Sigurd! There is no time to waste."

Sigurd grabbed Ceawlin's arm as the prince turned to leave the wall, forcing Ceawlin to swing around to look at him. "You go," Sigurd said with deadly seriousness. "I mean it, Ceawlin. Save yourself. The men are all at least half-drunk; you won't be able to move them fast enough. I'll try to rally them, do the best I can to clear them out of Calleva, but you must leave now. You are the one we cannot afford to lose."

"No," said Ceawlin, and pulled his arm out of Sigurd's grip. "We'll all get out of here together. Now, come on!"

Sigurd was never afterward quite sure how Ceawlin pulled his men away from the beer and the girls, but somehow he did it. Within fifteen minutes the entire war band was in the saddle. They took the north gate out of Calleva but ten minutes before Edric marched in through the gate from the south. Ceawlin's men were still clearly visible from the city walls as they fled northwest along the road toward Corinium. Edric, who had initiated a mounted troop himself since the summer, took off in hot pursuit, his horsemen first, his foot following after.

Within an hour, dark had fallen. "If they continue on this road," Onela said to Edric as the two eorls rode through the night, "the road will take them into British territory. Not friendly British territory, either."

Edric grunted. "He must turn toward the hills. It is his only chance. He cannot afford to get himself caught between the British in Corinium and us."

"He is probably heading toward the Badon pass again," said Onela grimly. "He will do the same thing to us he did once before, Edric. Take the pass from one side of the hills to the other, only this time he will be going in the opposite direction."

"I think that is what he will try to do," Edric agreed.

"He will escape us once more!"

"Not this time." Edric glanced back at the horsemen riding behind him. "I have taken care to learn the territory this time, Onela. The Corinium road here goes north as well as west, but Ceawlin will have to keep to it until he reaches the place where he can cut south for the pass. I propose to cut off the road now, onto a track that goes due west along the line of the hills. When Ceawlin turns south to head for the pass, we will be there before him."

Onela thought for a minute, playing out in his mind the strategy Edric had just described. Then, slowly: "Very good, Edric." Another pause. "Very good!" He gave a distinctly unpleasant laugh. "What a shock for the bastard, to find us in front of him when he will have thought us behind."

"Yes," replied Edric. "So I hope."

Onela was thinking further. "He will try to turn and run," he said. It was too dark to see his face, but Edric could hear the frown in his voice.

"We will post some men in position just off the road," Edric explained. "He will not see them in the dark and they will let him pass. But if he turns to run, he will find his way out blocked."

Onela laughed. "Trapped," he said. "The fox will finally be trapped."

"Exactly." Edric turned and called to the scout who was riding behind him.

"The track we must take is just up ahead, my lord," said the man, a Saxon, one of his own thanes whom Edric had dispatched weeks ago to spy out just this territory for just this purpose. This time he was not going to rely on the trustworthiness of a British farmer.

"Very good," said Edric. "You may take the lead, Wiglaf. We will follow."

It was pitch dark as Ceawlin's men rode along the road toward Corinium. Sigurd had long since come to the conclusion that Edric had just detailed for Onela. They would have to cut off the road and head south to the hills, to the Badon pass. He said as much to Ceawlin.

"That is what Edric will expect us to do," came the grim reply.

"But he is behind us," said Sigurd. "What can it matter if he guesses, so long as we outrun him? Once we are on the other side of the hills, we are in friendly territory, Atrebates territory, territory we know. We do not know the hills around here, Ceawlin."

"But suppose Edric does."

The night was dark and Ceawlin was but a shadowy figure to Sigurd, who was riding close beside him. The thanes behind them were silent. Silent, sober, and weary. The only sound in the night was the crunching of their horses' hooves on the gravel of the road.

"What do you mean?" asked Sigurd slowly.

"I mean that Edric planned this trap very carefully. He knew I have him watched, made sure I would think he was going to Winchester, made sure my thanes knew there were food and women in Calleva. It was a pretty certain thing I would come into Calleva once I thought he had left."

Sigurd strained to see an expression on Ceawlin's face, but saw only the shadow of his profile. "So he came back, hoping to catch you in Calleva. He almost did, too. If you had not been watching the road . . ."

He could just see that Ceawlin was shaking his head. "I'm sure he would have liked to catch me in Calleva. But I am equally sure he had made contingency plans in case he did not. If I were Edric, that is what I would have done."

"Edric is not as smart as you."

"Edric is not stupid, however. And he had time to plan this out. He was in Calleva for a whole month."

"Well, what are you afraid of, then, Ceawlin?" asked Sigurd impatiently.

"I am afraid that Edric has found a way to get between us and the hills," came the devastatingly simple reply.

"Name of the gods," said Sigurd.

"Yes."

Silence fell again. Behind him Sigurd heard one of the thanes complain to the man riding beside him that he felt sick to his stomach. "What are we going to do?" he asked Ceawlin at last.

"Turn around," came the unexpected reply.

"Turn around?"

"Yes." And, suiting action to words, Ceawlin halted Bayvard. "'We're going back!" he shouted to the men behind him.

A babble of protest greeted his words.

"Keep quiet and listen to me," Ceawlin said, his voice pitched just loud enough to carry to the last line of horse. "I think Edric is cutting between us and the hills. If we return to Calleva, we will avoid him."

"And if he is not cutting between us and the hills, we will run straight into him on the road." It was Penda. Sigurd recognized his voice.

"I don't think we will," said Ceawlin. "We go back."

The war band opened ranks to let Ceawlin and Sigurd pass through. Then they turned resignedly to follow their leader back along the road to Calleva.

For the next two hours the two war bands marched parallel to each other but heading in opposite directions. Edric, straining to catch a glimpse of Ceawlin in front of him striking south toward the hills, had no idea that the prince was in fact retracing his steps eastward to Calleva. It was not until he had waited a whole day at the Badon pass that Edric conceded that once again Ceawlin had managed to outmaneuver him.

For his part, Ceawlin did not allow his men to stop in Calleva to rest, but made them push on toward the west until they were safe in the friendly territory of the hills they knew. As his exhausted men dropped to the ground to sleep, Ceawlin prepared to take the first watch himself.

It occurred to him, as he posted himself on a convenient rock and tried to get comfortable, that if he had accepted the golden-haired girl's offer, Edric would have caught him in Calleva.

Once again Niniane had proved to be his luck.

Niniane sat on a stone bench and looked at the great mound of Glastonbury Tor outlined against the blue February sky. She had been looking at the Tor for months now, she was sick of looking at it, but it was the most imposing part of all the landscape surrounding Glastonbury. It drew one's eyes like a magnet, no matter where one was within the monastery grounds.

The sun felt warmer today, she thought. Winter was ending. Soon it would be spring; the season for war. Her eyes moved from the Tor to search for her son. She had brought him out into the garden with her for some fresh air and given him a trowel to dig with in the still-winter-hard dirt . . . no, he had found a mud puddle. He saw her looking at him and gave her a beatific smile before he squished his hand once more into the mud. Niniane winced, then laughed. Let him play, she thought. It was good for him to be outdoors again.

The child within her kicked and she shifted on her hard seat, then stood up. Cerdic was enthralled with his mud and she walked to the edge of the garden, folded her arms, and stared at the stone building that housed the religious women of Glastonbury who had given her refuge these last months.

They had been so kind to her. And all she wanted to do was to leave. To go home. Home to Bryn Atha and to Ceawlin.

The baby was restless today. He must sense his mother's mood, she thought, and sighed.

Niniane had not been surprised to learn for certain that she was again with child. She had known it since the very hour of the babe's conception: the night before she had left Bryn Atha for Glastonbury; the night of the weddings; the night she and Ceawlin had made up their quarrel over Cerdic's baptism. It had been a night of furious passion and she could swear she had felt it then, in her womb, the beginning of the new life they had made out of their love.

During the months of her stay at Glastonbury, Niniane had come to be deeply grateful for her children, both the one born and the one yet unborn. Cerdic filled her days with his needs. If she had not had him, she thought she would have gone mad. It was not the spareness of her accommodations that she found so difficult, although the good women lived a life that was Spartan indeed. It was the lack of something to do. She had grown accustomed to days that did not seem to have enough hours in them; in Glastonbury the days seemed to go on forever.

She prayed, of course, with the sisters and by herself. She tried very hard to fix her mind on God, particularly since she had such need of his blessing. But one thing her time in Glastonbury had shown her was how woefully worldly a person she truly was. She missed the busy life of Bryn Atha. She missed the striving for the future, missed the plotting and the planning she had thought she so disliked. She even missed the thanes, missed the constant effort to feed them and clothe them, missed the sound of male voices and male laughter. The monks within the abbey observed a vow of silence.

Most of all, she missed Ceawlin. She missed him and she fretted about her lack of information as to what was happening in Wessex. Glastonbury was in Dumnonia, and Dumnonia was still British, had always been British. The only communication Dumnonia had with the Saxon kingdoms was through the monks who went out from the Christian center of Glastonbury to minister to the Christian Britons in the Saxon-occupied lands to the east. And these monks were interested in bringing the sacraments to souls in need; they were not interested in the political squabbles of the Saxon overlords.

So Niniane was grateful for Cerdic, and grateful as well to be having another baby. As her body became heavier, slower, her bed did not seem so terribly empty. Her body did not seem so terribly empty. Even her mind seemed to become slower, more attuned to the rhythms of her body than to the world outside. Pregnancy cocooned her, cushioned her, and she welcomed this dullness. She took care of one child and nutured the other within her body and tried very hard not to think beyond the moment.

Chapter 22

GUTHFRID sat close to the hearth in the queen's hall and stared broodingly into the flames. By common consent her women kept to the corner of the room even though it was cold away from the fire. When the queen looked like this, it was better to be cold than to risk the heat of her wrath.

Guthfrid's thoughts were running along a too-familiar path. It was now more than two years since Ceawlin had fled from Winchester, and still he went free. Still he lived. It ate away at her, that knowledge. Guthfrid was Saxon to her very marrow, and would never lay Edwin to rest until she had had vengeance on his murderer.

The men were at the temple celebrating the Saxon spring festival, making offerings to the gods for the peace and the victory of the king. The war band was to leave Winchester within the next few days, to go north once again to try to capture Ceawlin. The eorls had been reluctant at first, but Guthfrid had been the one to point out that they would never be able safely to claim the rich lands of the Atrebates unless they had first got rid of the bastard. This had made sense to the land-greedy eorls and they were preparing to march yet again to Calleva.

The messenger came into Winchester while the men were still at the sacrificial banquet in the temple, so he delivered his unwelcome news to the queen. After all these months, Cutha had been seen, and seen leading a war band of some fifty or so men.

"Seen where?" Guthfrid demanded as the man paused to catch his breath.

"On the road south of Venta, my lady. Riding north. He is coming from Wight."

The news took longer to reach Ceawlin. It was the end of March before he learned that Cutha had reappeared in the south. "He must join with me," Ceawlin said to Sigurd, his eyes the intense blue-green they always turned with strong emotion. "By the hammer of Thor, if I can put my hand on fifty more men, I can face Edric. At last!"

"Why did we not think of Wight?" Sigurd asked. "My father has kin still in Wight. Witgar, the king, is his cousin. Witgar is *your* cousin,

Ceawlin. Your father and his father were brothers." Sigurd ran his hand through his light brown hair. "Why did we not think of Wight?" he asked again.

Ceawlin was pacing up and down the room. "Cutha may not be a great battle leader, but he is cunning when it comes to intrigue," he said over his shoulder, and did not notice Sigurd's frown. "I might have known he would not give up so easily!" Ceawlin stopped his pacing long enough to give Sigurd a crooked grin.

Sigurd did not answer the smile but said, his face still stern, "How do you mean to reach him?"

"I will ride south to meet him," came the instant reply. "No more waiting around for Cutha to come to me. This time *I* will go to him."

The following day, Ceawlin, with a war band that now numbered more than sixty men, left Bryn Atha and headed south toward Winchester.

The larks were trilling overhead in a clear blue sky on the day the war bands of Ceawlin and Cutha finally joined together. Cutha had avoided Venta and Winchester on his march north from Wight, gone west toward the Salisbury plain and then turned toward the northeast to pick up the Corinium road. After more than a week Ceawlin's scouts had located him, and the prince, who had come farther south, turned his own war band north and west to catch up with Cutha near to Anbyrg.

Ceawlin's thanes made camp in the same meadow as Cutha's, and Ceawlin, Sigurd, Cutha, and Cuthwulf sat down to talk. There was a strong breeze blowing and the wind whipped Ceawlin's thick, fine hair about like flax as he sat with his back against his saddle and talked to Cutha. The hair was as Cutha remembered it, but the face had changed. When last he had seen Ceawlin the prince had been a pink-cheeked beardless boy. Ceawlin's face was thinner these days, thinner and harder, and his cheeks were no longer pink. The close-clipped beard he now wore was the same impossibly fair color as his hair. The eyes had not changed; they were still the deep blue-green that was his legacy from his father.

"I have fifty-three men with me," Cutha said in response to Ceawlin's question. "After the . . . affair at Banford, I knew I would need more men if I was to be of any use to you. I was no older than you when I left Wight with your father, Ceawlin, but I have kin still on the island. They gave me a fair greeting."

"We could not imagine where you had gone," Ceawlin answered. "I tried for months to get word of you, but you seemed to have fallen off the map." He showed his teeth in a very white smile. "Nevertheless, I had a feeling you would reappear again someday, Cutha."

"Of course," said Cutha with cool composure.

"I hear you have been playing fox and hounds with Edric all this last year," boomed Cuthwulf.

Ceawlin's eyes moved from Cutha to his son. "I had little choice, cousin. I did not have enough men to face him in open battle."

"Well, now you do," said Cuthwulf, and showed his teeth.

"And now I do." Ceawlin finished with Cuthwulf and looked back to Cutha. "How many of your band are from Wight?"

"Thirty-seven."

The blue-green gaze was uncomfortably hard. "And what have you promised them?"

Cutha's highly arched eyebrows rose even higher. "Land. There is little land left on Wight or on the southern coast that belongs to Wight. Most of these men are young, Ceawlin, young and land-hungry."

"Thanes?"

"Ceorls, mostly," came the somewhat reluctant reply.

"So they know nothing of fighting."

"They know enough." Cutha's voice was sharp. "Enough to wield a sword and throw a spear."

"Ine made it to Bryn Atha after Banford, Father," Sigurd put in. "He and some fourteen others."

"I am glad to hear that," said Cutha. "I had hoped that that was what they would do. I myself deemed it best to go south, to recruit another war band to bring to Ceawlin's assistance." Sigurd understood that his father's pride had not allowed him to come to Ceawlin with fewer than the men he had originally raised. He hoped fervently that Ceawlin understood that too and would deal with Cutha carefully.

It seemed as if Ceawlin had read his thought, for now he grinned at Cutha and said, "My father always said you had the sharpest brain in Winchester, cousin. It was an inspired thought, to go to Wight. Your men are most welcome."

Cutha's eyebrows returned to their usual level and his thin, dark face relaxed as he returned Ceawlin's smile. "It is time for the true King of the West Saxons to claim his right," he said.

"We will all agree to that," said Sigurd fervently, and Ceawlin laughed and got to his feet. "Come," he said to the others, "I am starving. Let us go and get some food."

Ceawlin led his combined war band back to Calleva and spent a few weeks drilling the new recruits from Wight. Then the word he had been waiting for finally came: Edric had left Winchester and was marching north. His war band totaled, according to Bertred's report, some two hundred and fifty men.

Ceawlin had just over a hundred, but still the ratio was the best he had had in two years, and he was determined to confront Edric in open battle this time. He had, during the course of his travels around Wessex the previous spring, spied out a few likely battlegrounds, and now he decided he would go south toward Searo byrg. This was the scene of Cynric's first victory in his conquest of Wessex, and Ceawlin, always superstitious when it came to his luck, decided it should be the place where Cynric's son would make the throw for his father's crown.

Edric, learning that Ceawlin had left Calleva for the west, thought that the prince was once more on the run. This time, however, Ceawlin would be slowed by the new recruits from Wight, who did not have horses. This time Edric thought he could catch the prize that had eluded him for so long. Accordingly, he pushed his men onward relentlessly, west of the Corinium road, along the ancient track that led toward the Salisbury plain and the already historic village of Searo byrg.

It was early in the afternoon of May 18 when Ceawlin's war band reached Searo byrg. According to the scout reports, Edric was a day's march behind them, time enough to give Ceawlin the chance to reconnoiter the land and make his battle dispositions.

It was not for superstitious reasons alone that Ceawlin had chosen Searo byrg as the scene for this battle. The site had distinct advantages for an army that was outnumbered by its enemy. Searo byrg was less well known for its village, which consisted merely of an old Christian church, a smithy, and an inn, than it was for being one of the chief fords over the river Avon in the area. The ford was located just northwest of the village, and the ancient road which Ceawlin and his men had followed lay directly on either side of the Searo ford.

Just south of the ford was a hill, called by the local people Rom Hill. Rom Hill was steepest on the north side, which faced the ford, and fell off to a gentler slope on the east. It was on this hill that Ceawlin stationed his men, drawing them up into three commands and posting them in lines on the steep north slope so they would immediately be seen by anyone crossing the Searo ford. Edric would have to cross at the Searo ford. The spring had been a wet one and the banks of the river were boggy and marshy for miles at a stretch, making it impossible for Edric to cross the Avon upriver and steal in on Ceawlin's flank. The only way across the river this time of year was at Searo byrg.

Ceawlin's men remained on the hill for the rest of the day, ready but relaxed, as no one expected to see Edric before the morrow. Dusk fell and scouts came in to report that Edric's war band was but six miles away. Ceawlin posted sentries to keep watch during the night, taking no chances on a surprise night attack.

Sigurd slept but fitfully and was awake before almost everyone else. The sky was growing lighter but there was no sign of the sun. The visibility would be poor, Sigurd thought with dismay, and it was so essential that Edric see the men on the hill.

The hour advanced but the light remained poor. Sigurd watched Ceawlin as he walked up and down the lines of men, speaking to individual thanes as he went. He left a trail of laughter in his wake, but when he came up to Sigurd his face was sober.

"At last," said Sigurd, trying to keep his voice light. "Did you think this day would never come?"

His answer was a brief wry smile.

"I wish it were lighter!" Sigurd said, staring toward the mist that covered the river.

"If the mist does not clear, I will change our plans. The mist will favor us too, Sigurd. Do not worry." Ceawlin touched his shoulder, a reassuring pat, and turned away to walk over to Penda.

The mist began to lift, and within half an hour Sigurd was able to see the river. He was talking to the ceorls from Wight, joking and telling stories to hearten them, when there came a cry from the front: "My lord!" Sigurd turned instantly to look toward the river. The first line of Edric's men had appeared on the opposite shore.

Sigurd knew what the battle plan was, had approved it heartily when Ceawlin outlined it yesterday upon their arrival in Searo byrg. They all realized, of course, that Edric was sure to know that he outnumbered the prince by more than two to one. "He will not charge the hill," Ceawlin had said to Sigurd and Cutha and Cuthwulf as they stood together on the hill yesterday watching the ford. "He is not fool enough to give me that advantage. I wager he will try to bypass the north slope of Rom Hill and come at it from the east, where the ground is less steep," and Ceawlin pointed out the way he meant. "What Edric will not know," Ceawlin continued, "is that in marching east he will be marching into a bog."

They had stared at the ground beneath them as if mesmerized. "Not a good position to fight from," Cutha said at last, his face and his voice expressionless.

"No. Not a good position." Ceawlin then had gone on to detail the rest of his plan. They would fight under three commands. Cutha and Cuthwulf would have the thanes from Banford under them. To Sigurd, who would fight on the left, Ceawlin had given the best of the thanes from Bryn Atha—and the inexperienced ceorls from Wight. Ceawlin himself had taken the remaining Bryn Atha thanes and the Britons for the center.

Sigurd looked at the men lined up behind him now and gave them an encouraging grin. He was pleased to see Penda had taken his position on the far left. His strong presence would discourage any thoughts the inexperienced ceorls might have of breaking and running. The men all stood quietly and watched Edric's men crossing the ford. As Ceawlin had expected, Edric did not come toward the north face of the hill, but swerved to the right, to come at the hill from the gentler slope on the east. Ceawlin called to his leaders, and the line on the hill promptly swung around to face the direction from which Edric would now be coming.

The sky was still gray and promised rain, but the visibility was now fairly decent. There was dead silence on the hill as all eyes were trained on the marching war band below them. Sigurd saw Edric's thanes hit the bog, saw them waver and then halt.

For a brief moment Sigurd held his breath. What would Edric do? Would he come on or would he go back, perhaps try the hill from the north? Perhaps retreat until he could meet Ceawlin on better ground?

Edric was coming on, his men marching more slowly as the ground softened and pulled at their feet. Sigurd could feel the quiver of excitement from the men behind him. The scent of the battle was in their nostrils. He looked at Ceawlin but the prince was still, eyes trained on the war band below. He had told them yesterday that he did not want to charge until the enemy was directly below them. If they did not wait, the chance of being outflanked by Edric's larger numbers was too great.

A loud battle cry from the far right of their line caused Sigurd to jump. Then he stared in utter astonishment as his father and his brother went charging down the hill followed by the thanes of their command.

Sigurd's eyes flew to Ceawlin and saw a look of absolute fury on the prince's face. Sigurd's heart dropped into his stomach. What was his father thinking of? Ceawlin had told him distinctly to wait. . . .

His eyes went compulsively back to the charging Saxons, and as he watched, they smashed into the line on Edric's left. The line broke under the force of Cutha's charge.

Penda shouted, "Shall we go too?"

"No," Sigurd called back firmly. "Not until the prince gives the signal."

One of Edric's men was shouting furiously, trying to rally his men. Even at this distance, Sigurd recognized the gray head of Onela. The Winchester thanes began to reform on either side of Cutha's command; Ceawlin's men were now in danger of finding themselves surrounded.

"Sigurd!" Ceawlin shouted. "Get all the way to their right and press them toward the center. Now!"

Sigurd raised his sword, shouted first to Penda, then to the rest, and charged down the hill at Edric's right. As he ran, Sigurd saw that the battle-wise Winchester thanes were spreading their line thinner, to avoid being outflanked by Sigurd's men. Consequently the Winchester line was but three deep when Ceawlin and the Bryn Atha thanes hit it in the middle like an avalanche.

Edric's center crumpled like paper. Sigurd shouted with glee and began to close in from the right. On the opposite side of the battle, Cutha did the same. The thanes from Winchester wavered, then collapsed backward, turned, and ran for the ford.

Edric, the eorls, and the rest of the mounted men reached their horses, escaped across the ford, and headed back toward Winchester. Ceawlin's men pursued the men on foot, but they had been given orders earlier to capture and not to kill. Ceawlin wanted to begin his kingship with the blood of as few as possible on his hands. He ended the day with seventy men from the Winchester war band swearing to acknowledge him as their lord.

Next he marched for Winchester.

Edric had closed the gates and posted men with arrows on all the walls. Ceawlin camped outside the gate and prepared to conduct a siege. Edric could have but a few men inside Winchester with him, a few men and a large number of women. The food wagons that normally rolled into the royal enclave from the vils would be stopped. They could eat the horses, of course, and there would be vegetables from the gardens within, but come the fall the food would be gone. In the meanwhile, there was Venta close by to amuse his men, and all the food that would be stopped from going into Winchester.

Ceawlin settled down and prepared to wait.

Chapter 23

"CERDIC! Where are you, Cerdic?" Niniane peered around the corner of the chapel to the fields beyond. Where had that child gone to? And it was so cold . . . She pulled the folds of her cloak more closely around her and called once more. Never again would she entrust Cerdic to the care of that foolish serving girl.

There was little trouble Cerdic could get into around the monastery, but Niniane always feared the water. Glastonbury was virtually an island, with only one land bridge across the lake it sat within, and ever since Cerdic had begun to walk, Niniane had worried that he would fall into the water and drown. "Cerdic!" she called again, panic beginning to sound in the shrillness of her voice.

"Here, Mama." A small blond head peeked up from behind the woodpile. "I play in the wood," he said winningly as she strode across the chapel yard to grab him.

"You know you are not to go out of Riba's sight," Niniane scolded. "From now on you will have to stay with me. It seems I cannot trust you with anyone else."

His large blue-gray eyes, the same color as her own, looked up at her with blithe unconcern. Niniane held out her hand and he put his small, grubby paw into hers and walked beside her back toward the convent. It was a long time since Niniane had been able to carry this small, sturdy son of hers. At twenty-two months he was big for his age, and extremely independent. Too independent, she thought as she looked with a mixture of love and exasperation on the sunny golden head that seemed to reach higher against her with every passing day.

"Look, Mama," Cerdic said, and pointed. "What those men?" Niniane looked also and saw a group of horsemen riding over the land bridge and into the monastery grounds. With a great leap of her heart, she recognized the lead rider. It was Gereint. She began to run forward, dragging Cerdic along by the hand.

Gereint saw her coming as soon as his horse came off the bridge. He raised his hand to halt his men and dismounted to meet her. Niniane came to an abrupt halt about six feet from the young Briton, causing

Cerdic to trip and fall to his knees. She stared at Gereint out of fearful eyes, and waited.

"My lady," Naille's son said formally, "I have come to escort you back to Winchester to join the king." Then, as her eyes grew enormous, he grinned. "Edric surrendered three weeks ago. Ceawlin has exiled him and Guthfrid to East Anglia, where Guthfrid's father is king. It is all over, Niniane. Ceawlin is king."

Niniane moved forward again and flung herself into Gereint's arms. "I can't believe it," she kept repeating. "I can't believe it."

He was patting her on the back. "Believe it, for it is true. Ceawlin sent me to bring you to him at Winchester."

"Mama. Mama. Who that man? Mama . . ." Niniane finally heard her son's worried voice and let go of Gereint.

"Good God," said Gereint, looking down at the child, who was snatching at his mother's tan wool skirt. "This can't be Cerdic?"

"It certainly is Cerdic." Niniane wiped the tears from her eyes and Cerdic pushed himself between her and the Briton. "Go away," he said fiercely in British to Gereint. "Me no like you. You make my Mama cry."

"It's all right, my love," said Niniane, and knelt so she could look into his face. "I'm crying because I'm happy. This is Gereint and he has brought us good news. We are to go back with him to Winchester to join your father." And she smiled radiantly into the small face of her son.

"Oh," said Cerdic, unimpressed. His mother had told him much of his father, but Cerdic had no memory of Ceawlin at all. "Baby too?"

"Baby too."

"Baby?" asked Gereint.

Niniane turned the radiance of her face onto him and said, "Ceawlin has another son."

They had to take a litter because of the children. Ceawlin had sent Gereint and a British escort for obvious reasons, and Niniane's party encountered little difficulty as it passed through British Dumnonia on its way to the old Roman road that went from Aquae Sulis to Venta. The November weather was chill and damp, but Niniane kept the baby well-wrapped and within the relative shelter of the litter. The baby alternately ate and slept and gave his mother little trouble. The same could not be said for his older brother.

Cerdic hated the litter and he squirmed and complained and poked at the baby, of whom he was jealous, whenever Niniane was not looking. It was not until Gereint offered to take him up on his horse that Niniane had any peace from him. Thereafter he rode with Gereint until he was tired, and then he came into the litter and slept.

It was slow going and Niniane was heartily sick of the litter herself by the time they passed into Wessex. She would very much have liked to ride, but it was too cold to expose the baby to the wind, and she felt uneasy about leaving him alone. So she jolted along inside the litter, playing peekaboo games and singing to keep the baby amused and scolding Cerdic when he still took the occasional jealous swipe at his new little brother.

She learned the story of Ceawlin's campaign from Gereint when they stopped in the evenings to make camp.

"They besieged Winchester for six months?" Niniane asked incredulously when first she heard of Ceawlin's final tactic.

"Yes. There was no fighting, Niniane. Simply, Ceawlin starved them out."

"Dear God," said Niniane. "But there were women in Winchester!"

"I know." Gereint shrugged. "It wasn't easy on them, I fear. They all looked rather scrawny and hollow-eyed when finally it was over. But no one died. Or at least, very few."

Niniane thought of Nola and Hilda and all the girls from the bower. "Wasn't there any other way?"

"Edric could have ended it at any time. All he needed to do was surrender. Which he had to do in the end, anyway."

"But Ceawlin did not kill him?"

"No. He let the three of them go, Edric, Guthfrid, and Edgar. I thought he was wrong. But he said he did not want a blood feud with East Anglia and he was sure to have one if he killed Guthfrid. So he let them all go. Three of the eorls went with them, the ones who would not swear allegiance to Ceawlin."

"I'm glad," said Niniane. "Ceawlin was right. The Saxons have a terrible code of blood vengeance, Gereint. Ceawlin will be safer with Guthfrid alive than he would be if she were dead."

"I suppose so." Gereint was clearly unconvinced. "She is a very nasty woman. When she stared at Ceawlin she looked just like a snake."

Niniane shuddered. "I know. She hates him for killing her son Edwin. And Edwin tried to kill Ceawlin first, Gereint. I know. I was there and I saw it. So did almost everyone else in Winchester, including Guthfrid. But still she blames him, blames him and wants revenge. I don't think she will change until she is dead."

"Well, for the moment at least she is safe in East Anglia." Gereint smiled at her. "You will be the new queen, Niniane. How does it feel?"

"Ask me in a year," she replied, and at that he laughed.

Niniane did not want to enter Winchester in a litter, and so she rode the last few miles of the journey. Gereint had Cerdic before him on his horse and Niniane held the baby while Ferris walked before her holding the reins. Before she had moved from the litter she had combed her hair and washed her face. Her clothes were wrinkled and she smelled regrettably like the baby, but there was little she could do about that, she thought.

It had been one year and three months since last she had seen Ceawlin. She had longed for him during all that time, lived for nothing but the moment when they would be reunited, and now that that moment was at hand, she found she was afraid. A year was a very long time. What if he had changed, what if he had found another woman . . . ?

This was a subject she had refused to think about all during the time she had spent at Glastonbury, but now, with their reunion only a matter of moments away, she could think of nothing else.

He had been camped outside the walls of Winchester for six months, and Venta was only a mile away. If she had known that . . . She had not worried overly when she knew him to be at Bryn Atha, or flying around the countryside harassing Edric. But he had been near Venta for six months. Niniane knew why the thanes had gone so often to Venta, knew the kind of entertainment that was readily available in the city. She remembered Ceawlin's comment when she had balked about bringing women into Bryn Atha. "I have enough to keep me busy right here," he had said. But she had not been there this time to keep him busy. Perhaps he had found someone he liked better than her.

Stop this, she told herself. You are going to see your husband for the first time in over a year. You are bringing him a new baby. Do not ruin all your happiness by worrying about what may not ever have happened.

"There it is, my lady," said Gereint next to her. And she looked ahead and saw in the distance the great wooden stockade of Winchester. "It is hard to believe that a place like this has existed for nigh on twenty years and we knew nothing about it," he said.

"I know," Niniane replied. "I remember how I felt when first I saw Winchester." She went on to tell Gereint the tale of her first coming to the Saxon royal enclave, talking to keep herself from thinking, to keep herself from being afraid.

A few minutes later she interrupted herself to say, "They have seen us."

Gereint turned to look toward the gate. "Yes." Then, "Someone is coming to meet you."

A single horseman had ridden out through the gate, and she knew him instantly by the pale hood of his hair. He put his horse into a canter and Gereint's party stopped to wait. Niniane watched him come on, her heart thundering in her breast. The baby must have heard it, for he awoke from a sound sleep with a sharp cry of protest. Niniane shushed him and then Ceawlin was before her.

They stared into each other's eyes and for a moment neither spoke.

Then he looked at the bundle in her arms. "My lord," said Niniane with commendable steadiness, "will you take up your new son?"

He was off his horse and standing beside her before she had even seen him move. She bent to put the baby into his arms, and their faces touched. He looked into her eyes again, a quick brilliant look that held an unmistakable message. Her heartbeat was like a drumroll within her.

"Is that my father?" Cerdic asked Gereint. Ceawlin and Niniane had spoken in Saxon, but Cerdic spoke in British.

"Yes, lad," Gereint answered in the same language. "That is your father."

Ceawlin stared at his son. "Cerdic?" he asked.

"Cerdic," replied Niniane softly.

Ceawlin, still with the baby in his arms, walked over to stand beside Gereint's horse. "The last time I saw you," he said softly to the little boy in British, "you were a baby. Now you are a boy."

"Big boy," said Cerdic proudly.

Ceawlin grinned. "Very big."

"Me hate the litter," Cerdic said. "Want to ride the horse."

"Would you like to ride my horse with me?" Ceawlin asked.

Cerdic stared with big eyes at the splendid bay stallion his father was riding. "*That* horse?" he asked.

"That horse."

"Me want to ride that horse."

"All right," Ceawlin replied. "Let me give your little brother back to your mother, and you can ride Bayvard with me."

And so they rode in through the gates of Winchester together, Niniane with the baby in her arms, Cerdic seated before his father on Bayvard's back, pretending to steer with the ends of the reins.

Winchester looked just the same: the paved street, the great wooden halls. Niniane looked around, remembering, then turned to Ceawlin. "Where are you staying?" she asked.

He gave her a quick sidelong glance. "The king's hall," he replied.

Her breath caught and for the first time she took it in. The king's hall. It was really true. Ceawlin was really the king. A fear she had not yet thought of struck her heart. Did that mean she would have to live in the queen's hall?

"Ceawlin," she said in an urgent undertone, "I do not want to live in Guthfrid's hall."

They were alongside the temple now; the huge wooden pillar of Woden towered over the temple fence to their left. The great hall with its magnificent roof rose before them at the end of the road. "I am not going to put you in the queen's hall," he answered. "Guthfrid would be too . . . present."

"Yes," she answered fervently. That was it exactly. She would feel the contaminating presence of Cynric's queen in every nook and corner of that building. She knew it.

The horses were continuing their stately advance up the road. There were thanes in the great courtyard, many of whom Niniane recognized from Bryn Atha. She felt the eyes of all Winchester upon her, saw the smiles of greeting on both familiar and unfamiliar faces.

He would put her in the women's hall, then, where Fara had reigned. The women's hall and the bower. All the exotic marital arrangements of Winchester that had been so distant from her own marriage when they lived at Bryn Atha came rushing back into her memory. She bent to hide her face in the baby-softness of her infant son. Her heart felt like a stone in her breast. Dear God. How could she bear to live like that with Ceawlin?

"Here we are, Cerdic," she heard him saying to the child before him on Bayvard. "This is where you are to live." She felt her horse come to a halt and reluctantly she raised her head. They were in front of the king's hall. She turned her eyes to her husband.

"I thought we would be more comfortable living together," he said.

She smiled. The blood rushing to her head made her feel suddenly dizzy. His eyes had that look in them again. "Yes," she said, and laughed. Her laugh sounded dizzy too. "Much more comfortable."

There was a banquet in the great hall that night to celebrate Niniane's arrival in Winchester. Ceawlin sat in the king's high seat with his wife beside him, and for the first time Niniane bore the pledge cup around the hall, as Guthfrid used to do. Cutha had been given his old place at the king's side and Niniane proffered him the cup first. Sigurd, who had been placed next to Niniane, was the last guest she would come to, and he sat with his elbows propped upon the table and watched her as she circled the hall.

There was little outward change in her from the girl who had left Winchester three years before. She was as slender and fragile-looking as ever she had been; two children had not changed that. She wore her hair loose tonight, the fine, shimmering silk of it spilling all around her shoulders and down her back. She still held her small, lovely head like a flower on a stem. He watched her moving from thane to thane, greeting the men she knew with the gentle charm they all remembered so well from Bryn Atha. Then she was approaching him. She handed him the pledge horn and her fingers inadvertently touched his. She said something to him and he forced himself to smile and make a reply.

She took the horn back from him and looked at Ceawlin. Her eyes were like stars.

The harper sang. Ceawlin and Niniane listened gravely, but Sigurd noticed how they sat so that their shoulders touched. When the song was finished Ceawlin bent to say something into her ear, and when she replied, he covered her hand with his. Sigurd could see how her mouth had begun to tremble.

The wine cup went around and Sigurd drank deep. At last Niniane arose. "I won't be long," he heard Ceawlin murmur to her, and Sigurd watched dully as she left the hall. She walked beautifully. She had ever been the most graceful woman he knew.

Cutha offered Ceawlin more wine and Ceawlin laughed. "Not to-night," Sigurd heard him say. At that he turned and looked at his friend, at the king.

Ceawlin was not laughing any longer. He was looking at the door, looking at it as a hawk must look as it swoops down from the sky, ready to fall upon its prey. The look was there in his fiercely glittering eyes, the hard, severe line of his mouth. Sigurd drew a painful breath and said what he would never have said had he not been drunk. "If you go to her looking like that, you will frighten her half to death."

The glittering eyes turned toward him. "Looking like what?" Ceawlin asked.

"As if you were going to devour her."

"I am," Ceawlin answered, and his eyes did not change. Then, "Would you not feel the same if you were in my place?"

Sigurd felt the blood-red color rushing into his face. Ceawlin stared at him, eyes widening with sudden understanding. Sigurd stood up, backed away from that appalling recognition. Penda, on Sigurd's other side, said, "What is the matter?"

"I . . . I must relieve myself," Sigurd said wildly and, turning, weaved unevenly toward the rear door of the hall.

Penda looked across his empty place to Ceawlin. "What is wrong with him?" he asked.

"He's drunk too much, I think," Ceawlin replied somberly. Then, after a pause, "It is, after all, an occasion for celebration."

There was but one bedroom in the king's hall, and so Cerdic had been put to sleep on a bench near the hearth. The baby was asleep in his basket and Niniane was in the bed when Ceawlin came into the room.

"Ceawlin," she said as the door opened. "Ah, Ceawlin." Her voice trembled. An oil lamp was burning next to the bed and the room was soft with light. He saw that she had the blanket drawn over her breasts, but her shoulders were bare. The unease that his brief conversation with Sigurd had engendered disappeared in the flood of pure, uncluttered lust that swept through him at the sight of the pearllike sheen of those naked shoulders. He had waited for her for so long . . . for more than a year he had waited . . . too long. He walked to the bed and with a ruthless hand stripped the blanket away. She reached her arms up, her bright hair spilling over the white satin skin of her full breasts. He groaned deep in his throat and flung himself down onto the bed beside her.

They did not sleep that night, but made love, then talked, then made love, again and again. "The bed smells like sex," Niniane said as the lamp finally began to flicker and go out. "What will the handmaids think in the morning?"

Ceawlin yawned and stretched luxuriously. "They will think I was starved for it." He grinned at her through the tousled hair that had fallen across his face. "And they will be right."

Niniane leaned over and rained a shower of soft kisses along the line of his cheek. Then she sighed voluptuously and nestled her head into the hollow of his shoulder.

"Wait," he said. "I forgot. I've something for you." Reluctantly she moved so he could get out of the bed. He went to the chest in the corner and lifted something out. Her eyes widened when she saw what it was. A delicate circle of gold, beautifully engraved and set with precious jewels. It was the sort of rich adornment only a queen would wear, but Niniane had never seen it on Guthfrid. "I had it made in Venta," he said. "For you." His eyes were brilliant as he leaned over to place it on her long tangled copper-brown hair. "It is your morgengabe."

THE KING
(567–575)

Chapter 24

THE scop was singing of the coming of spring:

> The new year has come   to the dwellings of men
> Earth's lap is fair,   the sky roof shines bright
> The ring-prowed ship   drives over the water . . .

Sigurd listened to Alric's song, made in honor of Coenburg's wedding day, and let his eyes run idly around the great hall of Winchester. The benches were filled this bright May afternoon; eorls and thanes who had taken to living for at least part of the year on the lands given to them by the king had poured into Winchester this last week for the wedding of Cutha's daughter and Ceawlin's eorl, Penda. Even his brother Cuthwulf, who had been at odds with Ceawlin these last two years, had come into Winchester for Coenburg's day.

Sigurd looked at his sister's pretty flushed face and suddenly his mind flashed back eight years, to another day, another place, another marriage ceremony. It had been a Christian marriage ceremony, Penda's first one, performed by Father Mal at Bryn Atha. Sigurd remembered that day only too well. It had been the day before Ceawlin sent Niniane away to Glastonbury for safety, the day Ceawlin had first learned of his son's baptism, the day that Sigurd, for the first time in his life, had felt frightening rage burn in his heart against his friend.

Sigurd raised his wine cup and resolutely steered his mind away from such dangerous waters. Instead he remembered Penda's first wife, Wynne. How lovely she had been, he thought, and how brief her life . . . lost, as so many women's lives were lost, in childbirth. As he had almost lost his own wife two years before. They had told him after the birth of his twins that Edith would have no more children, and he had thought of Wynne and been glad. He bore enough guilt in his heart when it came to Edith; he did not want to bear the guilt of her death.

Alric's harp fell silent, and after a brief moment the hall rang with calls for yet another song. Sigurd watched as Penda bent his dark blond head to say something to Coenburg, saw his sister's swift shy smile in reply. This marriage had been Cutha's doing, Sigurd knew. It was a measure of how important Cutha thought Penda was, how important he thought Penda might become, that he had offered the young eorl his only daughter. Sigurd hoped Coenburg would be happy. Penda was not the most domestic of men. But then, one did not marry for happiness. One married for power. It was only the lucky ones who found something more.

Alric was gesturing toward the queen, and the noise in the hall rose even higher. Sigurd kept his eyes on the scop and saw the man holding out his harp. Then she was crossing the polished floor, her delicate cheeks flushed with color. Alric made her a bow and presented her with the harp. Sigurd looked quickly toward Ceawlin and saw him gesturing to the harper to join him on the high seat. Niniane touched the strings and the hall fell silent. After a moment her rich husky voice filled the room.

It was not often that Sigurd had such an excuse to look at her, and he stopped struggling, gave in to his need, and drank her in with his eyes.

She wore the gold circlet Ceawlin had given her when first she returned to Winchester, and her hair was loose, the way Sigurd liked it best. These days she usually wore it looped up and fastened on top of her head, but today it flowed around her shoulders and down her back, a shimmering mantle of autumnal silk. She wore a richly woven overgown of deep blue and there were jewels at her shoulders, throat, waist, and wrists. The garnets on her hands flashed in the torchlight as she moved her fingers on the harp strings.

Her figure was still slim and delicate-looking; as yet childbirth had not marked her. Yet she was not a girl any longer. Her face was thinner, her cheekbones more pronounced than they had been seven years before; her breasts were fuller, the breasts of a mother, not of a girl. The slightly wistful air that had so stirred his heart when first he met her was gone as well. There was a calm dignity about Niniane these days, the air of a woman who is accustomed to having her wishes obeyed. And there were four sons to sit around her hearth in the king's hall, four healthy sturdy heirs for Ceawlin.

The last note died away and she looked up from the harp, caught Sigurd's eye, and smiled. He moved his mouth in some kind of a response and watched as Alric came forward to claim his harp again.

"They say she can enchant people with her music," his wife said into his ear. "That it is witchcraft."

Sigurd swung around to stare into Edith's pale blue eyes. "Who says that?" he demanded.

She looked surprised by his vehemence. "The girls in the bower." Then, as he merely looked disgusted, "It is well known, Sigurd, that she has enchanted the king. And when our little Cutha was sick, Niniane played the harp and he grew better. And, too, her own sons are always so healthy. Surely it is enchantment."

"That is the most ridiculous thing I have ever heard." Sigurd was usually very kind to his young wife, but his eyes now were colder than she ever remembered seeing them. "I do not want to hear you say such a thing again, Edith. Do you understand me?"

"Yes, Sigurd." And her eyes filled with tears at his unusual abruptness.

The familiar guilt wrenched at his heart. It was not Edith's fault that he did not love her. It was not her fault that the very gentleness and sweetness that had attracted him to her in the first place had long since begun to cloy. As had her adoration. It had been so comforting at first, to find a woman who had eyes only for him; her love had soothed his ego as well as his heart. It was why he had married her, only to find out too quickly that it was not Edith's love he wanted. And now all he could feel for her was this miserable guilt. "Don't cry," he said more gently.

"I won't," she said, and her eyes brimmed over.

"What is the matter?" It was Cutha, who had noticed Edith's tears.

"Edith was just telling me some mad story that is going around the women's quarters," Sigurd said. "Something about Niniane having enchanted the king with her music."

Cutha's eyebrows drew together, making the ends seem to fly even higher. "Nonsense," he said.

"I know. But it could be dangerous nonsense, Father. I shouldn't like such a tale to reach unfriendly ears."

"Hmm." After a minute Cutha nodded. "I'll speak to Ceawlin." He gave his daughter-in-law an irritated look. "Do not cry, Edith. You were right to tell Sigurd of such a charge. Now, be a good girl and drink your wine."

Edith hastened to obey.

The priest put Coenburg's fingers into Penda's and tapped upon their joined hands with the sacred hammer of Thor. Then, with much laughter and encouragement to Penda, the eorls and thanes of Winchester escorted the bride and the groom from the great hall to the hall that Ceawlin had built for Penda when he had first named him an eorl five years before. Sigurd felt a brief flicker of sympathy for his sister as he saw her frightened eyes, but it had to be. And Penda would make it easy for her. One thing you could count on with Penda was his knowledge of women.

Sigurd found himself walking next to Ceawlin as the crowd of well-wishers returned to the great hall. The women had retired with the departure of the bride, but the men would continue to drink well on into the night. Behind him he heard Cuthwulf's drunken roar of laughter and suddenly Sigurd had no heart for it. "Edith said something to me today that I think you should know of," he found himself saying to Ceawlin.

"Oh?" Ceawlin cocked his silver-blond eyebrows in a familiar look of inquiry.

"It has to do with Niniane."

They walked in silence for a moment; then Ceawlin called to Ine, "I will be back later, Ine. The rest of you enjoy yourselves."

"We will, my lord!" came the boisterous reply.

"Come along with me to the king's hall," Ceawlin said to his friend. "Niniane will be putting the children to bed and we can be private."

The king's hall was indeed empty except for some servants and Ceawlin's old hound. Only their youngest child slept in the hall with Ceawlin and Niniane these days. At Ceawlin's insistence the older children and their nurses had been moved last year into the princes' hall.

"Get us some beer and then you can leave," Ceawlin said to the servants, and gestured Sigurd to a chair at Cynric's old table, which still stood in the middle of the room. When the cups of beer were before them and they were alone, Ceawlin turned to his friend and said, "What is this about Niniane?"

"It is some nonsense that Edith told me, but I thought you should hear it. They are saying in the women's hall that Niniane has enchanted you with her music."

Ceawlin's reaction was not at all what Sigurd had expected. The king threw back his head and roared with laughter.

"It may not be so funny if such a tale reaches unfriendly ears," Sigurd said when Ceawlin finally grew quiet.

"Do you mean Guthfrid?" Ceawlin took a long drink of beer. "Guthfrid has been saying far worse things about Niniane for years." The humor completely left his face. "It is not what Guthfrid says but what she does that concerns me."

"I know." Sigurd felt again the horror he had known last winter when they had apprehended a henchman of Guthfrid's right within the walls of Winchester. The man had been carrying poison, poison which he confessed was meant for the queen. Ceawlin had wanted to execute the man on the spot, but Niniane, with a scorn she was sure would infuriate Guthfrid even more, had sent the man back to East Anglia for Redwold, the East Anglian king, to deal with.

"You should have killed Guthfrid when you had the chance," Sigurd said.

Ceawlin shrugged. "I could not have won a war with East Anglia seven years ago, Sigurd. I had won Winchester, but any war band I put together at that point would have had divided loyalties. And if I killed Guthfrid, I would have had a war with East Anglia. Redwold accepted wergild from me for the death of Edwin, but he could not in honor have done anything but go to war if Guthfrid died. You know that."

Sigurd did know, and made no reply. Ceawlin suddenly pushed the cup away from him, stood up, and paced over to the hearth. The white boarhound raised its head from its paws at his master's approach. Ceawlin stooped to caress its long ears, then rose to his feet and began to poke at the fire. Sigurd watched him, comparing him in his mind with the Ceawlin of seven years ago, just as he had done with Niniane earlier in the great hall.

At twenty-seven, Ceawlin had lost all traces of his boyhood. His shoulders had broadened, the extreme slimness of adolescence turned into the lean, powerful strength of a mature man. His least conscious gesture bespoke the authority of a king who holds the power of life and death in the hollow of his hand. He was, as Bertred had once remarked to Sigurd, as close to being a god as a man was ever likely to get.

"I wanted to talk with you about Niniane too, Sigurd," he said at last over his shoulder. He put down the stick with which he had been stirring the fire. "You may have noticed we have been at odds of late."

"I noticed," Sigurd replied, his voice expressionless. Then, "You are easy to read, you two."

Indeed, Sigurd thought as he watched Ceawlin's broad shoulders move in a resigned shrug, all of Winchester had known there was strife between the king and his wife. Sigurd had come into the king's hall several times recently to find Ceawlin shouting and Niniane wearing a still, frozen, implacable look that was not at all like her usual serene expression. "Are you going to tell me what is the matter?" he asked when Ceawlin did not speak.

"Nan wants to see her brother."

Sigurd sat bolt upright in his chair. "What?"

"Her brother," Ceawlin repeated. He turned around. "Coinmail. The one who lives in Glevum. She wants to visit him."

"It would not be safe," Sigurd said. "Surely you won't allow her to go." But he knew as soon as he spoke that Ceawlin would. He would not be speaking thus to Sigurd if he had not already decided that. And he had called his wife Nan.

"I won't allow her to go to Glevum, certainly. She would be all too tempting a hostage for any British prince with illusions of power. But I have said she may meet him in Glastonbury if he will come there. The Christians have this belief in the sanctuary of the church. She swears she will be safe in Glastonbury."

"But why?" Sigurd asked. "What is the purpose of such a meeting?"

"The gods only know." Ceawlin shrugged again. "She wants to see her brother. She has not seen him in almost ten years and she wants to see him now. I don't understand it either, Sigurd, but it is important to Niniane."

"So you have told her she could go?"

"I have told her she could go to Glastonbury if Coinmail will meet her there . . . and if you will agree to be her escort." He looked at Sigurd out of narrowed blue-green eyes. "I must send someone I can trust with her. She would make an extremely valuable hostage. I will give you an escort of thirty men."

"Name of the gods, Ceawlin!" Anger flared in Sigurd's voice and eyes. "Are you mad? What good can possibly come of letting her go to Glastonbury? Keep her here in Winchester, where she is safe."

Ceawlin sighed. "Sigurd, about most things Nan is the mildest, most yielding of women. Rarely does she set her will against mine. Last year, for example, when I insisted she move the boys out of here so I could have a little peace, she did not want to do it, but she gave in, let me have my way. But every once in a while, something is important to her, really important. And then she does not give in. She was like that about having the children baptized Christian. And they have been, all of them. She was like that when I wanted her to get a wet nurse for Ceowulf." He began to walk back toward the table. "Do you know what she did?"

"No."

"She was so weak from childbed—that is why I wanted the wet nurse—and she got out of bed and took a knife to the woman. A knife!" Ceawlin shook his head in wonder. "She could hardly stand, and she held a knife to that woman's throat and said, 'Give me back my baby.'"

Sigurd felt a pain in his chest. "She loves her children well, does Niniane."

"So do most women love their children, but not like that. A knife! It had been a hard birth . . . she was not supposed to be out of bed . . . I was terrified she was going to start to bleed." Ceawlin had reached the table, and now he picked up his beer cup and drained it. "What could I do? I gave her the baby and she nursed it." He put down his empty cup and looked at Sigurd.

"There was nothing else you could do," Sigurd said.

"No." The grimness left Ceawlin's mouth, to be replaced by a look of distinct amusement. "This business of the women's bower. They say she has witchcraft because they know I sleep with no one else. But do you know how Niniane would take it if I did, Sigurd?"

The pain in Sigurd's chest deepened. "She would get out her knife again?"

Ceawlin came around the table and sat down. "She might. And I'm not at all sure she wouldn't use it on me!"

Sigurd looked resentfully at the man sitting beside him. Ceawlin had gone back to staring at his cup, and all Sigurd could see of him at the moment was the edge of his clear-cut profile and a thick curtain of pale hair. Was Ceawlin doing this deliberately? he wondered. Ceawlin knew how he felt about Niniane. Could he possibly be inflicting this pain on purpose?

"This business of Coinmail," Ceawlin was saying. "It is the same thing. She wants to see her brother, and that is that. Either I give in to her or I break her; there is no alternative. Under the circumstances, I think it best to let her go. But I must make certain that she will be safe."

"Gods!"

"Yes." Ceawlin turned his head to look at his friend. "I don't mean to burden you with my marital problems, old friend, but I wanted you to understand how it is." His sea-blue eyes looked confidently into Sigurd's. "Will you go?" he asked.

Sigurd heard himself answering that he would.

Niniane could not herself say why it was so important to her to see Coinmail. It had happened over the course of the last two years. First she had begun to dream about him at night. Next she had ridden to Bryn Atha to ask Naille if he ever heard from her brother. When Naille had been unable to tell her anything, she had sent some Britons to Glevum to see what they could learn. The Atrebates messengers had returned with the news that Coinmail was indeed married to the Dobunni chief's daughter and had become himself one of the important men in that tribe. It was then that Niniane had known that she must see him.

Ceawlin had kept his word to the Atrebates when he became king, and no Saxon had ever been given a hide of land that belonged to a Briton. There had, however, been plenty of open land, land that had once been farmed in the days of Rome but had stood empty ever since. This was the land he had given to his eorls and thanes, and now Saxon and Briton lived side by side throughout Wessex and peace reigned.

She wanted to tell this to Coinmail. She wanted her brother to understand that she had not betrayed her people, that accommodation with the Saxons was not something to be feared, but something to be striven for. She tried to explain this to Ceawlin, and though he understood what she was saying, he did not see the need for her to carry such a message to Coinmail. "I have no designs on his land, Niniane," Ceawlin had said. "I have enough to keep me occupied at the moment right here in Wessex. I am no threat to Coinmail and he certainly is no threat to me."

The problem was that in her heart, Niniane was not so sure. She was so happy with her husband and her children, with the life they led together. She felt this fierce necessity to protect it, to protect Ceawlin and her sons, and for some reason she could not explain even to herself, she felt that Coinmail was a threat.

She needed to see him. And so on a beautiful morning in early June she left Winchester with Sigurd and an escort of thirty thanes to go to Glastonbury, where Coinmail had said he would meet her. The only one of her children whom she had with her was the baby, Sigurd, who was still at the breast. The rest of the little band of brothers had remained in Winchester under the supervision of their nurses. She would not have brought them even if she thought Ceawlin would have allowed it. They were too like their father, too obviously Saxon, ever to soften the heart of her brother. But this new little babe—his hair was a downy red-gold in color, his eyes the dark blue that she knew would turn to gray. Sigurd was going to look like her, like Coinmail, like a Briton.

"Have I told you how grateful I am to you, Sigurd, for taking me to Glastonbury?" Niniane said as they rode along the road that went west from Winchester toward the old Roman city of Aquae Sulis.

"Yes, Niniane, you have," he answered, and gave her a teasing smile. "Many times."

She laughed. "Ceawlin is furious with me for insisting on making this trip," she confided. "He has this mad idea that someone will kidnap me and hold me as a hostage."

"Well, he is right. You are too valuable to be risked in enemy territory, Niniane. All the world does know how Ceawlin loves you. You would make an all-too-effective hostage." Sigurd's voice was stern, and when she turned to look at him, his face was stern as well.

"Well, no one will kidnap me with you to guard me, Sigurd," she answered. "All the world does also know how great a warrior you are." And she gave him her most enchanting smile.

Sigurd's face did not relax, and after a minute she gave up trying to coax him into a good humor and looked around with undisguised pleasure. She loved the spring best of all the seasons. The brown earth of the plowed fields was hidden by green spears of barley and wheat. The meadows were deep with grass and shimmered as a light breeze blew across them from the hills to the north. The smell of sap and growing things was in the air as they rode through the woods. She was young and strong and healthy. This last baby had been the easiest of all her children, both to birth and to care for. He slept now, cradled against her breast, and she bent her head to kiss his silky curls. When she looked up again it was to find Sigurd watching her. She smiled and this time he smiled back.

The country around Glastonbury was very wet; for this reason the British called it the Summer Country. Sigurd had never been this far west before and was surprised when the steep, odd-looking height of Glastonbury Tor reared up before them. "It was built long ago," Niniane told him, "by the Old Ones who made also the standing stones at Avebury and to the south."

The monastery itself was almost fully moated by a weed-strewn lake. Sigurd sent a contingent of men across the land bridge first, to make sure all was safe before he allowed Niniane to cross with him. They were met by Father Mal, who told them that Coinmail had arrived the day before.

Niniane wished to meet with her brother alone, and the priest offered to bring her to the room where Coinmail was lodged. Sigurd and his men made camp outdoors in the field and lighted the cook fires.

The first thing Niniane distinguished as she came into the darkness of the room from the bright sunshine outside was the color of his hair. She smiled and held out her hands. "Coinmail. I am so glad to see you."

He crossed the room with an unhurried stride and bent to kiss her forehead. "You look well, Niniane," he said in reply. Then, "Was it really necessary to bring half of your husband's thanes for protection? I have come alone."

Niniane flushed. How like Coinmail, she thought, to put her in the wrong from the start. "It was not my idea, Coinmail, but Ceawlin's. He has this mad notion that someone will try to kidnap me."

"Would he want to get you back?" Coinmail asked.

He was serious. She stared up into his face, at the beautiful, formidable features she remembered so well. He had not changed: the wide white brow was the same, the eyes still dark and gray as the northern sea. She had never seen aught of softness in those striking eyes, nor were they soft now as they regarded his only sister for the first time in eight long years. They looked merely curious.

"Yes," she answered after a long pause. "He would."

Coinmail raised an eyebrow. It was a trick of Ceawlin's to do that too, but it made Ceawlin look charmingly young and boyish. Coinmail looked like God on Judgment Day. "Do you come from him, then?" he asked.

This meeting was not going at all as she had expected. "Of course I don't come from Ceawlin! What could Ceawlin possibly have to say to you? I have come for myself."

"Why?"

"Why do you think?" she cried in exasperation. "Because you are my brother, my only living relative, that is why. I wanted to see you." Then, as he continued to look at her as if she were an enemy, "Is that so strange, Coinmail?" The exasperation had left her; she felt suddenly very sad.

There was no answering spark of recognition in his face. "Yes, Niniane, I find it strange. You have not wanted to see me for eight years. Why, all of a sudden, did it become so important?"

Niniane had not watched Ceawlin rule without learning something. So now she narrowed her own eyes and said in a voice quite as cool as Coinmail's had been, "Why did you agree to see me?"

"I was curious. I thought you were either coming as a messenger from your husband, in which case I was interested to hear what he could want with me. Or I thought you might be bringing me some information that could be used in the struggle against him."

"What?"

"Well, what else was I to think?" A muscle in his cheek jumped, the first indication of emotion he had displayed.

Her voice quivered with indignation. "I have brought you nothing, Coinmail, save a nephew who is sleeping in the convent with the nuns. I certainly did not come here to betray my husband."

He did not answer.

"Coinmail . . ." Niniane took a deep breath and put a hand upon her brother's arm. "Let us not quarrel."

His arm was stiff and unyielding under the pressure of her fingers. "There is little else for us to do, Niniane," he replied. "It is evident that you have thrown in your lot with my enemies. Do you expect me to love you for that?"

"But Ceawlin is not your enemy!" she cried passionately. Her fingers dug into his forearm with urgent insistence. "That is what I have come to tell you. Coinmail, listen to me. In Wessex today, Saxon and Briton live peacefully together. No Saxon thane has touched British land, I promise you. All live together in peace and harmony. Ask Father Mal. The priests from Glastonbury are welcome in Wessex. No British Christian need fear reprisals for practicing his religion."

His answer was immediate. "And a Saxon is king. And British children are learning to speak the Saxon tongue and British girls are wedding with Saxon thanes and breeding more Saxons to follow in their fathers' ways. Soon there will be no more Britons in Wessex, my sister. Soon there will be only Saxons. Did you think I would applaud that? Did you think I would be grateful to your husband for ruling over my people? For taking away my position? For turning the Atrebates into damned Saxons?"

Niniane dropped her hand as if he had slapped it away. "Coinmail . . . it is not like that."

"Is it not?" he answered ironically.

"Well . . . even if it is . . . is it so bad?"

"I will fight such a way of life till my dying breath, Niniane. I would sell my soul to the devil if I thought I could stop it. Never, never, will I willingly cede an inch of British land to a Saxon. Never."

She had begun to shake. "Ceawlin does not want to expand Wessex into the land of the Dobunni, Coinmail."

"Not yet."

"Not ever!"

His gray eyes were cold as ice. "How many sons have you, Niniane?"

She was shaking so much now that she was sure he could see it. "Four."

"Four sons. And they will need land, will want land. As will the sons of all your husband's thanes. Soon there will not be enough land in Wessex to hold them all. One day, Niniane, they will move into the land of the Dobunni, and from thence into Dumnonia itself." He was not a big man but he seemed to fill the room with the intensity of his passion. Niniane found herself taking a step away from him.

"No," she said, but her voice lacked conviction. The most horrible part of this whole nightmare conversation, she thought, was that Coinmail might be right.

"Go back to your Saxon, Niniane," her brother said. "Go back and tell him that he has an enemy in Glevum." And he pushed past her and walked out the door of the room.

She discovered, when she had composed herself enough to follow him some fifteen minutes later, that he had already ridden out of Glastonbury. He had not even stopped long enough to see her baby.

Chapter 25

~~~~~~

*T*HEY were tracked for miles as they rode east from Glastonbury through Dumnonia. Even Niniane could see British scouts watching the road from various points of vantage along the way. Sigurd placed her in the center of a living shield of mounted thanes, and she clutched her baby tightly to her breast and tried not to appear frightened.

"Do you think it is Coinmail?" she asked Sigurd, who was riding beside her and looking grim.

"I do not know who it is, Niniane, but it is certainly someone who knew we were in Glastonbury." Which meant, of course, that he thought it was Coinmail.

"Coinmail would never want to hurt me," she said.

"I don't think whoever it is wants to hurt you." Sigurd's eyes were traveling in a constant circle as he spoke, watching both sides of the road and before and behind as well. "That would only provoke bitter reprisals from Ceawlin. But as a hostage . . ." That was Niniane's fear also, the fear that Coinmail would try to use her to force Ceawlin to do something he did not wish to do.

She knew now she had been wrong to insist upon meeting with Coinmail. Instead of soothing her fears, the meeting with her brother had only served to confirm her suspicion that he was a danger. And it had also stirred up some uncomfortable doubts in her own heart, doubts she could not fully dismiss even as she rode in the middle of a Saxon shield wall raised to protect her from her own brother, her own people. She could not deny that there was truth in much of what Coinmail had said.

They passed out of Dumnonia and into the boundaries of Wessex. "I am sorry," Niniane said in a small voice to Sigurd as they made camp for the night within the safety of their own land. "Ceawlin was right. It was unsafe for me to go to Glastonbury. I am sorry you and your men were placed in danger because of me, Sigurd."

She was sitting before the fire, feeding her baby, and he squatted on his heels beside her and stared into the flames. "Was it worth it?" he asked.

"No." Her voice was oddly muffled, and he turned a little to look at

236

her. She too was staring into the fire, and the flames suddenly flared up and illuminated her, the baby at her breast, her shoulders, her neck, the line of her face, and her hair. Sigurd felt his throat cramp. He could not speak.

"He hates Ceawlin," Niniane said. "He will never be reconciled to Saxon rule, no matter how benign it may be. He is Ceawlin's enemy, Sigurd. Nothing I said could change that. You don't know Coinmail. He is like a stone; he never changes."

"He is like you," Sigurd managed to say, and saw her eyes fly to him in astonishment.

"I? I am not like that at all! I hate that in Coinmail, that . . . coldness . . . that inflexibility."

"And how do you think you were, Niniane, when Ceawlin said he did not want you to go to Glastonbury?"

Her eyes were enormous dark pools in the fine pale oval of her face. "What do you mean?"

"You just said almost the exact words about your brother that Ceawlin said to me when he asked me to take you to Glastonbury. He said that you were like a stone, that no matter what he said, you wouldn't change."

"I . . . I . . ." She was deadly pale. He was hurting her by talking this way, but suddenly he felt within himself a savage desire to hurt her. She had hurt him.

Sigurd went on relentlessly. "Ceawlin said he could either give in to you or break you, that he had no other choice." He stared at her out of eyes that were bleakly gray. "You are hard, Niniane, on those who do love you most." And only he knew he was speaking of himself.

Brilliant color flushed into her face. He saw the glitter of tears in her eyes. "You are right, Sigurd," she said. "Ceawlin is so good to me. Too good. I don't deserve his goodness to me." The tears glittered but did not spill over. "You're right too when you say that he is the only one I am so hard on. But you see, Sigurd, I fear for him. He is so unafraid for himself that I feel I must be the one to fear for both of us." The baby had finished nursing and she shifted him to her shoulder to burp. Sigurd had a brief glimpse of a white breast before she covered herself. She was completely unself-conscious, sitting there nursing her child before him. It never once crossed her mind that he might think of her in any way save as Ceawlin's wife.

"Why should you fear for him?" he asked, his voice hard. "If ever a man was able to take care of himself, it is Ceawlin."

"I don't know why," she said, and her own face was almost as somber as Sigurd's. She patted her son's back with a gentle hand. "But when I think of Ceawlin . . . of my children . . . when I think that anyone might be a danger to them . . . I feel . . . ferocious." She did not smile, was deadly serious. Nor, looking at her small, fragile figure, was he inclined to laugh.

There was a long silence. The baby burped loudly and Niniane murmured to him. Sigurd got to his feet. "I am going to check the sentries," he said, and left her to settle herself to sleep by the fire.

"Ceawlin pampers that woman ridiculously," said Cuthwulf.

"He should not have allowed her to leave Wessex," Cutha agreed. "But she is safe home now and naught has happened."

"Safe thanks to Sigurd." Cuthwulf raised his cup to his brother.

"There was no real danger," Sigurd said mildly.

"That is not what I understood from the other thanes." Cutha looked slantwise at Sigurd, but Sigurd's face did not change. He had been back in Winchester for two full days, but this was the first chance he had had to speak with his father. Cutha had not been in the royal enclave when Niniane's party returned.

Cutha's hall was the same as it had always been, but the rest of Winchester had changed. Much of the change reflected the different way of life that the king and the queen had adopted. The unmarried thanes still slept on the hall benches in the great hall, but more and more men had married and moved out of Winchester, onto the lands given to them by the king. The bower had become quarters for those girls who had lost their fathers or natural protectors and who in consequence must look to the king to see them properly married. New halls had been built for the men who had fought with Ceawlin in his struggle for the kingship, men whom he had named eorls, but these men spent at least half of the year on their own lands. Only Cutha remained in Winchester at the king's side, as of old. Cutha and Sigurd, who were known to be the king's right and left hands.

They sat this night in Cutha's hall, Cutha and Sigurd, and listened to Cuthwulf's familiar complaint. "Gods, but life is dull in Winchester these days! Ceawlin is turning us into a nation of farmers."

"Ceawlin is turning us into a nation," his father replied. "And I do not want to hear of any more foolish exploits by you, Cuthwulf. Ceawlin was remarkably tolerant of the last one, but his patience will not last forever."

Cuthwulf slammed his wine cup on the arm of his chair. The night was warm and they were sitting with the hall door open to let in a breeze. "Exploit!" he exploded. "What exploit? All I did was raid a few British farms. Gods, Cynric would weep if he could see the woman-ridden cur that Ceawlin has turned into."

"That is enough!" Cutha's voice clashed with and carried over Sigurd's angry protest. "Ceawlin realizes, as you do not," Cutha continued, his voice cold and controlled, "that the King of Wessex is no longer merely the leader of a war band. He is a law-giver, a peace-maker, a *king*, Cuthwulf; not just a ring lord, a king."

"And what have you got out of this kingship of Ceawlin's, Father?" Cuthwulf's lower lip jutted out belligerently. "Oh, he pays lip service to your advice, but does he really listen to you? Does he listen to anyone except that British wife of his? *That* is why he is so careful of the British, my father. It is Niniane's doing. Make no mistake about that." He leaned forward further in his chair. "And whom is Ceawlin to call upon if he does need to raise a war band? Who is left in Winchester these days to heed his call? All the eorls and thanes are scattered around the countryside on their farms! Where you have banished me." He shot his father an accusing look.

"I sent you out of Winchester to get you away from Ceawlin, Cuthwulf. You have too ready a tongue, my son, and not enough respect for your king."

Cuthwulf snorted eloquently, and Cutha frowned.

"The eorls and thanes are pledged to answer to a call to arms from the king," Sigurd put in, in answer to his brother. "You know that as well as we do, Cuthwulf. Your problem is that you are an inveterate brawler and don't know what to do with yourself when you are called upon to use your brain and not your sword."

"Your problem is that you are as bewitched as Ceawlin is by that redheaded British bitch," said Cuthwulf brutally. Then he jumped to his feet as Sigurd hurled a cup of wine full in his face.

"Cuthwulf!" His father's voice stayed the furious lunge Cuthwulf had launched toward Sigurd. Cutha looked from the panting Cuthwulf to the coldly furious face of his younger son. "Go home, Sigurd," he said softly. "Your brother is drunk. Go home to Edith and forget what he has said."

There was silence in the hall as Sigurd walked across the room, his footsteps sounding loud on the wooden floor. When he had gone out, Cutha turned to his eldest son. "You are a fool," he said, but without heat.

"What I said is obviously true." Cuthwulf flung himself back into his chair. "He is as besotted with her as Ceawlin is."

"Ceawlin saw too much of what happens to a man when he is caught between two women," Cutha said. "He grew up watching his father try to placate both Fara and Guthfrid, grew up in the midst of the discord that will always reign when a man has two wives. He holds to Niniane because it is easier that way. And she has given Ceawlin and Wessex four sons. She has done her duty as a queen, Cuthwulf. Give her her due. Nor is she vindictive or power-hungry, as Guthfrid was. Ceawlin could have done much worse." There was a pause as Cutha regarded the angry profile of his belligerent eldest. "Do not say such a thing about Niniane and Sigurd ever again."

Cuthwulf gave his father a startled look. "Why?"

"Because you have upset Sigurd."

"He is too much under Ceawlin's shadow," Cuthwulf said. "He has ever been too much under Ceawlin's shadow."

"Perhaps, but it is too late to change that now." Cutha's eyebrows rose. "I am surprised that you saw so clearly into Sigurd's feelings, Cuthwulf. You are not usually the most discerning of men."

Cuthwulf grunted. "I didn't see it," he said. "I just said it. He gave himself away."

"Yes, he did." Cutha leaned back in his chair. "I did not see it either," he said, and looked thoughtfully at the tips of his shoes.

In East Anglia a king was dying. Guthfrid's father, Redwold, who had reigned full thirty years from Sutton Hoo on the coast of the Narrow Sea, lay in his great hall dying. Around him were gathered his sword thanes, his eorls, his daughter, and his son and heir, Aethelbert. Aethelbert was forty years old, had waited a long time for this moment; at last he saw the kingship within his grasp.

Shadows crept across the land and the old king's life ebbed with the light. Guthfrid stood beside her brother and watched, her face set like stone. Her father had been too old to desire a war with the younger, more vigorous King of the West Saxons; her brother would be different.

Redwold's eyes opened and it seemed to Guthfrid that he looked directly at her. Then a strange rattling sound came from his throat and his face seemed to collapse inward upon itself. She stepped to the bed and bent to listen. "He is dead," she said and, straightening, met the eyes of her brother.

In East Anglia they cremated their kings. Redwold's queen had long been dead, so Guthfrid, as his only daughter, was the one to order the funeral. It was a woman's prerogative to send her man to the gods.

Guthfrid ordered a great pyre to be built, and men labored through the night to heap up the wood. It was not easy to burn a human body; it took a tremendous amount of heat. With those of lesser importance it did not matter so much if the entire body was not consumed; with a king they would be more careful. All knew that the higher the smoke rose into the air, the higher would rise the man whose pyre it was in the land of the dead.

The women dressed the old king in his finest garments and decked him with his jewelry. Then he was placed on an oaken pallet with his best bedding and carried to the pyre. His helmet was placed on the pyre with him, as well as assorted bronze drinking vessels for use in the other world.

The morning was gray and overcast and the pyre jutted up bleakly against the leaden sky. Guthfrid stood beside her brother; the eorls and thanes of East Anglia were grouped about the pyre. "Bring out the horse," Guthfrid said.

The only sound on the field was the crying of the birds overhead. The priest led Redwold's horse, a gray stallion, to stand before Aethelbert at the pyre. The stallion came quietly. He was old, like the king, and had been drugged as well. Redwold's son raised his father's ax. At the last minute, however, the old horse sensed danger, threw up his head, and tried to rear. The priests held tightly to the halter ropes, but Aethelbert missed the artery. The stallion screamed and thrashed and Aethelbert had to strike again and again; the sound of the horse's screaming drowned out the birds. Finally the stallion lay still and they dragged his carcass closer to the pyre. Aethelbert laid the ax he had used on his father's pallet.

"Bring out the woman," Guthfrid said next. Even the birds were silent as Redwold's slave girl was led across the field toward the pyre. She was escorted by three thanes and an old woman dressed in black. The girl walked as if she were drunk.

"Do you wish to die with the king?" Guthfrid asked.

"Yes," the girl replied. The pupils of her eyes were strangely dilated and she looked dazed. Guthfrid nodded to the old woman, who untied a rope from about her waist. She wrapped the rope once around the girl's neck and gave an end to two of the thanes. The third thane held the girl against him, pinning her arms to her sides. Then they strangled her and placed her body on the pallet next to Redwold.

"Light the fire," said Guthfrid. As the flames shot up, she commenced to wail and to weep. The funeral fire was soon roaring, the flames a brilliant orange against the heavy gray sky. The smoke rose higher and higher into the air. The onlookers saw the flames touch the bodies, saw the clothes ignite. Guthfrid led the women in dirge as the fire did its cleansing work, sent Redwold in glory to his gods.

> Then the East Anglian folk made for Redwold a great funeral pyre and hung it with all his household treasure. Then in its midst they laid their king, beloved ruler of thirty years. They lighted the fire, the wood smoke climbed, the people lamented their king and their lord.

So sang Redwold's scop in the great hall of Sutton Hoo later that evening. The funeral fire had died down and the remains of the bodies and the grave goods had been collected. The ashes had been put into a bronze vessel engraved with the swastika of Thunor for protection and carried to the royal burying grounds. On the morrow the thanes would erect a great barrow to mark for future generations the place of Redwold's grave.

Aethelbert, as Redwold's only surviving son, sat this night in his father's high seat. Beside him sat his wife, mother of his five children. To his left sat his sister, Guthfrid, with her husband, Edric. Aethelbert looked around the benches, at the anxious faces of his father's thanes, and thought of the morrow. He felt within himself all the zeal and impatience of a man too long kept from his own. East Anglia, once among the foremost of all the English kingdoms, had fallen of late years into the shadows. For too long had an elderly king steered at its helm.

It was common knowledge among the East Anglian eorls and thanes that the king had been at odds with his son. For many years now the two had not been able to meet without clashing. Aethelbert had actually spent the last five years in Kent, with his mother's folk, because of the antagonism between him and his father.

The chief cause of their falling-out had been the way his father chose to handle the return of Guthfrid. Aethelbert burned to avenge the humiliation of his sister, the death of his sister's son. And Redwold had accepted wergild! Aethelbert raged whenever he thought of it. Ceawlin had murdered his own brother and been allowed to pay wergild, to buy his way out of a blood feud that should demand nothing short of his life. It had made East Anglia a laughingstock; of that Aethelbert was sure. He had heard it spoken of more often than he cared to remember in Kent.

He looked now at his sister's still-bright hair and thought of Wessex. There had been a blood feud between his house and the house of the West Saxons even before the death of Edwin. The marriage of Guthfrid had been his father's attempt to heal the feud, another craven gesture of peace that had proved disastrous.

In vain had his sister begged his father all these years to redress her wrongs. Well, she would beg in vain no longer. Redwold had been a senile fool, had not seen the usefulness of having Guthfrid's son, the rightful claimant to the West Saxon throne, right here in his own hall.

He felt Guthfrid looking at him and turned to meet her burning dark eyes. Soon, my sister, he said to her in his heart. First I must get my house in order here at home. Then will I deal with Wessex.

Chapter 26

*T*HE years of exile in Kent had only served to drive Aethelbert's character ever more firmly into the tracks of a few unwavering obsessions. These were a burning desire to win back for East Anglia the pride he thought his father had betrayed by accepting wergild for the murder of Edwin, belief in his own military genius, hatred for the King of Wessex, and ambition to increase the boundaries of his own kingdom. All of these obsessions dovetailed neatly into one single course of action: the invasion of Wessex and the defeat and death of Wessex's king.

Unfortunately, this was not a plan Aethelbert could put into action immediately. First it was necessary to get rid of the older thanes who had abetted his father in Redwold's humiliating policy of reconciliation with Wessex, and replace them with younger, braver, more daring men. This task of revenge and rebuilding took Aethelbert the rest of the year 567 to accomplish. By the time winter was showing signs of relinquishing its grip upon the world, however, the King of East Anglia had assembled in Sutton Hoo a war band of more than five hundred men.

The wind was blowing raw off the Narrow Sea on the February afternoon that Aethelbert sat with his sister and his sister's husband to discuss his plan for the invasion of Wessex. The three were sitting around the hearth in the great hall, and with them was Guthfrid's son, Edgar, the boy Aethelbert was proposing to place upon the throne of Wessex. At twelve years of age, Edgar was old enough to understand what was being planned for his future.

"You will invade by the Icknield Way?" Edric asked.

"Yes. It is the most direct route into Wessex from East Anglia." Aethelbert's eyes, a lighter brown than his sister's, glowed with the fire of conquest. "For too long has Ceawlin been allowed to claim the upper Thames valley for Wessex. Another one of my father's mistakes. We will begin the war by reclaiming that land for East Anglia."

"Ceawlin has held that valley for eight years and more," Edric said. "He will not have left it unguarded."

"He has given it under the protection of one of his eorls," Aethelbert returned. "This much have I learned."

243

"Which eorl?" Guthrid asked.

"The one named Penda."

"Penda will stay loyal to Ceawlin," Edric said after a moment's thought. "I think he will fight, my lord."

"Perhaps," replied Aethelbert. "But I have near six hundred men, Edric. How many thanes can an eorl keep on his country manor? Twenty?"

"No more than twenty, certainly," said Guthfrid.

"Ceawlin will bring a war band out of Winchester as soon as he learns of your presence in the Thames valley," said Edric. "You will not long have the advantage of surprise, my lord."

Aethelbert smiled complacently. He was a heavy-shouldered man and he habitually hunched his shoulders forward, as if he could not wait to throw himself into whatever difficulties might be looming in the path before him. "You have not heard the rest of my plan," he said.

Guthfrid's dark brown eyes narrowed. "What else are you planning, Aethelbert?" she asked at last as her brother allowed the expectant silence to prolong itself.

"My kinsmen Oslaf and Cnebba will invade Wessex from Kent at the same time I am coming from East Anglia."

Edgar, who had been listening in silence, now said excitedly, "You will catch him in the middle of the two of you, uncle!"

Aethelbert's light brown eyes turned to his nephew. Edgar was a paler, less vigorous version of his brother Edwin, but he was still a handsome boy. Of greater importance to Aethelbert, he was completely dominated by Guthfrid. The boy's uncle anticipated little trouble ruling Edgar once the boy had been installed in Wessex. "That is my plan," he answered his nephew with a patronizing smile.

Edric was pulling at his mustache. "It sounds all right."

"It is a brilliant plan," Aethelbert snapped, his pride touched by the faint praise of his brother-in-law.

Edric stared at him bleakly. "With Ceawlin, brilliant plans have a way of going awry."

"Yes, well we all know that *you* had your troubles with Ceawlin, my brother," said Aethelbert as he rose to his feet. He was not a tall man, but he was very muscular. He gave Edric a stare of contempt before he strode away, shoulders characteristically hunched forward, eyes on the ground.

"May I go with the war band, Mother?" Edgar asked.

"No!" Guthfrid stared in horror at the fair, brown-eyed face of her only living son. "No, my love. You are too valuable to risk in battle. Your uncle will wage the war for you, never fear. By next Yule, Edgar, you will be sitting in the great hall of Winchester." And she gave him a brilliant smile.

* * *

Niniane looked around her sunny bedroom with satisfaction. Five years since Ceawlin had ordered the carpenters to cut a window into the wall of the king's hall for her, and he had had glass brought from one of the few remaining windows in the praetorium in Venta to glaze it. It was the only window in all of Winchester, and Niniane loved it.

The March day was chill, but the pool of sunshine on the bedroom floor was warm. Ceawlin's hound had long since discovered the pleasure of glass-filtered sun, and he lay now on one of the floor skins, basking in the warmth, sound asleep. Niniane had given up complaining about the hound in her bedroom and, to compromise, Ceawlin had taught him to stay off the bed. The bedcover was Niniane's other pride and joy, a blue wool rug with a border of white horses that had taken her half a year to weave on the great loom in the women's hall. She smoothed a proprietary hand along the cover, then went to the larger of the two clothes chests in the room and began to take out and inspect her gowns and tunics.

"What are you doing?" It was Ceawlin. The hound, hearing a beloved voice, raised his head, then got up and went to greet his master. Niniane, sitting on the floor, continued to sort clothes into piles.

"I am setting aside the things I want to take with me when I go to Wyckholm," she answered.

"Oh." He came over to the bed and sat down, watching her in silence for a few minutes. The hound followed, resting its head against Ceawlin's knee.

She finished folding a linen undergarment, then turned around to look at him. "Is something wrong, Ceawlin?"

He shrugged. "One of the vils close to Kent has been raided again."

"Oh." She searched his face. "Well, that is Oswald's area, is it not?"

"Yes. Oswald gave chase and his son was killed in the pursuit."

"Oh . . ." The word this time was long and drawn out.

"Yes." His eyes on her face were thoughtful. "I don't like it, Nan. There have been too many of these raids of late. And this last attack was more than just a cattle raid. There were near two hundred men, Oswald said. That is a war band. I have not forgot that Guthfrid's mother was from Kent. Nor have I forgot that Aethelbert spent the last five years of his father's life with his mother's kin."

Her delicate brows rose into two fine question marks. "Do you think that these Kentish raids are coming at Guthfrid's instigation?"

"Or East Anglian instigation. I certainly wouldn't dismiss the idea, Niniane. Nor do I think that this is the time for you to be going to Wyckholm."

She put a saffron-colored tunic on one of the piles and sat back on her heels. "Coenburg is due to deliver her baby, Ceawlin. I promised her I would be with her. You know that."

He reached down to rub the hound's ears, but his eyes were on his wife. "Cannot you send one of the other women?"

"It would not be the same. Coenburg is Cutha's daughter, Penda's wife. She is due the honor of having the queen attend her childbirth. You know that too."

Ceawlin continued to pet his dog and the hound sighed with pleasure. Niniane got to her feet and came to sit beside her husband on the bed. "What are you afraid of?" she asked softly.

"My spies in East Anglia tell an interesting tale," he answered. "They say that Aethelbert has purged his hall of all his father's old thanes. They say he has gathered around him a large number of new thanes, young thanes, land-hungry thanes." He had been bending over a little to stroke the dog, and now he straightened and looked directly down into her upturned face. "I think he means to come against me," Ceawlin said.

"Dear God."

He smiled a little wryly into her small, horrified face. "I cannot say such a decision would be unwelcome to me. I am not afraid of going to war with East Anglia. However, I am not particularly pleased with the idea of going to war with both East Anglia and Kent at the same time."

"I don't want you to go to war at all!" she said fiercely.

At that he grinned and his eyes danced as he said, "Of course you don't."

Even after all these years, that look turned her heart right over. But she wouldn't let him see that. "I realize," she said with delicate sarcasm, "that I am only a woman and so am incapable of understanding the pleasures of killing and murdering and maiming other people."

He raised an eyebrow and looked at her. "Guthfrid is a woman, and she understands it perfectly."

"Guthfrid is a monster."

"Mmm." His eyes were glinting as he watched her.

"What do you think is going to happen?" she asked.

"I think Aethelbert hopes to draw me to Kent with these border raids. Then, when I am safely occupied in the east, he will invade Wessex himself, coming from East Anglia by way of the Icknield Way into the Thames valley. Where Wyckholm lies. Under the circumstances, I would prefer that you were elsewhere."

"But what of Coenburg? I promised her I would be with her. It is her first child, Ceawlin. And now that her mother is dead, I am the woman she is closest to." He did not say anything, but got off the bed and began to pace up and down the floor. She watched him for a moment before she said flatly, "You have made some plan, Ceawlin. You are not simply going to leave Penda there alone to face an East Anglian invasion."

He continued to pace. "I am sending Penda a hundred men and five wagon loads of arrows and spears. Wyckholm has a strong stockade fence around it; all Penda need do is pull his ceorls and the British farmers who wish to come inside the stockade. He will be able to hold off Aethelbert easily with that number of men and that much ammunition. If Penda can slow Aethelbert down for me, give me time to deal with the situation on the Kentish border, that will be enough."

"Do you have word that Aethelbert is actually gathering a war band?"

"No."

"So none of this may come to pass after all?"

"That is true," he said. Regretfully.

"Then I am going to Wyckholm. If I do not go and Aethelbert does not come, it is not just Coenburg who will be upset. Penda will be offended, Ceawlin. You know how touchy he is about his position and his prerogatives. And if Aethelbert does come, I shall be perfectly safe inside the stockade with everyone else."

He came to a halt in front of her and looked down. His shoulders were so broad they blocked the light from the window. He was so big, she thought. So big and strong and fearless. He was really hoping for a war. She knew him too well. She was furious with him. She stuck her chin in the air and said, "I am going to Wyckholm." And was utterly dumbfounded when he agreed.

"Are you mad?" Sigurd asked Ceawlin incredulously. "You think there will be an invasion from East Anglia and you are sending Niniane to Wyckholm?"

"She will be perfectly safe," Ceawlin replied. "I would not send her if I thought otherwise. Nor would I permit Penda to keep your sister there."

"Coenburg is already there and it would be difficult to move a woman in her condition. But you are *sending* Niniane. That is different."

"Niniane insists upon going."

Ceawlin's face was as bland as his voice, and Sigurd stared at him with hard eyes. The two men were standing in the great hall while around them the trestle tables were being set for up for the thanes' dinner. "You have not given in to her on this," Sigurd said after a minute, and Ceawlin laughed.

"Not this time," he agreed. "She has to go, Sigurd. I cannot ask Penda to risk for his wife what I am not willing to risk for my own." Then, as Sigurd's face set into grim lines, "There is no risk, Sigurd. I am positive of that, else I would not let her go. However, if you wish to leave Edith here in Winchester, I will understand." Sigurd was also going to Wyckholm for the birth of his sister's child.

Sigurd did not answer immediately, and from halfway across the room there came the sound of a boy's voice. "Father!" Sigurd looked around and saw Ceawlin's two eldest sons threading their way through the slaves who were setting up the tables. "Father," said Cerdic once again as soon as he had come up before the men, "may we go to Wyckholm with Mother?"

Sigurd looked down into the two eager young faces as they waited for Ceawlin to answer. Cerdic, at ten, was a tall, well-grown youngster with butter-yellow hair and large slate-blue eyes. Crida, a year younger, was small-boned like his mother and fair-haired like his father. He looked at least three years younger than Cerdic as he stood there beside his taller brother, but Sigurd knew how much toughness and determination was in the small, seemingly delicate frame of Niniane's second son.

"Why?" Ceawlin asked.

Cerdic's eyes were glowing. "Because there is going to be a war! Please, Father, may we go?"

"There is no certainty that there will be a war," said Ceawlin. "And, no, you may not go."

The two faces fell ludicrously. "But you are letting Mother go!" said Crida.

"Mother is going because of Coenburg's baby; she does not need the additional burden of you two to worry about. You will stay right here in Winchester."

"If we stay here, we will never get to do any fighting," Cerdic muttered.

Crida gave his brother a warning look. "Of course, we would much rather go in your war band than in Penda's, Father," he said with his rare smile.

"You are too young to go in anyone's war band," Ceawlin answered pleasantly but firmly.

"But why can't we at least go with Mother?" Cerdic persisted. "We won't get in her way, Father. We won't bother her at all."

The corner of Ceawlin's mouth twitched. "I'm quite sure you would keep yourselves out of her sight, but that is not what I had in mind." Then, as Crida opened his mouth, "That is the end of the discussion. You will both stay right here in Winchester. Do I make myself clear?"

"Yes, sir." The two young faces were almost comically glum.

"You may go."

"Yes, sir."

Ceawlin and Sigurd watched the boys trail disconsolately off to the door, and then Ceawlin turned to his friend. "Do you remember how it felt?" he asked.

Sigurd grinned. "Yes."

"Actually, there is little trouble they could get into at Wyckholm, but Niniane would have my head if I let them go." There was someone else coming in the door of the great hall, and with a small shock of surprise Sigurd recognized his brother.

"Did you send for Cuthwulf?" he asked Ceawlin as his brother began to thread his way through the slaves and the tables.

"Yes." All the humor had left Ceawlin's face; his eyes were coldly reflective as they watched Cuthwulf approach. "I am going to send him to deal with the raiders from Kent," he said.

"Well, that should make him happy." Sigurd tried to keep his tone light. "We all know how Cuthwulf is longing for a fight. He's almost as bad as Cerdic and Crida."

"Cerdic and Crida are children," said Ceawlin. "Cuthwulf is not." He put his hand on Sigurd's shoulder in what might have been a gesture of affection or dismissal. "Let me talk with him," he said, and Sigurd nodded and left the hall, giving a greeting to his brother as he passed.

Aethelbert's war band left Sutton Hoo at dawn on a misty March morning and began its trek down the Icknield Way, the ancient track first used by the Old Ones that ran from East Anglia along the edge of the Chilton hills to the valley of the Thames. It was not paved or graveled, as were the roads left by the Romans; it was a dirt track but it cut across country where there was neither fen nor forest to hinder easy transit, and it was the most direct route into Wessex.

Six hundred men marched under Aethelbert's standard and the King of East Anglia's martial heart was filled with pride as he rode along in front of his thanes. At last, after all the years of frustration, the long years spent waiting for an old man to die, at last Aethelbert of East Anglia was on the war road.

He knew that Ceawlin had placed one of his eorls on the northern-most border of the land Wessex claimed; he knew that Penda had built a fortified manor there. But Aethelbert had six hundred men. He anticipated little difficulty in storming Penda's manor and from thence driving onward into the heart of Wessex itself. It was consequently a severe shock to find that he had scarce passed Verulamium when he was confronted with an ambush of bow-carrying horsemen, who struck with deadly accuracy and then fled.

"He knows we are coming." It was Edric, grim-faced and positive. "I told you, my lord, not to count on anything with Ceawlin."

"It is not Ceawlin," Aethelbert said. "It is Penda. Someone sent word ahead that we were on the march. But he cannot have enough men to mount an effective defense."

The farms in the area were rich and Aethelbert regarded them with an acquisitive eye. This part of England would soon be his. There was, however, no sign of anyone working on the farms; no one in the fields, no one in any of the houses that they passed. And then, in the distance, barring the way south to the river Thames, they saw the great stockade fence of Wyckholm.

It was considerably larger than Aethelbert had expected.

"This is the manor of an eorl?" he said to Edric. "Ceawlin must place great thrust in this man, to give him such a stronghold."

Edric too was surprised. Wyckholm would give any man who held it command of the whole valley of the upper Thames. He saw immediately the necessity of taking it for East Anglia and said as much to his brother-in-law. Aethelbert agreed. By now the day was far advanced and the East Anglian army settled down at little distance from the walls of Wyckholm and prepared to storm the stockade on the morrow.

Inside the great stockade fence, in the crowded women's hall of Wyckholm, Coenburg at last gave birth to a son. It was a long labor and Penda had broken away from his war preparations numerous times to come and inquire how things were progressing. As he told Sigurd, he had lost one wife in childbirth and did not wish to repeat the experience.

"Thank the gods," Sigurd said when at last Niniane told him that the baby had been born. Then, because the waiting had been so hard, because he had been reminded of that dreadful night when Cerdic was born, of the night when Edith had almost died giving birth to his own children, he said, "I wonder anew each time a babe is born that a woman who has been through that would ever again let a man near her bed."

He thought that Niniane was looking tired. Coenburg had been in labor for almost twenty hours and Niniane had been with her the whole while. She had tied her hair on top of her head to keep it out of her way, but several strands had slipped out of the knot and were wisping around her face and her neck. There were smudges of sleeplessness under her eyes and her gown was crumpled and flecked with stains of something he could not identify. But at his words she smiled and the dimple in the corner of her mouth flickered. "Oh," she said, and placed her fingers lightly on his sleeve, "you are worth it."

He did not return her smile, but regarded her somberly. "Are we?" he asked.

The dimple deepened. "Ceawlin is." Then, as Penda came in the door, her own face sobered. "My lord," she said with ceremonial formality, "you have a son."

Penda grinned and thrust a hand through his already disordered hair.

"Thank you, my lady," he said to Niniane. Then, as he noticed Sigurd, "Your sister is a good wife, Sigurd. A son!"

Niniane slipped her hand through Penda's arm. "Coenburg is waiting for you, my lord." Sigurd did not stay to see the two of them move off, but turned to go outside and see once again to his defenses.

The East Anglians charged Wyckholm at dawn and were met by a rain of arrows that felled dozens of them.

"In the name of Woden, how many men does he have on those walls?" Aethelbert yelled to Edric.

"Too many!" Edric yelled in return. "Pull back before you lose half your men!"

The East Anglians retreated out of arrow range and met to discuss this new development.

"He has at least two hundred men in there," Edric said. "Look." For now that the surprise was gone, Penda had allowed his men to show themselves on the walls.

"So that is where all the farmers have gone," said Aethelbert bitterly.

"Not just the farmers. Look." Edric pointed to a man on the wall. "Do you know who that is?"

"No."

"That is Sigurd. Cutha's son and Ceawlin's greatest friend. There can be only one reason for Sigurd being here; Ceawlin knew we were coming and sent him."

Aethelbert cursed. Then, "Who could have told him?"

"A pottery maker, a jeweler, a man who sells medicine; anyone who has been around Sutton Hoo long enough to realize that you were making preparations for war. It would not take much deduction to figure out whom you were planning to go against, or what route you would take."

Aethelbert jutted his head forward. "If that is so, then why did not Ceawlin come north himself?"

"I don't know."

"He may have decided to go east, to deal with the invasion from Kent."

"That may be so."

Aethelbert got to his feet and stared at the stockade of Wyckholm. "We will try again once it is dark," he said. "If we can get inside, we will have them. We outnumber them by nearly three to one."

"Perhaps we will have more success in the dark," Edric agreed, and Aethelbert summoned his eorls to give the order.

They did not have more success in the dark. Penda's men, all specially picked by Ceawlin for their superiority with a bow, cut down the oncoming East Anglians once again, and the few who did reach the walls were dispatched even more easily because they were more easily seen. Once again Aethelbert recalled his thanes.

"We can mount a siege," Aethelbert said to his council of eorls. "The area around here is rich with food and fodder. We could stay here for months, starve them out." He cast a quick look at Edric. "That is what Ceawlin did to Winchester."

"Yes, but all of Ceawlin's enemies were safely within Winchester," said Edric sourly. "That is not the case with us. Ceawlin himself is at large somewhere. I should not like to find myself caught between him and Penda, my lord."

"No," said one of the eorls, nervously glancing over his shoulder as if Ceawlin might somehow appear out of the dark. Edric gave him a look of amused contempt.

"I think," said Aethelbert sternly, "that we ought to try to join up with our allies from Kent. Chances are, that is where Ceawlin is. This stronghold," and he waved his hand dismissingly at Wyckholm, "is not important. I have come into Wessex to defeat Ceawlin, not to waste my time besieging his eorls."

"Yes, my lord."

"That is right, my lord."

"It is the bastard that we want."

Edric listened to the eager agreement of Aethelbert's council and curled his lip in the dark. He said nothing, however, for it seemed as if Aethelbert was inclined to get them away from Wyckholm, and Edric had spoken true when he said he did not want to find himself caught with Ceawlin on one side of him and Sigurd and Penda on the other.

"They are leaving!" The word ran around the walls of Wyckholm and then someone went running to bring the news to Penda. He and Sigurd came out to the gate and watched the retreating war band of East Anglia.

"They are marching south," said Sigurd.

"I had hoped to hold them longer." Penda's hazel eyes were narrowed in the morning sun.

"Ceawlin was counting on them wasting some time in a siege," Sigurd said in sober agreement. "He was hoping to give Cuthwulf time to deal with the Kentish invasion."

"Where is Ceawlin planning to meet up with Cuthwulf?"

"Silchester." Silchester was the Saxon name for Calleva.

Penda cursed, then turned to look at Sigurd. "It is a large war band, larger than I thought Aethelbert could muster." Penda looked worried. "How many men can Ceawlin muster? He has already sent me a hundred."

"And he gave Cuthwulf two hundred to deal with the raids from Kent."

Penda frowned. "Then he will have emptied Winchester. If the other eorls do not respond swiftly to his call, Winchester could be at risk."

"Bertred and Ine had come in with their men before I left," Sigurd said. "And Cynigils and Wuffa had sent word that they were coming."

Penda and Sigurd looked at each other. Then, "If you will remain here with your own men, the ceorls, and the women," Sigurd said, "I will take the men from Winchester and head for Silchester to join up with Ceawlin."

Penda nodded slowly. "Yes, I think you had better. I would come also, but someone must be here lest Aethelbert try to circle back."

Sigurd clapped his brother-by-marriage upon the shoulder. "We'll leave you most of the arrows. You can give your ceorls target practice until we return."

Penda grunted. "If it were not for the women, I would come with you."

"I know," said Sigurd sympathetically. "But there must be someone here to take charge."

"All right," said Penda. "Come along. You had better not delay in getting started."

Chapter 27

NINIANE stood beside Sigurd in front of the women's hall of Wyckholm and watched the thanes line up in the courtyard. "I wish they had stayed at Wyckholm longer," she said for perhaps the fifth time in the last hour.

"I know. So do we all. I would guess that Aethelbert did not want to take the chance of getting caught between Ceawlin and Penda. A wise choice on his part, however inconvenient it may be for us."

Niniane smiled a little wryly. "We should have had someone stand on the walls and pretend to be Ceawlin."

"It would be difficult to find someone who looks like Ceawlin."

She bent her head a little. "That is true." Then, looking up again, her face strained and white, "Sigurd, that army is so big. Ceawlin will never be able to collect that many men."

"He will know what to do, Niniane. Don't worry about Ceawlin."

Her voice was faintly bitter. "I spend my life worrying about Ceawlin. He has put all his trust in the eorls, has given them more power than any king has ever given out of his own keeping before. What if they fail him, Sigurd? What if they don't come to his call?"

"They will." Sigurd's voice was confident. "Ceawlin knows what he is about, Niniane. He has given the eorls such power because he knows that that is the best way to keep his borders safe, to protect his capital and his country. It is not possible for the king to maintain in Winchester the large numbers necessary for such constant readiness. The task of feeding and paying such a war band would be beyond any king's capacity. But if the responsibility is spread among the eorls as well, then it becomes possible to keep large numbers of men in arms. Look how the system has worked thus far. Penda was here in the north with his men to help counter Aethelbert's invasion while Oswald and Cuthwulf and their men are ready to fight in the east. This readiness gives Ceawlin time to gather his own war band together. If he had not had men on the borders—"

"I know, I know," Niniane interrupted. "Ceawlin tells me that all the time. But I worry . . ."

"I agree that in other hands such a sharing of power could be dangerous. But not in Ceawlin's hands, Niniane. Nor is it just that the eorls know they owe their lands and their power to him. They will be loyal to him because they love him. It is a knack Ceawlin has, the ability to win the hearts of his men."

Niniane smiled up at him with unshadowed affection. "*You* love him, Sigurd. I know that well. Your loyalty I have never doubted."

He looked down into her upturned face, and bitterness rose in his heart. Did she never once think that his love was not all for Ceawlin? Did she never remember . . . ? "Do you remember those days in Winchester before you and Ceawlin wed?" he heard himself saying. "How you and I would play with Coenburg and the other children?"

Her eyes reflected the blue of the sky. "Yes," she said softly. Then, "How long ago that seems, Sigurd. It is hard to believe that I am the same person as that girl."

"You always put me in mind of a dainty little woodland deer," he said. "So graceful, so shy . . ."

She laughed. "Well, I have learned to be a lion, not a deer. I have had to, living with Ceawlin."

He stared at her, an arrested look in his eyes. It was true, he thought, looking at her with suddenly enlightened eyes. She was small and delicate and lovely as ever, but she no longer put him in mind of a dainty woodland deer. The gentle girl who had so stirred his heart in Winchester would never have raised a knife to her child's wet nurse, would never have been able to force Ceawlin into letting her go to Glastonbury against his better judgment.

She wore her hair dressed high this morning, braided and clasped with golden pins on the top of her elegant little head. That head was held proudly on its long slim neck; there was nothing shy or timid about Niniane any longer.

Yet it was the Niniane of today who haunted his dreams. This was the face he hungered for as he lay in bed at night beside the sweet and gentle wife he had taken; not the maiden face of ten years since. It was the woman she had become whom he now loved, the woman who was Ceawlin's wife.

"Sigurd." He stared at her, his heart hammering. "Don't let anything happen to him," she said. "I will feel better if I know you are at his side. He thinks he can do anything."

No, she never thought of him. She never thought of any man save Ceawlin. The rest of them were merely shadows to her, not flesh and blood at all. "There is little that Ceawlin cannot do, Niniane," he said, and strove to keep his voice free of bitterness. "But I will look out for him, never fear."

She raised up on her toes and softly kissed his cheek. "God go with you, Sigurd," she said.

"Thank you," he answered, and strode off to join his men.

*   *   *

It was raining on the day that Ceawlin marched out of Winchester. Besides Cutha, he had with him two other of his father's old earls, Oswald and Cynigils, and three of the earls of his own creation, Bertred, Ine, and Wuffa. In his war band marched just over two hundred thanes. He had also sent word to Gereint and was hoping for a British contingent of at least another fifty to meet him at Silchester, which was also the rendezvous he had given to Cuthwulf. His whole plan hinged on Penda being able to hold Aethelbert long enough to give Cuthwulf time to crush the invasion from Kent and march to reinforce Ceawlin with his two hundred men.

They were ten miles south of Silchester when his scouts brought him a report that Aethelbert was no longer in the north, was in fact to the east of them and marching toward Kent. Ceawlin cursed long and fluently. "He is going to try to join up with the war band from Kent. Just what I did not want him to do."

"There are many of them, my lord," the scout, one of Bertred's thanes, reported. "They are heading in the direction of Odinham." Odinham was the name of Ine's stronghold, some ten miles east of the Winchester-Silchester road.

Ceawlin stood in the rain, his hair plastered to his head, water dripping off his eyelashes, and said grimly, "I cannot allow him to come up on Cuthwulf. Cuthwulf does not have the numbers to stand against Aethelbert's full army."

"What shall we do then?" asked Cutha.

"Go after him and stop him," said Ceawlin.

"We have no more men than Cuthwulf does," Cutha reminded him.

"But my men are experienced," Ceawlin replied. "Bertred, give the order to march."

Ceawlin's men all knew how to move quickly. They crossed the sodden countryside, marching along miry lanes with a speed that took Aethelbert, whose men, hunched against the weather, had slogged along at a snail's pace, by surprise in the fields just outside of Odinham. Aethelbert, who had given the order for his men to camp for the night, thinking that Ceawlin was still within the confines of Winchester, was stunned when he realized that the king was upon him. It was growing dark by now and the two armies, camped on opposite sides of a dreary mud-filled beanfield, settled in for the night and made preparations to fight on the morrow.

The West Saxons were outnumbered by almost three to one. "We have experience on our side," Ceawlin said to his earls as they took shelter from the rain under a hastily rigged tent. "The East Anglians are not tried in the kind of battle we will see tomorrow. We must carry the day early. The longer it goes on, the more will their numbers tell against us."

The following day was the feast of Eostre and the dawn rose gray and bitter. The rain had not ceased to fall all through the night, and the wind was blowing it into the faces of the men of Wessex as they formed up in battle order. Ceawlin had given the right wing to Bertred, the left to Ine, and the center to Cutha. He himself was commanding a flying wing of twenty men, ready to reinforce whatever line should need him most. The rain poured down and the men waited for the enemy on the other side of the field to make the first move.

"My lord!" The shout came from one of the men in Ceawlin's wing. "Listen!" Then they all heard it, the sound of horses' hooves coming fast. Out of the murk they swirled, a troop of horses mired in mud from the furious ride. It was Gereint, and with him were thirty men.

"There are more coming," Gereint said to Ceawlin breathlessly. "But they are on foot."

Ceawlin grinned and threw an arm across Gereint's shoulders. "By all the gods, but it is good to see you!" He looked around him, to Bertred and Ine. "Now that the old fellowship is together again, how can we lose?"

Just then the wind began to shift, driving the rain full into the faces of the men from East Anglia. "Use your arrows first!" Ceawlin shouted, then hastily sent the horses to the rear and deployed Gereint and his men in the center with Cutha.

There was a shout from the far side of the field and then the East Anglians were coming on. Ceawlin's archers delivered a volley into the oncoming enemy mass. Aethelbert's archers replied, but they were half-blinded by the heavy rain and most of their arrows fell short. Once again Ceawlin's archers shot into the close-packed mass of oncoming thanes. The East Anglians, infuriated by their vulnerability, flung themselves upon the enemy host.

Ceawlin's line gave way a little under the weight of the numbers. Up and down the field men hacked and thrust at each other with sword, spear, and battleax. Cutha bore the brunt of it in the center, slashing at the masses of the enemy like a madman until he saw that his line had steadied.

Ine's line on the left was the first to waver and Ceawlin took his detachment of men and plowed into the battle line, laying about him furiously, a silver-haired instrument of destruction and death. When the line stiffened, he withdrew to lead his detachment to another weak spot.

Slowly, as the deadly minutes passed, the numbers of the East Anglians began to tell. Foot by foot, the West Saxons yielded ground. Tirelessly Ceawlin, the most awesome warrior on all the field, hurled himself into gaps in the line to beat down the enemy advance and cheer the hearts of his men. But still his line was being forced back.

Sigurd heard the fight before he actually saw it. The West Saxon line had been forced back almost to the edge of the field when out of the rain the forces from Wyckholm appeared. With a shout they fell upon the right flank of the East Anglians. Ceawlin, seeing the shock of Sigurd's assault, stormed to the front of his own center and rallied his men. The West Saxons, given new heart by the impact of fresh troops, drove forward again. Fighting like maddened dogs, the men of Wessex thrust at the East Anglian line, and it gave. Back and back it went, and then it broke. All of a sudden the East Anglians were in retreat, fleeing toward their horses on the far side of the field.

Ceawlin called his men back, refusing to allow a pursuit that might cost him lives he could ill afford to lose. Then he set about burying his dead. A mile away, on a soaked and muddy cornfield, Aethelbert gathered his men together to lick their wounds. Ceawlin waited until darkness had fallen, then circled around Aethelbert's army and went east, to cut off the East Anglians' access to Kent.

"Hammer of Thor, but I was glad to see you!" Ceawlin draped his arm across Sigurd's shoulder as the two of them walked from the cook fire to their sleeping places. It had been full light for some hours; Ceawlin had got his army to the ford near Oswald's manor of Gildham, the place where he had decided to make his next stand against Aethelbert. He had not allowed his tired men to stop for even a few hours to rest, so insistent was he on reaching his destination.

"I went first to Silchester," Sigurd said. "It was a good thing you thought to send a man to the city with messages."

"I sent him for Gereint. I did not know you would be coming." Ceawlin's hand tightened momentarily. "I might have known you would not fail me."

"We repulsed Aethelbert from Wyckholm too easily. He saw he could not take it and so he went on." Ceawlin could feel Sigurd's shoulders move in a shrug. "We should have dissembled our strength."

"What you did was better." Ceawlin grinned, his teeth showing very white in his dirty face. "Now we are between Aethelbert and Kent and I anticipate reinforcements from Cuthwulf momentarily. Things could not be better, Sigurd. And it is thanks to your timely rescue, my friend."

Ceawlin was always generous in sharing credit. It was one of the things that made him so popular with his men. "What would you have done had I not arrived?" Sigurd asked curiously.

"I told the eorls beforehand that if I called a retreat they were to take their men and run like hounds out of hel for the gates of Odinham manor. Ine had sent earlier to make sure they would be opened for us. But if we had to do that, we would leave free passage for Aethelbert to head for Kent." Ceawlin ran a hand through his filthy hair. "This is much better," he said with satisfaction. "Now the command of the war has passed to me."

The men of Ceawlin's war band slept soundly on the cold and muddy ground near Gild Ford and waited for news from Kent. It came the following afternoon, with the arrival of Cuthwulf and his war band of nearly two hundred: his own thanes and the thanes Ceawlin had given him from Winchester. Sigurd took one look at his brother's exuberant face and knew that Cuthwulf had been successful.

"It was a war band, all right," Cuthwulf told Ceawlin and the rest of the eorls as they sat around a fire trying to keep warm. "The leaders were Aethelbert's kinsmen, Oslaf and Cnebba. They had rounded up a huge herd of cattle by the time I came up with them at Wibbandun." Cuthwulf's teeth flashed in the darkness of his beard. "We beat them into the ground," he boasted. "The two eorls are dead along with half of their men. The rest of them went running back to Kent."

"A good job, Cuthwulf," said Ceawlin. "Well done." Then, "What have you done with the cattle?"

A furtive look passed over Cuthwulf's face. "Oh," he said, and waved his hand, "we disposed of them."

"How?" said the king.

Cuthwulf's jaw jutted forward. "I left them under the guard of some of my men."

"They must be returned to their original owners."

"Those cattle are mine!" said Cuthwulf. "My booty. I promised them to my men."

"They are not yours, either to keep or to promise. Those cattle belong to the vils and farms from which they were stolen by the Kentmen. And you will return them."

Cuthwulf glared at Ceawlin. The king's eyes were as brilliant a turquoise as Sigurd had ever seen them. "Cuthwulf," said Sigurd quietly, "Ceawlin is right. If the cattle had come from Kent, then they would be booty. But they belong to West Saxons, to our own people."

"What about the cattle that belong to the Britons?" said Cuthwulf to Ceawlin.

"The Britons who live in Wessex are my subjects too. You will return all the cattle."

Cuthwulf cursed, got to his feet, and left the fire.

"You should have waited," Cutha said to Ceawlin in the sudden silence. "He has done you a great service, Ceawlin. You might have given him a chance to relish his victory."

Ceawlin's eyes still glittered. "I told him," he said to Cutha, and his voice was cold. "I told him before ever I sent him east that the cattle were not his. He knew. He had no right to promise them to his men."

The silence around the fire was heavy. Then Cutha got to his feet and left to join his son. Sigurd put his head into his hands and stared at the ground.

Aethelbert awoke the morning after the Battle of Odinham to discover that Ceawlin had gone. Edric was grim-faced and dour when told the news, but Aethelbert perceived it differently from his brother-by-marriage. "He did not wish to meet me again," he declared. "It was only luck that Sigurd came up at the last moment like that. It took the heart from our thanes. They did not know how many more fresh assaults they would have to withstand."

"It certainly took the heart from our troops, my lord," said Edric. "But I doubt if Ceawlin's departure has aught to do with fear."

"His victory was merely luck," Aethelbert repeated. "The rain was in our faces and then his men came up just in time."

The rest of the East Anglian eorls seconded their king. Edric looked bleakly over the field where men were at work burning the East Anglian dead. The fools, he thought. Ceawlin had beaten them. They had been three men to every one of his, and he had beaten them. And now he had gone to cut off their chance of joining up with the forces from Kent.

"In fact," said Aethelbert with sudden passion, "*we* are the ones left holding the field. By all the laws of battle, we may claim the victory."

It was pointless to argue, Edric thought. Nothing he said would alter Aethelbert's vision of himself as a great warrior. He could only hope that Oslaf and Cnebba had been successful against whoever it was that Ceawlin had sent to deal with them. That Ceawlin had sent someone, he had no doubt. He had fought against Cynric's son for so long that he thought he probably knew Ceawlin's mind better than any one of Ceawlin's own eorls.

"We will march for Kent tomorrow, when we have given honor to our dead," said Aethelbert. "Once we have joined forces with my kinsmen, there will not be luck enough in the world to enable Ceawlin to withstand us."

It took Aethelbert's war band two days to cover the twenty miles that Ceawlin had covered in one night. When they were five miles distant they learned that Ceawlin was awaiting them at Gild Ford. Then they learned of the defeat of Oslaf and Cnebba.

"We must fight," Edric said as the East Anglian eorls took council together. "If we turn back, he will only follow. And Penda bars the way back to East Anglia." He looked around the circle of gloomy faces. "The odds are even, my lords. He does not have advantage of us that way."

"We could not defeat them when we outnumbered them," one of the eorls said heavily. "How are we to beat them now?"

The myth of an East Anglian victory at Odinham could not weather the reality of Ceawlin and four hundred West Saxons staring them in the face.

"They had luck on their side last time," Edric said. He infused his voice with as much confidence as he could muster. "Come, my lords! Is East Anglia to be frightened by a battle against equal odds?"

"Of course not!" said Aethelbert, his passionate heart stirred by Edric's words.

The rest of the eorls agreed, although with noticeably less enthusiasm.

The Battle of Gild Ford was fought the following day and was a rout for the East Anglians. Aethelbert's men crumbled under the weight of the West Saxon charge. After less than ten minutes the East Anglian lines had broken up into swarms of fleeing thanes. Ceawlin gave the order to pursue, and slaughter was done as the West Saxons mercilessly cut down the fleeing East Anglians. By day's end the fields around Gild Ford were heaped with the slain.

When night fell, Aethelbert, who had got away on horseback, was safely in Kent. But the army he had brought so proudly from East Anglia lay in bloody ruins on the soil of Wessex. The king returned to Sutton Hoo, a reluctant herald of disaster. Not only did he have to tell his sister that her hopes of winning a throne for her son had perished at Gild Ford; he had also to tell her that Edric, her husband, was dead.

Ceawlin returned to Winchester with his eorls and his thanes after sending a messenger north to tell Penda that the threat from East Anglia was over. Word had gone before them of the king's victory, and most of the population of Winchester-Venta lined the road to welcome their defenders.

Sigurd rode with his father, one on either side of the gold-helmeted king. Cuthwulf had not accompanied the army back to Winchester; directly after the battle he had taken his men and returned to Banford, which manor he held for his father while Cutha remained in his hall at Winchester. When first Sigurd had learned that Ceawlin meant to give Cuthwulf command of the expedition to Kent, he had been pleased. His brother's growing discontent had been an increasing worry to him, and such a command was certain to placate Cuthwulf's pride. Now he was not so sure that Ceawlin's choice of Cuthwulf had been the honor Sigurd had originally deemed it. He was afraid rather that Ceawlin had bestowed it as a final test of Cuthwulf's allegiance; and he feared further that it was a test that Cuthwulf had failed.

Edith welcomed her husband with such heartfelt thanksgiving that Sigurd felt ashamed he had thought of her so little. The twins came running to fling their little arms around his legs, and his heart swelled with love as he stooped to encircle their sturdy little bodies with his arms. His love for his children was spontaneous, unshadowed—the only love he knew, he sometimes thought, that was untainted by guilt.

The night of their return to Winchester, Ceawlin held a huge victory feast in the great hall, which was crammed beyond capacity with the eorls who had returned with the army and their thanes, as well as the hall thanes belonging to Ceawlin himself. Alric outdid himself with his commemorative song. He could have heard the details of the battles only a few hours before, yet he had it all down in glorious music; Sigurd's own rescue march came in for great play.

"How did he manage it so quickly?" Sigurd asked Ceawlin across Niniane's empty seat.

Ceawlin grinned at him. "I sent someone back to Winchester right after the battle to regale Alric with the tale. I wanted him to be ready."

Sigurd started to laugh. "Gods. Do you never forget anything?"

"Rarely," Ceawlin answered, and turned to join in the chorus that was calling for a repeat of the song.

"Oh, Sigurd, that was wonderful." Edith's blue eyes were shining as she regarded her hero-husband. "You saved the king's war band. I am so proud of you."

The smile he gave her was faintly crooked. "Are you, Edith?"

"Oh, yes."

Her thin, fragile hand was lying on the table and he patted it gently. "I'm glad," he answered.

The singing continued and the wine passed around and around the hall. Then Alric retired to enjoy the wine cup himself and the roar of male voices and male laughter rose to the rafters. Bertred and Wuffa and Gereint were sitting on the other side of Edith, and Sigurd could hear them reminiscing about their days of chasing around Wessex after Edric. They were all eorls, all save Gereint, who had refused to accept the Saxon title in deference to his father, and all ruled over the large numbers of slaves and ceorls and thanes that were attached to their manors; yet tonight they sounded like boys again as they relived their coming-of-age exploits with Ceawlin.

"I think it is time for me to retire," Edith said in Sigurd's ear.

He laughed. "Yes. It is getting rather noisy." Around the hall the other women and girls were standing, making ready to depart, to leave the hall to their wine-guzzling men.

"Will you be coming soon, my love?"

Her blue eyes were so hopeful. Sigurd felt the familiar stab of guilt and said heartily, "Of course. Do not go to sleep just yet."

She smiled at him, her pretty face lighting to radiance. As she walked away Sigurd chanced to turn his head, and Ceawlin caught his eye.

"Lucky man," Ceawlin said. "The rest of us have wives at too great a distance this night."

"There are willing women enough in Venta!" Wuffa called, over-hearing Ceawlin's comment, and the men at the first table roared with approval.

"Not for the king," Sigurd heard himself saying.

There was a faint flicker of surprise in Ceawlin's eyes. Then Bertred said, "Ah, well, Niniane is worth the waiting for." He grinned, leaned around Sigurd, and said to Ceawlin, "Do you remember how she made us dig in the fields like slaves all that summer at Bryn Atha?"

"Do I not," Ceawlin said with feeling.

"Well, I will tell you this," said Wuffa boisterously. "Because of that summer, I can tell when my own coerls are slacking off. I know when a field is due to be harvested!"

"Do you remember . . ." Gereint said, and the old comrades were off on another round of reminiscences of bygone days. After half an hour, Sigurd left to go to his wife.

Chapter 28

T HE sun was shining the day the queen returned to Winchester. Sigurd was with his father at the armory when he heard the shouts.

"Niniane is back," Cutha said, and did not look at Sigurd.

"Yes." Sigurd continued to watch the thanes stacking the shields and swords and bows they had taken from the field at Gild Ford. Then, after a minute, "I'd better go. Ceawlin is not here this morning. I'll be back shortly." Cutha watched his son's figure all the way to the door, a frown between his high-arched brows.

There was quite a procession coming up the street and Sigurd saw immediately that Penda was riding beside Niniane. He stood in front of the great hall and watched the horses slowly advancing toward him.

Suddenly a small figure ran into the street crying "Mama!" Sigurd recognized Ceowulf's bright blond head and ran forward himself as the small boy crossed into the path of the oncoming horses. Then Cerdic and Crida appeared, following Ceowulf but walking more slowly. Cerdic had his two-year-old brother on his shoulders in the same way that Ceawlin had always carried his boys, and as Niniane's horse came to a halt her sons surrounded it. Sigurd slowed his own steps and moved to join Penda.

"I decided to escort the queen myself," Penda said as he jumped to the ground from his horse's back. He gave Sigurd a regretful smile. "I wanted to hear the whole tale firsthand. I gather you beat Aethelbert pretty decisively."

"We annihilated him," Sigurd said.

"And I missed it." The regret was even more noticeable.

Sigurd smiled. "You more than did your part, Penda." But his eyes were no longer on his brother-by-marriage; they were on Niniane as she was preparing to alight from her horse. "Let me," he said quickly and moved forward to lift her from the saddle.

Her waist was reed slim under his hands and she smiled up at him once she was on her feet. "Thank you, Sigurd."

"Mama! Mama!" Her youngest was holding out his arms to her and she reached to take him from Cerdic, saying, "You should not carry him like this, Cerdic. You could drop him. He is no lightweight anymore."

"I can carry him, Mother," Cerdic said impatiently. "He likes it." Then, in a burst of wounded feeling, "Father made us stay here in Winchester the whole time! We missed all the fun, Mother!"

Niniane laughed. "You sound remarkably like someone else I know," she said, and looked mischievously at Penda.

The eorl smiled back reluctantly. "Women never understand these things," he said.

"Well, that is a true word," she replied. Then, to Crida, "Where is your father?"

"He was judging a dispute in Venta this morning, Mother," Crida answered. "We did not know that you were so close to Winchester."

Niniane reached out to ruffle his shining fair hair and he ducked his head away from her hand, self-conscious of his mother's caress in front of the men. "Come along inside," she said to her sons, "and tell me what you have been doing while I was away." She bent to put little Sigurd on his feet, then took up his hand and began to walk toward the king's hall.

"Ceowulf," Sigurd said softly as the children turned to follow their mother. Ceawlin's third son turned to look at him inquiringly. "Do not run out in front of horses like that. You could frighten them. You would not want your mother to be thrown, would you?"

"My mother has never fallen from a horse," Ceowulf replied scornfully.

"Sigurd is right," said Penda. "You could get yourself trampled, running in front of horses like that, Prince."

"All right," said Ceowulf, anxious to be off and clearly not relishing this rebuke from his father's eorls. Without waiting to give them a chance to say more, he turned and ran after his brothers.

Penda shouted to the men who had ridden in with him to take the horses to the stables, then turned back to Sigurd. "Come into my hall with me. I want to hear all about the battle," he said, and Sigurd obligingly fell into step with him as they crossed the courtyard.

Ceawlin did not arrive back in Winchester until late in the afternoon. Niniane was in the women's hall with Nola. When Ceawlin had first become king, Niniane had seen to it that the bower girls were all offered decent marriages, either to thanes or to tradesmen from Venta. Nola had not married, however, had chosen to remain in Winchester as Niniane's chief handmaid, and she had long been in charge of the women's hall and the bower. Niniane was consulting with her this afternoon about a possible marriage for Brynhild, one of the bower maidens, when Brynhild herself came into the hall with two other girls and said, "My lady, the king has just ridden in."

Niniane's face lighted to beauty. "I'll speak with you about this again tomorrow, Nola," she said, smiled briefly at the three young faces she saw staring at her, and walked to the door of the hall. The three thanes' daughters who were under Nola's charge immediately went out to the porch, from which point they would have a good view of the courtyard.

The breeze was lifting Ceawlin's hair from his shoulders, and the color of his eyes was visible all the way to the porch of the women's hall. He had seen his wife, and as the girls watched, he swung down from his horse, threw his reins to a groom, and enveloped her in a ruthless embrace.

Merta, the youngest and most impressionable of the girls, sighed longingly. "She is so lucky," she said, wide eyes on Niniane, who was now laughing up into her husband's face.

"It isn't fair," the second girl answered. "No matter how fine a husband we may get, still there will never be another man like the king."

"How does she do it?" Brynhild, the eldest, repeated the most-oft-asked question in all the women's hall. "How does she bind him to her? A man like that . . . how does she do it?"

"It is very simple, really." The girls had not heard Nola come out onto the porch and they all jumped guiltily at the sound of her voice. "He loves her," said Nola. "That is all it is."

"But why, Nola?" asked Brynhild suddenly. "I like Niniane, I think she is very pretty, and for certain she has been a good wife to him, a good queen. Yet the same could be said for many wives, and their husbands do not honor them as the king does Niniane."

Nola looked at the three young faces that were regarding her so wistfully. It was true that Ceawlin had set a standard for husbands that most men would find it hard to follow. Nola smiled a little wryly. "That I cannot tell you." Her own eyes followed the retreating figures of the king and queen. "He was not always of so faithful a nature," she said. "I remember well the days of the old king, when the women in the bower would kill to get a call to go to Ceawlin's bed. But all that has changed since he took Niniane to wife."

Merta's eyes were enormous. "Nola, did you ever . . . ?"

"Enough of this talk," Nola snapped, jerking her eyes back to the girls. "It is lucky for you that things have changed, that you have a Christian queen who thinks it important that the honor of the girls under her care be safeguarded. Now you have the chance of making good marriages, bearing children who will carry on the honor of their fathers' names and lands. It is a good thing for all of us women that Niniane is queen in Winchester."

"Yes, Nola," the girls chorused in hasty agreement.

"I thought I had sent you to the dye house."

"Yes, Nola. We are going." And the girls fled from the hall and from the suddenly fiery look in Nola's brown eyes.

*   *   *

Sigurd pushed the platter away from him and drank a long draft from his wine cup.

"What is the matter, Sigurd?" It was Niniane's husky voice and he forced himself to look at her and to smile.

"Nothing," he answered with effort. "I am just tired, that is all."

Her slate-blue eyes searched his face. "You do look tired. Are you certain you are not ill?"

"Quite certain, Niniane. Don't fuss over me. I am perfectly fine."

Her eyes flickered a little at the unaccustomed irritation she heard in his voice. He could see that he had not convinced her, but she turned away as he had requested and gave her attention once more to Edith, who was sitting on her other side.

Sigurd himself did not understand what was the matter with him, why he was suddenly finding it so impossible to sit here with Ceawlin and Niniane in the familiar intimacy of the king's hall. Ceawlin had invited Penda to sup with him, and Sigurd and Edith as well; it was not an unusual invitation. There was no reason for Sigurd to suddenly feel that he could do it no longer—sit with her and talk with her and watch her and pretend that he did not care.

She and Edith were talking of their children. He pretended to listen to Ceawlin but in reality he heard only the soft voices of the women as they shared their favorite remedies of what to do for a child who is cutting a tooth. Edith's voice was faintly stiff. She had never been comfortable with Niniane. Sigurd sometimes feared that she suspected that his own feelings for the queen were deeper than they should be. It was certain that Niniane went out of her way to be kind to Edith; there was no other reason for his wife to be always so mistrustful of Niniane's obvious goodwill.

Supper was finally over and he could decently say it was time to leave. The king made no effort to keep his guests. After all, Sigurd thought, Ceawlin had not seen his wife in weeks. He would be anxious to get her to himself.

Would you not feel the same if you were in my place? Ceawlin had asked him that once, he remembered.

Name of the gods, why did it hurt so much? And it was not getting better. It was getting worse.

He went to bed in his own hall, the hall that had once belonged to Cynric's eorl Onela and that Ceawlin had bestowed upon Sigurd as soon as he became king, and lay awake staring into the darkness. Sigurd held to the traditional Saxon practice and did not share a room with his wife; Edith slept in the hall's second room with their children. It mattered not if he were restless. He would not disturb her.

His thoughts went round and round. For all these long years he had assumed he had made peace with this tormented love of his. It was not his fault, he had told himself, that he loved his friend's wife. He had loved her before Ceawlin even thought of her or had planned to make her his. If fate had not taken a hand, Niniane would have been lying beside him tonight and not beside Ceawlin.

So he had always thought. Then at Wyckholm she had said, "I have learned to be a lion, not a deer," and he had known that it was the lion that he loved. And for some reason, it was as if that knowledge had opened an old wound, a wound that bled and bled and would not stop.

And Ceawlin. The gods knew, he loved Ceawlin more than he did his own brother. Yet now he could scarce look upon his friend without seeing only the possessor of Niniane. He had even fantasized that if Ceawlin should be killed in the battle against Aethelbert, then would Niniane be a widow . . .

He thrashed about in the bed in his anguish. He could not go on like this. He would have to do something. He would have to be quit of those two. There was no other way. He would take Edith and the children and leave Winchester. The other eorls had done so; why should not he?

He would tell Ceawlin on the morrow.

He thought of the look of bewilderment he knew he would see in Ceawlin's eyes. Woden help me, he prayed. What am I going to say to him?

In the morning Sigurd learned that Ceawlin had taken his two older boys hunting, so he had to wait. He went instead to see his father.

"I have decided to live at Wokham," he said to Cutha. "Ceawlin granted me the lands when first he became king, and I have scarcely ever been there. It is time for me to take up my duties as an eorl, see to my own land and my own people. I owe it to my son." It was the speech he had prepared for Ceawlin, and he looked now to see how it fared with Cutha.

His father looked first surprised, then thoughtful. Cutha's brown hair was streaked with gray, but his thin dark face had aged surprisingly little in the years since Cynric's death. At the moment, Sigurd thought, he himself probably felt older than Cutha looked.

"I think that might be wise," Cutha answered at last.

Sigurd was surprised. He had expected an argument.

"Have you told Ceawlin?" Cutha asked.

"Not yet. He is out hunting with Cerdic and Crida. I will tell him this afternoon."

Cutha's blue eyes were shrewd. "He won't like it. You know how he relies on you, Sigurd."

Sigurd did know, and the knowledge made him feel wretched. "His sons are getting older. It will be well for Ceawlin to learn to turn to Cerdic and not to me."

"Yes . . ." said Cutha. "And I will still be here."

Sigurd forced a smile. "It will be best for Edith and the children for us to go to Wokham. It is time for me to think of them."

"Tell that to Ceawlin," Cutha advised.

"Yes," Sigurd said. "I will."

It was even harder than Sigurd had anticipated, telling Ceawlin he was leaving Winchester. The sight of Ceawlin riding in from the hunt with his sons brought back such forceful memories of the days when he and Ceawlin were boys and would steal out of Winchester to go hunting together. How happy they had been. How carefree.

Yet memory played tricks, he thought after a minute. The happy boyhood he was picturing had in fact been clouded with treachery, with the shadow of Edwin's hatred and Guthfrid's enmity. It was the friendship between him and Ceawlin that shone so crystal clear; the rest of Winchester had been muddy with strife and rivalry, struggling in the turbulent wake of an aging king. But the memory of their boyhood was still vivid in Sigurd's mind as he went to see Ceawlin to tell him of his decision to leave Winchester.

He went to the king's hall and found Ceawlin sitting at the table eating bread and cheese and drinking beer with his two eldest sons. The three were laughing when Sigurd came in, and Sigurd saw a flicker of resentment cross Cerdic's face as his father's friend approached the table. It was not often that his children got Ceawlin to themselves, and Sigurd was sorry to be the one to intrude upon what was obviously a treat for Cerdic and Crida. But it could not be helped.

"Ceawlin," he said, "I must speak with you."

"Of course," Ceawlin replied. He waved a hand to one of the chairs. "Sit down." His voice was both casual and commanding.

Sigurd came around and sat down next to Crida. Perhaps it would be easier to do this in the boys' presence. "I am going to take Edith and the children and go live at Wokham," he said baldly.

Ceawlin quirked an eyebrow. "You do not need to ask my permission to visit your manor, Sigurd. If you feel the need to go to Wokham, then go."

"You don't understand, Ceawlin. I am not talking about going for a visit. I am going to live there. Permanently. I am not coming back to Winchester."

Ceawlin put down the beer he had been about to drink and turned slowly to look at Sigurd. His face was very still. "Why?"

Sigurd could not meet his friend's eyes. "Your other eorls live upon their manors. It is time for me also to look to what is mine. I owe it to my son."

"You are not one of my 'other eorls,' " said Ceawlin. His voice was very quiet. Then, "Cerdic and Crida, you may leave us."

"Yes, Father." The boys recognized the note in Ceawlin's voice and got instantly to their feet and left the hall.

Ceawlin waited until the door had closed behind them before he said, "What is the matter, Sigurd? Is it Cuthwulf?"

"No!" Sigurd stared at him in surprise. "This has nothing to do with Cuthwulf."

"I see." Ceawlin ran a hand through the short hair on his forehead. "Then I don't understand, Sigurd. Of course you are perfectly free to do as you wish; you know that. Wokham is yours, and if you wish to live there, then that is your decision. But . . . I don't understand."

Sigurd stared into those familiar blue eyes and a sudden surge of love rushed into his heart. This was not Ceawlin's fault. And he knew his friend would miss him sorely. There was no forbidden love torturing Ceawlin's heart to mar the friendship he felt for Sigurd. No, of course Ceawlin could not understand. And not understanding, he was hurt.

Gods! He seemed to spread misery wherever he went. Sigurd put his elbows on the table and buried his head in his hands. "It is just . . . Ceawlin, I cannot bear to be around Niniane any longer!"

There was absolute silence. Finally Sigurd raised his head. Ceawlin was very pale, and as Sigurd watched, his thin mobile mouth twitched once at the corner. Yet the eyes that met Sigurd's were steady. "Once I suspected that you might . . . but, hammer of Thor, Sigurd, that was ten years ago!"

"And have your feelings changed in ten years?" Sigurd asked bitterly.

The corner of Ceawlin's mouth twitched once more. "No. No, they have not."

"So you see, it is best that I go."

"Has she . . . does she . . . ?"

Sigurd's laugh was not pleasant. "Niniane does not know there exists another man in the world but you, Ceawlin. You have seen how I feel, my brother, my father . . . gods, perhaps even my wife . . . but not her."

At last Ceawlin's eyes dropped. Sigurd stared with pain at the face of his friend, more familiar to him than was his own. "I wanted to marry her. I never told you that, but I was going to ask my father for his permission. And then came those intrigues of Guthfrid's, and you two were forced to leave Winchester . . ."

"I did not know." Ceawlin's voice was muffled. His long lashes, so much darker than his hair, lay against his cheeks, hiding his eyes. "Sigurd. I do not know what to say to you."

"There is nothing to say." Sigurd stood up. "When I came here I was not going to tell you this, but then I saw that you would not believe any other reason I gave you." He rubbed his forehead as though it ached. "In truth, Ceawlin, when I saw you ride in with your boys, I was put in mind of our own boyhood and I thought I owed you more than a feeble excuse."

"Sigurd." Ceawlin rose to his feet also. His eyes were purely turquoise. "Do you hate me?"

"*No!*" He took a step forward and then Ceawlin's arms were around his shoulders. "'Never that," Sigurd said shakily.

The two men stood thus for a long moment and then Ceawlin's arms dropped. "Go, then. And if you ever feel you can come back, know that you will be welcome."

Sigurd nodded, not trusting himself to speak, turned, and almost fled from the room.

Chapter 29

THE December night was bitterly cold, and all over Winchester men sat close to their hearths trying to keep warm. The enormous hearth in the great hall burned with two fierce fires and the king's-hall thanes clustered close, mending their gear or carving in wood and talking desultorily of this and that. Most of the eorls' halls lay empty save for Cutha's and Bertred's. Bertred had been in Winchester just that afternoon in order to consult with the king about Cuthwulf, whose manor lay near to Bertred's and who had been more restless than usual this autumn. Bertred was not in his own hall this night, however; he was in the king's hall with Ceawlin and his family.

Cutha sat with his own hall thanes and stared at the fire burning so brightly on his hearth. He was feeling old, old and alone. He had done what he wanted, had made Ceawlin King of Wessex, and this night he sat and wondered what he had got out of it. Both his sons were exiled from Winchester, Cuthwulf because he was at odds with Ceawlin and Sigurd . . . For over two years now Sigurd had been at Wokham, nor did he show any signs of planning to come back.

And himself? On the surface, his position in Winchester had not changed. Ceawlin had not taken any of his duties away from him, any of his honors. But all of Wessex knew that the only true power lay with the king, and with those who had the king's ear. And these last two years Cutha had slowly been forced to the humiliating realization that his was not one of the voices that counted with Ceawlin.

In truth, he had never enjoyed the same position under the son as he had under the father. It had been *his* son, Sigurd, who was Ceawlin's right hand, who had Ceawlin's trust. Now that Sigurd was gone, Ceawlin had ceased to make even a pretense that Cutha was a power in his government.

Oh, he was always amiable, always courteous. But that was not enough for Cutha. He felt within himself the urgent demands of his own talents, talents which he had no space to exercise within the confines of Ceawlin's kingship.

It was not enough for him to be the ruler of his own manor, his own thanes and ceorls and slaves. It seemed to satisfy the rest of them,

Ceawlin's eorls who were content to rule their property and their tenants and send tribute to Ceawlin to signify their bondage to him. Cutha wanted power on a larger scale.

His dissatisfaction had come to a head this past summer, when Ceawlin had betrothed Cerdic to the daughter of the King of Sussex without even consulting him.

The insult still burned whenever he thought of it. True, there had been no actual ceremony, just an agreement that when Cerdic turned sixteen the betrothal would be formalized. But Ceawlin had not even told him until it was all accomplished!

The fire hissed and one of the thanes got up to stir the logs. Cutha looked broodingly around at the circle of his men. He had begun to weigh in his mind his own power, those who would cleave to him as opposed to those who would cleave to Ceawlin. He had talked to Cynigils, one of Cynric's and Edric's old eorls who had stayed with Ceawlin after Edric's defeat, and Cynigils had some dissatisfactions with Ceawlin also. He thought, as did Cuthwulf, that Ceawlin showed too much favor to the British.

Outside, the wind howled, blowing from hall to hall, announcing with its noisy ferocity that once again winter had returned to Wessex. Those inside the king's hall this night heeded it not, however, so intent were they on their various pursuits. Cerdic and Crida sat cross-legged before the hearth, absorbed in a game of dice. Ceowulf looked on and persistently begged to be allowed to play too. Finally Ceawlin heeded his third son's pleas and, looking up from his conversation with Bertred, commanded the older two to let him join in the game.

"He *always* wants to do what we are doing, Father," Crida complained.

This was indisputably true. There were but fifteen months between Cerdic and Crida and the two eldest boys were fast friends and constant companions. Ceowulf was three years younger than Crida and almost as big, yet his elder brothers considered him one of the little ones, relegating him to the company of Sigurd and eighteen-month-old Eirik. Ceowulf resented this bitterly and there was constant strife among the brothers as he tried to keep up with Cerdic and Crida and was as constantly rejected. Occasionally, however, one of his parents, usually his mother, took a hand and made Cerdic and Crida play with him, and so it was this particularly cold and windy night.

Cerdic relinquished his dice to Ceowulf with unusual graciousness and went to sit on a skin at his father's feet. During the last year Ceawlin had been allowing his eldest son to watch as he went about the various duties of kingship. Cerdic would turn thirteen the following month and was very proud of the increased honor shown to him by his father. The legs he had to cross were growing longer by the month, but he folded himself onto the floor with the seemingly boneless ease of childhood and sat quietly, listening to the men talk.

"How many men has he gathered?" Ceawlin was asking Bertred.

"Eighty, I should say," came the grim reply.

Ceawlin cursed and fell silent, staring somberly into the flames.

"Is it Cuthwulf, Father?" Cerdic asked tentatively.

"Yes." Ceawlin did not look at his son, continued to stare into the flames. "He is forcing me to take action against him," he finally said.

Bertred rubbed his head. "I don't understand him, Ceawlin. Sword of Woden, what does he want?"

"I doubt that he knows. Cuthwulf does not think. He never did."

"Cannot you get Cutha to pull the reins in on him?"

There was a long silence. Then, "I do not think so."

Cerdic stared at his father. Ceawlin's face was iron hard. The boy looked next at Bertred. The eorl's pleasant face was no less serious than the king's. "What of Sigurd?" Bertred asked, his voice diffident.

Ceawlin leaned back in his chair, resting his head against its high back. "Sigurd has already spoken to him."

"I see." Then, "What are you going to do, Ceawlin?"

His father's blue-green glance rested for a moment on his face. For a terrible moment Cerdic thought Ceawlin was going to tell him to leave, but then his father looked at Bertred and said, "Make him leave Banford."

Bertred's eyes widened. "And send him where?"

"Back here, to Winchester. Where he will be under my eye."

"Cutha will not like that."

"Cutha either has not been able to control him, or does not wish to control him. He has left me no choice. I cannot have my eorls gathering their own war bands. A reasonable number of thanes to protect their borders is one thing. Eighty men is something else."

"Yes," said Bertred. "It is." Then, "Cutha and Cynigils have been very friendly of late."

"That has not escaped me." Ceawlin's voice was very cold.

The door to the hall opened and a gust of frigid air blew across the room. Cerdic looked around to see his mother coming in. She had been to the princes' hall seeing his two youngest brothers put to bed. She crossed the floor now, loosening her cloak and brushing back the hair that had been blown loose by the wind. Her cheeks were rosy with cold, and Cerdic, looking from Niniane to Bertred, was surprised to see a look of frank admiration on the eorl's face. "How do you stay so young, Niniane?" he asked, and Cerdic's mother laughed and took the third seat by the fire.

Cerdic had never thought of his mother in any light but as his mother. Ceawlin he saw as a man and a king, and it had been many years since first he thought that there was no one else in the world so splendid as his father. But Mother was Mother. Less important to him now than she had been when he was a child, but still a necessary and unquestioned part of his existence. Father belonged to his kingdom, his people. Mother belonged to them—to his father and him and his little brothers. Oh, she ordered the service, the women, the cooking, the weaving and such, but these things she did for them. Mother was . . . just Mother.

But he saw the admiration in Bertred's eyes, and for the first time he looked at his mother and saw a woman. Saw that her hair was smooth and shining and of a color he had never seen on anyone else. Saw her large gray-blue eyes, so like his own, her tip-tilted nose and delicately curved mouth that had Ceowulf's dimple in its corner. She *was* young, his mother. Young, and very pretty.

She was smiling at him. "How good of you, Cerdic, to let your brother play with Crida for a while."

At that Crida's silver-blond head turned. "He keeps forgetting the score," he said disgustedly. "Can't Ceowulf do *anything?*"

"You were not so good at keeping score when you were eight, Crida," Niniane said. Which was not true, Cerdic thought. Crida had always had a good brain for counting. He had, in fact, counted before Cerdic did. A fact which Cerdic would admit to himself if not to Crida.

"I will give you a game, Ceowulf," he said now, and was rewarded by his mother's grateful look. Crida threw down the dice and stood up, scowling.

"You may go to bed, Crida," Ceawlin said.

Crida threw his father a furious look, met Ceawlin's eyes, and muttered, "Yes, sir." He picked up his cloak and went out the door to go to the princes' hall.

Niniane sighed. "He has no patience with those who are less clever than himself."

"He will have to learn," said Ceawlin.

"I suppose." She smiled at Bertred and said, "How are Meghan and the children?"

Cerdic watched Bertred's face light with a returning smile before he turned to throw the dice with his brother.

The sleeping room was icy cold and Niniane pulled the rugs and furs up to her chin and said to Ceawlin, "What is Cuthwulf up to now? I imagine that was what brought Bertred to Winchester this time of year."

"Yes." Ceawlin finished undressing and got into the bed beside her. "He is gathering a war band."

"*What?*" She raised up on an elbow to stare into his face.

"There can be no other explanation. Bertred says he has at least eighty men in his hall."

"But where did he get so many men?"

"He has taken a number of ceorls off the land and made them thanes. And, from what Bertred hears, he has sent for some kinsmen from Wight."

"Dear God."

"Yes."

The candle still burned on the chest beside the bed, and Niniane looked down into her husband's eyes. They were pure turquoise. He was furious at Cuthwulf. Niniane could not blame him. "What will you do?" she asked.

"Make him come to Winchester. Make him live under my eye."

"But . . . Cutha."

He said to her what he could not say to Bertred. "I will see Cutha in hel, Niniane, before I allow his son to challenge my authority."

"Have you asked Cutha to speak to him?"

"Cutha has never made the slightest attempt to control Cuthwulf. I think he feels that Cuthwulf is in the right, feels that the split between us is my fault, not Cuthwulf's. The fact of the matter is, Niniane, that I do not greatly care what Cutha thinks anymore. Cuthwulf has been asking to be dealt with for years, and now he has gone too far."

Niniane chewed on her lip. He was right, she knew. Yet she had had an uneasy feeling of late about Cutha. There was an expression in Cutha's eyes when he looked at Ceawlin that she did not like at all. She said nothing, however, knowing Ceawlin would not listen even if she did. "When will you send for him?" she asked instead.

"After Yule. He is not likely to do much during the winter. I have time."

She shivered and he reached an arm over to draw her close. She nestled against him gratefully. "Why are you never cold? No matter how freezing it is, you are never cold."

"I have hot blood," he said, and growled and bit her ear.

She laughed, then said warningly, "Ceawlin, don't you dare push these blankets off me."

"I'll maneuver under them," he promised, and she put her arms around his neck and let him draw her under his warm and urgent weight.

Cerdic would turn thirteen on January 6, and on the day before his birthday it stormed and rained in torrents. He stood in the door of the princes' hall and looked gloomily outside at the weather. It was cold and dark and heavy with rain. And his father had promised to take him hunting tomorrow! There was to be a huge banquet for him in the great hall in honor of his turning thirteen, and the banquet would still go forward. But he had been looking forward to the hunt. It was to be just him and his father. Not even Crida was coming. And it had to rain! His mother would never let him go in the rain. He had been sick last week, sneezing and coughing; he knew she would not let him go.

Cerdic cursed under his breath, using words he had heard his father use when he was particularly angry. Then he saw the horse galloping up the slippery paved street.

"Cerdic, close the door. It is freezing in here!" It was Crida, and he said, without turning his head, "Something has happened, Crida. Look."

Crida's fair head appeared at his shoulder and the two of them watched together. "It's one of Bertred's thanes," Crida said. "I remember he came to Winchester with Bertred before Yule." Crida had an uncanny memory for men's faces.

The man was heading directly for the king's hall. As the two boys watched, he disappeared inside the door. "What can it be?" Cerdic asked.

"Whatever it is, it can't be good," said Crida.

"Close that door." It was Alric, one of the few voices in Winchester to exact obedience from the two eldest princes these days. Reluctantly Cerdic obliged, then turned to go back to his lessons with the scop.

The news brought by Bertred's thane was not good. The previous week Cuthwulf had taken his men and ridden north, into the land of the Dobunni. He had been met at Bedcanford by a hastily gathered troop of British and he had defeated them. The Saxons had then looted several of the towns in the area and returned in triumph to Banford.

"They say that the Dobunni chief was slain in the battle, my lord," Bertred's thane told Ceawlin. "We learned all this because my lady just happened to send a man to Banford on an errand to Cuthwulf's wife, and he arrived during the victory banquet. As soon as he discovered the story, he raced back to Romsey to tell the eorl."

"What chief was killed?" Ceawlin asked.

"I do not know, my lord. Lord Bertred is sending scouts north to try to discover more. He will report to you as soon as he receives further information."

"Very well." Ceawlin's eyes flicked over the man standing before him. "Go to the great hall and have them find you some dry clothes and get you something to eat and to drink."

"Yes, my lord. Thank you, my lord." The man backed away a few steps, then turned and rushed out the door. He had seen the king often during the past years, but never had he seen him look like this. The thane counted himself lucky that he had not been made the object of Ceawlin's all-too-obvious fury.

As the door swung closed, Ceawlin looked around the room. He had been talking to three of his most senior thanes when Bertred's man had been announced, and the thanes were still sitting on the wall bench to which he had dismissed them. They were staring assiduously at their feet. They had heard.

"Get me Cutha," Ceawlin said.

The men looked up, then looked away. "Yes, my lord," they said in unison, and exited almost as hastily as the previous thane had done.

The door opened, rain gusted once more into the hall, and Niniane came in. "What weather!" she said when she saw her husband sitting alone by the fire. Then, when he did not answer, she looked at him more closely. Her hands, which had been busy unpinning the brooch that held her cloak, stilled. "What has happened?" she asked, her voice suddenly sharp.

He did not look back at her. "Cuthwulf has invaded the land of the Dobunni," he said. "There was a battle. Cuthwulf won."

A sharp intake of breath was her only reply. Then she came slowly across the room to stand before him. His face was set and still. The Dobunni! she thought. What of Coinmail? Ceawlin seemed to read her thoughts, for he looked at her at last and said, "I do not know if Coinmail was involved. Bertred has sent scouts to try to learn exactly what happened."

There was a footstool near his chair and she sat down suddenly, as if her legs would not hold her. There was rain on her hair and on the shoulders of her blue wool cloak. "He is mad," she said. "Did he think you would allow this?"

"If he had any doubts, they will soon be set to rest." His voice was hard and cold.

She ran her tongue around suddenly dry lips. "What will you do?" she asked.

"I will kill him," Ceawlin said. She stared at him and saw that he meant it. She had seen him angry before, seen him furious, but never had she seen this merciless hardness. He meant it.

"Ceawlin . . . what of Sigurd?"

"What of Sigurd?"

This coldness was far more frightening than any of his hot-burning furies. Niniane wet her lips again. "Cuthwulf is his brother. I grant you there is little love lost between them, but still there is shared blood."

"There was shared blood between me and Edwin. Blood is not everything, Niniane. If Sigurd must choose between me and Cuthwulf, I have little doubt where his choice will fall." He looked over her head toward the door. "Ah, Cutha." A shiver ran up and down Niniane's back at the note in his voice. "Your son has taken a war band into the land of the Dobunni, given battle, and looted their towns."

Cutha's back was very straight as he approached Ceawlin's chair. "My son is a Saxon," he said.

"Your son has challenged my authority. I have been lenient with him before because he is Sigurd's brother and your son. But he has over-reached himself this time. I am King of Wessex, and no one leads a war band in this country save at my leave."

"You are King of Wessex because I made you such," said Cutha.

Ceawlin laughed. "How many battles did you win for me, cousin?"

Cutha had flushed when Ceawlin laughed, and now he went deadly pale. "You are not the only warrior in Wessex, Ceawlin. Whatever his failings, Cuthwulf is a war leader. He has always won."

"No." Ceawlin leaned slightly forward in his chair and stared at Cutha out of narrowed eyes. "No, cousin. This time Cuthwulf has lost."

There was no banquet for Cerdic's birthday. Instead, Ceawlin marched one hundred hall thanes out of Winchester in the predawn dark and fell upon Banford. Cuthwulf's men had not been expecting such swift retribution and were completely surprised. In the haphazard resistance that followed, Cuthwulf was able to flee. Ceawlin sent out a pursuit, but Cuthwulf and a small number of his men eluded it and fled south, toward Wight.

Niniane was relieved to hear that Cuthwulf still lived. She feared that the death of Cutha's son was the one thing that would drive his dissatisfaction with Ceawlin out into the open. For Niniane's ever-watchful eyes had not missed Cutha's growing alienation from Ceawlin, and she feared that her husband took Cutha too lightly. The eorl might be growing old, but he was not toothless yet.

Niniane thought that Cutha must in some way blame Ceawlin for Sigurd's exile from Winchester. Certainly the rift between the king and his chief eorl had first become noticeable to her after Sigurd's departure. Niniane had seen Ceawlin's own distress at Sigurd's leaving and she had been angry with Sigurd; this further development with Cuthwulf made her angrier still.

Sigurd was the only one with a chance of mending the breech between Ceawlin and his father and his brother, and still he stayed at Wokham, playing farmer. Niniane could not understand him. She said nothing of this to Ceawlin, however. Whenever she mentioned Sigurd, his face sealed absolutely shut. Something had happened between the two of them that he would not tell her about, and although Ceawlin went occasionally to Wokham to see Sigurd, Sigurd never once had returned to Winchester.

But Niniane was beginning to think that it was not just Sigurd's exile that had alienated Cutha. His words to Ceawlin upon hearing of Cuthwulf's battle were significant. Cutha thought he had made Ceawlin king, and he obviously did not think he was reaping a great enough reward.

There was a germ of truth in Cutha's belief. It was true that Ceawlin had needed the men Cutha had brought with him. But Cutha had been acting in his own interest as well as Ceawlin's. His position under Ceawlin was far greater than ever it had been under Edric. No, Niniane thought, Cutha had no cause for complaint.

But that obviously was not what Cutha thought.

After he returned from his raid upon Banford, Ceawlin rode north to Wokham to talk with Sigurd. Next he went to Bryn Atha to talk with Naille. Gereint offered to act as messenger between Wessex and the Dobunni and went to Glevum to offer restitution from Ceawlin for the damage done by his rebellious eorl. He was received with icy disdain by Coinmail, who had not been at the Battle of Bedcanford. Restitution was refused, and Gereint returned to Wessex furious at the scornful way he had been treated by his former prince.

Winter turned into spring and they learned that Cuthwulf was indeed in Wight. As the weather softened and became milder, the strain and bitterness between the king and his chief eorl became more and more noticeable. Finally, in May, Cutha announced that he would like to retire from Winchester. He would go to Banford, he told Ceawlin, who with undisguised relief granted him permission to withdraw to his manor.

In early June came news from Wight that Cuthwulf was dead.

"Killed in a brawl," Ceawlin said to Niniane. "Very fitting."

Niniane's reply was noncommittal, but she was not happy to hear of Cuthwulf's death. "Does Cutha know?" she asked.

"He probably knew before I did," Ceawlin replied acidly. "He is in constant touch with Wight."

"Ceawlin . . . do you think you ought to give him such a long rein?" Niniane asked. "I don't trust him. He would do you a mischief if he could. I know he would."

"You see trolls behind every tree, Nan," he said impatiently. It was his standard answer to all of the dangers she feared threatened him. Part of her knew he was right, knew she was overprotective of Ceawlin and her children. And what could Cutha possibly do to hurt Ceawlin?

Nothing, came the instant answer. But still she was uneasy. "I think you ought to set someone to watch Cutha," she said.

He kissed the top of her head. "I have," he answered, and went off to the great hall to give justice.

Chapter 30

*I*T was late August and the bees were thick. Sigurd was returning to his manor, his small tear-streaked daughter on the saddle before him, when he saw a group of horsemen approaching the gates of Wokham from the opposite direction. It was a moment before he recognized his father.

Foreboding struck his heart. He had heard, of course, of Cuthwulf's death. He could not feel personal grief; he and Cuthwulf had never been friends. But blood was blood and he regretted deeply that Cuthwulf had come to such an end.

"Look," he said softly to Hilda, who was still weeping over the bee sting on her finger, "there is your grandfather."

"Grandfather?" She looked up at him out of his own steady gray eyes. "Did you know Grandfather was coming, Papa?"

"No," Sigurd answered somberly, "I did not." Cutha had seen him and halted his party. With a reluctance he strove to conceal from his daughter, Sigurd spurred his horse forward to catch up with Cutha.

Once they were within the walls of Wokham, Sigurd consigned Hilda to the care of Edith and took his father to the manor's impressive hall. This was the first time he and Cutha had met since the death of Cuthwulf, and Sigurd was appalled by how gray his father's hair had grown, how much older he suddenly looked.

Cutha did not waste any time. "Sigurd," he said as soon as he was alone with his son, "I cannot stomach Ceawlin any longer."

The foreboding struck even deeper into Sigurd's heart. "What happened to Cuthwulf was not Ceawlin's fault, Father," he said around the tightness in his throat. "Cuthwulf brought all his ill fortune on himself."

"Ceawlin did not handle him properly," Cutha said. "Ceawlin made no attempt to reward Cuthwulf, to befriend him. Cuthwulf fought for him, and what did Cuthwulf receive? Where was his manor, Sigurd? His honors?"

"It was always understood, Father, that Cuthwulf would have Banford after you," Sigurd said. "Banford is one of the greatest manors in all of Wessex. I could not say that Cuthwulf was cheated."

"He gave you Wokham; to Penda he gave the whole of the upper

Thames valley; Bertred, Ine, even Cynigils, who fought for Edric—all of these were rewarded with manors. But not Cuthwulf."

Sigurd rubbed his forehead. "Father, Cuthwulf was not the most . . . trustworthy of men."

"He was trustworthy enough for Ceawlin to send him to deal with Cnebba and Oslaf. And he did deal with them, drove them back into Kent and reclaimed all the cattle they had stolen. He did that for Ceawlin, and what reward did he get? Insults. Insults because he had dared to be a true lord to his men and reward them for their bravery." Cutha's blue eyes were cold, his mouth thin with anger. "Cynric would never have dealt with him thus," he said.

Sigurd forbore to point out that the spoils Cuthwulf had divided among his men had not been his to give. "Perhaps not," he said instead. "But Cynric still thought like a warlord, Father. Ceawlin thinks like a king."

"Ceawlin thinks to advance himself, himself and his family. He has no thought for his eorls and his thanes. Do you know, Sigurd," and now Cutha's eyes glittered, "he has betrothed Cerdic to the daughter of the King of Sussex?"

"Yes, I know."

"Do you know that he did it without even consulting me? He just told me one day, as an afterthought, that he had arranged this marriage. He sent Bertred to Sussex to make the arrangements. Bertred!"

"I agree that it was not . . . thoughtful of him to do that, Father—"

"Not thoughtful?"

Sigurd rubbed his forehead again. In this he did agree with Cutha. Ceawlin had been careless of Cutha's feelings in this matter, should have at least made some show of consulting the eorl on a matter of such importance to Wessex.

"The only person Ceawlin listens to these days is his wife," said Cutha bitterly.

"Niniane is wiser than the ordinary woman. I would not scorn her advice myself." Sigurd was pleased his voice sounded so normal. "She has been with Ceawlin since first he fled from Winchester," he added. "He has ever been closer to her than most men are to their wives."

Cutha stared at him and Sigurd stared back. It was Cutha's eyes that fell first. "I am going to go to Wight," he said.

Ever since this conversation had begun, Sigurd had had a feeling that he was sitting with a sword suspended over his head. "Why?" he asked after a moment's tense silence.

"The King of Wight, Witgar, is the son of Cynric's elder brother," Cutha replied. "He has a better claim to the kingship of Wessex than does Cynric's bastard." And Sigurd saw that the sword was ready to fall.

"You cannot do this, Father," he said heavily. "You cannot so turn your back upon Ceawlin. Don't you remember? You were the one who befriended him when all else chose Edgar. You were the one who made him king."

Cutha's eyebrows rose high, and for a moment he looked young again. "I remember, Sigurd. It is your friend who has forgotten."

Sigurd slumped in his chair like an old man. "You cannot put Witgar on the throne of Wessex. Wight is a small kingdom, much smaller than Wessex. Ceawlin would destroy any war band Wight could collect to come against him."

"We shall see," said Cutha. "I still count for something in this kingdom, my son. Nor am I the only eorl to be dissatisfied with Ceawlin."

Sigurd masked the lower part of his face with his hand. "To whom have you been talking?"

Cutha shrugged and did not reply. Sigurd drew a deep, uneven breath. "Have you spoken with Witgar about this?"

This question Cutha deigned to answer. "Cuthwulf mentioned it. Witgar is a man in his fifties, Sigurd. It is an age when death begins to loom, and one sees that there is little time left to accomplish deeds of glory. Cynric was older than that when he decided to invade the land of the Atrebates."

Sigurd looked at his father and thought that perhaps Cutha was talking of himself. Then, "Ceawlin is still young," Cutha said, and Sigurd's suspicion was confirmed. "I am not. If I am to leave a name that the harpers will remember, I must act soon."

"Father . . . do not ask me to join with you in this. Ceawlin is my friend, my sworn lord. I cannot betray him. I cannot!"

Cutha rose and stared somberly down at his son's anguished face. "Think you, Sigurd. What has Ceawlin ever done for you? This manor," and he waved his hand to encompass the hall, "was no more than your just due, no more than he has given to the other men who aided him in winning the kingship. But you, you who are supposedly his greatest friend, what else has he given you?"

"There is naught else that I want," Sigurd answered steadily. "And if there were, I should only have to ask for it."

Cutha's blue eyes were narrow and hard. "You will not tell him of this conversation?"

"Of course not!" Sigurd was very white. "You are my father. How could you think such of me?"

"I do not know what to think of you, Sigurd," came the measured reply. "Blood seems to weigh less with you than this one-sided friendship." Cutha suddenly put a hand on Sigurd's shoulder. "I will tell you this, my son. There is only one rule in life and that is: when you want something, go and get it. It is the rule that Ceawlin lives by and it is

my rule as well. It would be well for you to think of it. Think also that if
Ceawlin should die, then would Niniane be a widow."

Every last ounce of color drained from Sigurd's face.

"Edith is no king's daughter," Cutha went on. "It would be easy to
put her aside." Then, as Sigurd still did not reply, "You owe him
nothing, Sigurd. Nothing! The past is the past. That is how Ceawlin
sees it, else he would never have acted as he has toward Cuthwulf and
toward me. Your duty lies with your kin, your own blood, not with this
ungrateful king. Remember that when I do send to you." And Cutha,
after a shrewd and satisfied look at his son's ashen face, left the hall,
gathered his men, and rode south to Wight.

The Romans had come to the Isle of Wight many centuries before
and built large villas and planted vineyards and done the best that they
could to create a corner of the civilized Middle Sea amidst the barbarian British. When Rome fell and the legions left Britain, the remaining
Romano-Celtic population of Wight had lived on in peace, cultivating
their farms in the mild island climate. Then, at the very end of the fifth
century, the Saxons had come.

They came from the land of the East Saxons and their leader's name
was Cerdic. He was a younger son of the East Saxon royal house,
banished from his homeland because in a fit of rage he had killed a son
of the neighboring East Anglian royal house, an action that had threatened to bring down a blood feud upon his own smaller, more vulnerable kingdom. Cerdic's brother the king had given him a ship and sent
him forth to win his fortune. With him had gone his own loyal thanes
and his two sons, Stuf and Cynric.

They had sailed out into the Narrow Sea and landed on the sands of
the small island the Romans called Vectis. The resident Romano-Celtic
population, safe since the days of Arthur, had not been able to put up
an effective resistance, and soon Cerdic had made himself lord of
Wight. The following years had seen the expansion of his kingdom to
several miles of shorefront land on the opposite side of Solent bay, but
when Cerdic died and left his lordship to his son Stuf, Wight was
largely an island kingdom.

Nor had it expanded its territory in the years that Witgar, son of Stuf,
had ruled. Wessex, the kingdom founded by Cerdic's younger son,
Cynric, was far larger and potentially far more powerful than the little
island kingdom left by Cerdic. Cutha had long sensed that there was
jealousy in Wight over the preeminence of the secondary kingdom. And
Winchester was little more than twenty miles from the coast. It would
make sense if the two kingdoms, smallest of all the English lands,
should combine under one king.

Who that king should be was the as-yet-unanswered question.

*   *   *

Witgar received Cutha with flattering attention. They were not strangers; Cutha had stayed in Wight after his defeat by Edric at Banford, before he had gone north to bring a war band to assist Ceawlin in his fight for Wessex's kingship.

The King of Wight was pleased by the turn of events that had brought the premier eorl of Wessex to his shores. Cutha had judged nicely when he had explained Witgar's character to Sigurd. Of late years, Wight, so rich, so settled, so confined, had been growing dull to Witgar. The king had been stirred by Cutha's first visit to take greater notice of his cousin's kingdom of Wessex, and the contrast between the burgeoning Wessex and his own small island had been more and more apparent as the years went by. The catalyst that had pushed Witgar from the role of envious onlooker to active conspirator was the proposed betrothal of Cerdic to the princess of Sussex. Sussex encompassed all the land along the southeastern shore of England and, along with Wessex, was the Saxon kingdom closest to Wight. Witgar had himself tried to arrange a dynastic marriage with Sussex for his own granddaughter and had been turned down. Ceawlin's success in the light of his failure was bitter indeed.

Witgar was fifty-three years of age. His two sons by his queen were dead. The heirs to Wight were either his two male grandchildren by his bastard son or his six legitimate granddaughters. In Witgar's view, the days of Wight as a separate kingdom were numbered. It was too small and he had no strong successor for his people to unite around. Ever since the death of his last son he had resigned himself to the fact that the only hope for Wight was to marry his eldest granddaughter, Auda, to the heir of either Wessex or Sussex. Thus would Wight be incorporated into one of the two larger kingdoms, and his blood would flow in the veins of its future rulers.

But Sussex had rejected a princess of Wight for its heir and had betrothed its prince into Northumbria. And Wessex had betrothed its heir to Sussex. It seemed no one wanted a princess from Wight; and Witgar's pride was severely wounded. Once more it was brought home to him how small and how unimportant a kingdom it was that he ruled.

Then Cuthwulf had come to Wight, hinting about dissatisfaction among the eorls with Ceawlin, hinting that the kingship of Wessex might not be as secure as it had hitherto seemed. Witgar had been interested and had let Cuthwulf see that he was interested. The arrival of Cutha was not a great surprise.

"Welcome once again to Wight, cousin," he said to Cutha as the eorl came into his hall on a warm and balmy August afternoon. "I trust you had an easy crossing."

"Nothing could have been easier," replied Cutha genially. "Your island is so fair, my lord. It is a joy to be here again."

Witgar offered Cutha beer and Cutha accepted. It was when the two men were seated, Witgar in his high seat and Cutha beside him, that they got down to the business of Cutha's visit.

Cutha minced no words. "My lord, would you like to be King of Wessex?" he asked.

"Wessex already has a king," Witgar replied.

"True. But Ceawlin is a bastard. You are the son of Cerdic's elder son. You have a truer claim to Wessex than does Ceawlin."

"That may be so, but Ceawlin has been king for ten years and more. He will not easily be dislodged."

"Not easily, no. But it is possible. Ceawlin is not as secure as he thinks he is." Cutha's blue eyes were very cold. "He has underestimated me, Witgar, and that is a serious mistake."

"How is it possible?" Witgar asked bluntly. "I do not have the numbers of men at my disposal necessary to unseat a king with the following that Ceawlin can command."

"Ah . . ." Cutha smiled. "But what following *can* Ceawlin command? That is the question, my lord. In Winchester he maintains about one hundred hall thanes, his own personal war band. The rest of his forces must be drawn from the followings of his eorls."

"And?" Witgar prompted as Cutha fell into a seemingly rapt silence.

"And his eorls are largely pledged to me," came the devastatingly simple reply.

There was a long silence. Then, "Who is pledged to you, cousin?" Witgar asked. "You must know that I have done some investigation of the situation in Wessex, and it seems to me that Ceawlin's eorls are remarkably loyal."

"They have been loyal, yes. But consider, Witgar. Sigurd is my son. Penda is my son-by-marriage. Ine was my thane before he became Ceawlin's eorl; his first pledge of loyalty was to me. Cynigils is as unhappy with Ceawlin as I am, is ready to follow me. I should say that the only two eorls who have a genuine loyalty to Ceawlin are Bertred and Wuffa."

Witgar's greenish-gray eyes were narrowed. "Are you saying that the eorls you have named will be willing to join a war band opposed to Ceawlin?"

"They will either join with us or they will hold aloof. At any rate, they will not join Ceawlin."

"You have pledges of this?"

Cutha's eyes did not flicker. "Yes, my lord. I do."

Witgar took a long drink from his beer cup. Then, "He has only a hundred men in Winchester?"

"A hundred hall thanes. He might be able to recruit more men if he were given the time. But we will not give him the time."

"What about his wife's people, the British?"

"I doubt not that the Atrebates would stand by him. But again, he must have time to rally them."

Witgar took another drink. Then, "It will not serve, cousin. To be successful, we must have a quick victory. To be blunt: to be successful, we must capture Ceawlin. And I do not have sufficient numbers of men to do it."

Cutha drained his cup and put it on the wooden table with a little thump. "We could get more men from East Anglia," he said.

Witgar stared at him. "How?"

"Marry your granddaughter to Guthfrid's son and promise him the kingship of Wessex after you."

Witgar's eyes began to grow very green. "Guthfrid's son," he said softly. Then, "But they are cousins."

"Not in blood," said Cutha dryly. "I would take my oath that Edgar is not Cynric's son. However," and he shrugged, "the boy is certainly Guthfrid's son, and she is a princess of East Anglia. Your granddaughter would be queen, my lord. Your great-grandson would be king."

"I thought you hated Guthfrid," Witgar said. "Ever since my uncle died you have been her sworn foe. And she must hate you as much as you hate her. Think you she will agree to join with you in such an enterprise?"

There was no more beer in Cutha's cup. "As you say, my lord, Guthfrid and I have been sworn enemies and mortal foes for all these many years. But now we need each other. She will accept me as an ally; for the sake of her son, she will accept me."

"If you can get promises of aid from East Anglia, we can do it," said Witgar. "I can raise a hundred men. If East Anglia can give us a hundred more and if some of Ceawlin's eorls will rally to our cause with their men, then we can do it."

"Yes," said Cutha grimly. "I think we can."

"And Ceawlin himself?"

Cutha's eyes were a clear sea of untroubled blue. "We cannot allow Ceawlin to live," he said. "He would be too dangerous."

Witgar nodded, satisfied. "That is my thought also. And his sons?"

Cutha shrugged. "They are but children yet. It is the father that we want, Witgar."

Witgar looked shrewdly at Cutha's face. Then, "Will you go yourself to East Anglia, cousin?"

Cutha smiled crookedly. "I would ask you first to send a request for safe conduct. Guthfrid is likely to have me murdered before ever she can hear my proposal."

"That is easy enough," Witgar replied. "I will send one of my own eorls to prepare your way."

"Thank you, my lord." The two men rose, looked at each other, and then joined hands. "You will be King of Wessex, Witgar," Cutha said. "I gave the power into Ceawlin's hands once and now I will give it into yours."

"You will not find me ungrateful, cousin," Witgar replied, and Cutha's returning smile was distinctly wry.

It was early October before Cutha was able to travel to East Anglia. It had taken a great deal of persuasion by Aethelbert to get his sister to see Ceawlin's traitor eorl. Guthfrid's passions had not cooled with time and, next to Ceawlin, there was no one she hated so much as Cutha. If it were not for him, she thought, Ceawlin would never have gained the throne of Wessex. In a sense, it was Cutha who was the author of all her woes, and she refused point-blank even to talk to him.

It took Aethelbert the better part of a month to convince Guthfrid that it was in her interest, in Edgar's interest, to come to terms with the eorl. Aethelbert himself was eager to avenge the defeat he had suffered at Ceawlin's hands upon the battlefield. The very name Gild Ford was an agonizing humiliation to his fierce pride. He had gathered a new crop of thanes into his hall at Sutton Hoo but his following was but a remnant of the proud war band he had taken into Wessex. He did not have the manpower to attack Ceawlin again by himself, and so this offer from Wight interested him mightily.

At last, driven by her own desire for revenge, her ambition for her son, and the unrelenting persuasions of her brother, Guthfrid agreed to see Cutha.

She received him in the great hall of Sutton Hoo, wearing her most magnificent jewelry and seated beside Aethelbert in the high seat. Her son, Edgar, sat on the bench on her other side.

The eleven years since she had been driven out of Winchester had set lines like scars into Guthfrid's face. But her hair had retained most of its gold, her figure was still slim, her pride was as high as ever it had been. When Cutha approached the queen he had dethroned, she said coldly, "You may kneel." Nor did she allow him to rise until he had begged her pardon for the wrongs he had done her and her son.

Cutha was properly repentant and humble and, after a good ten minutes, Guthfrid allowed him to regain his feet. It was then that the negotiations began.

Guthfrid agreed to marry her son to Witgar's granddaughter. She agreed to allow Witgar, an old man, she thought, surely not long for this world, to reign in Winchester until his death. Then Edgar would assume his rightful place. Guthfrid always thought of the kingship of Wessex as rightfully belonging to Edgar. It had been many years since she had troubled to remind herself that Edgar was not truly Cynric's son.

For his part, Aethelbert would send one hundred thanes into Wessex, to invade by way of Kent. The two war bands would converge at Winchester, where they would overcome Ceawlin's thanes and capture the king.

"The key is surprise," Cutha said to Aethelbert. "We must not give Ceawlin notice of our coming. We must reach Winchester on the first day of our march. Once Ceawlin has warning of our coming, he will have time to send for reinforcements. He is a dangerous man, my lord. A very dangerous man."

Aethelbert was silent. He had found out the truth of that statement for himself.

"What if Ceawlin is not at Winchester?" Guthfrid asked.

"Then will it be easy to take the royal enclave."

"But you have just been saying how dangerous this Ceawlin is!" said Edgar, brown eyes reflecting his confusion at the apparent contradiction.

"When once I . . . we . . . have control of Winchester, I will send word to my son Sigurd. Wherever Ceawlin is, he will send for Sigurd to join him with Sigurd's thanes. It is Sigurd who will capture Ceawlin."

"*Sigurd?*" said Guthfrid. "Sigurd was ever Ceawlin's staunchest supporter."

"Sigurd is the reason I was unable to consolidate my victory at Odinham," Aethelbert said bitterly. "It was his coming up at the last minute that gave fresh heart to Ceawlin's men."

Cutha forbore to remind Aethelbert that he too had been at Odinham. "Sigurd is my son and a Saxon," he answered confidently. "The claims of kinship will weigh with him more than the claims of friendship."

"Ceawlin will never suspect Sigurd," said Guthfrid.

Cutha smiled. "No," he answered. "He will not."

The sun was shining on the day that Cutha left Sutton Hoo. A good omen, he thought. All had fallen out much as he had desired. By the following summer, he should once more be back in his hall at Winchester.

If there was the slightest hint of doubt in his mind that he had misrepresented to both the kings with whom he had been dealing the disaffection of Ceawlin's eorls, he did not let it bother him. Penda he had not approached directly, but Penda was a pragmatic man. And Coenburg would work on him, keep him from taking the field against her father and her brother.

Sigurd . . . He had to admit he was not so certain of Sigurd as he had made himself seem to Guthfrid. Still, even if Sigurd decided to hold himself aloof and do nothing, still would that be a help to Witgar's cause. Between them, Sigurd and Penda commanded at least eighty thanes.

Never once, in all his ambitious devising of plots and schemes, never once did it occur to Cutha that he was forcing an impossible choice upon his son, placing him in an impossible situation.

Chapter 31

CRIDA was luckier on his thirteenth birthday than Cerdic had been. The April day was chill but springlike, with snatches of sunshine. Ceawlin took Crida hunting, just the two of them, as he had done for Cerdic the previous year, albeit belatedly. Crida was enormously pleased with the honor; it was rare that he had his father to himself.

The hounds got a scent almost instantly and gave chase, Ceawlin and Crida galloping after through the greening woods, over branches that had come down with the winter ice, ducking close to their horses' necks when the overhanging trees swept too close to their heads. After a run of perhaps twenty minutes the hounds lost the scent and began to cast around again. Ceawlin pulled his horse up and looked at his second son.

Crida was an excellent horseman; the best in Winchester, Ceawlin thought proudly. His small size made it easy for him to balance in the saddle, and his legs were extremely strong. He would never have the height that Cerdic had and that Ceowulf was going to have, and suddenly Ceawlin wondered if that bothered him. It was often difficult to know what Crida was thinking or feeling. Cerdic's was a far more open nature than was his younger brother's.

"You are the best horseman in Winchester," Ceawlin said now to his son. "I have always loved to watch you ride."

Crida looked over at Ceawlin, his eyes widening with surprise. "You are the best horseman in Winchester, Father. Everyone knows that."

Ceawlin shook his head. "I am too tall. You are better."

Crida's fair skin, so like Ceawlin's own when he was a boy, flushed with betraying color. "Well, I suppose being small has some uses."

"You have my coloring but you are built like your mother," Ceawlin said.

"I know." The answer was flat. "I used to think that I would grow, would be as tall as Cerdic, but I have long since resigned myself to the fact that I will not."

"You will grow," Ceawlin replied. "Your mother's brother is not a small man. But you are never going to be as tall as Cerdic." He looked seriously at his son. "What does that matter, Crida? You have gifts of more importance than size."

Crida's eyes were Ceawlin's also, although more green than blue. They gave nothing away as he answered, "What do I have, Father?"

"You have intelligence," Ceawlin said. "Extraordinary intelligence." He grinned. "Your mother would say you got that from her also."

Crida's usually reserved face lit with a reciprocal smile.

"You will be of great value to your brother when he is king," Ceawlin told his son. "I am very proud of you, Crida." He watched Crida try to hide his pleasure and thought that it had been a good idea to spend some time alone with the boy, that he should do it again. Then the hounds gave voice and once again father and son were off in pursuit.

Niniane stood on the steps of the princes' hall and watched her husband and her son coming back from the stables. They were walking very close together. In his left hand Ceawlin was carrying a bow. His right arm was laid across Crida's shoulders. The top of Crida's head just cleared his father's shoulder. Niniane looked at the two blond heads, shining like silver in the spring sun, and blinked back a tear.

Crida saw her first. "We got a boar, Mother!" he called.

"Very good." She smiled at the two of them. "I'll wager you also got an appetite."

"One of the reasons I have held so steadfastly to your mother for all these years, Crida," Ceawlin said seriously, "is that she understands how important food is to a man."

Crida laughed. "You hold to Mother because she is the finest lady in all the world," he said.

Ceawlin's eyes went to his wife. "That is true also," he agreed, his eyes brimming with amusement.

"You are a credit to me, Crida," said Niniane. Then she added to her husband, "Gereint rode in while you were gone, Ceawlin. Naille is dying."

All the amusement left Ceawlin's face. "Where is he?" he asked.

"In the king's hall. He has come to ask you to go north with him. Naille wants to see you."

Ceawlin nodded, patted Crida on the shoulder, and went off to talk with Gereint.

"How was the hunt?" Niniane asked Crida. "Come inside and tell me all about it." He was beginning his story before ever they entered the princes'-hall door.

"I will go, of course," Ceawlin said to Niniane. They were alone in their sleeping room preparing for bed. "I owe a great deal to Naille."

"Yes." Niniane sighed. "He is a good man. We shall miss him." She got into the bed and pulled the blankets up around her.

Silence fell as Ceawlin continued to undress. Niniane watched him in the flickering candlelight. "I am glad you took Crida out hunting today," she said then. "He was so full of excitement! He even deigned to tell the story of the boar hunt to Ceowulf."

"I think it bothers him, the fact that he is so small."

Niniane cast a rueful look upon her husband's splendid body, now fully undressed. "I feel so guilty," she said. "It is my fault that Crida is small."

Ceawlin laughed and got into the bed. "It is also your 'fault' that he was born." Then, when she wrinkled her small tilted nose, "He will come to terms with it, Nan. Upon first glance it is Cerdic who is the more impressive, but it is Crida who has the brain."

"Cerdic has a brain too!" said Niniane in instant defense of her firstborn.

He snorted. "I did not mean to imply that he did not. Cerdic has a gift for understanding people and will do very well as king. But Crida is quicker. That is all I meant."

"Well, that is true," said Niniane, placated. "He has to hear Alric recite but once and he knows it. It is sometimes difficult for Cerdic, the fact that Crida is so much quicker. But Crida makes allowances for Cerdic. It is Ceowulf who comes in for the brunt of his scorn."

"Perhaps I ought to take Ceowulf hunting too," said Ceawlin humorously.

"I think that is a good idea," replied his wife. "The two eldest boys and the two youngest boys have each other. It is Ceowulf who is left out. I often think it is a great pity that I miscarried of the child I was bearing after Ceowulf. Then would he have had a friend."

"All these sons!" said Ceawlin. "When am I to have a daughter?"

Niniane smiled at him. Since the birth of Ceowulf he had asked for nothing but a daughter. Niniane, who was well content with her sons, thought it endearing that Ceawlin was so anxious to have a girl. "I think I will come with you to see Naille," she murmured.

"No children," he said warningly. "I will be happy to have you, but Eirik must stay in Winchester."

"He is not a baby anymore and will do very well with his nurses," Niniane replied. She raised herself a little and bent over him to kiss him softly on the lips. "We can stay at Bryn Atha," she said. "Like the old days. Perhaps we will even make a daughter for you."

"Hmmm." Her loose hair hung down, encasing both of them in a silken tent. "That would be nice," he said, drew her down to him, and kissed her again.

*   *   *

Niniane and Ceawlin left Winchester two days after. With them went four of the hall thanes as well as Gereint and his escort of three Britons. Had the men been alone, they would have ridden straight through to Silchester, a long ride for one day but one that Ceawlin had often made. Niniane was with them, however, and so they made camp beside the road when they were still some ten miles from the city, cooked supper, and went to bed early. The ground was hard but Niniane was warm within the shelter of Ceawlin's arms, and she slept soundly, awaking with the birds at dawn.

They did not stop at Silchester but turned west toward Bryn Atha. Niniane had not been to the villa in several years and the sight of it in the bright April sun brought a smile to her face. "It is always the same," she said to Ceawlin. "Do you remember when once you said to me that when Winchester was but ashes, these stones would still be standing?"

He grunted, his mind clearly on other things.

Niniane's mind was on the past. For some reason, she found the first time she and Ceawlin had come to Bryn Atha vividly present in her mind. She remembered how surprised she had been to find the villa uninhabited, Coinmail and all the servants and the livestock gone. She remembered their visit to Geara to learn the news, and how they had gobbled Geara's bread and cheese. She remembered their first visit to Naille, how he had recognized Ceawlin from Beranbyrg.

How many years ago? she thought. Well, Cerdic was fourteen, so it must be fifteen years ago. How young we were, she thought. "Remember when you fixed up the slave quarters for the thanes?" she asked as they dismounted in the courtyard.

He grunted again and she flashed him an annoyed look. He did not even notice. Obviously he was not interested in sharing nostalgic reminiscences of their early married days at Bryn Atha. Niniane went into the house before him, her back very straight.

There was a steward at Bryn Atha these days, and servants to see to the upkeep of the villa. Ceawlin intended the property to go to one of his sons and wanted to keep it well-maintained. The steward, a Briton named Budd, had been warned of their probable coming by Gereint and so was prepared with food and fresh linen. Gereint continued on home with the message that Ceawlin and Niniane would come to see Naille on the morrow.

There was chicken fried in oil for dinner and the food was what finally put Ceawlin in a nostalgic mood. The four thanes eating with them in the dining room listened eagerly as the king and queen told stories of the old days in Bryn Atha, when Ceawlin was waiting to claim his father's kingship. They seemed to find the picture of their awesome king and his powerful eorls laboring like ceorls in the fields particularly riveting.

"It sounds like fun," said Sigbert, the leader of the thanes. He sounded distinctly wistful.

Ceawlin's blue-green eyes narrowed and he looked at the four young faces across the table. For the first time he realized that he had chosen the four youngest of all the hall thanes to come with him on this errand. The boys looking back at him were scarcely older than he himself had been when he and Niniane had first come to Bryn Atha. Niniane's sentimentality must be infectious, he thought with wry humor.

"Life is not so exciting these days, is it?" he said sympathetically, and the four thanes earnestly assured him that that was not so at all.

But it was so, Ceawlin thought, at least for these young ones. They had not been old enough to go with the war band to Gild Ford, and in the two years since they had slept in his hall, little of excitement had happened in Wessex.

I must think up something for the young ones to do, he thought. All the thanes, for that matter. They are men trained for war and they will rust away unless I use them.

Niniane was telling another story and the thanes were listening with rapt attention. "Did Bertred do so?" Sigbert inquired with awe. It was obvious to Ceawlin's amused eye that it was difficult for these boys to recognize in Niniane's tale the great and powerful eorl they themselves were familiar with.

Niniane was laughing at the boys as well, her nose crinkling, her large eyes dancing. "Bertred was once no older than you," she said. "Just think, even *I* was but seventeen."

"You have not aged at all, my lady," said one of the other boys respectfully.

Niniane threw him a disbelieving look from under her partially lowered lashes. But it was true, Ceawlin thought, that his wife did not look her age. It was her skin, he decided after thinking for a minute. It still retained the same baby-fine texture it had had when first he knew her. And her nose was still lightly dusted with golden freckles. She did not look seventeen, but she did not look like the mother of five children, either. Well, he was not doing so badly himself, he thought complacently. He could still outwrestle any man in Winchester.

Dinner was finished and Ceawlin took the four boys off to the thanes' quarters. Suddenly he too was curious to see his handiwork again. He stayed to share a cup of beer with the boys, and when he returned to the house one of the serving girls told him that Niniane had gone to bed. Good, he thought, and walked down the hall with an eager stride. He had been in the saddle for the better part of two days, but he still had energy enough for other things. He remembered her words to him in Winchester and his pace quickened. He and Niniane had made their first two sons in this bed, he thought as he pushed open the door and went into their room.

She was sound asleep. Ceawlin held his candle to his wife's quiet face. She never moved. Evidently two days in the saddle had taken a greater toll on her than on him.

Ceawlin cursed. He was not ready to sleep, not after the thoughts he had just been thinking. He stamped around the room, making noise and hoping to wake her. She murmured something indistinguishable and curled into a little ball. Her eyes remained closed.

Hel, thought Ceawlin. She was the one who had started all this business about the good old days at Bryn Atha. She was the one who had mentioned a daughter. Then what had she done? Gone to sleep and left him unsatisfied. Hel. He took off his shoe and threw it against the wall. Niniane's eyes opened.

"Ceawlin?" Her voice was fogged with sleep.

"Yes. Who did you think it was?" He was very annoyed with her.

"I don't know." Her eyes were closing again.

"No, you don't." He was bending over her now. "Nan. You can't go to sleep now. Wake up."

Dimly she heard the urgent note in his voice. "I'm so tired, Ceawlin," she mumbled. "I think I had too much wine at supper."

"Nan." He was beside her in the bed, his hands rough on her shoulders. He shook her and her eyes opened. He said her name again. She put her arms around his neck, and when he began to pull her sleeping gown up, she yawned and obediently shifted a little to help him.

It was sad, seeing Naille so weak and so ill. Alanna too looked old and worn. The two of them had worked hard all their lives, Niniane thought. Her own life in Winchester was so much easier than Alanna's had ever been as a farmer's wife.

How lucky I have been, she thought. How good God has been to me. She had borne five children to the man she loved, and all those children still lived. Lived and thrived. She was so lucky. Just thinking about it frightened her a little. As though the thought itself could put that luck into jeopardy.

The April day was warm as June and the world smelled of spring. Niniane's sorrow lifted as she and Ceawlin rode back to Bryn Atha. It was difficult to stay sad on such a day as this.

"Do you think I ought to make Gereint an eorl?" Ceawlin asked her. "He would accept the title, I think, once Naille is gone. But would it ruin his standing with the Atrebates?"

The track was wide enough for their horses to go side by side, and they rode in silence while she thought about his question. "No, I don't think it would," she answered at last. "The men of Naille's generation won't like it, but the younger ones, the ones that fought with you and know you, will be pleased."

He nodded. "That was my thought also."

"Coinmail will despise him for it, of course."

Ceawlin shrugged. "What does Coinmail matter? He has not had aught to do with the Atrebates since he went to Glevum."

"He is one of the chiefs of the Dobunni now."

"The Dobunni are no care of mine."

"No, I suppose they are not."

"I don't understand this concern you have with Coinmail, Niniane," Ceawlin said impatiently. "From what you have told me, he bullied you the whole of your childhood. Why should you care what he may think?"

"It is not so much what he may think as what he may do that worries me, Ceawlin."

"What can he do? He has sworn never to fight me."

Niniane halted her gelding, and Caewlin's stallion stopped as well. "Ceawlin, I should not count on that old promise."

"He gave his word," Ceawlin said.

"I do not think Coinmail would count as binding a word given to a pagan."

He shook his head. "You see trolls behind every tree, Nan." He started his horse forward again. "Coinmail is in no position to do me harm. Nor is he in any position to do Gereint harm. I think I shall make Gereint an eorl."

"Will you give him a manor?" she asked after a moment.

"He has his own land already. It is more the idea that I will have recognized a Briton as equal in power to my other most trusted men. Anyone who knows me knows that I have always held Gereint as highly in my heart as Penda or Bertred. But now it will be clear to all."

Niniane smiled at him. "You are a man of your word, Ceawlin. You promised Naille all those years ago that you would be a king for the Atrebates as well as the Saxons, and you have made your word good."

He did not answer, but she could see that her words had pleased him.

They were skirting the fields of Bryn Atha, going through a small copse of wood that had been left when the land was cleared, when Ceawlin said, "I'm thirsty. Let's stop to get a drink from the stream."

She followed him toward a small rushing brook and they got off their horses and tied them to a tree. Caewlin lay on his stomach and leaned forward to drink from the stream. Niniane watched him, a smile in her eyes. "Your hair is getting wet," she said.

He straightened up. The edges of his hair, where it had fallen into the water, dripped onto his shoulders. "Aren't you thirsty?" he asked.

"I am not going to push my face into that stream. I'll wait until we get back to Bryn Atha, thank you."

He made a cup of his hands, scooped up some of the crystal-clear water, and offered it to her. She bent her head and drank from his hands. "More?" he asked softly when she had finished.

"Yes," she said, and drank again. When she had finished, she looked up into his eyes and knew why he had really stopped in the wood. "Someone may come along, Ceawlin," she said.

"They won't." He caressed her cheekbones with gentle fingers and, bending his head began to kiss her. She closed her eyes and felt excitement ignite deep in her belly. The air was so warm, so springlike. His wet hair tickled her cheek. She put her arms around his waist and rubbed her body against his.

"Over there," he said. "The ground is clear." He lifted her by her elbows and walked to the place he had indicated. Then they both crumpled to the ground.

"Nan," he muttered, kissing her again, deeply, and sliding a hand up under the skirt of her gown. Niniane whimpered. The stallion, restless at being tied, began to paw the ground. Ceawlin pulled their clothes out of his way with a ruthless hand, then he was where she wanted him, deep, hard, stabbing again and again until her whole body convulsed with sensation, waves of intense pleasure radiating all the way up her back and down her legs. They collapsed around each other, Ceawlin panting hard and drenched with sweat.

"I love you," he murmured against her ear after he had begun to get his breath back.

She let out a long, deeply satisfied sigh and he raised his head so he could see her face. He grinned. She smiled back and drew his head down so she could softly kiss his mouth.

The stallion snorted and pawed the ground once more. "He's jealous," said Ceawlin, and pushed up to his knees. "There's a little patch of grass over there," he said. "I'll let him graze. That will take his mind off it."

Niniane straightened her clothes and her hair as Ceawlin went to take care of the horses. She was sitting with her back against a tree, looking dreamily at the swiftly moving stream, when he came back to her. "The grass will occupy them for a bit," he said, and lay down with his head in her lap.

Niniane looked down at him, at the tousled silver-blond hair, the long dark gold lashes and short silver beard; at the thin, mobile mouth; at the scar from the cut she had sewn for him, faint and white beside his left eye. Lying there, with his head resting so trustingly in her lap, he looked scarcely older than the boy she had first come to Bryn Atha with fifteen years before. Only the beard was different. She ran her fingers through his thick, silky hair. He looked up at her lazily and said, "That was what I brought you to Bryn Atha for. Last night I thought I was making love to a corpse."

"I was asleep," she said.

"I noticed."

She felt a flash of anger. "Then you should have let me be." She almost said it, but then held her tongue. She had long since learned that it was far easier for her to accommodate Ceawlin sexually than it was to put him off. His ill temper the following day was not worth the extra sleep she might have gained. But he would be furious if she told him that; she would wound his pride. She smoothed his hair from his temple and her brief anger died. She did not want to quarrel with him. She was too happy. She touched her lips to his forehead. "I have a feeling that within the year you will be getting your daughter," she said.

He captured her hand and held it to his lips. "That would be nice."

They stayed thus until the horses grazed down the patch of grass, and then they returned to the villa. Ten days later a thane came galloping in to tell them that Cutha, Witgar, and Aethelbert had taken Winchester.

Chapter 32

SIGURD had passed a miserable winter worrying over what his father would do and avoiding Ceawlin. He knew he could not look into Ceawlin's eyes while the knowledge of Cutha's planned treachery burned like acid in his heart, and so whenever it seemed that the king might come to Wokham, Sigurd had left. The only thought that gave him any consolation over the course of the winter was his belief that Cutha's plans would come to naught. Wight did not have the manpower to attack successfully the King of Wessex.

April came and Sigurd saw his fields planted, his fences mended, his roofs repaired. He conducted practice drills with his thanes in all the arts of weaponry. He began to teach his six-year-old son to ride.

Toward the end of the month several of his thanes returned to Wokham from Venta with the news that the king and queen had gone to Bryn Atha to visit the dying Naille. Sigurd had been at the stables when the men rode in and, after hearing their news, the eorl saddled a horse and rode out across the richly planted fields alone.

It was evening by now, and the ceorls were all at home eating their suppers. The fields were empty save for the birds. The air seemed strangely quite and full of peace.

So Niniane and Ceawlin were at Bryn Atha. Sigurd's thoughts, like those of the two he was thinking of, flew back in years to that time fifteen years before when he had first come to join Ceawlin in the land of the Atrebates. He remembered vividly now his first sight of Niniane as he had ridden into the Roman courtyard of Bryn Atha. She had been drying her hair in the sun, he remembered, and in his mind's eye he saw once again its beautiful color, gold and bronze and warm brown, glistening in the bright June sun.

The picture of her was so clear in his mind that for a moment it seemed as if she were there before him in the field. He could feel her presence, smell the sweetness of her hair . . . and all of a sudden it came on him that it was not so terrible a thing after all, this love of his for Niniane. It was as if all the evil, hateful dreams that had tortured his nights for years had finally been vanquished, leaving him only the pure sweet first love of his youth. It was as if bondage chains had broken, as if he had stepped out from the dank murk of shadow into the warmth and health of the sun.

He halted his horse and looked up. The evening sky was filled with the late sun's golden glow; he felt it in his heart. As he sat there wrapped in the peace and tranquility of the warm evening, a shout came from behind him. He wheeled his horse and saw a man galloping madly toward him across the fields, a man whom Sigurd recognized as belonging to his father. Sigurd felt the blood began to thump in his neck. The man pulled his horse up so abruptly that he was rocked forward onto its neck.

"My lord!" Cutha's thane said breathlessly when he had righted himself and got the stallion under control. "I bear an urgent message to you from your father!"

"Yes," said Sigurd, and his heart beat strangely and unsteadily. "What have you to tell me?"

"My lord . . ." Even though they were alone, the man lowered his voice. "Your father the eorl, the King of Wight, and the King of East Anglia have taken the royal enclave of Winchester."

Sigurd closed his eyes. This time, he knew, the sword had truly fallen.

"The children." It was all Niniane could say, could think. Ceawlin looked at her ashen face and reached out to grip her arm.

"The children will be all right, Nan. So long as I am free, Cutha will have naught to gain by harming my heirs."

The pain of his grip helped her to collect herself. She nodded to show him she was all right, then went to sit on one of the old wicker chairs, as her legs were trembling so much she did not think they would hold her. She sat there shivering, trying desperately to get her panic under control while on the other side of the room Ceawlin issued orders to his men. Within fifteen minutes the thanes were galloping out of Bryn Atha, bearing messages from the king to his eorls.

The news had been brought by two of Ceawlin's hall thanes who had been in Venta when the stockade of Winchester was taken. "There were at least three hundred men, my lord," one of them told Ceawlin. "We had no word of their coming until they were upon us. Our men closed the gate, but there was no time to man the walls properly."

The men had no idea what had happened to Ceawlin's hall thanes or to the princes who were caught within the royal enclave. They had ridden out of Venta almost immediately to bring word to the king of the invasion.

"What will you do?" Niniane asked her husband when the two messengers had gone to the kitchen for food and she and Ceawlin were alone.

"Gather my own men," Ceawlin replied. "Cutha and Aethelbert will not be content merely to hold Winchester. They will want to defeat me on the battlefield; they will *have* to defeat me on the battlefield. So long as I am alive, they will never have peace in Wessex."

So long as I am alive. Dear God, dear God, dear God. Niniane bit her lip so hard she drew blood. "Ceawlin . . . Ceawlin, whom can you count on for men?"

He looked at her as she sat huddled on her chair, white and desperate. "It is not so bad as it might have been, Nan," he said. "The gods know, I had not expected this." His voice was bitter. "Cutha and Witgar, yes. But Cutha and Guthfrid!" His laugh was as bitter as his voice. "They might have caught me had I been in Winchester. It was the sheerest good fortune that I was not."

He had not answered her question. "Ceawlin," she said, "whom have you sent to?"

"I have sent to Sigurd," he answered. Her heart jumped with fright at his words, but Ceawlin looked perfectly confident, perfectly normal. "And to Penda and Bertred and Ine and Wuffa," he continued. "They are to meet me in Silchester in two days' time." He bent down to kiss her mouth, and tasted blood from her bitten lip. "It will be all right," he said to her, and she knew from his brilliant eyes that he was looking forward to the challenge. "I have naught to fear from Cutha on the battlefield. He thinks he is a great war leader but I know differently. Sigurd has ever been the only true warrior in Cutha's family, Nan."

She said none of the things she was thinking, but instead forced herself to smile. "You have never lost a battle," she said.

"And I certainly do not intend to start losing battles now." He ran a hand through his hair and looked around the room. "Hammer of Thor," he said. "Little did I think, when I sat here the other night planning activities to bring some excitement into the lives of my thanes, that fate would take such a hand as this!"

Gereint and a contingent of armed Britons rode into Bryn Atha the following afternoon. The next day they would all march to Silchester to join up with the forces of Sigurd, Penda, Bertred, Ine, and Wuffa. Niniane was to stay at Bryn Atha until Ceawlin sent her word.

They were having dinner, the king, queen, Gereint, Ferris, and others of Ceawlin's original British followers in the dining room, the rest in the thanes' quarters, when a horseman came galloping in through the gates of Bryn Atha. Ceawlin and the others were already standing when the man was escorted into the dining room by a white-faced Budd.

The dirt- and sweat-covered horseman threw himself on his knees before Ceawlin. "My lord! My lord! There is a war band coming against you! By now they are but six miles away!"

Ceawlin's face was hard as flint. "Who are you?" he asked.

"I know him, my lord," Gereint answered. "He is the blacksmith from Silchester."

"How do you know they are not coming to join me?" Ceawlin demanded of the man.

"My lord, they carry the standard of the red boar."

Of late years it had become a fashion for each West Saxon eorl to choose an insignia to distinguish his thanes from the thanes of the other eorls and the king. Ceawlin's insignia was the white horse, Cutha's the red boar. "Is it Cutha?" Ceawlin demanded. "Did they come by the road from Winchester?"

"No, my lord. They did not come from Winchester. They came from the east."

I cannot believe it, Ceawlin thought. I will *not* believe it. He turned to Gereint. "Send a horseman out to verify this story."

"I'll go myself," said Gereint, and ran from the room.

"My lord . . ." It was Ferris, white-faced with fear.

Ceawlin gestured impatiently. "We can do nothing until we discover who it is," he said. Then, "Go and tell the rest of your men what is happening."

The room cleared, leaving Ceawlin alone with his wife. He did not look at her, but went to the window and stared out into the courtyard, watching as Gereint galloped out through the gates.

There was only one eorl whose manor was directly to the east of Silchester. Flying the banner of the red boar. He could not believe it.

"It is Sigurd," said Niniane behind him.

He drew a ragged, shallow breath. "Yes. It can be no one else."

"Ceawlin . . . what shall we do?"

He closed his eyes. Never in all his life had he been so frightened. My sons, he thought. My boys. Once I am dead, Cutha will kill them. He will have to kill them. They are my heirs. He was frozen, paralyzed with fear. He couldn't think.

"Can we close the gates of Bryn Atha?" Niniane was asking. "Can we withstand a siege?"

"No." He rocked his head from side to side, feeling the cool glass of the windowpane under his forehead. The doors of the thanes' quarters opened and the courtyard was suddenly filled with men, bows and swords in hand.

My loyal Britons, Ceawlin thought. Cutha will deal hardly with them too.

"A siege would mean either capture or death," Ceawlin said. "That is the last thing we should do."

"Then you must get away." Her voice was at his side now, and finally he turned his head to look at her. "You must save yourself, Ceawlin. Cutha has . . . he has our children."

The face at his shoulder was white and pinched-looking; there was a fine beading of sweat on her upper lip. But her large blue-gray eyes were full of trust that he would know what to do. "They have blocked the east and the south," she said. "Can you go north, to Penda?"

"Have you forgotten, Nan? Penda is Cutha's son-by-marriage."

Now fear crept into her eyes. "Dear God. I had forgotten. Ceawlin . . . do you think perhaps Sigurd is coming to join you after all?"

"No. He would not be flying the banner of the red boar if he were." It was like a blow at the heart even to think of what Sigurd was doing, what Sigurd must be feeling. "He did it to warn me, Nan. He came at his father's behest, but he is flying that miserable banner to give me a chance."

"What chance?" cried Niniane. "He has got you trapped, Ceawlin. Oh, my God . . ." and she pressed her knuckles to her mouth to force herself to stop talking.

He drew another breath, this one deep and steady. "You are right when you say I must get away. Too many lives would be forfeit should Cutha once get his hands on me. And there is only one way to go, Nan. Into British territory. To Corinium."

Niniane thought instantly of Coinmail. "No. You would not be safe, Ceawlin. Not in Corinium. It is under the control of the Dobunni."

"I will not be safe if I go as a Saxon. But what if I go as a Briton?"

Her eyes widened as she took this thought in.

"I can pass as British with my speech," he said.

"Yes. Yes, you can."

"Well, then," and he gave her a crooked grin. "Perhaps you had better find your father's old razor. And a scissors to cut my hair."

By the time Gereint galloped back to Bryn Atha with confirmation of what they already knew, Ceawlin had sent most of the British back to their farms.

"I am riding for Corinium," Ceawlin said to Gereint. "Sigurd will not harm the Atrebates, I am certain of that. Nor is Cutha likely to attempt any forays until he knows I am safely dead."

Gereint stared at his king. Ceawlin's fair hair was now as short as his own, and he was as cleanly shaven. "I see," he said slowly. "You will pretend to be British?"

"Yes."

"I am coming with you."

Ceawlin clapped him on the shoulder. "I won't deny I'd find your company helpful."

"If Coinmail ever discovers you are in his territory," Gereint said grimly, "he will be as merciless as Cutha."

Ceawlin shrugged. "One danger at a time, please. Let us get away from Bryn Atha before I begin to worry about Coinmail."

"Yes," said Niniane urgently. "Do not delay any longer!"

"I'll get the horses," said Gereint.

"Ferris is insisting he come also," said Ceawlin, and Gereint, on his way to the door, looked over his shoulder and grinned.

Ceawlin and Niniane were alone. He put his hands on her shoulders. "I hate to leave you like this, Nan, but you cannot come with me."

"I know." She looked up at him bravely. "It will be better for the boys if I am with them. They must be so frightened . . ." She rubbed her palm along his newly shaven jaw. "Sigurd will not harm me," she said.

"I know." The look he gave her was strange. "Sigurd would never harm you," he said.

"Once you get away . . . then what?"

He put his hand over hers and moved it to his mouth. "I don't know, shall have to see. Be patient, Nan. Be patient and wait. I shall come for you. Be sure of that."

"I know." She raised up to cling around his neck. He held her against him, feeling the slenderness of her, and hoped suddenly, desperately, that she was not in fact carrying his daughter. It was going to be hard enough for her without having to face childbirth as well.

"I must go," he said, and she released him. Gereint and Ferris were in the courtyard with the horses.

"God keep you, my love," she said. He nodded and was gone.

When Sigurd's war band marched into Bryn Atha an hour later, the only people they found were the queen and the villa servants. Niniane was standing in the courtyard directly before the house, and when Sigurd's horse stopped in front of her, she said clearly, "The king is not here." Sigurd's back was to his men and so Niniane was the only one to see the flare of wild relief in the eorl's gray eyes.

"Where has he gone?" It was a man Niniane recognized as Cutha's chief thane who now pushed his horse forward to stand beside Sigurd.

Niniane smiled with genuine amusement. "Do you expect me to tell you?"

The man's hard face tightened and he turned to Sigurd. "I told you, my lord, not to fly the red boar. Had we come under your own banner, we would have caught him."

Sigurd's gray eyes were cold. "If I am fighting for my father, then it is right that I fly my father's banner. Ceawlin has probably gone north, to Penda. There is nothing more for us to do here."

"Sigurd," said Niniane urgently, "what of my sons?"

His eyes turned toward her, though he looked not at her face but at a point somewhere to the left of it. "Your sons are safe, Niniane. I go now to Winchester myself. No harm will come to them, I promise you that."

"Take me with you," she said.

At that he did not look at her. "I don't think—" he was beginning, when Cutha's thane, whose name was Harold, cut in.

"Of course we will take you. Ceawlin's wife! Did you think we would leave you free, my lady?" His laugh was harsh and brutal.

Niniane ignored him, kept her eyes on Sigurd. "I want to be with my children," she said.

He hesitated, then nodded, turned, and said to one of his foot thanes abruptly, "Go saddle a horse for the queen. We leave Bryn Atha immediately for Winchester."

Riding south with the war band reminded Niniane of the first time she had come to Winchester as Cynric's prize of war. But the fear she had felt then seemed to her as nothing compared with the fear she felt now. Then she had been afraid for herself. Now her fear was for those she loved more than her own life.

Ceawlin had been certain that the boys would be safe so long as he lived. Niniane, thinking things out for herself, thought he was right so far as Cutha was concerned. It would gain Cutha nothing to kill Ceawlin's sons so long as the king was alive to get more. But would Guthfrid be so rational? Would not Guthfrid demand her vengeance? Ceawlin's sons for Edwin?

Guthfrid was not yet in Winchester; that she had learned from Sigurd. And Sigurd would never permit harm to befall Ceawlin's sons. He had promised her. . . . Desperately Niniane clung to that hope as the walls of Winchester rose before her.

The stockade gate was manned by strangers. Niniane rode between Sigurd and Harold, with Sigurd's men marching behind as they advanced slowly up the main street toward the great hall. The door of the king's hall opened and Cutha came out with two men who Niniane guessed must be Witgar and Aethelbert, the king of Wight and East Anglia. Cutha gave his son a smile in which welcome and relief were evenly mixed.

"Where is Ceawlin?" It was the thick-set man with the hunched shoulders who spoke. His eyes went once more over the men, searching for a distinctive blond head.

"We were too late at Bryn Atha," Sigurd replied evenly. He spoke to his father only. "The king had gone."

"Where?" demanded Aethelbert, his head jutting forward as well as his shoulders.

"I do not know, my lord," said Sigurd.

"Who is the woman?" It was the other, older man speaking now. Niniane stared haughtily at the King of Wight and answered.

"I am Niniane, the queen."

"You *were* the queen, my lady," the man replied. "Ceawlin is no longer King of Wessex. I am."

All the way south, Niniane had resolved not to be antagonistic to the men who would be her captors, to be pleasant and accommodating. But to see these . . . usurpers standing so brazenly in front of Ceawlin's hall . . . White fury burned through her veins and she said, scorn death-cold in her voice, "You are not fit to kiss the ground before my husband's feet."

"Niniane." It was Sigurd's voice, low and urgent. Bright, choleric color had flooded into the insulted Witgar's face. "The queen is upset, my lords," he said to the three men standing before him. "She is worried about her children. Let me escort her to them."

Cutha nodded. "Yes, get her away from here, Sigurd. The boys are in the princes' hall."

Sigurd reached over to take Niniane's reins, and she let him lead her across the courtyard. He dismounted and lifted her down from her horse. "Thank you," she said stonily, opened the door of the hall, and closed it behind her with a loud bang.

It took a minute for her eyes to adjust from the bright sunlight outside.

"Mama!" There was a rush of feet and then Eirik was in her arms, with Sigurd clinging to her knees and the older boys pressing so close she could scarcely find floor space to put her feet.

"Where is Father? Do they have him?" It was Crida's voice that cut through the general babble.

Niniane shook her head. "Your father is safe, my sons. He escaped from Bryn Atha before Sigurd could catch him."

"The gods are good," said Cerdic fervently, and Crida's laugh was unsteady with relief.

"But why are you here, Mama?" Cerdic asked. It was a measure of how he was feeling that he had reverted to the childhood name.

"Your father had to ride hard, Cerdic. I could not go with him." Her arms tightened on the warm, heavy weight of Eirik. "Besides, I was worried about you."

"They came out of nowhere, Mama," Cerdic said grimly. "We had no warning until they were but a few miles away. If Father had been here, he might have been able to organize a defense, but—"

"The hall thanes tried," Crida put in. "But they got in through the postern gate. Cutha knew where it was, of course." Crida's voice was hard and bitter.

"What has happened to the hall thanes?" Niniane asked.

"Cutha has locked them all into Bertred's hall," Cerdic said. "He first gave them a choice, Mama. He said they could either swear loyalty to him or be prisoners. Not a single thane would betray my father." Cerdic's voice rang with pride.

Niniane kissed Eirik's blond hair and bent to put him back on his feet. "Where has Father gone?" asked Ceowulf.

Niniane glanced at the two youngest children before looking meaningfully at the eldest three. "To a place where Cutha cannot get him."

"But where—?" Ceowulf was beginning, when Crida cut in.

"Be quiet, idiot. Can't you see Mama does not want to talk in front of the babies?"

"I am not a baby," said Sigurd indignantly. "Am I, Mama? I'm a big boy now. Eirik is a baby."

"Am not!" said Eirik instantly.

Niniane laughed unsteadily. "Well, it doesn't sound as if much has changed around here."

Crida shoved his hand through the short hair on his forehead in Ceawlin's own gesture. "I wish that were true," he said.

Cerdic took charge. "Come into my room, Mother. We must talk." Then, when the two youngest made as if to follow them, "No." With an imperious gesture he summoned a nurse. "Find my little brothers some food," he said. "Mother, Crida, come with me."

"And me!" cried Ceowulf in anguish.

Cerdic shrugged. "All right, Ceowulf. You too." Niniane's tall eldest son put an arm around her shoulders and led her toward his bedroom. Crida and Ceowulf obediently followed their brother's lead.

Chapter 33

FERRIS had a cousin whose farm was about halfway between Byrn Atha and Corinium, and it was at this farm that the three fugitives from Bryn Atha finally halted sometime shortly after midnight. Ferris' cousin was a man of about thirty, their own age, and he brought the three weary horsemen into his kitchen, sent his wife back to bed, and sat down to listen with horror to the tale of betrayal his cousin had to tell.

When Ferris had finished, the cousin, whose name was Owain, stared in amazed bewilderment at the three men before him. Gereint he had met before. The other very tall, very blond man he did not know. Ferris had introduced him as Rhys. "But I don't understand," Owain finally said. "Why did you have to flee? From what you tell me, they were only after the king."

"It is well known that we are the king's men," Gereint replied grimly. "Our lives would be worth naught should Cutha get his hands on us."

"Well, Ferris . . . Gereint, you know what we have ever thought of the Atrebates' support of the Saxons," said Owain piously. "I do not mean to be harsh, but you have brought this trouble on yourselves."

Ferris and Gereint both looked quickly at the fair-haired man who was accompanying them. The blond smiled. "Well, all is not lost yet." His voice was mild. "God willing, Ceawlin is safe and may still prevail."

"Yes, that is so." Ferris' voice sounded oddly choked. "God willing."

The blond crossed himself and Ferris began to cough. "Are you all right?" the man called Rhys asked.

"Yes, fine." Ferris looked at his cousin. "I should be glad of some water, though."

"Of course." Owain jumped up. "How stupid of me. You must all be thirsty . . . and hungry too, after such a ride."

As the men fell on the food and beer he put out, Owain looked from one face to the other. "What are you going to do?" he finally asked.

It was the blond, whose eyes were the most startling color Owain had ever seen, who answered. "If you would not mind, we should like to stay here for a while. It will give us a chance to see how things go in Wessex, assess how safe it might be for us to return." The man's blue-green eyes were vivid in the dancing light of the candle. "We are all experienced farmers, Owain. We will be glad to help you with your work."

Gereint's smile was luminous. "That is so, Rhys," he agreed.

"Well . . ." Owain looked at his cousin. There was more here than he had been told, of that he was certain. "Are you waiting to hear from Ceawlin?" he asked Ferris bluntly.

Ferris met his cousin's eyes and then smiled wryly and shrugged. "Yes," he said. "We are. And we need a place to stay while we wait. Will you help us, Owain?"

"I think you are mad," the man of the Dobunni, whose mother had been an Atrebates, said.

The blond grinned. "Doubtless you are right."

Owain looked at the three of them again and sighed. "Oh, all right. You can stay here for a while."

"One more thing." It was the blond again, and this time his pleasant voice was unmistakably giving a command. "It would be better to keep our presence as quiet as possible. Your prince, Coinmail, is not known to be overly fond of his old kinsmen."

"Are you related to Coinmail?" Owain asked curiously.

"Yes," said the man called Rhys, and there was a note of ironic amusement in his voice. "I'm afraid that I am."

Summer came to Winchester. Cutha spent his time in trying to keep Aethelbert and Witgar from falling out and in wooing the eorls. When Ceawlin came back—for Cutha, who knew the king well, had little doubt that Ceawlin would try to regain his kingdom—when Ceawlin came back, much of what happened would depend upon how many friends Cutha was able to win.

The country seemed to Cutha to be sunk in silence. No one knew exactly where Ceawlin was, though it seemed most probable that he was somewhere in Dumnonia. It was Bertred whom Cutha thought the king would try to reach first, and as Banford was not far from Bertred's manor, it was possible to keep a close watch on Bertred without seeming to do so. Bertred himself Cutha did not attempt to win over. Bertred would be Ceawlin's man until he died; all Cutha could do there was try to keep the eorl isolated from the king.

Penda was ominously silent. He had been pleasant to the man sent to him by Cutha, but had refused to come to Winchester with his thanes, saying he would be better employed guarding the northern boundary of Wessex. Guarding it from whom or for whom, he did not say.

Cutha's chief allies from among the eorls were Cynigils, who had come into Winchester to assist Cutha and to claim the spoils of victory he had been promised, and Cutha's own son, Sigurd. Ine and Wuffa had made brief appearances in Winchester, listened politely to Cutha, and then had gone home. For the first time Cutha was fully appreciative of just how much power Ceawlin had bestowed upon his eorls.

And yet, under Ceawlin that power had also been strictly limited, as Cuthwulf had found out. The eorls were free to exercise their power only on the direction of the king. Cutha drummed this message into the ears of Penda and Ine and Wuffa and hoped that his words fell upon fertile soil. Under a new king, he told them, their power would be even greater.

To Cutha's immense relief, Guthfrid had refused her brother's demand that she and Edgar come to Wessex. The wolf-mother had but one cub left, and she was not going to risk him until she was certain he would be safe. Not until Ceawlin was dead, she answered Aethelbert, would she come to Winchester.

Cutha was not the only one to be glad that Guthfrid chose to stay in Sutton Hoo. Niniane thanked God fervently when she heard this news from Sigurd. She feared Guthfrid more than she feared the men.

The months went by and there was no word from Ceawlin.

"Your father must keep his identity secret while he lies in British lands," Niniane told her sons. "It will take time for him to gather a war band."

"Yes, Mother," Cerdic and Crida said. "We know. Do not fear. Father will come."

"But how can he gather a war band?" Cerdic asked his brother when they were alone. "Cutha has all his men locked up here in Winchester."

"Bertred will aid him," said Crida stoutly.

"Will he?" said Cerdic. "Last year you would have said the same of Sigurd."

The two boys looked at each other. "The Atrebates will rally for him, then," said Crida.

"Perhaps, but they are not really warriors, Crida. Except for Gereint and Ferris and a few others, they are farmers. Gods!" added Cerdic passionately. "I hate being trapped here like this! If only I could get out of Winchester!"

"What would you do if you escaped from Winchester?" Crida asked impatiently.

"Find Father," said Cedric. "At least then he would not be alone."

Crida shook his head so hard that his fair, silky hair swung from side to side. "Do not try anything foolish," he advised. "As you just pointed out, we cannot be certain who is friend and who is foe. You are better off here in Winchester."

"Crida . . . has it not occurred to you what will happen to us should Father die?" Cerdic's eyes had lost all their blue, were large and dark and very gray.

"Yes." Crida's fair skin was paler than usual, but his voice remained calm. "Witgar will never reign unchallenged while we live. I know that. He knows that. You can be certain that Mother and Father know that as well."

"Then . . . do you not see why we should try to escape from Winchester?"

"No. I think we should wait for Father." Crida's eyes were only on a level with his brother's mouth, but his boy's voice for a moment sounded uncannily like Ceawlin's. "He will do something, we can be sure of that. Nor does he need his hostages scattered around the countryside, Cerdic." After a moment the younger brother added, "And at least in Winchester we have Sigurd."

"Sigurd." Cerdic's voice was full of loathing. "That traitor!"

"Sigurd will protect us," said Crida. The two boys looked at each other. Then Crida added slowly, "If he can."

The months were long for Ceawlin as well. Ferris, whose face was not so well-known as Gereint's, spent the summer carrying messages from Ceawlin to his eorls. Cutha by now, Ceawlin reckoned, must have under his command at least four hundred men. Cutha also had one hundred of Ceawlin's men locked up in Winchester, effectively depriving him of their services. The collected forces of Penda, Ine, Wuffa, and Bertred would not number two hundred. The eorls, who could count as well as their king, were inclined to wait.

The summer slipped by. True to his word, Ceawlin helped with the field work and did his best to remain inconspicuous. He was not a man it was possible not to notice, however, and all too soon for comfort the presence of the tall blond stranger was a cause for comment in the valley where Owain's farm lay.

Owain's wife was nervous.

"I don't like it," she told him night after night. "Ferris is in and out of Wessex all the time. They are in league with Ceawlin. I know it."

"What if they are?" Owain answered. "It has nothing to do with us."

"It might." Maire was a dark-eyed, dark-haired woman with strong bones and very white teeth. "That Rhys. He is someone important, Owain. Your cousin and Gereint are one thing, but he is another matter altogether."

"How important can he be, Maire? He is a Briton, after all."

"He doesn't look British."

Owain shrugged. "No Saxon could speak British like he does. Besides, he is related to Coinmail."

"But he does not want Coinmail to know he is here."

Owain shrugged again.

"He may have had a British mother, Owain, but I would wager you his father was a Saxon." Maire's brown eyes were somber. "He is important, my husband. You must know that yourself. Ferris and Gereint defer to him. You defer to him . . . yes you do! Even *I* find myself deferring to him. It's not that he is demanding, it's just that he . . . it is something about him . . . I cannot say what . . . but it is there, Owain!"

Owain sighed. He knew his wife was right. "He is very likable, Maire."

Her smile was rueful. "Too likable, my husband. And too striking. His presence has not gone unnoticed, we can be certain of that. What will happen if people learn we have been harboring a Saxon from Wessex? You know how hated the Saxons are after Bedcanford. We must think of our children, Owain. I think you should tell them it is time to move on."

Ceawlin was coming to the same conclusion as his hosts. The farm wagons from the valley, loaded with produce to sell in the city, were now rolling regularly to Corinium. Ceawlin could not fail to realize that his presence, along with that of Ferris and Gereint, was causing a great deal of local gossip.

Owain himself took a load of food into Corinium and returned with the news that Coinmail had recently come to the city. The chief of the Dobunni, Coinmail's father-by-marriage, was ill and the prince had gradually been assuming more and more of the chief's role. It was accepted that Coinmail's son would be the next chief, but as the child was but six, Coinmail would be the real chief of the Dobunni for many years. And Corinium was less than twenty miles from Owain's farm.

"The prince is known to be interested in Wessex," Owain reported to his cousin upon return to the farm. "He knows Gereint. It will not be long before he learns of your presence in this valley. Glevum was far enough away for secrecy, but now that he has come to Corinium . . ." Owain's voice trailed off as he looked unhappily at his three unwanted guests. "You did say you did not wish Coinmail to know of your presence," he added.

They all waited for the man called Rhys to answer. As Maire had noted, they always waited for Rhys. A fly hovered around the cheese on the table, its buzz loud in the suddenly quiet room. Owain looked at the man sitting opposite him at the kitchen table. His hair had bleached almost white in the summer sun, and his skin had tanned a surprising golden brown. One would not think skin that fair could tan, Owain found himself thinking. Rhys appeared to be watching the fly with utter absorption. The insect lighted on the table and Rhys's strong, callused hand came down like lightning. The buzzing stopped. Rhys looked at Gereint and said, "It is time to return to Wessex."

The temper of Wessex was sullen. Cutha felt it when he went into Venta, felt it in the inimical stares of the merchants who sold to

Winchester as always but with a surliness which was new. Ceawlin, Cutha was coming to realize, had been a very popular king.

Aethelbert was restless. His warrior soul lusted to meet Ceawlin once more on the battlefield and he was frustrated and angry by the absence of his enemy. Witgar was not happy either. The continued absence of the West Saxon eorls told him all too clearly that so long as Ceawlin was still at large, he would be king in name only.

Cutha was unhappily coming to the conclusion that his victory had been almost too easy. Sigurd's betrayal, which had driven Ceawlin from the kingdom, had left Wessex in a state of uneasy suspension. There had been no battle, no decisive trying of strengths, and consequently no clear victor. Ceawlin's presence, even in exile, was proving to cast a very long shadow.

Consequently, Sigurd's defection to Cutha, which had seemed such a great coup at the time, seemed less and less a triumph as the months went by. It had left Wessex in this ungovernable state, for one thing; and it was obviously preying on Sigurd's heart, for another. It was all too clear to Cutha that his son could not forget that he had betrayed his friend. Nor did Cutha's repeated assurances that he had done so in order not to betray his father seem to soothe Sigurd's agony of mind.

Cutha suggested that Sigurd return to Wokham, but his son refused to leave Winchester. Sigurd was afraid for Ceawlin's sons; Cutha knew that well enough. And he had reason to fear, as Cutha admitted to himself in his more honest moments. When he had first plotted to overthrow Ceawlin, Cutha had not for a moment envisioned what would necessarily be the fate of Ceawlin's sons. Or if the thought had crossed his mind, he had resolutely pushed it away. But now the boys in the princes' hall were all too obvious, all too present. All too popular. Perhaps, Cutha began to think, perhaps Witgar's granddaughter could marry Cerdic.

His mind resolutely refused to contemplate what Aethelbert and Guthfrid would think of this change in plan.

Then, to make matters even worse, Nola had told him that Niniane was expecting another child. Gods, Cutha thought, why could Ceawlin not have been like Cynric? Six children . . . six heirs to Wessex. He could not even begin to contemplate what he was to do with Ceawlin's six children.

The heat in the hall and the smell of the food were making Niniane feel nauseated. She wiped the sweat from her forehead and said to Cerdic, who was seated next to her at the table, "I am going outside for some air, Cerdic."

He looked at her with worried eyes and she forced herself to smile at him. "I shall be fine; I just need some air."

He smiled back, although his eyes still looked worried. "All right, Mother."

It was hot outside the hall as well; the air was heavy and still. Niniane looked hopefully at the sky, searching for signs of rain. There were men in the courtyard, walking purposefully from one hall to the other. Niniane looked at them, her face blank. Cutha's men. Aethelbert's men. Witgar's men. Enemies.

The door of the king's hall opened and a man came out. Niniane recognized him instantly. Sigurd.

The day was so stifling, so airless. She felt the sweat on her forehead, between her shoulder blades and breasts. Then the air went dark.

"Niniane!" Sigurd was beside her, his arm around her waist. She sagged against him and he lifted her up into his arms. "You are ill," he said. "Let me take you inside."

"No!" She closed her eyes tightly, then opened them again. "No, Sigurd," she said more steadily. "I cannot go back into that stuffy hall. Just let me sit down outdoors for a moment."

He looked around, searching for a place to take her. Then, "There is a breeze near the dueling grounds," he said.

Her small head, pillowed now against his shoulder nodded. "Can you walk?" he asked.

"No," she answered. "Carry me."

She kept her eyes closed as Sigurd walked with her around the hall in the direction of the dueling grounds. She felt immensely weary. It was not wrong of her to rest for a few minutes, she thought, to savor the strength of strong arms around her, a broad shoulder under her cheek. She could not lean thus on her sons; for them must she be strong and confident. But she was so frightened . . . so lonely . . . so very, very weary. And it was just for a moment.

"Here we are. Do you want to sit on the grass for a while?" Sigurd asked.

"Yes," she said. "That would be nice." Sigurd put her carefully on her feet and she folded to the ground in a graceful billow of skirts. He stood there looking at her, his mouth very grim. She patted the ground beside her, and slowly, almost reluctantly, he sat down as well.

For months now he had been avoiding Niniane. She would hate him, of that he was sure. And certainly she had made no attempt to seek him out, sequestering herself in the princes' hall with her sons and Alric, leaving only to go occasionally to the women's hall for a visit with Nola. He did not want to hold speech with Niniane, or with Ceawlin's sons either. He was in little doubt as to what they thought of him; how could he be, when he thought the same of himself?

So he sat cross-legged beside Ceawlin's wife on the grass and braced himself. She had wanted to speak to him, that was obvious. There was no other reason he could think of that would account for her behavior just now. But she said nothing, just sat with slightly bent head regarding the sunburned grass on which she reclined. "Are you all right?" he asked after a minute, his voice harsh to his own ears.

"Oh, yes." She raised her head and looked at him. "Just feeling the heat, that is all. I am with child again," she added, as if the news were of no importance.

He felt as if someone had just punched him in the stomach. "Oh, no," he said before he could stop himself.

Her eyes looked almost gray as they regarded him soberly. "Ceawlin did not know what was going to happen in Wessex," she said.

He could feel himself color. He wanted to look away from her, but he could not. She wouldn't let him, he realized, was holding him captive with those steady smoke-blue eyes. "Do you know where he is?" she asked.

"No." There was a small silence while they sat there side by side, eyes locked in a strange kind of duel. Then, "I thought you would know," he said.

"We had little time to make plans."

He tore his eyes away and put his hand on the grass to push himself upright. Her own hand shot out to cover his and hold him there. He froze, eyes on the small narrow hand that was holding him. She was wearing short sleeves in the heat, and he could see clearly the delicate bones of her wrist, the soft silky skin of her inner arm. "Sigurd," she said, and her husky voice sent a shiver up and down his spine. "Don't go."

His heart began to slam in his chest. "I know what you think of me, Niniane," he said. "I don't need to stay here to hear it."

"You don't know what I think of you," she answered. Then, "Ceawlin knew why you were showing your father's banner. He said to me, 'Sigurd is flying that miserable banner to give me a chance.'"

He pulled his fingers from under hers and, bending forward as if in pain, buried his face in his hands. Niniane sat watching and, unseen by him, her eyes held a distinctly speculative look. She said now, "Ceawlin is trusting you to keep his sons safe."

He did not move.

"Sigurd," she said relentlessly.

"I know." His voice was muffled by his hands. "I will get them away if it comes to that, Niniane. But this game has not been played out yet. Ceawlin will come back."

"I know he will."

Finally he raised his head. She smiled at him, a smile full of pity, and he said suddenly, "Do you know why I left Winchester to go and live at Wokham?"

She shook her head, and a strand of hair, which she had tied on the top of her head for coolness, loosened and slipped down her neck. "Ceawlin would never tell me." A delicately arched brow rose a little higher. "Are you going to tell me, Sigurd? Does it have aught to do with what has happened?"

He was surprised by how strong was the temptation to tell her. To say, "I have loved you since you were sixteen years old; since the time we were playing ring-toss with the children and you took the ring from my hand, accidentally touched my fingers, and looked at me like a startled fawn. I loved you before Ceawlin ever thought of you, Niniane. And that is why I left Winchester." Even to himself he could not say that that was why he had finally betrayed Ceawlin.

"No," he answered, his voice low. "No, it has nothing to do with what happened." And now he did rise to his feet.

"If you do hear news of Ceawlin," she said quickly, "you will tell me?"

"Yes. I will tell you." He turned on his heel and walked away as swiftly as he could.

Chapter 34

"IT is not just Coinmail," Ceawlin said to his two faithful followers when they met privately to discuss Owain's news. "I am convinced that if I stay out of Wessex much longer, I will lose it. I cannot give Cutha the time to establish himself."

"You have no war band, my lord," said Gereint.

Ceawlin cocked his eyebrow in a gesture they had not seen for months. "And I will never have a war band unless I show myself in Wessex to collect one."

Gereint found himself smiling. "After all," he said. "It is not the first time you have been in this position."

Ceawlin grinned. "The eorls have been reluctant in my absence. We shall see what they will do once they find me at their hall doors."

Ferris bit his lip. "It is risky."

"It is riskier to do nothing," Ceawlin replied positively. "I have wasted the entire summer and have naught to show for it but the crops stacked in Owain's storehouse. I dare delay no longer. It is time to throw the dice."

"Where shall we go first, my lord?" Gereint asked.

"To Wyckholm."

Ferris swallowed hard. He had been the one to speak to all the eorls on Ceawlin's behalf. "My lord, Penda has promised to stay neutral. I do not think he will betray you, but neither do I think he will come to your aid. He is one to look out for himself, is Penda."

"He came to Bryn Atha for me once," said Ceawlin. His eyes looked lighter than usual in his tanned face. "I think Penda will find it difficult to refuse me once I am under his roof."

"His wife is Cutha's daughter," Gereint reminded his king.

"Penda is not a man to be swayed by a woman," Ceawlin said. "We will go to Wyckholm."

It was the last day of August when Ceawlin and his two companions rode away from the farm that had sheltered them for the last four months. Owain and his wife stood by the gate and watched the horses disappear into the haze of the hot, still morning. "Thank God," said Maire.

Owain sighed. "Yes," he agreed, but his voice sounded regretful.

"The wagon is ready to go into Corinium," his wife reminded him.

"All right." The farmer cast one more glance up the road, then turned dutifully to return to his work.

Penda was stunned when a thane brought him the news that the king was at his gates. He did not really believe it was true until the tall, sunburned figure of Ceawlin was actually standing before him. "My lord!" he said, his hazel eyes going searchingly from Ceawlin to the two Britons who accompanied him. "What are you doing here?"

Ceawlin stretched the muscles of his back as if they were stiff. "I came to see you, of course. Gods, Penda, but I'm thirsty. We came straight through from Ufton."

Penda pulled himself together. They were all standing in the center of his hall, and now he gestured his guests to the benches along the wall. "Please sit down. You must be tired. I'll send for some food and beer."

When he turned back from giving orders, he saw that Ceawlin had made himself comfortable on one of the benches, big shoulders propped against the wall, long legs stretched in front of him. As Penda approached him, the king grinned and rubbed his hand along his bare jaw. "I'm surprised you recognized me," he said.

Penda found himself smiling back. "It would be impossible not to recognize you, Ceawlin."

The beer came and the three new arrivals drank thirstily. Penda waited. Ceawlin finished, put the cup on the bench beside him, and said, "I cannot wait longer, Penda. I am gathering a war band. Are you with me or against me?"

"I am not against you, Ceawlin," his eorl replied carefully. "But I must think of the welfare of my own people. Cutha has far more men than you can possibly hope to collect."

Ceawlin leaned against the wall, looking perfectly relaxed, perfectly at ease. "If we collect only thanes, yes. But not if we take the ceorls."

Penda stared at his king. "If we make the ceorls thanes, then, when the war is over, who will be left to till the soil?"

"I did not say make the ceorls thanes. I said make the ceorls fight. They are your men. You are my man. I need bodies, Penda."

The eorls's stare widened. What Ceawlin was proposing was something that was new among the Saxon kingdoms. More than a century before, when the invaders were still pouring in from Germany, the Saxon armies had numbered in the thousands. Every men who was of age to fight, fought. Then Arthur had pushed them back into their kingdoms along the eastern and southern shore and they had settled down to farm and to become civilized. For the last hundred years or so, all the fighting among the Saxons had been done by small bands of professional warriors, the thanes. The ceorls had worked the land. To ask a ceorl to fight had been to elevate him in class, make him one of the warrior elite. He had not gone back to the farm after.

"You have thirty thanes," said Ceawlin. "You can arm at least thirty ceorls as well."

"And after, they will go back to the land?" said Penda.

"Yes. I will pay them, Penda. Or I will pay you, and you can pay them. A man should have some reward for risking his life. But they will not become thanes."

"It has never been done before," Penda said.

Ceawlin slid his shoulders a little lower on the wall and contemplated his feet. "Life has been good in Wessex under my reign," he said. "They owe me something for that." He looked up and his eyes met Penda's. He added very softly, "And so do you."

For the briefest of minutes, his eyes caught in that turquoise gaze, Penda found that he had forgotten to breathe. Then, "I swore allegiance to you twice, Ceawlin," he said, his voice gruffer than usual. "If you are determined on this course, then I am with you."

Ceawlin smiled, teeth very white in his sunburned face. He got to his feet and put a friendly hand on Penda's shoulder. "Good man," he said. "I knew I could count on you."

Penda gave his lord a rueful look. He had not intended to involve himself in this struggle between Ceawlin and his father-by-marriage. "Fate does smile on you, Ceawlin. It always has."

"Fate smiles on those whose courage does not fail," Ceawlin replied, and for the first time since he had arrived at Wyckholm, his voice sounded grim.

Two days after Ceawlin had left the Ufton valley, riders from Corinium galloped into Owain's farmyard. The leading rider was a red-haired man with a beautiful austere face. Maire came out of the house to see what they wanted.

"This is Prince Coinmail," one of the riders said to Owain's wife. "Where is your husband?"

Maire stared at the prince, then hastily bobbed her head. "He is in the fields, my lord. Shall I send for him?"

"It is not your husband I wish to see, but your guests," Coinmail replied. He spoke British with the accent of the Atrebates.

Maire's heart began to pound. "Our guests?" She opened her eyes very wide in a look of innocence. "Do you mean my husband's cousin?"

"His cousin," came the grim reply. "And the tall blond man who is with him."

Maire wet her lips. "They are gone, my lord."

Coinmail stared at her. Maire did not think she had ever seen so cold a face. "Gone? Gone where?"

"Back to Wessex, my lord."

"When?"

"Two days since."

There was a long, very uncomfortable silence. Finally the horses began to paw the ground with impatience. Coinmail asked, "This man with your cousin, I understand he was British?"

"So my husband's cousin said. And he spoke British, my lord. As you do, with the accent of the Atrebates."

"What color were his eyes?" the prince asked.

Maire knew then that her guess had been right. Rhys was important. "They were a mixture of blue and green, my lord," she said with great reluctance. She would have lied if she had thought she could get away with it.

Coinmail's face looked like chiseled marble, but his eyes glittered strangely. "You stupid cow," he said to the woman who stood before him in the farmyard. "Do you know whom you have been sheltering all these months?"

"N-no, my lord."

"Ceawlin. Ceawlin himself. God in heaven, if only I had known!"

"Ceawlin?" Maire stared at her prince as if he were speaking a strange language. "Do you mean the West Saxon king? Rhys was the king?"

"I mean that the man you knew as Rhys was Ceawlin, the King of Wessex. The deposed King of Wessex. My brother-by-marriage." Coinmail's voice was icy with bitterness. "I knew as soon as I heard the description of the man who was here with Gereint who he must be."

"We did not know, my lord!" Maire cried desperately. "You must believe me, we did not know. Ferris told us he was a Briton, a friend who was fleeing the wrath of the new king, just as he was."

Coinmail looked at her as if she were some kind of an unpleasant insect. Then he said to his men, "It is too late to catch him now. God knows where he will have gone." He wheeled his horse and, without another look at the trembling Maire, galloped his horse out of the farmyard, almost trampling on the chickens as he went.

Maire waited a few minutes to make certain they were down the road before she ran to the fields to tell Owain.

On the first of September Witgar and his thanes left Winchester to march south. The shoreline across the bay from Wight had been part of Wight's territory since the days of Cerdic, and reports had come to Witgar in Winchester of raiding from across the Sussex border. Evidently the neighboring kingdom was testing the stability of the new government in Wessex, and Witgar thought it wise to assert his authority in his old kingdom without delay. Cutha concurred, albeit reluctantly. He did not like to deplete Winchester of men.

The second week in September brought the news that Ceawlin's family had long been awaiting. The king was in Wyckholm with Penda.

It was Sigurd who told Niniane and her two eldest sons. "My father received word from Coenburg," Sigurd said, his eyes on the queen alone.

"What did the messenger say?" Niniane asked tensely.

"Just that. Ceawlin is at Wyckholm and Penda is joining him."

The three were alone in a corner of the princes' hall and now Cerdic laughed. "If Penda holds to my father, then will the other eorls do so also."

Even in the dimness of the hall's corner, Niniane could see the strain on Sigurd's face. "Yes," he said. "They will."

There was silence as three pairs of eyes stared at Cutha's son, Ceawlin's traitor-friend. "What is Cutha going to do?" Niniane asked at last.

"Nothing, for the moment. It will come to a battle eventually. There can be no clear victor otherwise, and Wessex will continue in this uneasy state of waiting."

"So he will let Ceawlin gather a war band?"

"I think so."

Silence fell once more. "Well," Sigurd said as the air seemed to grow heavier, "I thought you would like to know." He turned and walked to the door; Niniane thought briefly that he looked very alone, very vulnerable. Then Crida said something and she turned back to her sons. She had no extra sympathy to spare for Sigurd.

The two boys' faces were blazing. "At last!" Cerdic said.

"Can Sigurd be telling the truth, Mother? Will Cutha allow Father to gather a war band?"

"I think so," Niniane replied slowly, thinking as she spoke. "Sigurd is right when he says it must come to a battle. Witgar cannot rule unless he proves himself on the battlefield. The eorls will not follow him."

"Father has never been beaten in battle," Cerdic said proudly.

But Crida knew the arithmetic. "Cutha has Father's men locked up here in Winchester. The eorls have only thirty or forty thanes each. That means Father will be able to command fewer than two hundred men. Cutha must have four hundred, at least." He looked at his mother, his silvery brows drawn together in worry.

"Your father has won with the odds against him before, my son," Niniane said with more confidence than she felt. "There is no greater warrior in England than Ceawlin. We must trust him to know what to do."

"Hammer of Thor!" said Cerdic, using Ceawlin's favorite oath. "If only I could be at his side. I am so useless sitting here in Winchester."

"Waiting is ever the hardest part of any endeavor, Cerdic," Niniane said with a sigh. "Best to learn that now, while you are young."

"Father needs all the men he can get," the prince said.

Niniane closed her eyes. She had longed for so many months to hear news of him, but now that she had . . . A strong young arm went around her shoulders. "It will be all right, Mother," Crida's voice said in her ear. She looked up into his eyes, so like Ceawlin's own. He had grown these last months, she thought. He was inches taller than she. "You look pale," he said to her now. "Come and sit down."

"Yes," she said. "I think I will."

She was sleepless in the night, tossing restlessly on the narrow bed that had belonged to Crida, and before him to Ceawlin. Crida had moved into Cerdic's room when Niniane came back to Winchester. She had not ever slept well in this windowless room, in this narrow lonely bed, but tonight she could not sleep at all. Consequently, when the door to her room opened softly, she sat up at once.

"Who is it?" she asked.

"Crida."

Niniane reached for the tinder on the table beside her bed. "Come in, Crida," she said, and lit a candle.

He closed the door behind him and came across the floor. "I can't find Cerdic," he said in a low voice. "I woke up a half-hour ago and he was gone."

"Gone? How can he be gone?" Cutha posted a guard at the door of the princes' hall every night.

"The guard is asleep," Crida said. "I think he is drunk."

"Dear God." Niniane stared up at her second son. "Where can he gave gone, Crida?"

"I think he may be trying to get out of Winchester, Mother. He has been fretting about his captivity, and now that he knows where to go to find Father . . ."

"He can't do that!" Niniane got out of bed and clutched Crida's arm. "He would not have gone without telling you!"

"He knew I would try to dissuade him." Crida's face in the flickering candlelight did not look young at all. "We have talked of this before. Gods, Mother. What shall we do?"

"We cannot do anything," Niniane said. She sat down again on the bed, heavily. "Where did you look?"

"The stables. The gates. All is quiet. I saw no sign of Cerdic."

"He cannot possibly get out of Winchester," Niniane said.

"Not by horse. But suppose he tries to go over the wall?"

"There are guards on the walls." She pushed her tangled hair off her face. "'If he tries it, the guards will simply catch him and return him to us. Or he will get away and go to your father. One or the other.'"

"Yes," Crida said slowly. "I suppose you are right. One or the other." They did not look at each other.

"No one saw him leave?" Niniane asked after a minute, referring to the servants who slept on benches in the main part of the hall.

"Everyone is asleep."

"Then we must just wait, Crida," Niniane said. "Perhaps he will see it is impossible and come back himself."

"That is so." Crida sounded more hopeful. "I'm sorry, Mother, I should not have awakened you. But I did not know what I should do . . ."

"I was not asleep," she said. "Come. The two of us will wait together in your room. I'll wager Cerdic returns within the hour."

It was but ten minutes after Crida awakened Niniane that a shadowy figure appeared from out of nowhere to take a flying leap at the stockade wall on the south side of the enclave, behind Bertred's hall. The guard on duty there was yawning and looking up at the three-quarter moon, trying to assess the time, when his attention was caught by the noise. He was usually posted farther down the wall but had moved his position this night simply for a change. He had had guard duty all week and was heartily bored with it.

"Who is there?" he called sharply, and began to run toward the figure lurking on the sentry walk in the shadow of the wall. There was no answer, and the figure began to climb over the wall. The sentry saw fingers holding on to the top of the stockade, then heard the thud as the escapee landed on the hard ground below. The sentry fitted a bow into his arrow with steady fingers and shouted again. The figure, whose hair shone blond in the moonlight, never turned, but began to run toward the fields. He looked to be limping; it was a long drop from the wall to the ground. The sentry raised his bow, aimed, and shot. The figure fell forward onto his face and lay still, arms spread-eagled at its sides.

A few other thanes came running up. "What is it?" they asked.

"I don't know. Someone tried to get over the wall. I shot him."

A thane shouted for help and then they set a ladder over the wall and climbed down. They broke off the arrow embedded in the center of the back, turned the figure over, and for the first time saw the face of Ceawlin's eldest son. The sentry had shot true. Cerdic was dead.

It was Cutha who brought the news to Niniane. Sigurd refused to do it. Cutha woke the guard at the door of the princes' hall by the simple expedient of kicking him in the stomach. After a brief interchange with the retching guard, he entered the hall, to find Niniane and Crida waiting for him. Niniane had pulled a cloak over her sleeping gown and her hair hung in a tangle of brown and bronze to her waist. She was barefoot. In the dim light of the candle perched on the edge of the hearthplace, Cutha thought that she looked scarcely older than the boy who was standing beside her. Crida's hair too was tousled and he was wearing only a pair of linen trousers. His young chest and shoulders were more muscled than Cutha would have thought.

These impressions flitted through the eorl's mind in the brief moment's silence before Niniane said, "What is it?"

"Do you know where Cerdic is, Niniane?" he asked, not knowing how to begin.

"No. Crida came to tell me just a short while ago that Cerdic was not in his bed. Where is he, Cutha? What has happened?"

"He gave wine to the guard," Cutha said, trying to delay the moment when he would have to tell her. "That is how he got out of the princes' hall."

"*Where is he?*"

"Niniane . . ." He looked away from Cerdic's mother to Crida. In this light the boy looked uncannily like his father. Cutha found himself remembering suddenly, vividly, the seventeen-year-old who had come to him for help when Cynric died. And now Ceawlin's son was dead. Ceawlin's son for his son. But he had not wanted this. Standing here in the hall, watching the dawning understanding on Crida's young face, Cutha knew he had not wanted this.

"Cerdic is dead," he said, his voice harsh with suppressed feeling.

The two in front of him did not move. Did not speak.

"He tried to climb over the wall," Cutha went on, the words coming with more and more difficulty. "It was dark and the sentry did not know who it was. He shot. Cerdic was dead when they got to him."

"I don't believe it," Niniane said. "It can't be true."

"Niniane, the gods know I wish it were not true," said Cutha. "But it is."

In the background there was the noise of children, and female voices hushing them. "Can I see him?" Crida asked.

"I had them bring the body to the women's hall. I did not think you would want it here . . . with the children . . ."

Niniane moved forward, like a sleepwalker who sees but does not see. "I will come," she said. Crida hastened to her side and together the two of them left the princes' hall and crossed the courtyard in the light of the moon that Cerdic would see no more.

Chapter 35

*I*T was Crida who conducted the funeral rite for Cerdic. At first Niniane had refused, thinking he was too young, that it would be too much for him, but then she saw that it would comfort the boy to be the one to do this for his brother, and so she relented. It would mean something to Ceawlin also, she thought, that it was Crida who officiated at Cerdic's burial.

So Crida said the prayer of dedication and killed the ox that Cutha had provided to honor Cerdic's rank. There was a small gathering in the temple: Crida, Ceowulf, who had begged and begged his mother to allow him to attend, Alric, and a handful of the younger thanes with whom Cerdic had been friends. Sigurd did not show his face.

Crida went faultlessly through the ceremonies, and he and Ceowulf kept watch by Cerdic's body through the night. Ceowulf fell asleep but Crida did not. He sat motionless on the king's bench, his eyes on the still face of his dead brother, his composed face giving no hint of the confusion within.

Where was Cerdic now? he wondered. His mother had told him Cerdic was in heaven, with her God, who was a Father to all. He would like to believe that. He could not bear to think of Cerdic anywhere cold or bleak or dim. Not Cerdic, who had been so full of joy, so full of life. His father did not believe as his mother did, but Crida was not so sure. There must be something good after this life for those who were pure of heart, he thought almost desperately, his eyes on the unrevealing face of his brother. It only made sense to believe that there was something for them after this life. He was still sitting in the same position hours later when Ceowulf awakened.

"Crida?" The younger boy's voice was thick with sleep.

"Yes."

"I . . . I fell asleep. I'm sorry."

"That is all right." Crida's voice sounded distant, impersonal.

The two boys were alone in the temple; the priests had gone to prepare for the trek to the burial site. The candles had all burned down. The smell of the cooked oxen from the funeral banquet lingered in the air. Ceowulf walked hesitatingly to stand beside his brother's

325

dead body. He looked at Crida, however, not at Cerdic, as he asked, "What do we do now?"

"The priests and Alric should be coming soon," Crida answered. "We will take Cerdic to the burial grounds and put him in the earth."

"Oh." At last Ceowulf looked at Cerdic's quiet face. "Crida . . ." he said, his eyes on Cerdic, his voice choked with emotion, "Crida, I cannot believe that we will never see him again."

Crida's face clenched. "Ceowulf, don't . . ." But the younger boy had begun to cry, great sobbing gulps that racked his whole body.

Crida got to his feet. He wanted to run, to get away from the tearing sorrow he heard in his brother's voice. He couldn't let Ceowulf break him down, he had to get through the funeral. Ceowulf lifted his grief-stricken face. "Crida . . ." Crida hesitated. Ceowulf was only ten. He could not leave him like this. He held out his arms and the younger boy, as tall as he but not as strong, came stumbling to him. Holding Ceowulf, Crida too began to cry. Ceowulf's arms came around his shoulders and the two brothers, who in the happy days of the past had so often been at odds, stood together in their sorrow and comforted each other.

The funeral procession was small. Nola walked with Niniane, while Alric accompanied Crida and Ceowulf. There were the marks of tears on the boys' faces and on Alric's as well. Nola sobbed uncontrollably as the grave goods were dedicated and Cerdic's body lowered into the grave.

I cannot believe this is happening . . . I cannot believe this is happening . . . It was the one thought that kept running over and over again in Niniane's brain. Yesterday at this time, Cerdic had been alive. Today he was dead. They were burying him.

Crida's voice was steady as he made the dedications, but Niniane could see the effort it was taking him to keep it thus. I cannot cry, she thought. It will upset the boys if I cry; they will not be able to get through this. I cannot cry.

She did not even feel like crying. She was numb. I cannot believe this is happening, she thought. I cannot believe this is happening.

Cutha had actually been relieved to hear news of Ceawlin. It was necessary to put the sovereignty of Wessex to the test of the battlefield; that lesson had become crystal clear to him during the course of the last few months. And while he was surprised, and disappointed, to learn that Penda had declared for Ceawlin, still Cutha thought he had reason to be sanguine. He had his own men and Aethelbert's men here with him in Winchester. Cynigils had forty men of his own at his manor of Alford, some fifteen miles to Winchester's east. Sigurd had thirty thanes at Wokham. Witgar was in the south with a strong following of thanes from Wight. And Cutha was holding the core of Ceawlin's men captive right here in Winchester. The numbers were most definitely on Cutha's side.

Cutha asked Sigurd to send for his men and Sigurd did so, seizing the excuse to leave Winchester with a look upon his face that suggested he was riding out of hel. Sigurd had taken the death of Cerdic very hard. Cutha had once tried to say that Fate had taken Cerdic in vengeance for Cuthwulf, but Sigurd had given him such a look that Cutha had dropped the subject and never brought it up again.

Sigurd returned to Winchester with the further news that Ine had joined Ceawlin at Wyckholm. Cutha contemplated sending a war band to Romsey to keep Bertred out of the fray, but in the end did not. Let the eorls make their own decisions, he thought. Even if they all went with Ceawlin, their numbers would not be able to make up the half of his. Sigurd had left horsemen stationed at Wokham and Silchester to keep watch on the roads south from Wyckholm. Cutha sat with his men in Winchester and waited; he had decided to let Ceawlin make the first move.

In October Ceawlin moved to Silchester. He had almost a hundred and fifty men with him, the thanes and ceorls of Penda and Ine and a contingent of Atrebates. Bertred and Wuffa had sent word that they would join the king in Silchester within the week. They too would be bringing their ceorls.

Wokham was fifteen miles to the east of Silchester, but Ceawlin's scouts had informed him that Sigurd had moved his thanes to Winchester, and so the king's forces took possession of the city with confidence. The scouts that Sigurd had left posted in Silchester counted the number of Ceawlin's men and rode south to tell their eorl.

"Bertred and Wuffa must be there," Cutha said when he heard the news from Sigurd. "There is no way Ceawlin could have collected that number of men without them."

Sigurd shrugged. "Speak to the scouts yourself if you like. They are trustworthy men, Father. They know Bertred and Wuffa. They know their thanes. If my men say there are not in Silchester, you may be sure that they are not."

"But where did Ceawlin get that many men?"

"I don't know," Sigurd said. "But he has them. And if I know Bertred and Wuffa, he will shortly have more."

Sure enough, the following week brought the unwelcome news that the eorls Bertred and Wuffa had joined Ceawlin at Silchester with some hundred and twenty more men. Finally the truth dawned on Cutha. "He has armed the coerls," he said to Aethelbert and Sigurd as they sat around Ceawlin's table in the king's hall. "That is how he has gotten the men. Sword of Woden, he has armed the ceorls!"

"Such a simple solution," Sigurd said with a laugh. "So simple that it would only occur to Ceawlin to do it."

"This is not a laughing matter," Cutha said angrily. "He has a war band of close on three hundred men!"

"We have more," Aethelbert said. "And if we want to be safe, then we can arm our ceorls too."

"The Winchester ceorls owe allegiance to Ceawlin," Sigurd pointed out.

"They owe allegiance to whatever king holds Winchester," Aethelbert answered, fire in his eyes. "If we command them to fight for us, then they will fight."

"We can give them arms," Cutha said grimly. "But once the battle begins, can we count on for whom they would fight?" There was a devastating silence. "Ceawlin is well-liked," Cutha added at last. "I would not trust my back to his ceorls."

"We are still a hundred men stronger than he," said Aethelbert.

"That is so." Cutha squared his shoulders. He had aged these last months, Sigurd thought. He was beginning to look like an old man. "And ceorls do not know how to fight. We have the advantage yet." He turned to look at Aethelbert, "We must not let Ceawlin frighten us into doing anything foolish."

Aethelbert jutted his jaw forward. "Ceawlin does not frighten me!"

"Then he should," Sigurd said. "I have fought beside him often enough. Ceawlin has never been defeated. You have seen him in battle, both of you. He is matchless."

Cutha was quick to point out to his son, "You have never been defeated either."

Sigurd smiled crookedly. "But you see, I have always had Ceawlin to tell me what to do."

Aethelbert slammed his hand upon the table. "I will hear no talk of defeat!" he shouted. He got to his feet. "Let him come, this warrior-hero, and I shall show him what defeat means!" He strode out of the room, shoulders hunched forward, eyes on the ground. Cutha and Sigurd watched him go; then Sigurd put a hand upon the table and pushed himself to his feet. "You had better send immediately to Cynigils and Witgar," he advised his father. "It would be wise to gather our forces without delay."

Cutha nodded. "I will be in the great hall if you want me," Sigurd added before he too left the room.

He went not to the great hall, however, but sought out Niniane. He had not had private speech with her since the death of Cerdic, but now he forced his unwilling feet to take the path to the princes' hall.

Silence fell when Sigurd came in the door. He had the distinct impression that everyone in the room had taken a step backward and the iron bands that seemed to be constricting his chest squeezed tighter. Then Crida was coming forward to meet him.

"I have come to speak to your mother," Sigurd said to Ceawlin's eldest surviving son.

Crida's eyes told all too clearly what he was feeling, but his voice was coldly polite as he said, "My mother is resting."

Sigurd had to see Niniane now, knew he would not be able to come back here again. "Will you ask her if she will see me, Prince?"

Crida nodded once, shortly, and turned to go into Ceawlin's old room. The wait seemed to Sigurd to last forever. No one spoke. Even the younger children were staring at him with hostility, or so it seemed to him. Finally Crida returned. "My mother will see you," he said. "Come with me."

Sigurd followed Crida to the sleeping room. Crida came in with him and closed the door. Sigurd looked at Niniane.

She had been resting; the bed still bore the imprint of her body. She was standing now, near the clothes chest along the far wall. Her face was thin, he thought. Too thin. There were shadows beneath her large smoke-gray eyes. She was now obviously pregnant. His heart was wrung with pity for her. "Niniane," he said. "Ceawlin is in Silchester with nigh on three hundred men. He should shortly be setting out to come south. Do you want me to send a messenger to tell him about Cerdic?"

Niniane sat down on the chest. Crida moved as if to come to her side, but she shook her head at him and looked to Sigurd. "I keep thinking of that," she said. "He does not know. All this time, Cerdic has been in the earth, and Ceawlin does not know."

The band around Sigurd's chest tightened still more. "I realize that, Niniane. It is up to you. If you think he should know now, I will send someone to tell him. Or you can wait and tell him yourself."

Her lips were very pale. She looked into his face and said, "I think he should know."

Their eyes held. Then, "I think so too," Sigurd replied.

She lowered her lashes very slightly. "All right. Send someone, then."

He nodded and turned toward the door. He put his hand on the handle and paused for a moment, hoping she would say something else, but she did not. He pushed the door open and went out, closing it softly behind him.

Sigurd sent one of his own thanes, a man whom Ceawlin knew well. The king stood like a rock all through the man's recital. "When did this happen?" Ceawlin asked when the thane finally fell silent.

"The beginning of September, my lord. It was when the young prince first learned you were at Wyckholm. Apparently he was trying to join you."

Ceawlin still had much of his summer tan, but under the sunburn he was very white. "How is my wife?" he asked.

"She is living with your sons in the princes' hall, my lord. She is . . . she is with child."

Ceawlin closed his eyes. Very briefly. When they opened again they were glittering, but his voice was steady and cool. "You may return to Winchester," he said.

"Yes, my lord." The thane took a step backward. "Do . . . do you have any message, my lord?"

"No," said Ceawlin. His eyes were a brilliant turquoise. "My message is my sword."

Sigurd's thane looked away from the king, nodded, and backed out of the room.

Sigurd's messenger was not gone five minutes before Ceawlin ordered his war band to make ready to march. It was late afternoon but the king did not delay; he moved his men onto the Roman road and began to push south. The main body of the army he allowed to halt as darkness fell, but a scouting party on horseback was sent ahead to Alford, the manor of Cutha's partner in treachery, Cynigils.

Cynigils had not yet moved his men to Winchester and in the dead of night he was roused by one of his thanes with the news that Ceawlin was almost upon him. Cynigils' men had mistaken the king's advance scouts for his whole force. The eorl routed out his men in a panic and fled from Alford, fled east, away from Winchester and the battle that now was looming so ominously near.

When this news was brought to Ceawlin at eight the following morning, he quickly resumed his southward march. By afternoon he was within sight of the walls of Winchester.

Witgar was not yet in Winchester either. No one had expected Ceawlin to move so quickly. Cutha stood on the walls of the royal enclave and watched with incredulity the array of the king's war band drawn up out of the reach of arrow shot. Without Witgar the numbers within and without were even, and Cutha did not want to meet Ceawlin on even terms. He turned to Aethelbert, who was standing beside him. "I have sent a messenger to Witgar. If he will only advance boldly, we will have Ceawlin caught between the two of us."

Aethelbert nodded shortly. His searching eyes had caught sight of a tall fair-haired figure standing with a group to the left of the large mass of men. "There he is," he said. His brown eyes burned. "There is no mistaking Ceawlin."

Cutha looked also. "No. There is not." He turned away from the wall. "He will not try to force his way into Winchester, not with his family here. We have time. We will wait for Witgar."

Ceawlin, however, was not waiting for Witgar. Hours before his war band had reached Winchester he had sent a messenger to seek out the King of Wight. What he offered Witgar was simple: a marriage between Crida, heir to the kingdom of Wessex, and Witgar's granddaughter, the Princess Auda. The price of such a marriage would be Witgar's recognition of Ceawlin as king and his consequent desertion of Cutha.

The King of Wight looked at the situation, remembered how uncomfortable it had been trying to reign in Winchester in Ceawlin's stead, and agreed. After all, he told himself, he was getting what he had wanted in the first place. A union of Wessex and Wight, with his blood flowing in the nation's future kings.

Once Ceawlin had Witgar's acceptance, he sent a messenger to Winchester bearing the white banner on a raised sword that signaled truce. The messenger was let in the gate and was brought to Cutha and Aethelbert in the king's hall. Sigurd was there as well, seated at the end of the table in such a way that seemed to indicate he was not going to be an active participant in the discussion.

The messenger was Sigbert, the young thane who had accompanied Ceawlin to Bryn Atha and so had missed being taken captive. "My lord," he said to Cutha, his face wooden, "I have come to tell you that the King of Wight has made peace with Ceawlin."

"*What?*" The outraged voice belonged to Aethelbert.

Cutha sat silent. Not even to himself had he admitted this possibility, but he had known, in his heart, that he feared it.

"What were the terms?" It was Sigurd speaking, his voice quiet, almost conversational.

"My lord, a marriage between Prince Crida and the Princess Auda."

"I see." Sigurd looked at his father. "Very clever, Father. Just what Witgar originally wanted."

Cutha felt ill. "Is that all?" he asked Sigbert.

"No, my lord. I am empowered to offer you terms for surrender."

Cutha let out a long harsh breath. "What are they?"

"The King of East Anglia will be allowed free passage for himself and his men back to his own country." Beside him Aethelbert began to breathe heavily through his nose. Cutha made a gesture for him to keep quiet.

"And?" he said.

"For yourself, my lord, the king does offer you your life."

My life, thought Cutha. But his property would be gone, given to one of the men who had kept faith with Ceawlin. His influence, his power, all gone. . . .

"For the eorl Sigurd . . ." Sigbert was going on. He paused and turned to Cutha's son. Sigurd did not meet the young thane's gaze but sat with his eyes focused on the table as if he were utterly absorbed in studying the pattern of the wood. "The king does offer you full pardon, my lord," Sigbert said to him, "if you will accept his offers of peace."

There was absolute silence in the room. Cutha and Aethelbert would keep their lives; Sigurd would be forgiven.

"Wait outside," Cutha said to Ceawlin's messenger, and the young thane nodded and left the room.

"The nerve of him," Aethelbert snarled. "As if I would go back to East Anglia like a beaten dog, with no battle fought, no victor decided."

Cutha ignored the king and turned to his son. "Sigurd?" he asked.

Sigurd was looking away. "Whatever you decide, I will abide by, Father," he answered.

Thank the gods, Cutha thought. He put his head into his hands and thought of Ceawlin, seeing in his mind's eye the boy he had helped to put in the high seat of Wessex not so many years ago. But the picture of that smiling boy was overlain by a newer picture, a hard-eyed Ceawlin who meant to rule and would not suffer his authority to be brooked. Ceawlin would let him live, but the life he faced—a pensioner at Wokham, surely—was not attractive.

He sent once more for Sigbert, and when the king's messenger was standing before him, he looked up and said, "I will not yield to kiss the ground before Ceawlin's feet." His glance went briefly to the bent head of his son, then back to Sigbert. He said, "We will fight."

The battle site was chosen—a field some five miles from Winchester. Sigurd knew it well. It was as level as the dueling grounds; appropriate, for this battle would be the final bout in a duel that had started between Ceawlin and Cutha some two years ago and more. An hour after the return of Sigbert to Ceawlin, the watchers on the walls of Winchester saw the king's war band break camp and depart. Ceawlin would wait for Cutha at the appointed grounds.

Cutha sent word round to his men that they should make ready to fight. They would march the following morning for Torfield, the designated scene of battle.

Aethelbert bustled among his men, barking orders, inspecting weapons, tense and excited about the coming fight. He looked forward to the morrow, burning to redeem his reputation from the humiliating defeat at Gild Ford.

Cutha sat by himself as the torches cast flickering shadows on the walls of his hall and the long night stretched out ahead. His heart was heavy. All his great plans, his schemes, his allies . . . gone. Oh, Aethelbert remained, but Aethelbert was a fool. The single experienced battle leader he had left to him was his son. Sigurd was the only one he could trust not to change sides at the last minute and betray him. And Sigurd's heart was with Ceawlin.

Ceawlin. Cutha had underestimated him, had underestimated how secure was his hold on his kingdom. He had seemed to rule so lightly, had given so much power into the hands of others. But Wessex had been prosperous these last ten years and more; merchants and ceorls and thanes had eaten well and slept quietly in the knowledge that their rights were protected. If their immediate overlords became too overbearing, they always knew they could appeal to the king.

Cutha had not dared to raise Ceawlin's ceorls or ask the merchants of Venta for men. He had been reduced to calling on his own primal loyalties, the men who had sworn to follow him as lord and the men who had sworn to follow his son. And even among these, there was lingering affection for Ceawlin. Cutha would not be leading a high-hearted army tomorrow, and he knew it.

Sigurd knew this also.

Cutha's son was glad, though. Glad this ordeal would finally be coming to an end. He was so immensely weary of it all. Years and years of a divided heart had worn him out.

Before he went to bed, Sigurd sought out Niniane. This time she sent Crida away and the two of them were alone together in the small bedroom that had been meant for one of the royal princes. "You know what is happening?" he asked her.

"Yes."

"It will be over tomorrow."

"Yes." She looked at him gravely, her small, lovely head held proudly on its long, slim neck. He had always loved the way she carried her head. "I heard also that Ceawlin offered you pardon," she said.

"Yes." His face was strained; the skin over his cheekbones seemed too tightly stretched. "He did."

"Why did you not take it, Sigurd?" Her voice was soft.

"I cannot. Niniane . . . I cannot desert my father . . . not now."

She looked at him and then she nodded.

"It is my fault, Niniane," he said wretchedly. "I know that. All my fault. If I had not come to Bryn Atha when I did, Cerdic might still be alive."

She went very pale. "Sigurd." She swallowed and tried again. "Ceawlin offered you that pardon after he learned about Cerdic. He does not blame you."

"And you? Do you blame me?"

She gestured, as if she were pushing cobwebs from in front of her face. "I blame you. I blame myself for not realizing what it was he was thinking. I blame the sentry who shot him. I blame Cerdic for being so foolhardy. I keep thinking if only I could roll back time, make it that night again, could stop it from happening. But I can't."

"No." His voice sounded hopeless. "No, we cannot turn back time."

"Why did you want to see me?" she asked.

"Niniane . . . I know I have no right to ask you this, not after Cerdic. But . . . will you look after my children for me? Edith is . . . well, you know Edith. She loves them but she is not very sensible."

Her eyes widened and she searched his face. "Sigurd . . ." The tip of her nose was white with strain. "Even if you fight tomorrow, Ceawlin will still forgive you. You must know that."

He forced himself to smile at her. "I know that. This is . . . just in case."

"Of course I will look after your children. So will Ceawlin. You need have no fears for them."

"Thank you. You are . . . you are very good."

He thought he had kept his voice perfectly normal. But she stared at him and the pupils of her eyes dilated and he knew she understood that he did not intend to come back from the battle. She reached her hands out toward him. "Sigurd . . . my dear . . ." and she came to lay her cheek against his shoulder.

He circled her body lightly with his arms. The child she carried pressed against him. The bones of her shoulders and narrow back were so small and light. He let himself touch her hair with his lips before he stepped back. He wanted to tell her how much he loved her, even opened his mouth to say it, then did not. It was too late for that as well.

"Good-bye Niniane," he said, dropped his hands from her shoulders, and went out the door.

Chapter 36

*I*T was raining the morning the Battle of Torfield was to be fought. Cutha led some two hundred men—his thanes, Sigurd's thanes, and Aethelbert's East Anglians—out of the gates of Winchester shortly after dawn. The cold gray morning matched the mood of Cutha's war band. Most of the West Saxons who marched to Torfield that day had fought with Ceawlin. They knew what he was like in battle. They did not relish being on the opposing side, and they knew they were outnumbered.

The rain was lessened to a fine mist by the time they reached the appointed site. There, drawn up in battle formation on the far side of the flat, grazed-down field, were the lines of the king's war band. The figure of Ceawlin himself was clearly visible to all of Cutha's men. The king was astride a large gray stallion, walking the horse up and down the lines of his men. He appeared to be chatting with them.

It was the first time Sigurd had seen Ceawlin since he had turned against him. The eorl had not been one of those to line the walls of Winchester a few days back. He looked now at that tall, lean figure, that familiar blond head, and the whole back of his throat seemed to close down. Then Ceawlin turned and scanned the groups of Cutha's men who were forming into battle lines of their own. The king's head suddenly ceased moving; he had found what he was looking for.

Ceawlin's eyesight had ever been unusually keen. Sigurd had no doubt that the king had spied him, was even able to see the expression on his face. The distance was too great for Sigurd to see Ceawlin clearly, but there could be no doubt as to the direction of the king's gaze. Sigurd raised his head and looked back somberly. Then, in full view of both their armies, Ceawlin raised his hand in a gesture of greeting. Sigurd's own hand rose slightly, feebly, then fell again to his side. He could scarcely see for the tears that suddenly blinded his eyes.

"Sigurd, you will have the right." It was his father's voice, and he shut his eyes hard, opened them, blinked, and turned around to answer.

Ceawlin had the greater number of men, but half of them were coerls, untried in battle. Cutha's men were all professionals. This was a point that Cutha made to his troops once again as he prepared to raise his banner. "Do you want it to be said that you were beaten by a pack of farmers?" he asked his men, his raised voice ringing with scorn.

"No!" the answer came back dutifully.

"Hit them hard enough and the ceorls will break and run," Cutha said. "Then will we be masters of Wessex."

Who would be King of Wessex was a question he had not yet had time to decide.

On the opposite side of the field Ceawlin too was rallying his men. He himself was leading the center, with Penda on his right and Bertred on his left. His battle formation consisted of two lines of thanes, four lines of ceorls, and then two more lines of thanes to discourage any attempt by the ceorls to turn and run. The rear lines were commanded by Ine and Wuffa.

"Follow your battle leaders," Ceawlin said. He spoke from horseback so he could be seen by all the men. "We outnumber them by at least a hundred men. Just keep pressing forward and the victory will be ours." He looked up and down the lines once more. Then, "I want the eorl Sigurd taken alive. Cutha and Aethelbert are to die, but not the eorl Sigurd."

There came a rumble of assent from the thanes.

"Very well. Then we are ready." Ceawlin grinned at his men and at that moment a ray of sun broke through the clouds. "Woden has sent us a sign!" he cried, and dismounted to take up his arms. The king's army sent up a battle roar that was heard a mile away. Then Ceawlin gave the signal to advance.

Cutha's men came on to meet him. The two war bands clashed, the strengthening sun gleamed on sword and shield, and the battle began.

Ceawlin's ceorls, none of whom had seen battle before, none of whom had been trained for battle, wavered a little at the first shock. But Penda and Bertred charged directly into the ranks of the opposing army and their thanes followed with gusto. The ceorls, pressed from behind by the rest of the thanes, who were shouting encouragement and obviously eager to engage their swords, suddenly caught fire. In the very center of the fray, laying about him with deadly skill and petrifying ferocity, was the king.

Ceawlin, Cutha thought as he caught a glimpse of the dominant figure on the field. Then the king's army surged forward irresistibly, the sheer weight of numbers pressing Cutha's men back and back and back again. Cutha too was in the front line. He deflected one sword blow, then another. Then he was surrounded. A sword was raised, came down on his head, and Cutha fell to the ground. The oncoming mass of men trampled over his body as they overwhelmed the traitor's troops.

Sigurd did not see Ceawlin. He was a warrior himself and knew his task was to break the king's charge before it could gather momentum and feed upon itself. He had to get through to the ceorls, shake them, make them run.

It was surprisingly easy for Sigurd to get through the line of thanes. It was not until he was deep in the middle of Ceawlin's army that he realized his men were not behind him. Ceawlin's thanes had let him through, but not his men. Sigurd's brain, always cool even under the press of battle, understood immediately what had happened. Ceawlin had given orders that he was not to be harmed.

He couldn't bear it. Couldn't face Ceawlin after all that had happened. He looked around him at Ceawlin's ceorls. They did not know who he was, assumed at the moment that he was one of the king's thanes. Sigurd raised his sword.

"May Woden take you and all of Ceawlin's men!" he snarled to the startled man beside him. The ceorl shouted a warning as he raised his own sword. The ceorl behind Sigurd saw what was happening and slammed the eorl on his leather-protected shoulder with his spear. The farmer was an ox of a man and the blow drove Sigurd to his knees. The eorl was still for a moment, seemingly dazed, making no attempt to protect himself. While he knelt there, vulnerable, the first ceorl slashed open the artery in his unprotected neck.

With Cutha down and Sigurd lost, Aethelbert was the only opposing leader still on the field. They were losing, he could see that. But his hungry heart could not accept the thought of another defeat. Better to die on the field, he thought despairingly, than go home vanquished to East Anglia once again. Valiantly he raised his sword and pressed on, even as his men melted away and Ceawlin's men closed in around him.

In less than half an hour the Battle of Torfield was over. The once-peaceful field, where sheep had grazed all summer, was littered with the bodies of the slain. Cutha's slain. Ceawlin had lost but twenty men.

The rebels had not lost as many men as they might have had Ceawlin allowed his thanes to pursue their fleeing opponents. But the king had held his eager men back. Ceawlin never allowed blood lust to cloud his judgment, and he knew that, with Cutha and Aethelbert dead, the leaderless men were harmless. Further, they would be looking for a new lord. Far better to give mercy and add to his own following.

It was Penda who came to him as he stood surveying the blood-soaked field and taking a drink from the horn a thane had given to him. "Ceawlin . . ." Penda's face was grim. "Ceawlin, they have found Sigurd."

He knew. Just looking at Penda's face, he knew. Fury shook him. "I gave orders he was not to be harmed!"

"It was the ceorls, Ceawlin. They did not know who he was. They had never had any occasion to see him."

The fury left him as quickly as it had come. He dropped the drinking horn to the ground and rubbed a hand across his mouth. A muscle twitched uncontrollably in his cheek. "Take me to him," he said.

It was Bertred who brought the news of Ceawlin's victory to Winchester. "Cutha is dead," he told Niniane and her sons as he met with them in the princes' hall. "Aethelbert too."

"And Sigurd?" Crida asked when his mother said nothing.

"Sigurd was killed as well," Bertred replied. "Ceawlin had given orders that he was not to be hurt, but he got in among the ceorls and they did not know who he was."

"But where is my father?" Ceowulf asked in bewilderment. "Why has he not come with you?"

"Ceawlin sent me on ahead to secure things in Winchester." Bertred spoke to Niniane, not to the children. "Word is to be sent to Venta of his victory as well. Tomorrow morning Ceawlin and his war band will ride through Venta and into Winchester."

"A victory procession," said Crida with satisfaction.

"Yes." Bertred looked at Ceawlin's silver-haired son. "Your father thinks it important to make a show, emphasize his victory, and allay any fears and insecurities that may be left in people's hearts."

Crida nodded solemnly.

"He wishes you to ride beside him, Prince Crida," Bertred said then.

Crida's eyebrows rose in a familiar gesture. "Me?"

"Yes." There was no smile on Bertred's face. "You are his heir."

Color stained Crida's fair skin and he looked to his mother. Niniane put a hand upon her son's arm and said quietly to Bertred, "Crida will accompany you whenever you are ready to leave, Bertred."

Bertred nodded. Then, his voice helpless and aching, "Niniane, I am so sorry about Cerdic."

"I know." Her voice was kind and very composed. "Thank you." She looked at Crida. "Come along with me," she said. "Before you leave, I am going to wash your hair."

Bertred spent an hour speaking to Ceawlin's thanes who had been held prisoner by Cutha, then went into Venta. He returned from the city in midafternoon, collected Crida, and went back to Torfield to rejoin Ceawlin. After Bertred and Crida had gone, Niniane walked slowly across the courtyard, and for the first time since she had left it to go with Ceawlin to Bryn Atha, she entered the king's hall. She stayed but a few minutes before she left and walked to the women's hall to seek out Nola.

Within half an hour the king's hall was being torn apart to be cleaned. The wooden floors were scrubbed, as were the benches, the table, and the chairs. The bed was stripped, the old straw burned, and the bed remade with sweet fresh straw covered by clean linens. The rugs and furs, Niniane had taken outside to be beaten and aired. She even had the hearthplace stones scrubbed. Niniane and Nola supervised the handmaids, and it was dark before the job was finished. Niniane's back ached with tiredness and her legs could scarcely hold her up, but as she sat her sons down at their father's table to eat a late supper, the satisfaction she felt was worth the fatigue. Her house was her own again.

The dead had been taken off the field by the time Crida arrived at Torfield, and the cookfires were burning cheerfully. Ceawlin was talking to a group of Sigurd's thanes who had come in to surrender to him, when someone came to tell him that his son was in camp.

Crida was standing by Bertred's side, his slim, boyish frame looking very vulnerable next to the bigger man. Ceawlin called his son's name and the boy turned, his face suddenly lighting. "Father!" He took a step forward, then stopped himself. If he had been a few years younger, Ceawlin thought, he would have run to throw himself into his father's arms.

"It is good to see you, my son," Ceawlin said and, putting an arm around Crida's shoulders, gave him a quick, rough hug. "How is your mother?"

"Brave," said Niniane's son.

Ceawlin looked at him for a moment in silence, then nodded. He turned to Bertred. "Is all arranged for tomorrow?"

"Yes," said Bertred. The two men discussed plans for a few minutes while Crida stood in silence, listening. Then Ceawlin turned to his son.

"Come," he said. "You and I will go for a walk."

The field was surrounded by a thicket of woods, all red and gold with autumn, and it was into the privacy of these that Ceawlin led his son. After they had walked a little way in silence, he said to Crida, his voice very steady, "Who conducted the funeral rite for Cerdic?"

"I did." Crida's voice was as carefully controlled as Ceawlin's. "And Ceowulf helped me watch through the night." He did not tell his father that Ceowulf had fallen asleep.

"I am glad," Ceawlin said. Then, with obvious difficulty, "Crida, I know how close you and Cerdic were. I know how hard this must be for you."

"Father." Crida stopped and drew a long breath. His voice sounded constricted. "I feel I must tell you this. I *have* to tell you this. I loved Cerdic; you know I loved him. But . . . but . . ." Then the words came out in a guilty rush: "I am glad that I am going to be king."

They had stopped walking and were standing under the flaming canopy of trees. The fire above them was only visual, however. It was cold in the woods, and damp. Ceawlin looked into his son's face. Crida would not look back at him, was staring desperately at the ground. Ceawlin let out his own breath in what sounded very much like a sigh and said, "When I was seventeen years old I killed my brother so I could be king. At least you do not have that kind of blood guilt to live with."

Crida's eyes flew to his father's face. There was a moment's silence; then Crida said, "You killed your brother in a duel. He had poisoned his sword. You acted in self-defense. Mother told us all about it."

"I did not have to kill him," Ceawlin said. "But I hated him. And I wanted to be king."

Crida searched his face with worried eyes. Ceawlin reached out and pushed the flyaway, newly washed hair off his son's cheek with a gentle hand. "I am glad that you want to be king," he said. "To be a good king, you must want it very much."

"But . . ." Crida's voice was anguished. "If I were given a choice to bring Cerdic back . . . Father! I don't know what I would do!"

Ceawlin was tempted to speak words of comfort, to assure the boy that of course he would choose to bring his brother back. As Crida undoubtedly would. But it was the very possibility that he might consider choosing the other, the very real reluctance to give up what now he had won—that was what was causing Crida such agonizing guilt. Ceawlin would not help the boy by making light of this. "That is something you are going to have to live with, Crida," he said. "It is part of the burden of being a man."

There was a long silence. Ceawlin could hear the voices of his men in the camp. There was a rustling in the woods as a small animal scurried by. Overhead, a bird began to trill. Finally Crida spoke. "Yes," he said. His eyes met his father's and held them. "I understand."

Ceawlin's return to his capital the following day was a triumph. He and Crida rode at the head of his war band, followed by his eorls, also on horseback. The thanes and the ceorls marched behind. For many of the ceorls, that day of adulation and rejoicing was the high point of their lives.

The main street of Venta was lined with people. The road from Venta to Winchester was similarly packed with ceorls from the Winchester vils. Ceawlin's name rang out in the cool, crisp autumn air, again and again and again as the war band progressed along its triumphant way.

Crida was flushed with excitement. A few times the path in front of them became clogged with people, but the eorls rode forward and cleared the way with their horses. Saxon and Briton together greeted Ceawlin as if he had been a god.

Crida's eyes shone like stars. As they left the road to turn toward the open gates of Winchester, he said to his father, "You are the greatest warrior in the world, Father. That is why they cheer you so."

Ceawlin's returning smile was crooked. "I am not a god, Crida. Fate will turn against me someday. In the end, we all must die. It is well to remember that, my son, and not to let yourself be too swayed by the adoration of others."

Then they were inside the gates, back in Winchester, back home. The steps of the great hall held a welcoming party. Niniane and all his sons. No . . . not all. One he would never see again.

He pushed that thought aside, pushed it down and away as he had done since first he heard the news of Cerdic's death. The horses came closer and closer to the hall. Niniane had Sigurd and Eirik standing before her, so he could not see her below breast level. Her hair was dressed high with jewels; jewels glittered at her throat and shoulders and on the arms that encircled the boys. She had decked herself for victory.

"Mother looks splendid," Crida said proudly.

"Yes," said Ceawlin. "She does."

They had reached the steps of the great hall and all the horsemen dismounted. Sigurd pulled away from Niniane and rushed to meet his father. Eirik came after, then Ceowulf, more aware of his dignity than the younger boys. Ceawlin looked from the children who surrounded him to his wife.

She wore a full blue cloak pinned with a great golden brooch. He would not have known she was pregnant if he had not been told. He left the boys and came forward to take her into his arms. Then he felt the baby. "I am very glad to see you," she said, her voice shaking.

"And I you." He released her, backed away from the emotion in her voice, and said to his eorls, "Let us go inside."

There was a great banquet that evening. Alric, prepared by Bertred the previous day, was ready with a song of the Battle of Torfield. Crida sat in Cerdic's old place, and for the first time Ceowulf attended a thanes' banquet. Crida had asked that he be allowed to come.

Niniane retired immediately after Alric's first series of songs. It was almost two more hours before Ceawlin left the banquet and walked with slow, almost reluctant steps toward the king's hall.

The servants were asleep along the wall benches. The door to their bedroom was closed, but he could see a light shining in the crack between door and floor. Niniane was still awake.

She was sitting on the cushioned bench that ran under the window. Her hair was loose and she wore a cloak over her sleeping gown. She was looking out the window and did not turn her head when he came in. "Is the banquet over?" she asked.

"No. It is still roaring on."

"I hope you sent Crida and Ceowulf to bed?"

"Yes. Shortly after you left."

Finally she turned to face him. They had not been alone together for more than five minutes all day. He looked at her, at the small, delicate face, the great haunted eyes, the mouth curved with sorrow. The only person in the world, he thought, who understood what he had lost. For these last weeks he had been like a man standing with his back against a dam, utterly concentrated on nothing but holding back the flood that threatened to overwhelm him. He looked now at his wife, and the dam began to give way. He crossed the room, no longer trying to guard his face, and knelt in front of her. He put his hand on her swollen stomach. "I remember the night you bore him," he said. "I remember how grievously you cried."

She looked down at his hand and then covered it with both of her own, pressing its strong sinewy hardness against her. "Do you remember the day I told you I was expecting him?" she asked, her voice very low.

"Yes." He turned his hand, easily grasping both her small hands within his own large clasp. "It was the day I learned of my mother's death." He closed his eyes, and the dam within him shattered. "Oh, Nan." It was a cry of anguish. "Our beautiful boy!" And burying his face in her lap, he began to cry. Awkwardly at first, wrenchingly, in the way of one unused to tears, but finally with a flooding release of grief that eased at last to exhausted quiet.

Niniane held him, tears pouring down her own face, but the tears were more for Ceawlin than they were for Cerdic. Finally she got him into bed and he fell asleep still cradled in her arms.

Chapter 37

THE March day was unusually warm, and after Niniane had nursed her daughter, she took a horse and rode out of Winchester toward the woods. It was muddy underfoot but there was a woodland clearing she had been going to for the last month and it was usually drier there. That was her destination on this warm March day, the six-month anniversary of the death of Cerdic.

The sky was pale blue and cloudless. Niniane dismounted, tied her horse, and went to sit on the decaying trunk of an oak tree that had come down in some storm years before. The sun was warm on her head and back but she scarcely noticed. She sat and stared sightlessly at the small pool in the middle of the clearing. She sat so quietly and for so long that two deer, feeling themselves safe, appeared from the woods to drink from the pond's clear fresh water.

The anniversaries were the worst, Niniane thought as she sat there motionless in the early-spring sun. Anniversaries, marking the inexorable flow of time, taking you further and further from the one you loved.

Today she could say: Six months ago he lived. Tomorrow she would not be able to say that anymore. Soon it would be seven months, eight months, a year. It was a fine day; she noticed it for almost the first time. A fine day for hunting. Cerdic had loved to hunt. And so, finally, she began to cry.

The deer fled as soon as she moved. After a while she struggled to gain control of herself and went to the pond to splash cold water on her eyes. She wet a corner of her cloak and laid it against them. She did not want to return to Winchester with swollen eyes, did not want Ceawlin to know she had been crying again.

He grieved too. She knew that. But after that one outburst on the night of his return to Winchester, he grieved in silence. He did not want to talk about Cerdic, not to her, not to anyone.

"Nan, I can't," he had said desperately once when she had tried to share her feelings with him. "I can't keep going through it again and again. Don't ask it of me. I just can't."

That was the difference between them, she thought now as she tightened her girth and prepared to mount from the log. He had accepted Cerdic's death when it happened, had experienced it, had gone through it. She had not. She had been so strong, so brave, simply for that very reason: she had not accepted it.

And now she could not get over it. Ceawlin was coping, was going on with his life, but she could not. She was stuck in it, reliving it over and over and over in her mind.

The nights were the worst. She could not sleep, would lie there going over the possibilities of its not happening. Two scenes played themselves again and again in her mind.

In the first scene, she heard Cerdic getting up, heard him moving stealthily out of his sleeping-room door. In this scene she would get up herself and follow him, follow him and catch up to him just as he was going to try to climb over the wall. His blond hair was bright in the moonlight and he would smile at her and say, "What are you doing here, Mother?" And she would touch his arm and say, "Do not do this, Cerdic. Come back to the princes' hall with me." And he would come, so tall, so healthy, so full of life, back to the princes' hall and safety.

In the other scene he was shot, but the wound was not fatal. She would take him back to the hall and nurse him. He would look up at her out of heavy blue eyes and say, "I'm sorry, Mother. Sorry I caused you such worry."

She would think of these scenes so long and so hard that almost, it seemed to her, they were true. And then came the awful realization, the slow dawning that she could not stave off, that she was dreaming, that what she was thinking was not true, that it really had happened. Cerdic was dead.

Then she would begin to cry, holding herself very still, trying not to wake Ceawlin, weeping in silent anguish as the slow hours of the night slipped by.

She got back to Winchester in time for supper. Ceawlin gave her a long hard look and she knew he saw that she had been crying. He said nothing, but as he passed her chair he laid a gentle hand on the top of her head.

One of Niniane's problems during this time was that it was so difficult for her to be alone. The halls in Winchester were arranged for communal living. The fires burned continually in the hearthplaces and there were always thanes or servants or family members underfoot. There was rarely privacy even in her own sleeping room; the baby was sharing the room with them these days, and Niniane feared to disturb her daughter's sleep.

These were the living arrangements that had always prevailed in Winchester, nor had Niniane found them fretful in the past. But now she needed to be alone, and there was no place for her to go. This was why she had begun to ride out to the woodland clearing. She went as often as she could; the weather never stopped her. If she could get away from all the people who seemed constantly to claim her attention, she would take a horse and go. She had to have a place where she could be alone to think and to cry.

The baby comforted her more than anything. Her daughter. The small, fuzzy baby head, the little mouth pulling at the breast; when she was with Fara she was happy. But the baby slept for most of the day.

A week after Cerdic's six-month anniversary Bertred and Meghan came to Winchester for a visit. Niniane was surprised. This was a busy time of year on the manors; rarely did they see the eorls in springtime. It was when Meghan sat talking with her around the hearthplace in the king's hall the following afternoon that Niniane realized why they had come.

"I know how you are feeling, Niniane," Bertred's British wife said gently. "I also have lost a son."

Niniane sat politely and let her talk. It was not that she belittled Meghan's sorrow. Meghan's son had been five years old when he died of fever, and obviously the hurt was still there. But it was not the same. Couldn't Meghan understand that? Niniane knew that death was something that happened to everyone. She knew that other people's children had died. But that was not what she *felt*. What she felt was that this was something that had happened only to her. To her and to Cerdic.

"Did Ceawlin ask you to come?" she asked after Meghan had finished talking.

Meghan hesitated, obviously not sure how she should answer. Finally she nodded. "He is worried about you, Niniane."

Niniane knew he was worried about her. He could not help her himself, but he tried very hard to find someone who could. He even sent to Glastonbury for Father Mal, who came and was very kind and talked to her about heaven. It did not help. She did believe that Cerdic was in heaven, but that did not stop her from missing him.

In the end it was the most unlikely person who helped her, someone whose coming she had resented and feared. The person who helped her was Auda.

The day after Crida turned fourteen, Ceawlin said, "I am going to send for the Princess of Wight. We will have the betrothal ceremony next month and she will live here in Winchester until they marry."

Niniane protested. She did not want a strange girl in Winchester, someone else for whom she would be responsible. It was enough that Edith and her two children were now living in the royal enclave and had to be included in almost all family occasions. And this girl was

Witgar's granddaughter. Niniane blamed Witgar bitterly for siding with Cutha; Cutha's rebellion would never have been able to take place had it not been for Witgar, she thought. Except for Witgar, Cerdic would still be alive. She did not want Witgar's grandchild to come and live in Winchester.

But Ceawlin was adamant. "I want her here, Nan," he said when she protested again in the privacy of their sleeping room. "She will be safer that way."

Niniane understood what he meant. The reports they had had from East Anglia were that Guthfrid had gone mad when she learned that Witgar had betrayed her. Niniane met Ceawlin's eyes and knew he was thinking, as was she, of the poison Guthfrid had once sent to her. "I want this marriage for Crida," Ceawlin said. "As much as Guthfrid wants it for her own whelp." The line of his mouth was grim. "Auda must come to Winchester."

Crida understood as well as Ceawlin the value to Wessex of this marriage. It was not just the bargain his father had struck with Witgar on the eve of his battle with Cutha. There were other advantages to a marriage with Wight: it would expand Wessex' territory to the sea, gain them a much-needed port, and eliminate a potential enemy to their south.

Crida understood all this and approved. Nevertheless, the reality of the marriage had remained vague to him. It was so far in the future. Then, suddenly, it was not in the future at all, but here and now. Suddenly the flesh-and-blood girl was coming to Winchester. Within a month he would be betrothed to a stranger.

She was his age, so that was all right. But suppose he did not like her. Suppose she was ugly. Worst of all, suppose she was taller than he! Crida was growing, as Ceawlin had promised he would, but he would never be a tall man, never have the height of his father and his little brothers. He would find it unbearable to have a wife who was taller than he. But Crida was a prince and he knew where his duty lay. He kept his own counsel and said nothing about his apprehensions.

These were the circumstances under which Auda came to Winchester. She was escorted by Witgar himself, who greeted Ceawlin with smiling ease, as if nothing had ever divided him from the affectionate trust of his cousin. Witgar brought with him a train of thanes and women who would have to be accommodated with sleeping spaces and fed with Winchester's best meals.

Crida met his intended wife for the first time just before the banquet Ceawlin gave in the great hall the evening of her arrival. The chief guests from Wight had been accommodated in the old queen's hall, and it was from there that Ceawlin sent for Crida a half-hour before the banquet was due to commence.

Auda was standing between her grandfather and Ceawlin as Crida came in the door. The first thing he saw, to his intense relief, was that she was as small as his mother. The eyes of everyone in the room were on him as he crossed the floor, but he scarcely noticed. He stopped in front of the two kings, bowed slightly, and looked with grave courtesy at his father.

"Crida," Ceawlin said, "this is Auda, the princess of Wight. I thought you should meet before we go into the great hall for the banquet." Having been officially presented, Crida then looked directly at the girl who was to be his wife.

She was pretty. That was his second, relieved impression. Her hair was pale brown, her features small and regular. She had been looking somewhere in the vicinity of his chest and now she raised her long gold-tipped lashes and glanced fleetingly into his face. Her eyes were a golden hazel.

"I am pleased to welcome you to Winchester," Crida said.

"Thank you, my lord." Her voice was soft and low. She had dropped her eyes once more.

"A pretty pair," said Witgar jovially. "Eh, Ceawlin?"

Ceawlin's eyebrow quirked but he replied with perfect blandness, "Exceedingly."

Auda's face was withdrawn; she might not have heard for all the sign she gave. Crida looked at her, and once more, for barely a flicker of an eyelash, her eyes lifted to meet his.

"And this is Auda's mother, the Lady Geata," Ceawlin said. A thin, sharp-faced woman stepped forward to claim Crida's attention.

The welcoming banquet was not one of the more riotous occasions ever seen in Winchester. There was still a great deal of bitterness in Wessex over Witgar's attempt to overthrow Ceawlin, and, while the Winchester thanes were polite, they were not jolly. Ceawlin was relieved that they were polite. He had threatened them all with expulsion from his service should any incidents arise during the stay of the folk from Wight.

Auda was seated next to the queen, and the girl spoke scarcely a word during the entire banquet. Niniane, splendidly dressed in a beautifully woven white overgown with the gold circlet Ceawlin had given her set on her brow, made a token effort to be polite to Auda and then, thankfully, gave up. What a mouse the girl was, she thought. Poor Crida.

Auda had not wanted to come to Winchester, but she, like Crida, understood her duty. She knew Witgar had offered her to the prince of Sussex and been refused. She knew her grandfather had been furious when Ceawlin betrothed his eldest son elsewhere without even considering a marriage with Wight. She was a quiet girl but she heard and understood a good deal more than her mother and her mother's second husband gave her credit for.

And so she also knew that Ceawlin had been forced to take this marriage at point of arms. Her grandfather was well pleased; it was what he had long wanted for Wight. Her mother was pleased; her daughter would be Queen of Wessex. Auda was frightened. They did not want her in Wessex, she thought. The prince who was to be her husband could not want her. They were only going through with the marriage because Witgar had forced them into it.

The reality of Wessex proved to be as bad as she had feared. The king was courteous enough, but his eyes were aloof. And he was so big. Too big. Auda could see that her grandfather, who was afraid of no one, was afraid of Ceawlin. He frightened and intimidated Auda too.

The queen was even worse. If Ceawlin was indifferent to Auda, Niniane disliked her. Auda could see that immediately. It did not take long for the girl to hear the full tale of how Cerdic had died, and then Niniane's behavior was made perfectly clear; the queen hated Auda because her grandfather's plot had been the cause of Niniane's son's death.

But it was not my fault, Auda wanted to cry when Niniane spoke to her with frost in her voice and ice in her blue-gray eyes. *I was not consulted.* But, of course, such a plea would be useless. It was better to make herself as quiet and as inconspicuous as possible and thus hope to slip beneath the queen's notice.

The only ray of hope for Auda all during that first miserable week in Winchester was Crida. She had been delighted when she saw that he was not a giant like his father, but a slim, elegant boy with a pure, chiseled face and beautiful silver fair hair. Nor did he look at her as if he hated her. His extraordinary blue-green eyes were much warmer than his father's; not at all indifferent. He was the only person she had met in Winchester who made her believe that it just might be possible for her to live there.

The banquet Ceawlin had given on the day of their arrival was the most lavish Auda had ever attended. The great hall of Winchester was far grander than her grandfather's hall in Wight. The arms that hung on the walls were more splendid, the harper far more accomplished. The drinking horns that were passed around were engraved and set with jewels. The folk from Wight had been rather overcome by all the splendor.

The betrothal banquet was still more magnificent. Auda's mother had dressed her in a pale saffron-colored overgown that brought out the gold in her eyes, but the moment she saw the Winchester women she felt underdressed and inadequate. Her jewelry was so plain beside the brooches and belt buckles and necklaces worn by the wives of Ceawlin's eorls.

She was given the place of honor beside the queen. Niniane looked beautiful. Auda had been astonished when first she saw how young Crida's mother was. There was a look of strain on her face this night, however, and Auda was aware of the quick looks of concern the king threw to his wife from time to time. Niniane was remembering her dead son, Auda thought; that was why she looked so stern. For some strange reason, Auda felt guilty and could not bring herself to meet the queen's eyes.

For a betrothal banquet it was surprisingly subdued. The jokes were perfunctory, the good humor only surface deep. Auda, always sensitive to atmosphere, realized this and understood its causes. Standing beside Crida in front of all these people to receive the betrothal gifts was the hardest thing she had ever done.

The gifts were lavish beyond belief. She gave Crida an involuntary look of astonishment as the mounds of clothing and jewelry and linens were piled before her. He was watching her, and when her eyes caught his, he gave her a very faint smile.

She and Crida were standing together before the high seats, and as the last of the gifts was placed ceremoniously at Auda's feet, Ceawlin rose and called for the witnesses. Three eorls, those Auda had heard addressed as Penda, Bertred, and Gereint, came forward to swear legal witness to the transferral of goods. Then, as the eorls resumed their places, Crida took her hand into his. She knew there had to be a kiss to seal the betrothal, and obediently she held up her face. His lips were cool and dry on hers, then he was stepping back, allowing her to return to her place beside the queen.

She would much rather have stayed with him.

Chapter 38

ONCE the betrothal was concluded, Witgar and the rest of the folk from Wight returned home, leaving Auda in Winchester. Niniane moved the princess into the bower with the other unmarried girls. It would be better for her to have the company of girls her age, Niniane told Crida, less lonely. What she did not say was that if Auda lived in the bower, Nola would have charge of her and not Niniane.

"Once you are married, your father will give you the old queen's hall for you both to live in," Niniane said to her son. "For now, while you are still both so young, it will be best if you go on as usual."

"Yes, Mother," Crida agreed. He was more aware than Niniane realized of the difficulty she was having accepting this girl of Witgar's blood. Crida was the least demonstrative of all her sons, but he was probably the one who was most attached to Niniane. He saw how she still grieved for Cerdic. And he thought, also, that since the way his mother felt about Auda had not escaped his betrothed's notice, it would be best for Auda to be in someone else's charge.

The weeks went by. Nola reported to Niniane that Auda gave her no trouble but that she kept herself to herself. She had not become friends with any of the other girls. "She is a dreadful needlewoman," Nola said, "but she spends a great deal of time doing needlework."

Niniane, who was an exquisite needlewoman, gave Nola a scornful look and did not reply.

Then one day in mid-June, before the feast to bring in the summer, Niniane came into her sleeping room to feed Fara, only to be told that one of the handmaids had taken the baby into the herb garden for some air. Niniane, who had been cooped up in the dye house all morning, decided to go in search of her daughter herself.

She found the baby in the garden, lying on a rug someone had spread on the grass for her. Kneeling beside her, watching the infant kick its feet in high delight, a small tender smile on her lips, was Auda. Niniane halted for a minute in surprise, then spoke the girl's name. Auda started violently, and looked up. Faint color stained her cheeks. "Your maid had to leave for a few minutes and I offered to watch the baby," she said, her voice defensive, her eyes lowered.

Niniane felt a flash of irritation. Why would the girl never look into her face? Whatever was Crida going to do with such a mouse?

"Thank you, Auda," she replied coolly. "That was good of you but I will take her now." And she dropped to her knees on the rug beside the baby. Startled by the sudden movement, Auda jumped. Niniane frowned and turned to look at her. For a brief moment she was able to see into Auda's unguarded eyes; then the girl's long lashes dropped once again.

"Auda . . ." Niniane was appalled. The girl had flinched away from her as if she thought she was going to be struck. And for that brief, revealing moment, her eyes had been those of a child in fear.

"Shall I find a handmaid for you, my lady?" the girl asked. Her voice was even, her face composed. She was looking at Fara.

"No," Niniane said helplessly. "No. In fact, why don't you carry Fara back to the hall for me?"

Auda stiffened infinitesimally, but then she bent and lifted the baby into her arms. Niniane saw that she cradled the small bundle with instinctive tenderness. Niniane walked beside her as they returned to the hall, talking easily about the baby, but although Auda listened politely, she responded only with monosyllables.

The girl left the king's hall as soon as she had put Fara into her basket. Niniane watched the small, slim figure retreat out the door and was smitten by a terrible feeling of guilt. The poor child, she thought. What can I have been thinking of?

Now that her eyes were open, it became clear to Niniane that Auda was frightened and lonely in Winchester. Niniane was filled with remorse for the way she had been treating the child. There was no excuse for her, she thought. She of all people knew what it was like to be set down among strangers, and strangers whom one regarded as enemies. Niniane thought of how kind Ceawlin's mother had been to her and felt even worse. She began to plan ways to try to make friends with Auda.

It was hard going. All of her efforts at goodwill were met with rigid courtesy. Auda did not trust her, that was abundantly clear. The only time Niniane saw the child looking even faintly happy was when she was with Fara. She loved the baby. The only success Niniane ever had in talking to Auda was when she talked about the baby.

Ceawlin gave her no help in her campaign to win over Auda. He was always courteous to the girl, but it was enough for him that she gave no trouble. Her happiness was not his concern. Ceawlin had proved a wonderful father, but he had never been interested in children who did not belong to him. He was making an effort with Sigurd's twins; Niniane could see that. But it did not come naturally to him. It was only with his own flesh and blood that Ceawlin's heart was truly engaged.

But Niniane's maternal heart was wrung. What a terrible fate royal princesses faced, she thought. Married off like chattel into lands and people that were not their own. Never, she determined with ferocious intensity, never would she allow that to happen to her little girl.

In the meanwhile, she made effort after effort to extend the branch of peace to Auda, and in trying to heal the wounds in the heart of the living child, she was unknowingly helping to heal the wounds in her own. She thought more of Auda and less of Cerdic. But her efforts went unrewarded.

I cannot blame her, she thought one afternoon after she had invited Auda to come out riding with her and had been stiffly refused. She does not trust me. Why should she? She has been warned against me, and God knows I was unkind enough when first she came here. Why should she trust me? She is not my child. Just like a wild animal in a strange environment, Auda had to think of self-protection first.

July began with a week of rain, but then the skies finally relented and sent day after day of brilliant hot sun. It was one such afternoon, after she had fed Fara and put her into her basket to sleep, that Niniane decided to go sit in the Winchester herb garden. She had been going out to the woods less frequently of late, being too much concerned with the happenings within the confines of her family.

She was walking slowly along the neatly planted rows of herbs, enjoying the sun and for once not thinking much of anything, when the sound of voices made her realize that someone was in the garden with her. She looked up and saw, on the far side of the wooden shed which held the gardener's tools, Crida's unmistakable blond head. She stopped. Whatever was Crida doing in the garden? She thought he had been with Ceawlin. Then she heard the sound of a girl's voice. In a moment a figure, which had evidently been bending over the plants, came into view. It was Auda.

Niniane stood still. The boy and girl had not seen her, were too absorbed in what they were saying to notice her approach. Auda had a can of water in her hand, and now, as Crida said something that evidently surprised her, her hand jerked and the water tipped and spilled. It spilled all over Crida's feet. There was a moment of silence and then Crida began to laugh.

Auda had first recoiled in dismay, but now, tentatively at first, then with almost hysterical abandon, she joined in his laughter. Niniane began to back away. After she had taken a few steps, Crida's laughter stopped and he reached out a hand to draw Auda to him. In response the girl's arms went around his neck and she clung to him as if he were her only hope in all the world. Her long brown hair streamed down over Crida's arm and her face was pressed against his shoulder. Niniane turned and walked away.

For the first time in months, she felt happy. The day was beautiful and warm, and quite suddenly she longed for Ceawlin. But he was listening to a particularly difficult case this day, and she knew she could not disturb him. The case involved the abduction of the daughter of a land-owning thane by one of Wuffa's hall thanes. This abduction, in the eyes of the law, was rape, and the rape of a freewoman was punishable by death.

However, the girl had apparently been willing. She and her paramour were now appealing to the king to recognize their marriage and grant her her rights of inheritance. The main participants in the case were all in Winchester this day for Ceawlin to render his decision.

Niniane decided to go and have a gossip with Nola.

Ceawlin finished in the great hall late in the afternoon, and when he came into their sleeping room, Niniane was there, sitting on the window cushions nursing the baby. She smiled up at him and said, "How did you fare?"

He grunted and stretched the muscles in his back. He hated to spend the whole day sitting. "You know the sort of case it was, Nan. The girl is an only child, an heiress, and the man is trying to gain land and power in the only way that is open to him. He would never have been allowed to marry the girl, so he abducted her."

"And the girl?" she asked.

"The girl was clearly willing. However, it is much better not to prove that she was willing, as I pointed out to her father. The union has been consummated, the girl is no longer a virgin, and is therefore useless. She will even lose her rights of inheritance if it is proved she willingly went with the man. So it is best to accept the man as her husband and save everyone's honor." He shrugged. "That is always the best solution to these cases. I don't know why they have to come to me to hear it."

She lifted Fara from the breast and laid her across her shoulder. "It saves their face to have you be the one to make the decision," she said.

"I suppose." He looked fretfully over her head out the window. "It is perfect weather for hunting, and I was kenneled in the hall all day."

"Do you want to go for a ride now?" she asked impulsively.

His eyes rested on her face. "With you?"

"With me. It will be good to get away together for a little."

He smiled. He had actually been hunting three days this week and his skin was brown from the sun. "I'll give orders for the horses," he said.

She took him to the clearing. The air had become heavy and still and the sound of the bees was unusually loud.

"I think we may have a storm," Ceawlin said. He looked at the pond. "I'm thirsty." He went to get a drink.

Niniane sat on the log and watched him. "I don't think I need to worry about Auda any longer," she said when he came back to join her.

"Oh?" He raised an eyebrow. "Why not?"

"I think I can safely leave her to Crida," Niniane replied. She felt so peaceful all of a sudden. She moved closer to him on the log, and when his arm went around her, she laid her head on his shoulder. They sat for a few minutes in silence, both busy with their own thoughts.

"This is the third such case of abduction I have had within a year," Ceawlin said finally. "I am going to have to raise the fines."

"Too many handsome landless men trying to raise themselves in the world," Niniane murmured.

"So it seems." He bent his head to look down at her. "Why are you suddenly so sure you can leave Auda to Crida?"

She told him about what she had seen earlier in the afternoon.

"Hmm," said Ceawlin. "If that is the case, we had better get them married as soon as Crida turns fifteen."

"Fifteen is too young!" Niniane protested. "You didn't marry until you were eighteen. I thought we said we would wait."

"I had my first woman when I was fifteen," Ceawlin replied. "My father sent one of the bower women to my bed."

"I think that is disgusting," Niniane said.

"I know you do." His voice was amused. "That is why we haven't got any bower women in Winchester. Witgar and his men thought we were uncivilized. I had to send them into Venta. I thought I would have to take Crida into Venta too—"

"What?"

"The boy has to learn from someone, Niniane," her husband said practically.

"They can learn together. We did."

"I had somewhat of a head start." His voice was dry.

There was a long silence. Then she said, "You are so good to me, Ceawlin." Her voice sounded perfectly serene. He smiled and touched her hair with his mouth.

"I couldn't get from any other woman what I get from you," he said. "That is all."

By the time they got back to Winchester, it had begun to rain. All of the children were gathered into the main room of the king's hall when Niniane and Ceawlin came in. Niniane sent for some food, and as she and Ceawlin ate, she listened to Ceawlin explaining to Crida the case he had decided today.

"Why was Crida not there?" Niniane asked at last.

Ceawlin shrugged. "The girl asked for as few people as possible. As if the whole of Wessex does not know her shame by now."

"We need more land," said Crida.

Niniane stiffened. "Nonsense. There is plenty of land in Wessex."

Ceawlin gave his son a warning look. Then he said, "We should begin to invite Auda to spend her evenings in the king's hall. It must be boring for the girl to be cooped up all the time with women."

"What a good idea." Niniane gave Ceawlin a grateful look. She had not suggested such a thing herself because she knew how he was always trying to clear the children out of the hall.

Crida too looked pleased. "She would learn to be less afraid of us that way. I will tell her, Father."

The window in their sleeping room was open, letting the fresh scent of summer rain into the room. Niniane took off her clothes and lay down on the bed, stretching luxuriously. "This was a good day," she said to Ceawlin.

"What can I do to make it better?" He sat down on the bed and, putting his hands on either side of her shoulders, leaned over her to look into her face. Her eyes were voluptuous. "It has been a long time," he said.

She knew what he meant. They had made love, of course, since Cerdic's death, but there had been no joy in it for her. Tonight, for the first time since *before*, she wanted him. She ran her hands up and down his torso, reveling in the lean-muscled strength of him. "I'm too old to feel like this," she murmured.

His teeth were very white against his tan. "Don't be absurd."

"It's true. I look at Auda and I realize how old I am. My stomach is all stretched out from having babies, my breasts are beginning to sag . . ."

His eyes flicked up and down her naked body and a delicious shiver ran all through her. "True," he said. "I shall have to find myself a friedlehe."

Her eyes narrowed. "I will kill her."

He began to laugh. "You would kill me first," he said. "I know it."

She stared up at him. His hair was hanging in his eyes. "I would torture you first."

"Mmm." He stretched out beside her and without haste took her into his arms. "You are beautiful," he said. "And those are my babies you are complaining about."

"You are the best husband in the world," she said.

"I know," he answered, and began to kiss her.

III

THE BRETWALDA
(576–577)

Chapter 39

THIS was not the first visit Coinmail had paid to Wales. During the last two years, since the death of his father-by-marriage had made him the undisputed chief of the Dobunni, he had been to Wales numerous times. The chiefs he was consulting with this day were two of the principal princes of Gwent: Condidan and Farinmail. Both had lands bordering on the Sabrina Sea, the ocean channel that separated Wales from Dumnonia. And both had previously proved receptive to Coinmail's warnings about the encroachment of Saxon Wessex into British territory.

The three men were meeting at Caer, Farinmail's chief stronghold. Caer was a typical Welsh fort, a group of small stone halls, huts almost, surrounded by earth-and-timber ramparts. The king's hall in which they were meeting was perhaps sixty feet by thirty and had a hearthplace on the end wall. The three princes were alone, seated in a small semicircle of chairs in front of the hearth. No fire was burning; it was summer.

Coinmail opened the conference. "Witgar is dead," he said. "Wight is now part of Wessex."

There was a moment of silence. "Well, we knew it was going to happen," Condidan said. "It comes as no surprise."

"It is an expansion to the south," Farinmail agreed. "I cannot like to see Ceawlin's influence grow, but Wight is far removed from us."

Coinmail did not respond to these comments. Instead he said next, "I have just had word from Dumnonia. Do you know the villa of Dynas, to the east of Aquae Sulis?"

The two Welsh princes sat straighter in their chairs. "Of course we know it," Condidan answered. For centuries Dynas had belonged to a Romano-Celtic prince of the Durotriges tribe. It stood in relation to Aquae Sulis much in the same way that Bryn Atha did to Calleva-Silchester. In the days of Roman rule the chief of Dynas had been a magistrate of the city. In the last two hundred years Dynas, like all the other Roman-built villas, had become virtually an island unto itself. But it was still a famous name. Not so famous as Avalon, perhaps, but more so than Bryn Atha.

Condidan looked piercingly at Coinmail. The Welsh prince was a man of perhaps fifty, with graying brown hair and beard. The Welsh had never adopted the Roman custom of shaving. "What of Dynas?" he asked. "I thought Bevan was still prince there."

"He is. But he has only one daughter; she will inherit Dynas when he dies. And he has betrothed the girl to a son of one of Ceawlin's eorls."

There was a shocked silence. "How can this be?" Farinmail said at last. "Bevan is Christian."

"Easily." Coinmail's voice was bitter. "Ceawlin's eorl Bertred is married to a Briton and their children were baptized. As were my sister's. Not that that means anything; they are all being reared as pagans. But the baptism makes the marriage possible."

"I do not understand." Farinmail gripped the arms of his chair. "Why should Bevan do such a thing, put the property of Dynas into the hands of a Saxon?"

"He thinks it is the best way to protect the property." Coinmail's lips were thin. "He is a fool."

"With the annexation of Wight, Wessex will extend from the Narrow Sea to the Aildon hills." Condidan's bushy graying brows were drawn together. "And once Ceawlin gets a foothold in Dumnonia . . ."

"Wales will be next." Farinmail's thin dark face was grim.

Condidan's frown deepened. "He has shown no signs of warlike intent."

Coinmail answered. "He has not had to. Why fight when you can win bloodless victories by marriages? It is the same even among my own people. Marriages between the Dobunni who live near Ufton and the Atrebates are common. Ufton is directly on the Roman road to Corinium, Glevum, and Wales, and the Atrebates are Ceawlin's devoted subjects."

There was a heavy silence as the two Welsh chiefs looked at the Atrebates prince who was now the leader of a different tribe. Coinmail was nearing forty, yet there was no gray in the burnished auburn hair he still wore clipped short in Roman style. His chiseled features were as sternly beautiful as in his youth. He was, if anything, more imposing and impressive than ever and, in pursuit of his life's mission, as inexorable as death.

"Perhaps you should communicate with your sister," Condidan suggested at last. "Tell her of our concerns . . ."

Coinmail's lips tightened. "My sister has become a Saxon."

"She is still a Christian, surely?"

Coinmail shrugged. "What matter? She has borne Ceawlin six children. She has a stake in all these marriages as well. Niniane will do nothing for us, my lords. If we wish to stop Ceawlin, we must do it ourselves."

*   *   *

Niniane and Auda sat together in the herb garden spinning wool. Fara, a small and agile three-year-old, chased a butterfly while Auda's infant son slept peacefully in the basket at his mother's feet.

"Ceawlin insists that the thanes from Wight must come to Winchester to swear allegiance to him and to Crida," Niniane said with a sigh. "I must confess I tried to persuade him it would be easier for him to go to Wight, but he says no. I suppose he is right. He usually is." Niniane gave her daughter-by-marriage a rueful look. "Of course, I am the one who has the housing and feeding of them."

Auda was amused. "You will manage, Mother. Like the king, you usually do."

A little silence fell as the women peacefully spun their wool. The baby smacked his lips in his sleep and Auda began to laugh. "He is so greedy. Even in his sleep he thinks only of food."

"He is a fine, healthy boy," said Niniane. "You and Crida have been blessed."

"I know." Auda's voice was very soft. She turned to Niniane and smiled. "You have lived in Winchester for so long, Mother, that I don't think you realize how unusual life is here. There are none of the petty jealousies, the intrigues, the spites, that pervaded my grandfather's enclave in Wight. And I know from my sister Fritha, who is married into East Anglia, that it is the same there. But here . . . all is peace."

Niniane's skillful fingers continued to work even as her mind was busy elsewhere. East Anglia, she thought. No, from all reports they had received, things had been far from peaceful in East Anglia these last few years. With the death of Guthfrid's brother and the accession of her brother's son, Redwold, to the kingship, Guthfrid had been pushed from her previous position of influence. She and her son had found themselves an embarrassment to the new king, a galling reminder of East Anglia's double defeats at the hands of Ceawlin of Wessex. But even in enforced retirement, Guthfrid had been a source of bitterness and discord at Sutton Hoo. She had, by all accounts, been a raving fury when Redwold had married his brother and not his cousin to Auda's sister, Fritha of Wight.

Then word had come only last month that Guthfrid was dead. By poison, it was whispered; but then, poison was always whispered when royalty died of aught else besides battle wounds or childbirth.

Guthfrid, the implacable enemy of all that Niniane loved, dead at last. Niniane still felt a flash of wickedly un-Christian pleasure when she thought of Guthfrid, safe at last in the earth.

Guthfrid had sowed discord enough in Winchester in her time as well. But Niniane did not want to remind Auda of the intrigues that her own family had been so much a part of. Auda was extremely sensitive on that subject. So she turned now to her son's wife and said with a small laugh, "You would not be lauding the peace of Winchester if you had heard the fight I had to mediate this morning between the baker and the cook."

Auda's face was grave. "I was not talking about the servants," she said.

"I know." Niniane rested her hands in her lap and watched Fara fall into a patch of thyme. The little girl got up, unhurt, and continued her pursuit of the elusive butterfly. "There will never be peace in a household where two women vie for power," Niniane said at last, turning to Auda and raising her delicate brows a little. "Ceawlin grew up in the middle of the war that waged between his mother and Guthfrid. He learned his lesson well." Her eyebrows returned to their normal position and once more she began to spin her wool.

"I see . . ." Auda's voice was thoughtful.

Niniane shot her a sideways look. "See what?"

Color stained Auda's cheeks. "Well, you must know, Mother, how unusual it is for a man . . . well, I mean, the king is not like other men . . ." Niniane's amusement was now visible and Auda pushed her pale brown hair off her brow and said sheepishly, "You know what I mean."

"I know what you mean." Niniane's dimple was much in evidence. "And it *partly* explains it."

Auda looked at her son. "I hope I can have as good a marriage with Crida as you have had with the king." Her eyes flicked toward Niniane, then went back to her son. After a moment's hesitation she added, "And I am not just thinking of my own personal happiness when I say that."

Niniane's head tilted. "What do you mean?"

Auda replied, her voice slow and thoughtful, "I think that if there is peace in the king's family, then there is peace in the kingdom. When my father was alive, he was always at odds with my grandfather. He did not think my grandfather gave him enough power. There were always schemes and plots between him and various thanes and eorls who saw in his dissatisfaction their own chance for advancement." Now Auda looked directly at Niniane. "Crida does not feel like that about the king. Crida admires his father, loves him. All your children feel that way, about the king, about you, about each other. There is no rivalry. And this . . . goodwill . . . trickles down to the rest of the kingdom. To the eorls and the thanes."

Niniane looked at Auda with startled pleasure and respect. "That is very astute of you, Auda."

Auda blushed. How grateful the child was for praise, Niniane thought as she smiled at Auda and smoothed out her wool. She had long thought that Crida's marriage was going to turn out to be a success for the kingdom as well as for the principals. Auda was proving surprisingly shrewd about matters of statecraft. She also obviously adored Crida, and Niniane thought that her son would be like Ceawlin, able to find contentment with one woman. Auda had already given Wessex an heir. As Niniane's thoughts reached this point, Ceolwulf hiccuped in his sleep and Auda bent to see if he was all right.

Crida had wanted to name the baby Cerdic, but Niniane had said no. She was not yet ready for another Cerdic.

Auda was right, she thought now as she looked at the girl's slender back bending over the baby. Her family was at peace.

It was a conversation she was to remember with aching nostalgia in the not-too-distant future.

Ceawlin was furious. It was a long time since Niniane had seen him in such a rage. He paced back and forth across the floor of their sleeping room, his long strides making the room seem very small. "I will not allow it," he said. "He has chosen to challenge me and he will find he has made a mistake."

Niniane sat huddled on the window seat and watched him. The cause of Ceawlin's ire was the withdrawal of the prince of Dynas from his daughter's betrothal to Bertred's son. It was not so much the withdrawal that had infuriated Ceawlin as the reason for it.

"Dynas does not fall within your brother's territory," he flung at Niniane now as he paced in front of her. "Coinmail has gone beyond what is allowable in forbidding Bevan to go through with this marriage. And Bevan is a spineless coward for allowing Coinmail to intimidate him."

It was, of course, Bevan's cowardice that had led him to seek a Saxon marriage for his daughter in the first place, but Niniane did not think this was the time to point that out to Ceawlin.

"What does Bertred say?" she ventured after he had paced in silence for a few minutes. Bertred himself had ridden into Winchester that afternoon with the news of the broken betrothal.

"Bertred wants to hold Bevan to the betrothal. I cannot blame him. Dynas, like all the British villas," and here he cast a look of scorn at Niniane, "has been allowed to fall into decay, but it is potentially a rich property. It will make a very nice settlement for Bertred's second son."

"But, Ceawlin, how can you hold Bevan to the betrothal? Dynas does not lie within the boundaries of Wessex. It is part of Dumnonia. I can understand Coinmail's concern that it should fall into Saxon hands . . ." Her voice trailed off. He had stopped his pacing and was standing in front of her, towering over her, and his eyes were blazing.

"Dumnonia is not Coinmail's concern," he said.

"Well"—she swallowed—"neither is it yours."

"Dynas is my concern. It was promised to the son of one of my eorls and I am going to see to it that he gets it."

Niniane stared up into her husband's face. It had been a very long time since anyone had dared to cross Ceawlin, she thought. He could rule with a light hand because his rule was so unquestionably accepted. But this was going to be different. Let Ceawlin get entangled in a dispute with Coinmail, and the allegiance of his British subjects would be sorely strained. She knew it. A confrontation with Coinmail would threaten the very stability of Wessex. But now was not the time to say that, not when he was so angry. He would not listen. Later, perhaps, when she had got him into bed . . .

"I have held my hand for all these years," he was saying now, and the line of his mouth was thin. "We need more land, but I have not reached my hand to take it, have done my best to expand Wessex by peaceful means. I have ever been conscious of British rights. But if Coinmail challenges me, Niniane, all of that will change."

Dear God. "Ceawlin . . . there is no need to be thinking of a war," she said quickly. "It is only a betrothal that has been broken!"

"No. It is a challenge, Niniane. I know it. Coinmail knows it. And if I do not answer it, my eorls and my thanes will despise me. I will despise myself. I promised Bertred this afternoon that we will hold Bevan to the betrothal."

The prince of Dynas was a man of middle age who had married late in life and had one daughter. The girl, the Princess Alys, was fourteen and of an age to marry. Upon Bevan's death, Alys' husband would become the owner of the villa of Dynas.

Dynas was set on the river Avon, some six miles to the east of Aquae Sulis. It consisted of a lovely old stone manor house with outbuildings and many tilled acres of farmland. It was a rich prize and Bevan had worried long over how to dispose of it safely. He was a lazy, idle man but he was of a line of princes, and it was important to him that his blood descendants hold the land of his ancestors. In the end, to the horror of all his acquaintances, he had chosen the son of a Saxon eorl.

Two things had prompted Bevan to the choice of Cedric, son of Bertred. The first was his conviction that it was inevitable one day for Wessex to expand into the area of Aquae Sulis. It would happen, if not under Ceawlin, then under the rule of Ceawlin's son. And when it happened, properties like Dynas would be the first to be handed over to new Saxon eorls. A marriage with the son of one of those eorls would safeguard Dynas from such a fate. His daughter and his grandchildren would be assured of keeping their family's ancestral home.

The second thing that had made such a marriage possible in the eyes of Bevan was that Bertred's wife was British and a Christian. The boy, Cedric, had been baptized and his father had agreed without protest to a Christian marriage ceremony.

So the betrothal had been accomplished. Alys was pleased with Cedric, a slim, handsome boy with soft brown hair and frank blue eyes. He was of an age with her and the two young people had seemed to agree very well during the short time that the eorl and his wife were at Dynas.

Bevan had been pleased and relieved. Then had come the visit from Coinmail.

Bevan knew Coinmail had no authority over him. Bevan was the Durotriges prince in this part of the world and he need answer to no one. But his weak and timid personality was incapable of standing up to Coinmail, who had always intimidated him.

The red-haired prince rode into the villa one hot summer afternoon accompanied by an escort of six men. He met with Bevan in the room that had served for centuries as the prince's study. Scrolls were still piled upon the walnut tables, but they were coated with dust. Bevan was not one to pass his days imbibing the great literature of the past. He was much fonder of imbibing wine.

Coinmail cast an appraising glance around the room. He had never learned to read or write and had always envied those who could. He looked scornfully at the chubby figure of the man in front of him. Here was a prince who had had the sort of Roman upbringing Coinmail was trying so desperately to save for Britain, and he was betrothing his daughter to a pagan! Coinmail's gray eyes held the pale blue ones of the prince of Dynas in a merciless glare.

"Allow this marriage and you will cut yourself off from the princes of Britain," he said, going directly to the reason for his visit.

Bevan blustered a little. "You have no authority in Dumnonia, Prince. Nor have I heard you have been given leave to speak for the princes of Britain."

"I speak for the princes of Wales," Coinmail returned. "For Condidan and Farinmail."

"The King of Dumnonia is my lord," Bevan said.

"The King of Dumnonia keeps his court far to the south of you, Bevan. You are on the northeastern boundaries of Dumnonia, and I doubt he troubles his mind about you. What you do will affect my people and the Welsh far more than it will affect Cador in distant Cornwall."

This, of course, was true. The King of Dumnonia was Bevan's official lord, but the area around Aquae Sulis had been self-ruling since the days of Arthur. Cador would not concern himself with the marriage of Bevan's daughter.

"They are already betrothed," Bevan protested. "There is nothing I can do."

"Break the betrothal," Coinmail said.

"I cannot! You don't understand. It was done formally, in front of witnesses. I cannot break it now."

'You will break it, Bevan, or I will take your daughter back to Glevum with me and marry her into Wales."

"You cannot do that!"

"I have a hundred of my men in Aquae Sulis," Coinmail said. "I can do it."

In the end, Bevan had agreed to break the betrothal. Alys cried bitterly; she had been well pleased with Cedric. And Bertred had ridden to Winchester to tell the king. Bevan sat at Dynas waiting in trembling fear for what was to happen next.

The weather was sultry. It had been years since Bevan could remember such heat. He sat in his study, drinking wine and sweating heavily. There had been no response from Bertred since Bevan had sent a messenger to Romsey to inform the eorl that the betrothal was broken. Bevan was beginning to hope that the Saxon would understand his problems with Coinmail and accept his withdrawal with good grace.

"My lord." One of his house servants stood in the doorway. "My lord, the eorl Bertred has just ridden in with a troop of men."

Bevan put down his wine cup and groaned. "My lord," the servant was going on, his eyes huge, "there is someone with him. . . . My lord, I think it is Ceawlin himself!"

"What?"

"A silver-haired man, very tall, riding a white stallion, my lord."

"Oh, my dear God." Bevan stumbled to his feet. "What am I going to do?"

"My lord, the lady Alys has gone to greet them."

Bevan gave a hunted look around his study, as if he would like to hide. Then, as he felt the servant's eyes on him, he straightened and said with dignity, "I will come also."

He knew as soon as he saw him that the man standing beside Bertred was Ceawlin. He had never seen Ceawlin before, but it was not difficult to know that this man was a king. Bevan went forward to greet his unwanted guests and conduct them into his house.

"We have come to discuss the marriage of the lady Alys to Cedric, son of Bertred," the king said when the three men were seated in the marble-floored great hall of the villa, which had not been used in decades.

"My lord king . . ." Bevan's pale eyes were desperate. "You must understand that it was not my wish to withdraw from the marriage. But

Prince Coinmail came here—with a hundred men, my lord!—and threatened to take Alys to Wales with him should I not agree to break the betrothal."

Ceawlin's face was unreadable. Bevan had never seen a more splendid-looking man than the Saxon king. "I did not know Prince Coinmail was overlord in this part of the world." His voice was faintly surprised.

"My lord, you know he is not. But Coinmail . . . well, it is hard to say no to Coinmail. Especially when he comes with a hundred men to enforce his will!"

"Ah." Ceawlin took a sip of his wine and smiled at Bevan. The British prince felt himself relaxing. The king's smile was full of charm. "But I have a hundred men with me also," he said. "And I am going to hold you to the marriage."

It took Bevan a moment to understand. Then all the wine-rich color drained from his face. "H-hold me to it?"

"Yes." The extraordinary blue-green eyes were positively friendly. "Your daughter says she is willing. And you have sworn in front of witnesses, Bevan. The marriage will go forward."

"I . . ." Bevan was now white to the lips. "But what of Coinmail?"

All the good humor left the king's face. In the heat of the room Bevan crossed his arms on his chest as if he were cold. "I will deal with Coinmail," Ceawlin said. "You need not worry about him."

Chapter 40

C EAWLIN brought Alys and Bevan to Winchester and sent to Glastonbury for a priest.

"You are putting yourself in an impossible situation," Niniane said to her husband. "You can force the marriage, but that does not mean Cedric will ever be able to claim the villa. It is in British territory, Ceawlin! Coinmail will be able to arrange his death with little trouble. And he will do it. Then what will you have? Instead of gaining a manor, Bertred and Meghan will have lost a son."

"This is not woman's business," he answered.

Quite suddenly Niniane was furious. "You were able to claim this kingdom because of British help," she said, her voice shaking. "And you got British help because of me. You kept this kingdom, Ceawlin, because of British help. Were it not for Gereint and Ferris providing shelter for you, Cutha would have caught and killed you. Do not dare to tell me this is not my business. Everything that affects you and my sons is my business. And I tell you now you are making a mistake."

His eyes narrowed to blue-green slits. He was as angry as she was. "When someone crowns you king, you can make the decisions," he said. "Until that time, I rule, and I say the marriage will go forward. I do not want to hear your voice on the subject again."

Niniane tried to talk to Meghan. "Do you not see, Meghan," she said as the two women met in the king's hall to plan the marriage ceremony, "this marriage is a danger to Cedric. He will never be able to live safely at Dynas, not with Coinmail's enmity. It would be much better to choose a nice Saxon girl for him to marry."

But Meghan was no help. "Bertred says this is a splendid match for Cedric," she said to Niniane. "The girl is an heiress of the kind not often given to younger sons. It is an opportunity for Cedric to establish himself on a much larger scale than we could have hoped for. Bertred is determined that the marriage should go forward."

"Meghan," Niniane tried again, "think. You are a Briton. You must understand how this marriage will divide the kingdom. Ceawlin's British subjects have proven their loyalty to him again and again, but never has he asked them to choose between Wessex and their own people. All that will be changed if Coinmail takes up this challenge."

"Bertred says it will be all right," said Meghan, and that, for her, it seemed, was that. Niniane's love for her husband was not so blind. Ceawlin could make a mistake. True, he made very few, but this was one of them. She knew it. And he would not listen to her.

She tried Crida. He listened with more patience than Ceawlin. "I understand what you are saying, Mother," he said when she had finished. "But what you don't understand is that Father has no choice in this matter. He cannot allow your brother to outface him. You worry that he will lose the allegiance of his British subjects if he goes to war against Coinmail. I tell you this: he will lose the respect of his Saxon subjects if he does not."

It seemed to Niniane supremely ironic that now, after all these years, after she had long ceased to worry about Coinmail as a potential threat to Ceawlin, the confrontation had come. She had let herself be lulled into complacency these last peaceful years in Winchester. The kingdom was prosperous. Her children were strong and healthy. Ceawlin was content.

How happy her world had been. How foolish she had been to rest secure, to forget. She felt, obscurely, as if this challenge by Coinmail was her fault, as if for all those years she had kept him at bay simply by worrying about him, fearing him. Once she had forgotten, had let him slip to the back of her mind, it was as if she had set him loose to do as he chose.

She had not been happy when first she learned of the betrothal between Bertred's son and the heiress to Dynas. She had lived among the Saxons for so long that in some ways she had taken on their colors, but still she was a Briton. Dynas was in Dumnonia, and no Saxon had ever gained a foothold in Dumnonia. No Briton would rejoice at this marriage. In approving it, Ceawlin had given Coinmail the very rallying call he had always lacked. Dumnonia was the very heartland of Celtic Briton. Dumnonia was where Arthur had built Camelot. Dumnonia and Wales were the only places in Britain where Saxon feet had never trodden. Coinmail would be able to rally the Britons to fight for Dumnonia.

It was raining. Niniane sat at the window of her sleeping room and stared out at the gray day. Her body felt heavy and dull as her mood. She was with child again and was just getting over weeks of morning sickness. Now she just felt tired.

In the end, brave soldier, death will defeat you. The line had been running around and around in her head ever since the banquet the previous night. The actual marriage was to take place tomorrow in the old Christian church in Venta, but last night had been a traditional Saxon banquet to honor the bride and bridegroom. Alric had sung one of his greatest compositions, the story of an old Scandinavian hero from deep in the Saxon past. It was a song Niniane had heard before, but last night it had made a great impression upon her.

"Avoid pride, great hero." The lines that Niniane could not forget came toward the end of the song, when the hero, after many great deeds, returned home to his own people and received the advice of his king. "Now you are at the height of your strength," the old king cautioned the young adventurer. "But it will not be long before sickness or the sword, or the blaze of fire, or the raging sea, a thrust of the knife or a whizzing arrow, will rob you of your might. In the end, brave soldier, death will defeat you."

Ceawlin was Saxon to his fingertips. He knew he was not invulnerable. Why, then, did he persist in living his life as if he were?

The door opened and she heard her husband come into the room. "Are you all right?" His voice was rough but she could hear the concern underneath.

"Yes. Just weary. It's the weather, I suppose."

He came to stand beside her and stare out at the day as well. She turned her head slightly so she could see him. There was rain on his hair and on his shoulders. His profile was as clear as the profiles on some of the old Roman coins she had seen; and as unreadable.

"Gereint has not come for the wedding," she said.

"No." His profile did not change. "After the marriage, we will go to Bryn Atha and speak with him."

Niniane felt her heart jump. He was worried. Why had he not listened to her? "Ceawlin. It is not yet too late." She laid her hand on his bare forearm. "They are not married yet."

He turned his head and looked at her. "They will be tomorrow," he answered, removed his arm from beneath her fingers, and left the room.

A young priest from Glastonbury married Alys and Cedric, and after a restrained banquet in Bertred's hall, the new husband and wife were put to bed. Alys lost her virginity and it was done; Dynas' next lord would be a Saxon. If he lived.

Ceawlin was well aware that he could not send Cedric to live at Dynas just yet. The newly wedded couple were to live at Romsey until matters were settled between Ceawlin and Coinmail. Bevan, the unhappy pawn in this power struggle, went miserably home by himself and rued the day he had ever promised his daughter to the son of a Saxon eorl and thus brought this catastrophe down upon his head.

A week after the marriage, Ceawlin, Niniane, and an escort of ten thanes paid a visit to Bryn Atha.

The sight of her old home lifted Niniane's spirits, as it always did. But then the shadow of Coinmail seemed to descend. Things were not the same in the land of the Atrebates since the marriage of Alys and Cedric.

Gereint was blunt when he met with Ceawlin and Niniane in the sitting room at Bryn Atha. "You have made a mistake, Ceawlin. You have given Coinmail just the weapon he has always needed to rally the Britons against you. You have threatened the integrity of Dumnonia."

Ceawlin ran his hand through his hair and stared at Gereint in exasperation. "I am not moving against Dumnonia, Gereint. This is a marriage, not a rape. The girl's father sought out Bertred."

Gereint's thin dark face was somber. The older he got, Niniane found herself thinking, the more he looked like Naille. "Bertred should not have accepted the offer."

Ceawlin was beginning to get angry. "Why not? If he were offered a good marriage into Sussex, he would have taken it. Why is Dumnonia so sacred?"

"You don't understand, Ceawlin." The two men and Niniane were sitting in the ancient wicker chairs that furnished the sitting room, and now Gereint bent forward and stared at the mosaic floor.

"No, I don't." Niniane saw that Ceawlin's eyes were beginning to deepen in color. "Are you saying that if the King of Dumnonia offered to marry one of his sons to my daughter, I would have to refuse?"

"Cador would never make such an offer." Gereint looked up at Niniane. "Don't you understand, Niniane? Haven't you told him how it is?"

"Niniane was against the marriage." Ceawlin's face was set hard.

"Then for God's sake, why didn't you listen to her?" Gereint's voice was almost despairing. "You don't understand what you have done, Ceawlin. You can't. If you did understand, you would never have done it."

Ceawlin let out his breath in a long, slow release. When he did that, it was always a sign that he was trying to keep his temper. He couldn't lose his temper, Niniane thought suddenly. To lose his temper with Gereint would be the very worst thing he could do.

"You see, Gereint," she put in smoothly before Ceawlin had a chance to speak, "when the marriage was first proposed, no one had any idea that there would be a confrontation. Cador made no protest. It was, as Ceawlin told you, Bevan's idea. Then Coinmail got hold of the news. Coinmail has no authority in Dumnonia, but he bullied Bevan into withdrawing from the betrothal. This was after the betrothal vows had been sworn. Bertred, not unnaturally, was furious and came to Ceawlin to ask him to hold Bevan to the marriage." She shrugged slim shoulders. "What was Ceawlin to do? If he refused to back Bertred, he would have lost the respect of all his Saxon eorls and thanes."

"I see." Gereint was very pale. He looked from Niniane to Ceawlin. "So, given a choice between your British and your Saxon subjects, you chose the Saxon."

Niniane's intervention had had the desired effect. There was no sign of temper in Ceawlin's face or voice as he replied, "I did not issue this challenge, Gereint. Coinmail did. I am perfectly willing to continue to live in peace with British Dumnonia. I am ready to swear to you that I will never use Dynas as an excuse to invade British-held territory. But if Coinmail raises an army and comes against me, I cannot say what will happen."

The two men looked into each other's eyes and Niniane held her breath. Then Gereint said, raw pain throbbing in his voice, "I have always loved you, Ceawlin. Do not make me choose between you and my people."

Tears stung Niniane's eyes and rose in her throat. "By the hammer of Thor," Ceawlin said softly, "is it as bad as that?"

"Yes," said Gereint. "It is."

A muscle twitched in Ceawlin's cheek. "Crida is half-British," he said, "and Crida will be the next King of Wessex."

"Crida may be half-British by blood," Gereint replied, "but he is wholly Saxon by upbringing."

Ceawlin said, "You underestimate Niniane."

Niniane whisked the tears from beneath her eyes with her forefinger. "Gereint . . . have you heard from Coinmail?"

"Yes." Gereint's dark tan had taken on a sallow tinge. "It will come to a fight, Niniane. Coinmail has wanted this for a long time and now he has the Welsh princes with him."

"Stay out of it." Ceawlin's voice was harsh with suppressed feeling. "If there is to be a fight, I will keep it away from Atrebates territory. Just stay home, Gereint. Will you do that for me?"

"I . . . will try," came the Briton's answer.

Ceawlin went out to the courtyard with Gereint to see him off home, and when he came back to the sitting room he found Niniane still sitting in the old wicker chair, with silent tears pouring down her face. "I tried to tell you," she said when he had dropped into a chair himself.

"Why is there this feeling about Dumnonia?" His voice was hard, abrupt.

"Dumnonia is . . . oh, I suppose you could say it has always been the heartland of Celtic Britain. Arthur ruled from Dumnonia. And in all the years since the Saxons first invaded Britain, Ceawlin, there have never been Saxons in Dumnonia."

"Until now."

"Until now." She sniffled and wiped her cheeks again.

He shrugged. "I am sorry for it, Nan, but once Bevan approached

Bertred about that cursed marriage, there was nothing I could do. I could not forbid Bertred to marry his son into Dynas. I would not even if I could. I have been willing to leave Dumnonia in peace but I am not willing to allow Coinmail to dictate to me whom my subjects may or may not marry."

"I see."

"Gods, Nan," he said, and now the feeling he had been suppressing in front of Gereint was evident. "Is Gereint going to be another Sigurd?"

Her heart ached for him, but she understood Gereint as well. "He doesn't want to be, Ceawlin." Then, "His heart is breaking over this, couldn't you see that?"

He was staring fixedly at his feet, and all she could see was the top of his head. His voice was muffled as he answered, "So, I imagine, did Sigurd's."

There was nothing she could say in response to that.

Coinmail was delighted when he heard that the marriage between Cedric and Alys had been accomplished. As he said to his wife in a rare moment of confidence, "Ceawlin's power has ever lain in the loyalty of his British subjects. I do not think he will be able to count upon that loyalty any longer."

Coinmail's wife was the Princess Eithne, a blue-eyed, blond-haired Celtic daughter of the Dobunni who had married the Atrebates prince when she was but fourteen. She had thought he was wonderful then, with his beautiful face and his fanatic devotion to the cause of Britain. She had dreamed he was another Arthur. Years of marriage to him had dampened her ardor. Men of Coinmail's stamp might make strong leaders, but they were no joy to live with. She had long since realized that he had no personal feelings for her. He prized her as a soldier might prize a particularly good sword. She had given him power in the Dobunni tribe and she had given him a son to rule through. For Eithne, the woman, he had no thought at all.

"They might not be happy with this marriage," she answered him now, "but that does not mean they will actively oppose Ceawlin."

"I think they will. I spoke to Gereint personally. Gereint, as you know, has ever been Ceawlin's staunchest supporter. Ceawlin even named him eorl for the loyalty Gereint showed in his struggle with Cutha." Coinmail's beautifully cut mouth smiled. "When I asked Gereint to join with me in opposing Ceawlin's invasion of Dumnonia, he did not refuse."

"He did not accept, either," said Eithne.

Coinmail frowned. "You don't understand, Eithne, how great a thing it is for Gereint even to contemplate going against Ceawlin. If he has come this far, he will go the whole way. I know it. In the end, blood will tell. And Gereint, eorl or no, is a Briton."

"Still," said Eithne, "Ceawlin will have all his Saxon eorls and thanes."

"If I can raise southern Wales, the Dobunni, and the Atrebates, I will have almost a thousand men," said Coinmail. "No Saxon war band ever comes near that number."

"Coinmail . . ." Eithne's blue eyes searched her husband's face. "What will you do should you win? Surely you don't think you can annex Wessex?"

"No, I suppose not," came the reluctant reply. "The Welsh will not go so far."

"Then all you wish to accomplish is to keep Ceawlin out of Dumnonia?"

"I want Ceawlin dead," came the immediate, implacable reply. "Ceawlin is the reason why Wessex has grown so strong, and under him it will continue to get stronger. I have known for years that I must get rid of Ceawlin."

"But he is your sister's husband."

Coinmail's expression did not change as he replied in level, carefully measured tones, "I have no sister."

Four weeks after Ceawlin had returned to Winchester from Bryn Atha, his scouts rode in with the news that the Welsh were mustering in large numbers near Caer.

"How large?" Ceawlin asked.

"My lord, the princes are calling up all their clansmen who are of an age to fight."

"How many?" Ceawlin repeated.

"My lord, when we left they had perhaps five hundred men. But they were still coming in."

After Ceawlin had dismissed the scouts, he began to pace. He had met with the men in the king's hall, dismissing the servants for the sake of privacy, and so he was alone and could think without having to guard his face.

If the Welsh could muster that many men . . . Hammer of Thor! Coinmail might collect a war band of nearly a thousand. A thousand men was not a war band; it was an army. Numbers like that had not been seen in Britain since the wars of Arthur.

He was still pacing like a caged tiger when Niniane came in ten minutes later. He looked up frowning when the door opened, saw who it was, and went back to prowling up and down the length of the hearthplace. Niniane came to take her usual seat in front of the small afternoon fire. She said nothing.

It was a full two minutes before he said to her over his shoulder, "The Welsh are mustering. In large numbers."

"How large?" she asked, her voice quiet.

"Too large. It looks as if Coinmail might raise a thousand men."

Niniane's cheeks were thin with pregnancy, making her eyes look very large. Now they dilated almost to blackness. "A thousand men!"

"So it seems."

"You will have to call up the ceorls again."

"Yes. And the men of Wight."

"What . . . what of the Atrebates?"

"I do not expect Gereint to join with me, but I will tell you this, Niniane: if he goes against me, I will be in trouble."

"There . . . there are not so many fighters among the Atrebates, Ceawlin. Their numbers cannot make much of a difference."

"Coinmail is not raising just the fighters. He is taking every man of an age to hold a bow or a sword. If Gereint declares for him, they will empty the farms. And those numbers *will* count."

Their eyes met. "You predicted this, I know," he said. "But if it were all to do again, I would do the same. If I am to be king, I could do no other."

He meant it, she thought. Even now, facing what was probably the greatest challenge to his rule ever, he meant it. If he could, he would not undo the marriage. For Ceawlin, to have backed down would have been worse.

She did not agree with him. But she stood with him. She would always stand with him. It did not have to be said; he knew it. "Let me go by myself to talk to Gereint," she said.

"No." At last he stopped his pacing and came to drop down on his heels in front of her. "You are almost five months gone with child."

"I will go by litter if you wish." She smoothed the short hair on his brow into order. "If the Atrebates stay loyal, they will not only deprive Coinmail of a number of fighting men, they will keep him from entering Wessex by way of Silchester."

"I know." His eyes searched her face. "I still do not understand it, Nan. I have been as good a king to Gereint's people as I have been to my own."

"Yes. You have." She leaned forward to touch his forehead with her lips. "Let me go and talk with him."

He drew a long uneven breath. "All right," he said. "Shall I send Crida with you?"

"No. It will be best for me to go alone. Gereint and I . . . we share the same loyalties. He will be better able to speak with me if no one else is there."

"All right," he said again. "I would not ask it, but you are right. I cannot afford to have the Atrebates go out against me. But take a litter. And an escort of twenty thanes."

"Ten thanes. I do not want to look as if I am coming to threaten them. And I will take a litter." She wrinkled her nose. "Much as I hate them."

"It will be safer for you."

"I know." She laid her cheek against his. "Gereint does love you, Ceawlin. I do not think he will go against you, no matter what you have done."

His arms came around her. "No one loves me like that," he said, "except you."

Chapter 41

*F*ALL was coming early this year, Niniane thought as she looked from the back windows of Bryn Atha toward the woods that separated the house from the pig pens and chicken coops. September had been chill and rainy; some of the leaves were already beginning to turn. She had had the hypocaust lit as soon as she arrived.

She saw three of the thanes who had escorted her going toward the stable, leading their horses. They had just returned from carrying news to Gereint of her presence at Bryn Atha. Gereint had returned word that he would come to see her on the morrow. She had one more night to think about what she was going to say to him.

She was tired. The long trip by litter had been exhausting. She had not gone five miles before she knew she should have ridden; she had ridden the previous month when she came north with Ceawlin, and she had been fine. But Ceawlin had insisted on the litter. Nor could she deny that she was feeling this pregnancy more than she had her others. She supposed she should not be surprised; she was getting old. Thirty-five did not bear as easily as seventeen, she thought with a sigh.

She turned and walked toward one of the wicker chairs, stopped before it, but then did not sit down. No, she thought. She was so weary, she would go straight to bed. She would tell Budd to send some bread and cheese to her room; then she could just crawl in under her old blue blanket and go to sleep. She rubbed the back of her neck, turned, and walked with unusual heaviness down the hall toward the kitchen.

Gereint did not come until late in the afternoon the following day. Niniane had not slept as well as she had expected to. She missed Ceawlin's big body next to her in the bed. She rose early, dragged around for half of the morning, then went back to bed and napped for half the afternoon. She was just waking up when Gereint rode in.

The day was damp and gray. Gereint looked as cheerless as the weather as he held Niniane's hand in his for a minute before leading her to one of the old wicker chairs. "You are not looking well," he said bluntly.

"I am with child again, that is all." She smiled at him ruefully as she sat down and gestured for him to take the chair beside her. "I am not as young as I used to be, Gereint."

"Nonsense. You still look like a girl."

She watched as he lowered his slim, lithe frame into the sagging old chair. It was Gereint who had kept his youthfulness, she thought. "You are a very kind liar," she said, and sighed. She looked slowly around the faded Roman room. "There are so many memories waiting for me here at Bryn Atha," she said softly, her eyes on the peacock scroll. "Do you remember the night your father made you stay with me while Ceawlin was gone? You were fifteen and horrified that there was a Saxon at Bryn Atha. I can still remember how you challenged Ceawlin when he came home. He swore to you then that he would be a good king to the Atrebates, Gereint, and you ended the evening by going with him to help with the horses. Do you remember?"

"Niniane . . . this is not going to do any good." Gereint's voice was constricted.

"He said to me before I left, 'I do not understand, Niniane. I have been as good a king to the Atrebates as I have been to the Saxons.' And he has been, Gereint. You cannot deny that."

"That is not the question." His voice was even more constricted. "I do not question that Ceawlin is a good king. But it is more than that, Niniane. It is a matter of . . . of racial loyalty now." His brown eyes were very somber. "It is a matter of racial survival."

"Listen to what I am going to say, Gereint," Niniane said. "It is something I have thought about for a long time and I am convinced it is the truth. The way to British survival is intermarriage with the Saxons."

Gereint made a gesture of impatience. "That is what Ceawlin tried to say when he pointed out that Crida is half-British. But the truth is, Niniane, that Crida is Saxon. He speaks Saxon. He thinks like a Saxon. He will bring his children up to be Saxon. It is only an accident of birth that his mother is a Briton."

Niniane's pale mouth set in a stern line. "That is Coinmail talking," she said. "And it is not true. Ceawlin told you true when he said that you underestimate me. My children are part British. They are British in the most important way of all, Gereint. They were baptized."

"They are not Christians for all that, Niniane. I have been in Winchester often enough to see that. They worship with Ceawlin, not with you."

"They follow the rites of the Saxon religion, and the form gives them a sense of comradeship with the rest of the men, but they do not worship Saxon gods, Gereint. Even Ceawlin does not really believe in those gods. He sees Woden as some kind of glorified ancestor, but he does not believe in him as God. If he believes in anything, he believes in Fate."

Gereint was staring at her intently. She began to pleat the fold of her linen overgown with careful deliberation, looking at her fingers and not at Gereint. "Ceawlin would not tell you that, of course. And he is very wary of Christianity; he thinks it is the religion of the weak." She smoothed out the pleats she had made and began to do them again. "But my sons are farther down the road than their father. I think Crida believes in God. Not Christ, maybe, but a God. One God. He is not quite sure, and because he is young, he has other things to think about." Niniane looked at Gereint out of the corner of her eye. "I have to be careful, you see. I cannot talk about Christ. Ceawlin would not be able to accept that."

"What are you telling me, Niniane?" Gereint asked quietly.

"I am telling you that even if the Saxons move into Dumnonia, and perhaps into Wales; even if the language eventually spoken in those lands is Saxon and not British, still we will have won in the most important way. It is we who have kept the spark of faith alive in Britain, Gereint, and someday, a day not too far in the future, the Saxons will convert. I know this will happen. If the pope sent an apostle to Crida, I think Crida would listen." She smiled wryly. "Ceawlin, no. But Crida would. So would Ceowulf and Eirik and my little Fara. And it will happen because we will have prepared the ground for it."

"Coinmail still wants to drive the Saxons out."

"You cannot. Arthur could not do it a hundred years ago, Gereint. Coinmail cannot do it today. The Saxons will never leave Britain."

Gereint's long-fingered hands moved restlessly on the arms of his chair and then were still. "I think you are right," he answered finally, his voice very low.

"But don't you see what has happened?" She bent a little toward him in her eagerness to convince. "Arthur has proved victorious after all. He gave us almost a century of peace, Gereint, and during that century the Saxons became civilized. I remember that Ceawlin said that to you once. The sea wolves who first landed on Britain's shores have turned into farmers and merchants. They are civilized people, Gereint."

"Coinmail says—"

"I know what Coinmail says," she put in impatiently. "He said it to me too, and he can be very persuasive. It was Coinmail's words that made me think all this out. Coinmail says that we Britons are the repository of Roman civilization, that we must save it from the ravages of the pagans. But the bitter truth is that we have not been very good at saving Roman civilization, Gereint. The cities left by Rome are falling down. It is the Saxons who have rebuilt the cities. We just let them fall into decay. Why do you think Bevan turned to Wessex for a husband for his daughter? Because he loves Dynas and wants to see it survive. It has not survived very well under British custody. But do you know something? Under Cedric it will flourish."

"You are not very flattering about your own people, Niniane," Gereint said. His face was unreadable.

"There is much that is great in the Celtic people. I like Saxon poetry, but ours is finer. There is a fire in us, a quicksilver quality that no Saxon possesses. But we are not a city people. Think, Gereint. What city in Britain was built by the British?"

"Camelot," came the instant reply.

"Ceawlin would tell you that Arthur was more Roman than Briton. Whatever he was, Arthur was unique. The rest of the cities on this island were built by the Romans. And a hundred years after the Romans had left, the cities were falling apart."

"Well, what is so important about cities?"

Niniane laughed. "That is the Briton talking."

There was a long silence. Then Gereint sighed. "You and Coinmail would make Roman orators."

"I don't know about that." Niniane rested her head against the back of her chair and closed her eyes. "I understand that you are torn by this, Gereint. I have been married to Ceawlin for some eighteen years, but I have always remembered that I am a Briton. I also know Ceawlin, and I will tell you this: he is as great a king as Arthur ever was, and Coinmail is not his equal. Not as a man, not as a king." She opened her eyes and stared at Ceawlin's only British eorl.

Gereint had slumped down in his chair and a shock of dark brown hair hung forward over his forehead and hid his eyes. When Niniane finished speaking he peered up at her, a look that recalled vividly the boy he had been. He said, "I agree."

There was a long silence. Then Gereint pushed himself upright. "I do not think I can take up arms against Coinmail, Niniane, but I will promise not to fight for him either. Will that do?"

Niniane's smile was tremulous. "It will have to," she said. "Stay for dinner."

It was during dinner that it happened. The sound of thundering hooves in the courtyard, the shouts of the thanes as they erupted out of the thanes' quarters, the clashing sound of sword upon sword.

"Dear God in heaven, what is happening?" Niniane cried as she ran to a window with Gereint close behind her. It was growing dark but they could see that the courtyard was filled with horsemen. Ceawlin's thanes had drawn up into a circle facing out, but they were outnumbered four to one. "Sigbert!" Niniane screamed as one of the thanes went down. She turned to run to the villa door.

Gereint caught her arm. "No! Stay here, Niniane. You can do nothing for the thanes now."

"Let me go!" She pulled frantically at the hand that was holding her.

"No. Niniane, didn't you see who it is?"

She stopped struggling and stared at him. "Who?"

"Coinmail."

She went white to the lips. "Coinmail?"

"Yes." Gereint looked around the room. "How did he know you were here? God, where can I hide you?"

"Hide me?" she repeated blankly.

From down the hall came the sound of the front door opening. "It's too late," Gereint said despairingly. "He will know you are still here because of the thanes."

Niniane drew a deep shuddering breath. There came the sound of feet tramping down the hall. They had left the dining-room door open. "Greetings, Coinmail," Niniane said to the man who entered first. "I am sorry I cannot say welcome." Gereint gave her a startled look. She had collected herself with astonishing quickness.

Coinmail stopped two feet inside the door and looked from his sister to Gereint. A flicker of satisfaction showed on his austere features. "So," he said. "I am in time."

"How did you know Niniane was here?" Gereint demanded.

"I have friends in the neighborhood," Coinmail replied. "Fortunately I was at Corinium and able to move quickly."

"If you wished to speak to me so desperately, my brother, you had only to send word." Niniane was still very pale but her small chin was high.

"I have nothing I want to say to you," Coinmail replied. They were the first words he had spoken directly to her and his voice was cold. "But you will come with me, Niniane. You have polluted yourself in Ceawlin's bed long enough."

"My lord." It was one of Coinmail's men at the door. "We have taken four of the Saxons alive. What shall we do with them?"

"Kill them."

The Briton's "Yes, sir" clashed with Niniane's anguished *"No!"*

"The fewer West Saxons in the world, the fewer men for Ceawlin's war band," Coinmail said. He spoke to Gereint, who had also made a protest.

"You could hold them captive," said Gereint. "It is not necessary to kill them."

"They are pagans," Coinmail said. Then, to Niniane, "Where is your horse?"

"I have no horse. I came by litter."

"You will have to ride with one of my men, then."

"Where are you taking me?"

"Glevum."

"Coinmail, you cannot take Niniane all that long way!" It was Gereint. "She is with child. That is why Ceawlin sent her in a litter."

Coinmail's gray eyes looked his sister up and down. Then, "It cannot be helped," he said. "If she loses it, that will be one less son of Ceawlin's for me to worry about."

"She is your sister!"

"Coinmail cares nothing for that." Niniane's voice was as cold as her brother's. Gereint had never heard her sound like that. "He is incapable of any of the human ties that most people feel, that bind together families and societies. He is a man with a Great Cause, and he will sacrifice everything that is real and decent in life in order to achieve it. It is really Coinmail and not Ceawlin who is uncivilized, Gereint. Isn't that ironic?"

There was a spark of anger in Coinmail's dark gray eyes. "You have been in bed with the Saxon for so long that now you think like him," he said.

Niniane's delicate brows rose. "Then send me back to him. I am of no use to you."

"You are of use to him," came the uncompromising reply. "That is why you will go with me."

Gereint protested again, but for naught. He was forced to stand by helplessly and watch Niniane being lifted to the saddle of one of her brother's men. Her whole face had clenched when she saw the dead thanes lying in the courtyard.

"I will see them buried," was all Gereint could think to say in comfort.

She nodded, clearly not trusting herself to speak. As Gereint watched the cadre of horsemen riding out of Bryn Atha, he was filled with despair. How in the name of God was he going to tell Ceawlin that Coinmail had taken Niniane?

Gereint sent for some men and together they dug graves for the thanes. All of the men he buried were known to him; they had been with the king for years. Several of them had wives, children. But Coinmail did not care for that. He saw only that they were the enemy.

Ceawlin would not have done this, Gereint found himself thinking as he shoveled dirt over the inert bodies. He would not have cold-bloodedly executed the men who survived the fight in the courtyard. Ceawlin could be ruthless, but he also knew how to show mercy.

When Gereint had sent for the burial party, he had also sent out a call for a tribal meeting the following morning. The first men began to ride into his farmyard shortly after dawn. By eight o'clock there were some fifty men and boys assembled to hear what Gereint had to say. The men of Gereint's age and older made up the bulk of the group, but to the side was a collection of youngsters surrounding Naille, Gereint's fourteen-year-old son. There was an air of determination about them that caught Gereint's attention. Naille must have sent for the boys, Gereint thought. He certainly had not requested their presence.

"You are all aware of what has been happening between Wessex and the Dobunni and the Welsh over this matter of Wessex marrying into Dumnonia," he began. The faces watching him were all sober. By now there was no one who had not learned of the kidnapping of the queen. "You know I represented our feelings to Ceawlin and that the marriage went forward anyway." He paused, testing their attention. No one moved. "I told the queen yesterday, before Prince Coinmail's arrival, that the Atrebates would not take up arms in this struggle; not for Ceawlin and not for Coinmail."

A sigh seemed to go up from the assembled men. What that sigh portended, Gereint did not know, was never to know, because just then his son spoke out, clear and passionate in the morning air. "I cannot believe, Father, that you are not going to back the king!"

There was a movement as if everyone present had snapped to attention. All of the boys with Naille were signaling violent agreement.

"I explained to you, Naille," Gereint said carefully, trying not to show his surprise. "Never before have we been faced with a choice between Ceawlin and our people."

"What people?" It was Ferris' son speaking now. "Our people are not in Wales. Or Dumnonia. Our people are here!" A gesture to encompass all the men standing together in the farmyard. "We are the Atrebates and Ceawlin is our king!" the ringing young voice cried. "He is the greatest king in all the world, and if he wants my sword, he shall have it!"

Gereint stared at the glowing young faces of his son and his son's friend. These boys, he suddenly realized, had not been brought up on tales of Arthur and Arthur's wars against the Saxons. They had been brought up on tales of Ceawlin. He had told them himself, night after night, the stories of how the Atrebates had helped Ceawlin win a kingdom. And he remembered also the time he too had defied his father to take up a sword for Ceawlin. It was a tale he had recounted often to his own children.

He looked at the boys and suddenly it was as if a great weight had lifted from his back. For the first time in months he felt young again. He grinned at his son and said, above the agitated rumble of male voices in the yard, "He can have my sword too."

Chapter 42

*I*T proved surprisingly easy to convince the Atrebates to take up arms for Ceawlin. The young ones who had grown up thinking themselves part of Wessex, who had never known another king, were eager. But the resistance Gereint had expected from the older ones, the ones who remembered the days when the Saxon king was an object of fear and hatred, never materialized.

"He is a good king," one of Gereint's older cousins said as they met in council after the larger meeting. "Two years ago, when the crops were so bad, there would have been famine had Ceawlin not sent to Gaul for food and fodder. He paid for it himself, and we got an equal share with all the Saxon vils and manors. We could not ask for a better king than Ceawlin. I say he deserves our support."

It gave Gereint a little comfort to know that he could go to Winchester with news of Atrebates support to soften the blow of Niniane's kidnapping.

Ceawlin was not in Winchester when Gereint rode in, and he was directed instead to Crida, whose headquarters as heir was now the old queen's hall. When he had made Gereint eorl, Ceawlin had given him Cynigils' old hall, and it was at his Winchester home that Gereint washed the dust of the road off hands and face before going, on reluctant feet, to see Crida.

The autumn day was chill and a fire was going in the hearthplace, which in Crida's hall had the usual central position in the main room. Crida was alone, standing at the end of the hearth facing the door; the fire from behind lit his hair like a halo. From another room there came the sound of a baby crying, then silence. It was a moment before Gereint realized how rigidly the boy was holding himself.

"Where is my mother?" Crida said, and suddenly Gereint understood what Crida had braced himself to hear.

"She is all right," he replied hastily. "She is not dead, Crida."

The boy relaxed visibly; Gereint thought he could almost see the blood begin to flow again through Crida's veins. His blue-green eyes, so like Ceawlin's, grew glitteringly bright. "I thought . . . when you rode in without her . . ."

"I am sorry. I did not mean to frighten you so." Gereint drew a deep breath. "She is not dead, Crida, but still the news I bring you is not good. Coinmail came to Bryn Atha while she was there and took her by force to Glevum."

Crida took a step forward. "Took Mother?"

"Yes." Then, hastily, "He did not harm her. He will not harm her, I am sure of that. But she is being held hostage. There was nothing the thanes or I could do. He came with a hundred men and he took us by surprise."

"Where are the thanes?" Crida was frowning now.

"Dead," Gereint replied, his voice harsh. Then, as Crida's face began to look very grim, "Where is Ceawlin?"

"He went to Wight. He will be back on the morrow." Crida gestured Gereint to a chair, then slowly took one himself. "Are you sure they were going to Glevum?"

"That is what Coinmail said. It is probably true. Glevum is close to Wales."

Crida bent his head a little and Gereint watched him. He knew Ceawlin's son, of course, but they had never dealt before as prince and subject. Crida had Ceawlin's spectacular coloring, Gereint found himself thinking, but his face was different. The clean bones and planes of Ceawlin's face gave an impression of strength; Crida's bones were more like Niniane's. Yet, although he was almost beautiful, there was nothing feminine about Crida. At last the prince looked up and said, "What are the Atrebates going to do?"

"We will fight for Ceawlin."

"Good." Crida's finely drawn fair brows were sharply knit. "I don't understand," he said. "What was the point of kidnapping Mother?"

Gereint was surprised. "As I said, she is a hostage."

"But a hostage for what? I doubt that Coinmail will use her to try to get my father to annul Cedric's marriage. From what Mother says, Coinmail has been looking for a reason to raise the Britons against my father for years; he certainly won't want to remove the reason before ever he gets his fight."

Gereint looked at the young prince sitting beside him with surprise and respect. "That is so." Crida's lashes were shadowing his eyes; his face looked somber. Gereint tried once more to reassure Niniane's son. "I am certain that Coinmail will not harm her, Crida." His voice was gentle.

The blue-green eyes lifted in surprise. "Of course he will not harm her. She is his sister," said Crida, to whom treachery within a family was almost unimaginable. "In fact, I think my mother will deal with being taken hostage better than my father will. He is going to be very upset when he hears what has happened."

*   *   *

Ceawlin was even more upset than Gereint had expected. He was so upset that it took a few minutes for him to react to the news that Gereint was also bringing him word of Atrebates support.

He stared at Gereint, his eyes narrowed to mere slits of color. "How many men can you raise, Gereint?"

It was with great pride that Gereint answered, "Nearly two hundred."

Ceawlin's eyes opened wider. "Two hundred!"

"All the men who can carry a sword will come, Ceawlin."

Ceawlin's mouth twisted in a smile that held no humor. "Niniane will be pleased to know she was not kidnapped in vain."

"It was not just Niniane," Gereint replied, "but that was certainly part of it."

There was silence as Ceawlin paced up and down the length of the hearth. They were meeting in the king's hall the day after Gereint had spoken to Crida. After a minute's silence Ceawlin said, "I can raise perhaps seven hundred men without the Atrebates. It should be enough."

Gereint frowned and stared at the restlessly pacing figure of his king. "What do you mean? I have said that we will fight for you."

Ceawlin came to a halt at the far end of the hearth, put his hands behind his back, and stared at Gereint. "I want you to tell Coinmail that you have two hundred men willing to fight for me. Then I want you to tell him that you will stay home if he will return Niniane to Winchester."

Gereint's eyes opened wide. "Ceawlin . . . Niniane would not want you to do that. She would say that the best way to get her back would be to best Coinmail in battle. He will not harm her; I am confident of that. Coinmail is not cruel, you know. He does not love Niniane, but killing her or hurting her would have no purpose. He will keep her safe for you."

"It is not that. . . ." Ceawlin turned to put a foot up on the hearth. He bent a little forward so that his hair swung forward, a thick curtain to screen his face. "She is with child, Gereint. That is what is worrying me."

"Niniane has ever been lucky in childbirth, Ceawlin. Six children she has borne you and always come through healthy and strong. What reason to worry now?"

"You cannot escape fate forever," Ceawlin said. "And I have bad feelings about this pregnancy. She does not look well." Then, violently, "*Gods!* I should never have let her go to Bryn Atha!"

Gereint had never heard such a voice from Ceawlin before. He stared at the king's profile, most of which was still hidden by that silver screen of hair. Then, "Ceawlin, if he thinks you want her back as badly as that, he will never let her go."

Ceawlin's head jerked up. "Think," Gereint said. "It was Crida who asked the crucial question. What is the point in taking Niniane hostage?"

Ceawlin's head moved a little, but he did not reply.

"The last thing Coinmail wants is for you to back out of Cedric's marriage. He will not use Niniane to try to get that concession from you. So . . . why?"

"You tell me," Ceawlin said.

"He hates you." Gereint's mouth twisted. "And it is a very personal hatred too. He would deny that, say he is only doing his duty as a Briton, but he hates you, Ceawlin. I think he cannot forgive you for defeating him that time at Beranbyrg; he cannot forgive you for giving him his life. I think he took Niniane because he hoped it would hurt you. If he knows how much he has hurt you, he will never return her."

There was a white line around Ceawlin's mouth. "She is afraid of him," he said.

"She was always afraid for you, not for herself." Gereint searched for words that would help. "In her own way," he finally said, "Niniane is as tough as Coinmail."

Ceawlin's response was a sound somewhere between a laugh and a sob. "I know that. If only she were not with child!"

Niniane's feelings echoed Ceawlin's. It was nearly sixty miles from Bryn Atha to Glevum, and by the time they arrived in the city Niniane was thoroughly exhausted. Coinmail had actually slowed his pace slightly to accommodate his sister, but it had still been too long and too arduous a journey. She scarcely looked around her as the horses came through the town gate. Glevum, she knew, had never been more than a market town for the Romans, and the quick glimpse she had of a small, unimpressive forum and decayed-looking town hall only confirmed what she had expected to see.

Coinmail's residence was of timber and had been built by his father-by-marriage a decade before. It was rougher-looking than the houses in Winchester, but the hall inside had a glowing hearth and there were outside stairs to the loft, which was used for sleeping. Coinmail's wife took one look at Niniane and immediately put her to bed with a hot drink. The bedstead straw was sweet and the linens fresh and Niniane slept like the dead for ten hours. She woke with a pain in her back.

She said nothing, hoping it was just a muscle ache from the long ride. She rose and dressed in the clothes from her saddlebags that a maid brought to her, and went slowly and carefully down the loft stairs. Coinmail's wife was in the hall below, and when she saw Niniane she ordered a bowl of steaming porridge and insisted that Niniane sit and eat.

Coinmail's wife was named Eithne and she had golden hair and blue eyes and looked kind. Niniane made a great effort to respond to her questions, but with every passing minute the pain in her back was growing worse. She was terrified she was going to lose her baby.

She ate the porridge, thinking it would strengthen her. The pains got strong. Finally she could no longer hide her distress; the air in the hall was chill and damp, but she was sweating and there were marks like bruises under her eyes. When Eithne said, "Are you ill, my sister?" she made herself answer, "I . . . I fear I am going to miscarry."

Eithne came to put an arm around her shoulders. "Come back to bed," she said. "I will send for the midwife."

After an hour of fierce contractions, the blood began to flow out of her. The baby, Niniane thought as blood gushed from between her legs, I am losing our baby, Ceawlin.

"Mother of God," she heard Eithne say. "Can you not get it to stop?"

The pain had let up a little, but now instead of being hot she was cold. Very cold. Her skin felt clammy. "Niniane." It was a voice she did not recognize. "How do you feel, Niniane?"

She opened her eyes and saw strange blue eyes. She closed her eyes again. "Bring more cloths," she heard someone say. "We must stop this bleeding."

She was at a very great distance, floating, floating. Her body hurt but it did not seem to have anything to do with her. She felt free. Dimly, as if from very far away, she heard the voices of women.

And then she saw Ceawlin. He was so vividly present to her that she opened her eyes, expecting him to be there. But there were only the women.

I am so tired, she thought. So tired. But if she floated away she might never see Ceawlin again. I must stay awake, she thought, and frowned with the effort of it.

After what seemed to her a long time, someone said, "We must get her into a clean bed." She looked down. There was blood everywhere. Someone was washing her and then the women were trying to get her into a clean sleeping gown. She tried to help. "Don't move," an authoritative feminine voice said. "I will get someone to lift you into the other bed."

A man came in and she was put into a bed with clean, fresh linens. "Thank you," she said, and fell asleep.

She was ill for days. She lay in bed, weak and bloodless, and grieved. Coinmail's wife was very kind, but Niniane longed for Nola. And for Ceawlin. He loved his children so . . . he would grieve as much as she. Then, when the midwife told her that she would bear no more, her heart was near to breaking.

She saw nothing of her brother. It was not until she was finally out of bed and able to go down to the hall that she met him again. His gray eyes looked her up and down. "I am glad you are feeling better," he said.

Niniane's face was very still and for a moment her delicate features bore an uncanny likeness to his. "You murdered my baby," she said, her voice cold as death. "I hope Ceawlin drives you and your followers into the sea."

"There is little likelihood of that," Coinmail replied. "I am raising almost the whole of South Wales."

"Ceawlin has never lost a battle, my brother," Niniane returned with relish. "And you have never won one. Consider that. Your men certainly will."

"Get her out of here," Coinmail said to his wife.

"You brought me here, Coinmail." Niniane's eyes were pure smoke. "Your mistake." And she turned with arrogant disdain to walk away with Eithne.

Gereint sent a British spy into Glevum to gather what news he could, and it was from this source that Ceawlin learned of Niniane's miscarriage.

"The girl I talked to is one of Eithne's handmaids," the youngster who had been posing as a Dobunni tribesman told Ceawlin. "She said the queen was near to death but that she is growing stronger now."

The relief Ceawlin felt was overwhelming. He was sorry about the baby, but, considering the circumstances, he thought things had turned out for the best. It was over and she was all right. Now he could give his full attention to the war.

The armorers were put into production day and night, forging spears and making arrows. The ceorls would have to be given arms; unlike the thanes, they had none of their own. Ceawlin rode from manor to manor, consulting with his eorls, checking supplies, speaking personally to the thanes and then the ceorls, rallying enthusiasm.

Autumn advanced into winter. News came that the armies of Condidan and Farinmail had marched out of Wales and were camping to the north of Glevum, on the banks of the river Severn. The Welsh chieftains together had raised an incredible eight hundred men.

"Coinmail has raised four hundred more," Ceawlin said to Crida as the two of them sat late one December night by the fire in the king's hall. "The Dobunni and a goodly number from northern Dumnonia. Or so goes the word from my scouts."

"You have near a thousand yourself, Father," Crida said. "And the Britons will be no match for the thanes."

"I want to force this battle now, Crida," Ceawlin said. "Hearts are high. Now is the time to strike."

Crida frowned. "But the weather. Would it not be better to wait for the end of winter?"

"Easier but not better. We have arms enough. The ceorls will not be worrying about planting their fields. Coinmail will not be expecting us to move. The time is now."

Crida's eyes had begun to glow. "Where?"

Ceawlin grinned. "I think we ought to hold Yule at Dynas this year," he said. And Crida laughed.

Bevan, prince of Dynas, was appalled when the messenger came from the king stating his intention of holding Yule at the villa. When a messenger came from Bertred the following day inviting the British prince to sojourn with his daughter at Romsey for the month, Bevan accepted with alacrity. He remained at Dynas only long enough to greet Ceawlin and hastily assure him that the villa was at his disposal. Then, to the well-concealed contempt and amusement of the West Saxon king, he took horse for Romsey.

"What a worm the man is," Ceowulf said with incredulity after Bevan had left the room.

"True, but he has served us well," Ceawlin answered. He looked at the two sons who had accompanied him and his hall thanes to Dynas. Ceowulf was inches taller than Crida but he was yet only fourteen. He would never have been allowed to join this expedition if Niniane had been in Winchester. Ceawlin knew that, yet he had not had the heart to deny his son's plea. This would be the greatest confrontation between Briton and Saxon since Badon. How could he refuse the boy a part in it? Ceowulf was a son to be proud of, full of courage and skilled in weaponry. Freed of Niniane's maternal anxiety, Ceawlin had allowed Ceowulf to join the army.

Ceawlin looked at the charcoal brazier glowing in the corner of the Roman room. "Pleasant as it would be to stay here in the warmth," he told his boys, "I'm afraid we must first see to the supplies." Ceawlin had brought wagon loads of food with him for the men whom he expected to be gathering within the week. The king placed little reliance on his army being able to live off the winter-bare countryside of Dynas. "And I want to assign camping places to each of the eorls," he added. "The more organized and comfortable the army is in camp, the better they will fight."

"Yes, sir," said two bright-eyed boys, and with absolutely no sign of reluctance they followed Ceawlin out into the cold.

It was hours later, after the food had been got in out of the weather, after the hall thanes had been bedded down, after the excited princes had fallen into the bed they were to share in one of the villa sleeping rooms; Ceawlin was sitting alone in front of the glowing brazier in Bevan's sleeping room. Outside the window a light snow had begun to fall.

Ceawlin sat comfortably in the silent room, his long legs stretched out before him, a cup of wine in his hand. He was well pleased with the way this campaign was going. Before a month had passed he fully expected to have extended Wessex all the way to the Sabrina Sea.

He sipped the wine, then stood and went to look out the window. It was too dark to see the snow. A little snow would be all right, he thought, but he did not want too much. He did not want to delay this coming battle. All his instincts told him to press for it quickly; Ceawlin always followed his instincts. They had never failed him yet.

Coinmail had played right into his hands, he thought as he gazed out into the unrevealing dark. Niniane had thought the opposite, but it was not true. His wife did not know that Ceawlin had long coveted the rich lands to the west of Wessex. He had coveted them but he had also understood that to conquer them by force would be to incur the enmity of his British subjects. What he would gain by such a move would not offset what he would lose.

Then had come Bevan's marriage offer. At first it had seemed a splendid chance to gain a foothold in Dumnonia by peaceful means. Then had come Coinmail's challenge, and the vision of a far greater gain had loomed before him. Aquae Sulis. Glevum. Corinium. Wessex would be the largest kingdom in England. And for the first time in Saxon history, the Britons of Dumnonia would be cut off from the Britons of Wales. Ceawlin's eyes glittered as he considered the possibilities. He would be the most powerful king in all of England. He would be the Bretwalda, the High King.

He finished his wine and put the cup down on a small table of inlaid walnut. There was no doubt in his mind that the lands of the Dobunni would do better under his rule than they had under Coinmail's. Ceawlin had been a good and a just king to his Atrebates subjects; he would be the same to the Dobunni. The blood of Woden ran strong in his veins. He had been born to be king; to be a great king; to be Bretwalda. It was his fate.

Ceawlin stripped off his tunic and prepared to go to bed.

Chapter 43

A_S soon as Ceawlin and his men rode into Dynas, a British scout took horse for Glevum to report to Coinmail. Then, in successive days, as more and more Saxons poured into the villa, the reports to the British prince were updated.

"He has garrisoned Dynas with an army of near seven hundred men," Coinmail told his fellow princes as they met to discuss the situation in Coinmail's hall in Glevum. "It is a direct challenge to us."

"So it is." Farinmail blew his nose vigorously and spoke around the loud honking noise he made.

Coinmail, fastidious Roman that he was, looked faintly disgusted. "He has moved an army into Dumnonia," Farinmail said, wiping his still-dripping nose on his sleeve. "The question is, do we go to him or do we wait for him here?"

"Go to him," said Condidan immediately. "We will lose the confidence of our men if we let it look as if he has intimidated us."

Coinmail's auburn brows were drawn together into a fine straight line. "I would rather not march through this weather. It is looking like snow."

"I would prefer to wait for better weather also," Condidan answered, "but Ceawlin has forced the action. His reputation is too great. If we delay in moving to meet him, it will look as if we are afraid of him. We cannot afford that. We have the greater numbers; if our men keep their hearts high, we will win. If they have doubts, the battle will be lost before ever it is fought."

With deep reluctance Coinmail was forced to agree. He hated to admit to Ceawlin's superiority in anything, but the myth of the Saxon's invincibility in battle had spread even into Wales. They could not allow their men to begin to suspect that their leaders were apprehensive of facing the Saxon in battle. They would have to answer Ceawlin's challenge.

On January 1, the day of the New Year, the combined Brit-Welsh force of Coinmail, Farinmail, and Condidan marched out of Glevum and headed south. It was snowing.

* * *

The sheds and barns of Dynas were filled with men. Ceawlin walked from war band to war band, speaking to the leaders, joking with the men, inspecting arms. Overhead the sky was gray, full of snow yet to fall. The landscape was all gray and brown and white: colorless and bleak. Ceawlin's spirits were high. He had heard just that morning that the Brit-Welsh were coming south.

He did not intend to meet them at Dynas. Dynas was only the challenge. It was too far to the east to serve the purpose he needed. He wanted a victory that would ensure him the city of Aquae Sulis, yet he wanted to be on the road north to Glevum as well. He had decided the day after he arrived in Dynas to stand his ground at Deorham, a small market center six miles north of Aquae Sulis. There was a large field where on market day the wagons were set up; the fight on such a field would be fair and victory should go to the stronger force.

There was little doubt in Ceawlin's mind that he had the stronger force. He was not quite equal in number with the Brit-Welsh, but large numbers of his men were seasoned warriors. Even many of the ceorls had fought before. Face-to-face, man-to-man, he thought he was superior.

The last of his forces to ride in were the Atrebates under Gereint. Two hundred and seventeen of them, ranging in age from fifteen to fifty. Ceawlin's heart swelled with pride to see them. He had protected their lands, fed them in times of famine, stood as a shield between them and their enemies, been their lord. He felt now that their loyalty to him was a sign of his destiny: to be king of both Saxon and Briton. To be Bretwalda.

On the morning of January 2 the West Saxon army moved out of Dynas. Ceawlin and Crida, with their eorls beside them, rode at the head of the marching men. Over each band of thanes and marching ceorls floated the banner of the eorl whom they served. At the head of the whole, carried by a thane on a great bay stallion, floated Ceawlin's banner of the white horse. By late afternoon they had traveled the twelve miles to the field of Deorham. There was as yet no sign of the Brit-Welsh, so the West Saxons lit cookfires and settled down to wait.

It was cold, but Ceawlin had seen to it that food was plentiful. The men were in good spirits, and after the dinners were eaten, Alric, sitting close to the fire to keep his fingers warm, began to play. At a little distance from the harper, around another fire, sat Ceawlin and his eorls.

"My scouts say they are camped but five miles north of here," Ceawlin said. "We will rouse before light and take up battle positions. I do not desire to be surprised by a dawn attack."

Grunts of assent came from all around.

"The battle commands will be as follows," said Ceawlin, and there was sudden, absolute silence. "I will hold my own hall thanes and the

Atrebates as a reserve. When I see which way the battle is going, where the enemy is strongest, then will I commit the extra men to the field."

All nodded; no one spoke. This was a tactic Ceawlin had used before and it had always proved successful. It enabled the king to place his undoubtedly awesome powers where they were most needed.

"Penda," Ceawlin said into the silence, "you will have the center." This was no surprise, but still Penda smiled with pleasure.

"Yes, my lord," he said.

"Bertred, you will take the left."

Again, no surprise. Nods of acceptance.

"Crida," said Ceawlin, "you will have the right." Crida's face lit like a candle; the rest of the eorls frowned.

"Ceawlin. . . ." It was Ine speaking. "Is that wise? Crida is brave as a lion, no one doubts that. But he is inexperienced."

"He is prince of Wessex," said Ceawlin. "He will command the right."

Silence. Then Wuffa said practically, "Where do you want me to be, Ceawlin?"

"With Bertred, on the left. Ine, you will lend your support to Penda in the center. The men from Wokham and Gildham will fight under Crida on the right."

Nods all around. "Very well," said Ceawlin. He lifted his cup of beer. "May Woden take them," he said. His son and his eorls pledged likewise, "May Woden take them!" They drank, and then the eorls went off to see to their men.

They woke to snow. Not heavy, but steady. Thanes and ceorls unwrapped themselves from their cloaks, ate the hot porridge served up by Ceawlin's cooks, and took their places in the line of battle. They waited for an hour, stamping their feet to keep warm, cloaks draped over heads and shoulders, their banners flying bravely in the drifting whiteness.

Then, from the far side of the snow-filled field, came the noise of marching men. The Brit-Welsh, following the call of their princes and their blood, had come to fight.

The two armies facing each other this snowy morning numbered slightly more than two thousand men, the largest force assembled for battle in Britain since Arthur's victory at Badon a century before. And this coming battle on Deorham field was fully as crucial to Coinmail and his followers as Badon had been to their forebears. To lose was to divide the Welsh from the British in Dumnonia; to lose was to leave Dumnonia vulnerable to Saxon invasion; to lose was in all probability to say farewell to what remained of Celtic Britain.

The Brit-Welsh battle horns blew. Ceawlin's battle leaders, on foot like the rest of their men, shouted the order for readiness. Crida stood under his personal banner, felt the snow stinging cold on his face, and listened to the singing of the blood in his veins. There were two lines of archers before him, and as the line of the Brit-Welsh began to move forward, Ceawlin's archers fired once and then again before melting back into the ranks to allow the sword-wielding thanes to move to the fore. Incredibly, over all the noise of men and horns, Crida heard his father's voice. He lifted his sword and ran forward, his men beside and behind him.

The two armies came together with a crash.

It seemed to Crida, as the white world began to turn red with blood, that the two enemies were evenly matched. Both lines of battle were holding their own; neither side seemed able to push the other one back. He did not know who was commanding the wing opposing him, as the whole of the Brit-Welsh force was fighting under the banner of the red dragon which had been Arthur's emblem when he reigned as king.

He felt a blade glance off the chain mail on his shoulder and turned to return a blow that proved more deadly. Then one of his thanes was beside him. Crida set his teeth and began to press forward with all the force and skill that were in him. "Come on!" he shouted to his men. "Push them back!"

Ceawlin watched the battle from the saddle of his stallion. It was difficult to see in the snow, and it was a minute before he recognized that the deadlock was beginning to break a little on the right. Crida was pressing forward. The evenly matched battle line was showing its first crack. He had to move now, before the Brit-Welsh could recover.

"Gereint!" Ceawlin called. "A hundred men to reinforce Crida on the right! Now!" Then, as the Atrebates ran forward eagerly, "My hall thanes, to the center with me."

"And me, Father?" said Ceowulf eagerly.

"Listen, my son . . ." Ceawlin dismounted and threw his reins to a groom. He had not intended to give Ceowulf any command, had intended actually to keep him out of the fight if possible, but now . . . "If you see our center and right beginning to overwhelm them, and if I am still in the midst of the fight, take the rest of the Atrebates and join Bertred on the left."

He had a brief glimpse of glowing blue eyes and very white teeth and then he was gone, racing forward at the head of his thanes, to hurl himself into the battle. The ceorls at the rear moved aside to let him through; then he was well forward, his own thanes solidly beside and behind him. He caught a glimpse of Penda through the snow and knew where his front line was. Penda was always at the front. Crida was well before him.

"Follow me!" he shouted, and began to hew his way through the ranks of the Brit-Welsh, clearing a path for his men to follow. The fighting was so close that the snow fell on the men and not the ground. The Celts fell back before Ceawlin's ferocious assault, and Penda, seeing this, pressed forward with renewed vigor.

Coinmail, who was commanding the center, shouted to rally his men. The snow began to fall harder, limiting vision to a paltry few feet. It was then that the men who knew they were in the middle of Coinmail's line saw the great banner of the white horse driving toward them. It was merely a wing of men, Ceawlin and his hall thanes who had thrust their way into the heart of Coinmail's army, but the Brit-Welsh, who could not see, thought that their whole front line had been broken. They panicked and turned to run. The men behind them, who could not see either, followed suit.

Ceowulf also was blinded by the snow, but he heard the change in sound coming from the field. He did not see his father returning, and, desperate not to miss the battle, he finally commanded the remaining Atrebates to follow him and charged in to reinforce Bertred on the left.

Coinmail, seeing his men begin to drop their weapons and run from the field, worked desperately hard to shore up the front of his line. He was pushing his way toward the hated banner that waved over Ceawlin when a sword blow landed on his head. His helmet saved him. Stupid Saxons, he thought, they didn't wear helmets. He had cleaved a respectable number of blond heads in this battle, but the one blond head he most desperately wanted had eluded him. He had not seen Ceawlin in the battle at first, but he was here now. Here, and deep inside Coinmail's lines. If he did nothing else in his life, Coinmail was going to kill the West Saxon king.

His helmet had been loosened by the previous sword blow, and when the second blow landed on it, it slipped forward over his brow. Coinmail's head came up as he tried to see from under the leather blinder, and for a moment his neck was cleanly exposed. The moment was brief but fatal. One of Ceawlin's hall thanes cut his throat.

The Dobunni, who had been following Coinmail, halted when they saw their prince fall. Then a great victory shout came from the left; the voices were Saxon.

"We are beaten!" The cry went up and down the ranks of Brit-Welsh. More and more Celts, confused by loss of leadership, blinded by snow, followed their instincts and ran from the death they were sure was before them.

As the enemy began to disappear into the snow, Ceawlin sent orders to his commanders not to pursue. With ruthless efficiency the princes and eorls pulled back their rampaging men, who, hot with the blood lust of victory, were ready to hunt down and fell any Celt they could get within the reach of their swords.

"Their princes are all dead," Ceawlin said to Penda later when the eorl demanded why the victory had not been followed up. "They are no danger without leadership: the Welsh will simply flee back to their valleys, and the Dobunni I wish to make my people. I have sworn to be as good a lord to them as ever I have been to the Atrebates."

Ceawlin and his eorls and his sons were gathered together under the roof of a hastily rigged tent near the battlefield. On Deorham field itself the wounded were being separated from the dead, with the former being treated and the latter laid aside for burial. The question Ceawlin was answering belonged to Penda, but the king's eyes were on Gereint.

"Do we march next for Glevum?" Crida spoke the question into the accepting silence that had fallen after Ceawlin's last words.

"First we enter Aquae Sulis," Ceawlin replied. "If the city is anything like Silchester was under the Britons, it will be half-empty and crumbling. I will formally claim it for Wessex and hold an assembly for the people to reassure them." His eyes turned to Bertred. "Bertred, you I designate as my governor. Romsey is the manor closest to Aquae Sulis, and the city will need leadership if it is to become a useful part of the kingdom."

Bertred looked pleased. "Thank you, my lord. I shall not fail you."

"You never have," said Ceawlin, his matter-of-fact voice robbing the moment of any uncomfortable emotion.

"Then shall we go to Glevum?" asked Crida.

"Then Corinium," said Ceawlin.

"You are claiming all the lands of the Dobunni?" It was Gereint's voice this time.

"Yes." Ceawlin's eyes were level. "All the lands from Kent to the Sabrina Sea," he said. "The cities of Aquae Sulis, Corinium, and Glevum will become West Saxon chesters. And I promise you, Gereint, that under me they will prosper."

Gereint sighed and with a flicker of humor in the corners of his mouth said, "I don't doubt it."

"Who will govern in Corinium?" asked Ine.

"Ceowulf, with you to advise him," Ceawlin answered promptly. "I shall give you lands in the neighborhood of the city, Ine, to settle on whom in your family you will."

Ine smiled. He had a large number of sons and wished to keep his own manor of Odinham intact for the eldest. "I shall be pleased to accept such a charge," he said.

Ceowulf was scarlet but his face was perfectly serious as he answered formally, "I thank you, my father, for such a trust."

"You are a son to be proud of, Ceowulf," Ceawlin said with equal formality. "A fine and a brave warrior. In Corinium, which I shall rename Cirencester, you will learn how to be a lord."

Then he turned to his eldest. His heart swelled with pride as he regarded the boy. It was Crida who had given him the opening he had needed to win, and both of them knew it. "To you, Crida, my son, I give the thanks of my heart," he said. "To you I shall leave a kingdom unequaled in England for size and for power."

"My father," said Crida, and though his face was almost stern, his eyes glowed. "Your thanks and your love are all that I desire."

For a brief moment Ceawlin closed his hand on Crida's forearm; then he threw his head up and said briskly, "Once we are finished here, the ceorls are to be sent home. Each eorl may take twenty thanes for his following. Then we march for Aquae Sulis, the new West Saxon chester of Bath."

Niniane knew what had happened as soon as the British survivors of Deorham began to stream into Glevum. As ever, Ceawlin had triumphed. He always did. She wondered why she lived in such fear and trembling every time he went to war.

With Coinmail, Farinmail, and Condidan dead, the threat of panic hung in the air of Glevum. Frightened men told terrible tales of Saxon ferocity in battle. The Welsh did not tarry in Glevum but streamed west with all haste, crossing into the relative safety of Wales. Coinmail's men, who had fled instinctively to the place of their starting out, did not know what to do.

It was Niniane who took charge. Eithne was too frightened at the magnitude of the defeat to know what to do. Coinmail's ten-year-old son, who had inherited his father's spirit, was fierce in wanting to make a stand against the Saxons, but he was too young to get a hearing from the rest of the Dobunni chiefs.

"The king is a man of mercy," Niniane told Eithne and the tribe's leading men who had survived the Battle of Deorham. "He is like a lion in battle, but after, he is a man of mercy. You have naught to fear from him."

They said nothing, but looked distinctly dubious.

"Did he hunt you down as you left the field?" Niniane asked.

"No," came the reluctant reply. Then, "It was snowing so hard, it was difficult to see."

Niniane shrugged. "He could have sent his men after you like hounds after a fox, but he did not. He let you go. He does not wish to destroy the Dobunni; he wishes to be your lord and your king."

"Never will I bow my head to a Saxon!" It was Coinmail's son, Col. Niniane turned to the boy. He was all his mother to look at, golden curls, clear blue eyes. Niniane's son Sigurd looked more like her brother than this boy did. But that relentless voice—that was unmistakably Coinmail.

"You will bow your head to this Saxon," she said, unaware that her own voice held exactly the same note as her nephew's. "Your father began this conflict. It was he who challenged Bevan's right to marry his daughter where he would. Ceawlin had no choice but to act as he did."

"Ceawlin should never have allowed his eorl to marry his son into Dumnonia." It was one of the chief men of the Dobunni speaking now, a man of perhaps forty-five, who stood high in the councils of the tribe.

"It was Bevan who proposed the marriage." Niniane's small, delicate face was almost forbiddingly stern. "What would any of you have done should Bertred have offered Romsey to one of your sons?" There was silence. "Exactly," she said after a minute. "And would you not have expected your prince to uphold your rights as well?"

"There is some truth in what you say, my lady," another man reluctantly agreed. "The fault was Bevan's in that he made the offer in the first place."

"The fault was Coinmail's for demanding that he forswear the betrothal," Niniane snapped. Her small, tip-tilted nose was looking alarmingly imperious. "Coinmail has schemed for years to raise an army to fight Ceawlin," she told the circle of somber-faced men. "If you are not blind or deaf, you know that. Well, he got his wish and he died for it. Thanks to his plots, the Dobunni are about to become West Saxons. Which, let me tell you, my lords, is your good fortune. The Atrebates did not fight for you, they fought for Ceawlin. Not because they fear him, but because they love him."

"The Atrebates are slaves and cowards," said Col.

He was his father all over again. She would not have it, would not let it all begin again. "If you want to live, Col," his aunt said to him, her voice very, very quiet, "never let me hear you say such words again." The boy, who was not a coward, went suddenly pale. There was no doubt in any man's mind who heard her that Niniane meant every word she spoke.

Eithne, who had been silent for the whole time, put a hand on her son's arm. "Col is upset," she said. "He did not mean it."

Niniane ignored them. "This is what we will do," she said to the rest of the men. They all took a step closer, the better to hear.

Chapter 44

THE countryside of the Dobunni was bleak white with winter, but Crida thought that the rolling hills would be glorious in the spring and summer. Good land. Rich land. A great deal of empty land. A fine acquisition for Wessex.

Glevum itself was distinctly unimpressive. Bath had been magnificent even in decay, and Cirencester had also once been a fine city, the tribal capital of the Dobunni. But Glevum was very small, with few Roman buildings of any distinction. It had come into significance only in the last hundred years, mainly because it was the farthest west of all the Dobunni towns and thus the safest from Saxon invasion.

The Roman houses were interspersed with wooden structures, none of which approached the sophisticated architecture of Winchester. There was not a soul in sight under the broad gray sky. Crida glanced out the side of his eyes to his father, who was riding beside him at the head of their men. They were moving up the main street of the deserted town, and as his son watched, Ceawlin's eyes suddenly narrowed. Crida instantly looked back to the road and saw that a line of men had appeared on the front step of the large wooden building some three hundred feet before them. They were Britons. Ceawlin continued to walk his horse forward, his eyes on the men. When they had advanced another hundred feet, one of the Britons came forward to stand in the road. Ceawlin raised a hand to halt his thanes, then went forward himself, alone.

"Owain," Crida heard his father say with what sounded like real pleasure in his easy yet unmistakably authoritative voice. "Greetings." Ceawlin spoke in British.

"My lord king," the man replied. His face was reserved. "We bid you welcome to Glevum and we cry your mercy."

Ceawlin swung off his horse. "Of course you have my mercy. I will speak with your chiefs about it." Then he grinned, approached the smaller man, and lightly put a hand on his shoulder. "It is good to see you, old friend," the king said. "Gereint and Ferris are with me too."

The man's rigid face wavered, then cracked into a tentative return smile. Crida, watching, thought dispassionately that no small part of his

400

father's success came from knowing how to woo a man with smile and touch. The stiff Dobunni leader was actually laughing as he led Ceawlin forward to meet the men who were assembled to submit to their new lord. Ceawlin accepted the bows with smiling ease, talked for perhaps three minutes, then turned to signal Crida forward.

"This man will show us where to quarter the thanes," Ceawlin said as a Briton stepped forward into the road before Crida's horse. "Tell Penda he is in charge and then come back here. Bring Gereint and Ferris with you."

"Yes, my lord," said Crida, and trotted his chestnut back to the waiting men to convey his father's orders. Penda dismounted to walk beside the British guide, and Gereint and Ferris came eagerly forward to join Crida. They all three gave their horses into the care of Ceawlin's hall thanes and walked back to the hall where Ceawlin had been greeted. The men on the front steps had already gone inside. Crida pushed open the door and he and the two Britons followed.

The small hall was filled with lamplight and men. Arranged in the middle of the room were a golden-haired woman and a boy who was obviously her son. As Crida watched, the woman bent her head to Ceawlin in the age-old gesture of submission. The boy hesitated, then, as his mother's hand touched his arm, he too bowed his head. Coinmail's wife, Crida thought. And his son. He looked around the room, searching for someone else. Where was his mother?

Ceawlin's thoughts were evidently running along the same path as his son's. He made a gracious, generous reply to the Dobunni princess's obviously rehearsed speech and then said, "But where is my wife?"

The princess replied, "She said to send for her when the formal greeting was accomplished, my lord." Eithne gestured to a handmaid and the girl turned and hurried out a side door.

Ceawlin looked around the neat rows of solemn-faced men who flanked Eithne and her son and quirked an eyebrow. "You have received me most royally, Princess," he said. And Crida knew, suddenly, that his mother had probably arranged the whole thing. His father thought so, certainly. He could tell from the lift of Ceawlin's eyebrow.

The door in the side of the hall reopened and suddenly Niniane was there. A rush of relief and happiness swept through Crida at the sight of her small, graceful figure. She looked the same as always, he thought thankfully. Her God had looked after her well.

"Ceawlin," said Niniane in Saxon from the far side of the room, "you took your time getting here."

"I stopped first in Corinium," he replied. "To give you time to organize them." And he held out his arms.

She ran forward, light as a girl, to throw herself against her husband.

She was so small that when his arms closed tightly around her she was lifted right off the ground. Ceawlin's head was bent close to hers. Crida could not hear what his father was saying. He moved forward to claim his mother's attention next.

She saw him as soon as Ceawlin put her back on her feet. "Crida!" Her smile was luminous. "Oh, my son, how glad I am to see you." His own rare smile lighted his face and then he too scooped her into his arms.

The Britons stood in attentive silence. The men had all been at Deorham, had all seen the efficient killing machine that was Ceawlin loose on the field. Now he stood, surrounded by an obviously well-loved and loving wife and son, and gave them all an irresistibly beguiling smile.

"From henceforth I proclaim that the Dobunni are under my protection," Ceawlin said. "Your hunger is my hunger, your enemies are my enemies. Together we will forge such a kingdom as this island has never yet seen. Saxon and Briton, together." He was sober now, and utterly compelling. "Tonight we will feast together in token of our joining. Tonight you will swear allegiance, not to a Saxon king but to a King of Wessex. And to his son and heir, born of Saxon king and British princess." Crida felt a thrill run through his blood and raised his head with pride. "Tonight," his father concluded, "will see the birth of a new kingdom, and we will make it together. This I promise on my honor as a king."

There was a moment's intense silence and then a cheer went up from the Britons in the hall. Full-throated, relieved, excited, spontaneous. The only one who did not roar his approval was Coinmail's son, who stood beside his mother with a tense and frigid face. Only Crida appeared to notice him, however. All the rest were uproarious in their pleasure and approval.

"I always liked him," Owain said to Ferris.

Ferris gave his cousin a lopsided grin. "There is no gainsaying him, Owain. This is Arthur's heir. Not Coinmail, not any Briton, but this Saxon who will give us a kingdom and a prosperity and a peace such as we have not seen in Britain since Badon."

"And he will give us a half-British heir," Owain added quickly.

"Yes." Both men looked at the beautiful, slim silver-haired boy who stood beside his mother and father, looked at each other again, and smiled.

Niniane was so glad to see him. She had rallied all her physical and mental forces while she had to, had driven the Dobunni to see and to accept the inevitable. It had all gone better than she had ever dared to hope. Of course, it had helped immeasurably to discover Owain and the men who had known Ceawlin as Rhys. It had made him seem human to them, not just a petrifying Saxon giant ruthlessly felling all in his path.

She had prepared the way and Ceawlin had done the rest. He knew very well the strength of his own charm, and over the years he had learned to wield it as effectively as any other of his weapons. By the end of the banquet the Dobunni had been eating out of his hand.

She could let down. She could remember how grieved she was, how weary. She could creep, bloodless and cold, into his warmth and his strength. She did not even have the vigor to protest about his allowing Ceowulf to join the fight at Deorham. Ceowulf was not a child any longer. Her children were all growing up, growing away from her. And there would be no more babies to replace them.

She held off telling Ceawlin what the midwife had said. Deep down, she was afraid to tell him. She knew, had always known, that much of his love for her was bound up with her ability to give him children. He had never said such a thing to her, but her woman's heart knew it was so. Ceawlin's feelings for his children went deeper than most men's. His feelings for her were in good part gratitude for those children. If she could give him no more . . . She did not know what it would mean to him. She was afraid to find out.

In February they went back to Winchester. She had been gone for five months and Fara did not know her. The little girl clung to Auda when Niniane tried to pick her up, and said, "No!"

Auda made light of it, said, "She is only angry because you left her, Mother. She will come around."

But Niniane was devastated. Her last baby. She left Fara with Auda in Crida's hall and went back to her own house and her own room and wept bitterly. She was still there, her face visibly tearstained and swollen, when Ceawlin came in to change for the evening's feast in the great hall. He frowned when he saw her. "What is wrong?"

"Fara did not know me," she said.

"Nonsense. Of course she knew you." His voice was rough; impatient, she thought.

"She clung to Auda and stared at me as if I was going to kidnap her."

"She is punishing you for leaving her," Ceawlin said. "She will get over it. You must just give her time."

"That is what Auda said."

"Auda is right." Then, "Aren't you coming to the banquet this night?" She did not see the worried frown that furrowed his brow. She was looking out into the growing darkness, her back turned to him.

"I suppose I must," she replied listlessly.

"Nan." He had come up behind her noiselessly. She started a little to hear his voice so close to her ear. "What is wrong? It is not just Fara.

Are you well? You haven't been yourself at all, not even at Glevum. Are you still grieving because you lost the baby?"

She tried not to sob, failed, sobbed again, and then gave up trying to quell it. She was in his arms, her face pressed into his shoulder. "I'm sorry," he was saying. His hand gently stroked the smooth copper-brown hair on the top of her head. She waited for him to say that she would have another child. He did not.

She clutched the front of his tunic and clenched her hands into fists. "Ceawlin, I have something to tell you."

"Yes?" This as she paused and drew a deep uneven breath.

It came out in a rush. "When I miscarried of the child, I almost died and the midwife told me that I would never bear another."

He said nothing, but she was so close that he could not hide the shudder that ran all through him at her words. She shut her eyes tightly. She did not want to see his face.

He did not speak for a long minute. She thought in growing desolation that he was searching for something to say to her. "Nan," he said at last and, astonishingly, his voice held a note she had never expected to hear. "I am sorry if you are grieved, but I would not be honest if I did not confess myself relieved."

He meant it. Relief was the note that had sounded, unmistakable, in that well-known, well-loved voice. He was not dismayed at all.

She looked up at him, so accustomed to his height that she knew automatically how far back she would have to tilt her head. "I don't understand you," she said.

"That is because you are braver than I," he replied. There were faint shadows below his deep-colored eyes. "I was so worried for you this last time, so fearful." He put his hands over her clenched fists and she released the death-hold she had on the fabric of his tunic and turned her fingers to rest within his clasp. "I even tried to get Gereint to trade his two hundred Atrebates for you," he said.

Her eyes widened, began to go from gray to blue. "Did you really?"

"Yes. But he said that if Coinmail ever came to know how important you were to me, he would never give you back."

"Gereint was right," Niniane said.

"He convinced me that he was, and so I did not try it. But I feared for you. Childbed has been kind to you thus far, Nan, but one cannot outrun fate forever." His fingers tightened about hers. "I am sorry if you are grieved," he said again, "but I cannot find it in me but to be glad."

"I thought . . . I thought you would be sorry . . . you have ever been so glad to learn you were to have a new child."

"I have enough children," he said with unmistakable sincerity. "It is you I cannot afford to lose." He gave her the crooked, self-deprecating smile that was one of her favorite of all his expressions. "I am too old a stallion to have to search out a new mare."

She laughed, sniffled, then laughed again. "Is that all that is amiss with you?" he asked.

"Well . . . yes."

"You might have told me sooner."

"I . . . My heart was too sore."

He sighed and drew her close once more. "Mother Crida's babies if you must," he said. "From the looks of it, he and Auda should have more than enough to keep you busy."

Niniane gave a watery chuckle.

"And to think how I have been restraining myself." He was beginning to sound indignant. "Between thinking you were not feeling well, and fearing that I would get you with child again . . . and all for naught!" Now he did sound indignant.

He had been remarkably continent since their reunion in Glevum, Niniane thought. She had been too unhappy to mark it much, but now that she thought back on things . . . She bit her lip. The poor love.

He put his hands on her shoulders and held her away so he could look down into her face. She smiled up at him, radiant. "I'll make it up to you," she promised.

His eyes took on a glint that made her blood begin to race as it had not done in nigh on a year. "Tonight?"

"Tonight."

He grinned. "If it were not for this banquet, I would hold you to your word right now. But . . ."

"But Alric has a new song he has been waiting to sing, and your eorls and thanes are probably already in the hall waiting for us. It is time to get dressed, my lord, not undressed." And, suiting action to words, she poured some water into the pottery bowl on the bedside table and bent to splash it on her face and eyes.

Behind her he began to strip off his tunic. "Unfortunately, you are right." His ruffled head emerged and he dropped the tunic on the floor. "What new song?" he asked.

"His best yet. The song of Ceawlin, Bretwalda of England," she answered. She dried her face and turned to find him staring at her, his face very still. She smiled and added, her husky voice soft with love, "Get dressed if you want to hear it."

He reached out, tugged a strand of coiled hair that had slipped down onto her shoulder, then reached into the clothes chest for a fresh linen tunic.

Afterword

*B*RITAIN in the sixth century was truly the Dark Ages. This was the century in which the Anglo-Saxon kingdoms spread across the landscape of Britain; this was the century that saw the transformation of Romano-Celtic Britain into Anglo-Saxon England. Yet we know scarcely anything of how that transformation was accomplished.

Early Anglo-Saxon England was a pagan, preliterate society, and no written records from the time exist. The main source of information we have derives from the *Anglo-Saxon Chronicle*, which does give a list of names and dates detailing the establishment and expansion of the kingdom of Wessex. However, the *Anglo-Saxon Chronicle* was most probably compiled in the reign of Alfred the Great, some centuries later than the history it purports to report, and so it cannot be considered reliable.

The other source we have for sixth-century Britain is Bede's *Ecclesiastical History of the English Nation*. The *Ecclesiastical History* also makes mention of the conquest of Wessex; however, Bede lived a century later than the period of Ceawlin and so his facts must necessarily be somewhat suspect.

This lack of definite information is both a problem and a liberation for the author. What I have done is take the names and dates given in the *Anglo-Saxon Chronicle* and from them I have constructed a story of the way it might have been. It does seem certain that there did exist a man named Ceawlin of Wessex. He is named most definitely by the *Anglo-Saxon Chronicle* and by Bede as one of the few kings on whom the title of Bretwalda, or "ruler of Britain," was bestowed. Aside from his name, however, and a few untrustworthy dates, nothing is known of this early King of Wessex. I must confess, it was a great deal of fun to invent him.

The social background of the time is almost as obscure as the historical. I have used the descriptions of feasts and halls from *Beowulf* as background for life in the mythical capital of Winchester. And the description of the funeral of Redwold of East Anglia is based on the findings of the Sutton Hoo burials. The rest is imagination.

For anyone interested, the following is the excerpt from the *West*

Saxon Annals of the *Anglo-Saxon Chronicle* on which I have based my story:

530 Cerdic and Cynric took the Isle of Wight and slew a few men at Wihtgaraesbyrg.
534 Cerdic died: and his son Cynric reigned on for twenty-six winters, and they gave the Isle of Wight to their kinsfolk Stuf and Wihtgar.
552 Cynric fought with Britons at the place called Searo byrg and put the Brit-Welsh to flight.
556 Cynric and Ceawlin fought with Britons at Beran byrg.
560 Ceawlin began to reign in Wessex.
568 Ceawlin and Cutha fought with Aethelberht and drove him into Kent, and they slew two chieftains Oslaf and Cneba at Wibbandun.
571 Cuthwulf fought with Brit-Welsh at Bedcanford and took four townships, Lygeanburg and Aegelesburg, Benesington and Egonesham, and the same year he died.
577 Cuthwine and Ceawlin fought with Britons and slew three kings, Coinmail and Condidan and Farinmail, at the place called Deorham, and they took three "chesters," Gleawanceaster and Cirenceaster and Bathanceaster.

The only change I have made from the *Chronicle* is in the substitution of Crida for Cuthwine as Ceawlin's companion at the Battle of Deorham. The name of Crida appears linked with Ceawlin's at a later date and it seemed less complicated not to have to introduce another "Cuth" character into the action.

The battle of Deorham appears to have been historical and it was indeed a watershed in the transformation of Britain into England. Deorham is one of the place names that can be traced to an actual geographical site, and the site is the modern-date Dyrham, six miles north of Bath. For Ceawlin to have taken Bath and Cirencester and Gloucester would mean that for the first time English rule would extend to the western sea. For the first time in Saxon history, land communications between Wales and Dumnonia would be cut off. Apparently, however, Ceawlin did not actually invade Dumnonia. It was not until the next century that the West Saxons began to expand in that direction.

By the end of Ceawlin's reign, then, late in the sixth century, Wessex would have comprised the present English counties of Berkshire, Hampshire, Wiltshire, and a large part of Gloucestershire.

The lines of Anglo-Saxon poetry in the novel are from the poems *The Wanderer*, *The Ruin*, and (most of them) *Beowulf*.